Son of Tears

Prologue

The faculty of memory is a great one
(Confessions X, 8, 15).

I t was July of the year 430. The blanket of dark was spreading its folds over the earth and the ship-scarred Mediterranean. The figure of a man bowed with age slipped out of the Basilica of Peace and into the orange grove close by. He wore the simple black cotton robe of the servant of Christ, for this was Augustine, Bishop of Hippo, stealing away to his outdoor cell to meditate.

Of late, the bishop's parish had become swollen. The pressure of war had made it necessary to convert Hippo into a city of refuge for wounded soldiers, and for helpless Numidian men, women, and children, blown like leaves before the hordes of invading Vandals. Starved, half-naked, they had swarmed into the city, into the basilica, the chapels, the hospital, the convent, even the private home of the bishop, begging for food, medicine, and clothing. Augustine and his staff had responded with the generosity that had long established Hippo as a lighthouse for the sick and destitute.

The Vandals, fresh from their victories in Gaul and Spain, had crossed the Mediterranean. The situation in North Africa was critical. Most of the major cities had fallen to the invaders. They had seized Carthage and other centers of civilization, and now were closing in on Hippo, one of the few remaining outposts of freedom. They had thrown a cordon of troops around the city, and were pressing hard for the kill.

Augustine loved the orange grove. It was his secluded island in a river of feverish activity. Since his consecration to the office of bishop, he had lived a life of intense activity. He had traveled, preached, lectured, catechized, written books and tracts, engaged in endless correspondence with friend, stranger, and foe. His letters, like those of the great Apostle Paul, everywhere stimulated the cause of Christianity. He had arbitrated quarrels and lawsuits. He had served as judge and counselor. He had done the work of ten men. Pathetically few were the opportunities that allowed him to escape to his retreat, there to indulge in meditation and communion with his God.

Even now, the shouts of the barbarians bivouacked outside the city, and the cries of hurt and hungry children inside the walls, broke in upon the exhausted bishop. He paused under one of the orange trees, panting from exertion, and threw an arm around the trunk for support. The cloying scent of orange blossoms perfumed the air.

Augustine inhaled deeply, closed his eyes, and gave himself up to the passionate pleasure of reflection. Years before, he had cultivated the habit of carrying on conversations with his various members: the memory, the heart, the conscience, his soul, his will. It was as natural as sleep, therefore, that in this crisis he should draw apart, summon memory into play, and conjure up a cycle of images that time had covered but not destroyed.

Memory, like a mystic guide, led him back to Thagaste, and to loved ones he would soon see again, though not on earth. Tagaste was the place of his birth, his frantic youth, and the setting also of his own son's death.

Beloved Monica, his mother, he had lost at Ostia on the return from Rome to Thagaste. She had lived to witness the regeneration of her son. Augustine had heard her pray, "Let now your handmaiden depart in peace, for my eyes have seen your salvation blessedly applied to my son, and to his child as well." And God had kissed away her soul in sublime outgoing as gentle as the loosing of a ship from its moorings.

Memory whispered to the weary bishop, "Your son you lost, your mother you lost, but before these two you parted with the joy of your heart, remember?" I remember, he mused. How well do I remember, and with what bitter remorse!

He knew he would never see Melanie in this life. She had chosen to secrete herself in an obscure convent. Yet she was seldom out of his mind. He reflected: *I can never look at a drop of dew in a buttercup without beholding shafts of love in the retreats of her eyes. I cannot listen to an aria flung to the heavens by a lark without hearing the echo of her sweet voice. I cannot pass the nearest house in Hippo with-out calling to remembrance her last message to me: "Oh, how I long that we shall meet above in the glory of our Savior's house!"*

Suddenly, he heard a servant calling to him from the edge of the grove. He sighed, for it meant he must return to his duties. As he turned to leave his sequestered nook, fragmentary scenes flashed across his imagination: the orchard at Milan, where he had yielded his soul to Christ; Cassiacum, the Eden of springs and palms where he had convalesced spiritually; the Basilica of Peace, here in Hippo, and that terrifying moment when the congregation had seized him and dragged him before the Bishop Valerius, shouting, "Augustine a priest! Ordain Augustine!" He thought of the day he had stood before the Primate of Numidia to clear himself of charges his enemies had leveled against him of betraying a certain maid, and of his vindication and ordination to the office of bishop —

"Your Reverence!" the servant called, scurrying through the trees.

His memory was banished. Reluctantly, Augustine advanced to meet the man, and said, "Yes, what is it?"

"Your Reverence, a dying soldier needs you."

"Very well. Tell him I am on my way." Moving heavily, Augustine followed the servant out of the grove.

A moonless night frowned down on the Mediterranean port. The stars rained their fire from heaven, as though to burn away the pain from the soul of the exhausted bishop. The whimper of children came to him, homeless little ones huddling in the basilica, frightened and famished. Outside the city, fires kindled by the enemy threw a circle of phosphorus against the tapestry of the sky. The Vandals shouted coarse quips at each other, and vowed horrible retribution on the city defenders, in particular the virgins.

Augustine turned his eyes upward and wondered how long it would be, in God's program, before Hippo, city of shadows, symbol of every earthly center, should become the City of God, the city of substance, the New Jerusalem that had no need of the sun, nor the moon to shine in it: for the glory of God would shine in it, and the Lamb would be the light. . . .

As he hurried toward the basilica, Augustine prayed for strength. The man the Roman Empire had come to regard as the most brilliant of his era, the aristocrat of theologians, the prince of philosophers, the most compassionate of pastors, the most human of preachers, in his generation the noblest Roman of them all — this man prayed for strength.

Chapter 1

Where was I, and how far was I exiled from the joys of your house in that sixteenth year of my bodily age (Confessions II, 2,4).

The night was perfect for the assault. The clear desert air of North Africa so magnified the stars that they hung like amber lanterns over the city of Thagaste, giving enough, just enough, light to guide the attackers to their target. A quarter moon dawdled back of Mount Adas as if curious to see the outcome.

A band of eight boys, of fifteen or sixteen years, was advancing on a pear orchard that adjoined the vineyard of Patricius, father of Augustine, the leader.

The boys pushed their way stealthily into the orchard. They shook the trees, or leaped into the air and tore off the lower limbs, stripping them bare. The ground was soon littered with fruit, leaves and broken twigs.

Jubilant with success, the thieves grew noisier and noisier. They laughed. They jabbered. They cursed. They reviled the owner of the orchard for being an old fool too stupid to guard his property. All the while, they plucked green pears and stuffed them into their tunics. They tightened their belts to keep the pears from slipping through.

One of the boys was working near the edge of the orchard. Suddenly he shouted, "Somebody is coming!"

"Where?" called the others, startled.

"There! Across the field!"

In the barley field south of the orchard a blazing torch was seen bobbing toward them. Fear paralyzed sixteen pairs of arms and legs. A horrified silence gripped the thieves.

One boy let out a frantic oath.

Another whimpered.

Augustine took charge of the situation. "Stop that sniveling!" he snapped. "Run, everybody! Scatter, and meet at the Hollow!"

They abandoned their booty, spread out and melted like shadows before sunlight. Augustine, followed by his friend Alypius, skirted the orchard and dove into his father's vineyard. Well into the vineyard, they halted and listened. Only the barking of dogs in the city broke the stillness of the summer night.

Alypius drew the sleeve of his tunic over a perspiring forehead. "Looks as if we made it," he said. "Ah, that was close!"

"Not too close," Augustine said, affecting carelessness. "Just dangerous enough to be fun. Come on."

"To the Hollow?"

"To my house first."

"What for?"

"Wait and see."

They plodded through the vineyard until they came to a clearing near the farmhouse of Patricius. It contained a fenced enclosure where swine grunted.

"We will rest here," Augustine said.

He leaned against the fence, pulled a pear from his tunic and bit into it. His face puckered.

"No good?" Alypius said.

Augustine spat out the pieces. "Fah!" he said. "Bitter and hard. Hard as cork. Nothing like my father's."

Alypius fished in his tunic, produced a pear and took a cautious bite. "Hm, I must say I have tasted worse."

Augustine's answer was to empty his tunic and shower his entire supply on the hides of the black swine milling in the pen. These squealed their delight and dug their snouts into the mud-caked pears.

Fascinated, the two boys leaned over the fence and watched.

A mottled pig, not full-grown but more predatory than the rest, kept butting into the others as he foraged. Undisputed sovereign of the herd, he snarled, bit, gouged, scratched, stole, blustered. Always the herd yielded to him.

Augustine couldn't take his eyes from the bully. Alypius heard him chuckle, and thought he heard him say something in Latin — something like "Augustinus."

"What did you say?" Alypius sounded puzzled.

"Nothing."

"I thought you said —"

"Nonsense." Augustine pushed himself away from the fence. "You stay here a few minutes."

"Where are you going?"

"Never mind. Stay here."

He left Alypius, and ran toward his father's farmhouse, the curtain of night blocking out his slight form.

In ten minutes he was back, lugging a basket filled with pomegranates, figs, and ripe pears.

"What is this for?" Alypius said.

Augustine's smile acknowledged his purpose.

"My guess is it will not hurt your standing with your friends," Alypius said.

Augustine slapped him on the back. "My son," he said, "there are moments when your powers of deduction are stupendous."

"Thank you." Alypius screwed his face into a frown. "Did your father give them to you?"

"Shall we say I found them in the cellar? Here, you carry them."

Augustine handed over the basket and set out for town. He wore his white tunic knee-length, according to Roman custom. It allowed him greater freedom of motion than African garments. Alypius had on a Punic robe that fell to his ankles, forcing him to take shorter steps.

Augustine walked with a swagger. His school teacher said of him once, "Augustine is the only one of my pupils who can swagger while standing still."

He had the features of an actor. His changing moods were reflected in his expressive face; variously it registered pleasure, chagrin, rage, frustration, joy, offended innocence. This quality matched his incurable flair for the dramatic.

The friends hurried into town and picked their way through knots of figures crouching on rush mats in the narrow streets. Eventually they reached the Hollow, the pride of Thagaste. An oblong basin in the center of the city, it was the hub from which the streets fanned out like the spokes of a wheel up to the clay-formed hills ridging the city. The Hollow resembled a village green or the common of a New England town.

Two rows of snowy marble columns flanked its parkway. Porphyry vases set in the columns held petroleum lamps. Clumps of laurel roses, oleander, and cotton plants sprayed the carpet of grass. Overhead, spreading plane trees lifted their blond heads into the air, softening the marble columns.

In the center of the Hollow a fountain gurgled, flowing into a watering trough. Here caravans of camels toiling up from the desert stopped to rest and drink. Here also horsemen riding in from the lonely Plain of Medjerda paused to quench their thirst and give their horses drink. At this spot Thagaste's housewives, after their morning marketing, gathered to exchange local gossip. Here tonight half a dozen partners in crime waited for their leader to join them.

Augustine and Alypius approached the six.

"Augustine! Alypius!" they said. "We were beginning to think he caught you."

"Not us," Augustine said.

"Next time you pick a target," said a boy, "I hope you pick a better one."

"Yes," another grumbled. "Those pears were bitter as wormwood."

"We ought to make you eat them," a third said.

Augustine seized the basket Alypius was holding and tilted it. His peace offering scattered on the grass. Under the light of the petroleum lamps eyes gleamed hungrily as russet-red pomegranates, yellow pears, and black figs pyramided into a luscious mound.

"There you are, my squirrels," Augustine said, tossing away the empty basket. "Eat."

The boys needed no urging. They flung themselves on the ground, filled their mouths with the fruit and munched it contentedly. Augustine watched them with the condescension of a lord. He himself ate nothing.

"Augustine," said one named Evodius, "you are a fine fellow."

Augustine seated himself cross-legged in the circle. He plucked a blade of grass from the lawn and chewed it pensively. "Tell me," he said, "why is stolen stuff sweeter than other kinds?"

"Why?" Alypius said, nibbling a fig. "Who says it is?"

"My mother."

"Where did she get the idea?"

"From a book."

"What book?" Evodius said.

"The Bible. It says, 'Stolen waters are sweet and bread eaten in secret is pleasant.'"

"I find that hard to believe," another said as he helped himself to a pear. "How can anybody say stolen stuff is sweeter —?"

"If not," Augustine said, "why did we have to steal pears? Any of us can get better ones in our own homes."

They listened idly to his questions.

"Your trouble is you are too philosophical," an athletic-looking lad said. "You got an overdose of learning at Madaura. I say, why try to figure out a reason for everything, as you keep doing?"

"I think it is like this," said a boy with coarse features. He turned the subject into an obscene situation. It was all that was needed to kindle the fires of rivalry; for almost an hour the young libertines vied with each other in an effort to see which could tell the most vulgar tale. The contest declined into a series of personal confessions, some obviously exaggerated, others having the ring of reality.

Augustine waited until everyone else had finished before he told his story. "While I was going to school in Madaura," he began, "I boarded with a man and his wife who were about as poorly mated as a peacock and an ape. The woman was a beauty — ah, what a beauty she was! And the man, well, the man was a ghoul. More than that, the beauty had wit; the ghoul had a head as empty as a drum."

"So she fell in love with you," a listener broke in caustically.

Augustine's mouth twitched.

"You shut up!" the youth with the coarse features said to the caustic one. "Go on, Augustine."

"One day," Augustine said, "this simpleton went away and the wife lured me into an empty cask in the cellar that was open for cleaning, and started to make advances — like Potiphar's wife with Joseph."

"Who is Potiphar?"

"Never mind," Augustine said with a sweep of his hands as though to brush off the question.

His audience had forgotten all about the fruit. Every boy bent toward him eagerly, straining to catch every detail. Augustine loved it.

"She had no sooner got me into the cask when in walked her husband and found us in the cellar. 'Aha!' he said. 'How is it I find you two together down here?' 'Oh,' I said as we came out, 'your wife was just showing me your cask. You see, a friend of mine asked me to buy one for him. I will give you five denarii for this one.' 'Agreed,' said the simpleton. 'No,' the wife said. 'It is surely worth seven denarii.' I said, 'Seven denarii is too much. The cask has too many cracks to be worth seven denarii. If you do not believe me,' I said to the husband, 'go in yourself and examine it.'

"The jackass lighted a torch and went inside to look the cask over; the wife and I sat down on the edge and made love to each other all the time he was in there. Every few minutes she would stop kissing me long enough to poke her head inside and yell questions at him, and while he was yelling the answers we would go back to our amors." He smacked his lips. "I can assure you it was rich and risky business. I —"

"You lie!" The coarse-featured youth got up, dashed a pear to the ground and glared at Augustine. "You are a liar!"

His accusation was true. Augustine had lifted the story, point for point, from the writings of Apuleius, a second century writer of Madaura. The only exception was that he transferred the role of the lover to himself. He never dreamed anyone would detect the plagiarizing.

He put on the mask of innocence. "What did you say?"

"I say you are lying. You stole that story from *The Golden Ass.*"

Augustine exploded with mirth. He glanced around the circle and said, "The only golden ass I know is standing up." He cupped an ear and inclined his head toward his accuser. "Did I hear a braying over there or was that —?"

He didn't finish the sentence. A body catapulted through the air; a clawing mass of fury rammed into him with the power of a leopard. Attacker and attacked crashed to the ground, locked in each other's arms. They rolled over and over, wildly shrieking and cursing "Kill you!" the attacker shouted. "Kill you! Kill you, I will!"

It was the spark needed to touch off a tumult. The other six boys quickly took sides, three lining up with Augustine, three with his assailant. Blood flowed hot in Numidian veins. The eruption of tempers found outlet in kicking, choking, rabbit punching, every form of violence imaginable. Grunts, groans, howls of pain, sobs, imprecations, horrible threats punctuated the progress of the battle in the Hollow as limbs thudded savagely against bodies.

The town lamplighter happened to pass that way, coming to the Hollow to put out the lamps for the night. Attracted by the commotion, he bore down on the fighters and tried to break up the fight. It was a vain attempt. He soon gave up, grasped the ram's horn he always carried, and gave out a long blast calculated to bring the constable on the run.

Alarmed, the boys untangled themselves like angleworms receiving a charge of electricity, and churned away into the night.

Augustine started up the street that spiraled toward his father's farm, with Alypius trudging at his side. Silently they passed the chapel where Augustine's mother Monica worshiped every Sabbath. Augustine didn't look up as they walked by. The sight of the chapel always brought on an uncomfortable feeling, and he had had enough discomfort that evening.

He pressed a soiled finger against a tooth someone's elbow had jarred loose. "Ouch!" he said. "I hope I keep that."

Alypius was nursing an eye that an enemy knee had half closed. "I hope I can keep this."

"Alypius."

"Yes?"

"Why did we steal those pears?"

"Are you still worrying about that?" Alypius said.

"I wish I had the answer."

"Why?"

Augustine shrugged. "There has to be a reason. A man commits murder because he loves his victim's wife or wants his property. Nobody murders without a cause. A bandit robs because he sees something he needs, not just for the sake of robbing. They say not even Cataline loved his own villainies. You and I and our friends there," — he tossed his head backward — "had no cause to steal."

"You think too much" Alypius said, but failed to keep the admiration out of his voice.

They arrived at the corner where Alypius had to leave him.

"Shall I see you tomorrow?" Alypius said.

"Tomorrow. Come to my house."

"Good night, Augustine."

"Good night." Augustine looked at his comrade with affection. "I appreciate your coming to my help down there."

Alypius' smile was rueful. "Sorry we could not win."

"Next time," Augustine said with a wave of his hand.

As he moved on toward home he revived and reviewed his own question: "Why is stolen stuff sweeter than other kinds?" Try as he would, he could not come up with an answer.

Years later the answer would come, and he would put it down:

> The pears were beautiful, but it was not pears that my empty soul desired. I had any number of better pears of my own, and plucked those only that I might steal. For once I had gathered them I threw them away, tasting only my sin and savoring that with delight; for if once I took so much as a bite of any of those pears, it was the sin that sweetened it.

Chapter 2

This same father of mine was unconcerned about how I would grow up for you, and cared little that I should be chaste (Confessions II, 3, 6).

"I have made up my mind. The boy will go to Carthage." Patricius lolled on a couch covered with hippopotamus leather. He picked a grape out of the wooden bowl at his head and popped it into his cavernous mouth. A second grape emphasized the finality of his decision.

Across the white-walled room Monica sat at a spindle. She was weaving an undergarment for her husband. "But Carthage is a modern Sodom," she said, without raising her head. "It could be his ruination."

Patricius laughed uproariously, "His ruination!" Under the dark red toga his distended stomach bobbed up and down like the foot pedal of the spindle. "It depends on what you mean by ruination. By the standards of your Christian friends I am a ruined man . . . I can hear them whisper, 'Patricius is an uncircumcised Philistine,' 'Patricius is a moral leper,' 'Patricius is a corrupt politician,' 'Patricius is unfaithful to his wife.' Ha! They are right, by Pollux." He swung an open hand hard against a bee that had settled on the lower part of his toga, then snapped it, lifeless, to the earthen floor. "They are right. I am a ruined man. But" — he paused and chuckled — "I do enjoy it."

Monica's head bent lower over the spindle. With steady fingers she ran the shuttle through the white threads of the loom. Thirteen years younger than Patricius, she had married him when she was sixteen. During the years they had lived together she had been a constant student of his moods. She knew better than to engage him in argument, so she said nothing.

"Augustine is at the age when his gifts are like our barley crops. They need cultivating." Patricius closed his eyes and yawned. "He has milked our local teachers of what knowledge they have — the gods know it is precious little. He has drained the Madaura sages of their wisdom. He knows the rules of grammar better than any adult in this area. He must go on to the university."

"You are right, of course." Monica kept the spindle humming. "And you are no more anxious than I to see him go on with his studies at Carthage. Oh, but how I tremble — how I tremble when I think of a sixteen-year-old boy exposed to the evils of that cesspool!"

"Fetch me a drink."

In a corner of the room stood a jar of honey water. Monica stopped her work. She went to the jar, poured some of the water into a gourd, and carried it to Patricius. While he gulped the water down she hovered over his couch, a profile of meekness in her simple gray cotton gown and sandals of palm leaves.

Patricius drained the gourd, belched, and handed it back to her. He wiped the drops from his great beard and drew a sigh. "You are a fine woman," he said. "You deserve a better man."

"I happen to love the man I am married to."

She returned the gourd to the jar, then slipped to the front doorway. She parted the strands of esparto grass hanging from the top of the frame, peered up into the sky and studied the position of the moon. "It is late," she said. "I wonder where he is."

"Put your heart at rest," Patricius said. "Come here."

She went to him.

"Sit down."

He made a place for her on the outer part of the couch. She sat down and folded her hands submissively.

Patricius stretched out a hairy hand and put it over hers. "My little dove, hear this bit of news. Your son is no longer a child."

"How do you mean?"

He wagged his head. The wooden disks attached to the lobes of his ears rose and fell with the motion. "This afternoon I noticed the first beard of manhood upon him."

Monica's countenance revealed her emotions. Her eyes, like his too, were dark and penetrating. They pried beneath the person she was observing like the prongs of a trident.

"Yes," Patricius said, rubbing her hands, "our son is now a man. Would you have it otherwise?"

Monica released one of her hands, placed it over her heart and looked away. "No," she said. "Not otherwise. But about Carthage and its pitfalls. I cannot but have a foreboding —"

"Be at ease." He jabbed her playfully. "As for me, I am overjoyed. You should be too. At least we now have the assurance of grandparenthood. Junia wants to be a nun. Navigius is still impotent. It begins to look as though Augustine will be the one to father our grandchildren."

Always resourceful at turning her husband's romantic spells into spiritual channels, Monica murmured, "There are greater honors than those of grandparenthood, my husband."

"Such as — ?"

"Such as the honor of receiving Christian baptism."

Patricius had permitted himself to be enrolled as a catechumen, but further than that he had never gone in religious activity. He was forever parrying the matter of baptism.

He threw an arm around Monica and pulled her down to him. He stroked her head affectionately. She was forty-two, and threads of silver like pearly filaments were running through her hair.

"Do you love me, my husband?"

"I love you."

He told the truth. He philandered with other women in the city, but in his heart he loved Monica. A contradiction, perhaps, but then Patricius was a compound of contradictions. To Augustine he bequeathed a mass of them.

"If you love me," Monica said, "you will apply for baptism."

"You know I would make a poor follower of the Christ," Patricius said, still stroking her head. "Besides, at present I cannot afford to offend our local gentry."

Monica understood the statement.

In 353, the year before Augustine was born, the Roman Emperor Constantine II had issued an edict closing the doors of pagan temples and abolishing pagan sacrifices. The free city of Thagaste lay in the orbit of Roman jurisprudence, so the law had direct bearing on Thagastean politics. A few of the community patricians were wedded to pagan customs. They paid no attention whatever to the edict and continued to offer animal sacrifices in secret. The practice imposed a problem on the local *curia*, or council, of which body Patricius was a member. What should the politicians do? Should they close all non-Christian temples, do away with the sacrifices and so incur the wrath of the patricians? Or should they ignore the edict, look away from the pagan sacrifices, and thereby expose themselves to the possible disfavor of the Roman magistrates?

Christianity was currently enjoying an upsurge of popularity. This posed a real threat to pagan religions. Thus the *curia* found itself in the political-religious crossfire flaming over the Roman Empire. The situation bristled with complications.

With Machiavellian shrewdness, Patricius had worked out a solution to the problem. Was he not married to a Christian woman? He was. Would he be willing to enroll as a catechumen? He would indeed.

He enrolled as a catechumen. The step insured his standing with the state and with the leaders of the state religion. At the same time his practical paganism kept him in the good graces of the non-Christian patricians. Why then, he asked himself again and again, suffer the rite of baptism to be administered and jeopardize his position with the pagan aristocracy? One never knew when he would have to call on them for loans.

From this political expedience Monica sought prayerfully to turn him.

"Dear heart," she said, running her fingers through his thinning hair, "the cleansing you would find in the waters of baptism would more than make up for the meager political preferments you think you are enjoying. What does a man profit if he gain the whole world and lose his soul?"

"Someday I will yield. Someday."

"Is it a promise."

"You are not a bad man. In spite of your faults you are not a bad man at heart."

"At heart I am the vilest of the vile. I find it fun being vile."

She withdrew herself from his arms and sat up. "It is because you are out of grace that you think it fun."

"You have grace enough for us both, my lotus blossom."

"I do long that you may soon have the healing waters applied." Her delicately built-up sense of timing, developed across the years, warned her that it was the moment to withdraw. She smiled into his eyes. The smile transfigured her face so that it was, like Stephen's in martyrdom, the face of an angel. "I must go to prayer." She touched his cheeks and rose from the couch.

"Pray for my sin-riddled soul," he said.

She glided gracefully from the room. Patricius watched her go with reluctance, then rolled over on his side and promptly dropped off to sleep. His snoring was like the fury of a storm.

Half an hour later Augustine drew back the esparto grass and stepped into the room. With relief he noted the unconscious condition of his father. He tiptoed across the room and was about to enter the hall leading to his bedchamber when Patricius came to with a start. He rubbed his eyes, spotted his erring boy trying to escape, and snorted, "Good evening, my son. Sit down! I want some words with you."

Chapter 3

*In my mother's soul you had already begun
to build your temple (Confessions II, 3, 6)*

Augustine thought he heard an ominous note in
his father's voice. He halted near the entrance to the
hall, hesitating.

"I said sit down!" Patricius thundered.

Augustine chewed his lower lip as he wheeled about
and marched to the corner of the room furthest away
from Patricius. He sank down on a low cane stool,
leaned back against the whitewashed wall, crossed his
legs, locked and unlocked his fingers nervously.

He had chosen that particular corner for a purpose.
It was in the shadows. Monica's spindle intercepted the
light that fell from the clay lamp across the room, and
here Augustine had placed himself in a position where
he could study his father's face and at the same time
shield his own from Patricius' gaze.

Patricius sat up and stretched. "Where have you
been?" he said.

"Oh — playing."

"Playing at what?"

"Just playing." Augustine formed circles with his left
hand.

Patricius yawned noisily. Augustine kept watchful eyes on him, studying every move.

"Boy — " Patricius helped himself to a cluster of grapes from the bowl — "I have decided that you are to go on with your studies."

Augustine gave a start. His heart lurched. His eyes sparkled.

"This evening I went to see Romanianus." Patricius named a rich landowner who lived some distance from Thagaste.

"Oh, is he back from Carthage?"

"He came back yesterday."

"Oh."

"He promised to lend me money to send you to the university. In the autumn you shall go to Carthage."

"Father!" Augustine leaped up, dashed across the room and threw himself on the couch beside Patricius. "You really mean it?"

Patricius spat a volley of grape seeds on the earthen floor. "Am I in the habit of stating propositions I do not mean?" He put the question sharply.

Augustine's face was shining. "No, Father," he said. "But it sounded too good to believe."

"Mind you, I am taking this step for selfish motives. Already I am in capricious middle age and soon I shall wither like a sheaf of old wheat. Also, my physician tells me I have an internal growth. So when you become a successful professor of rhetoric — as you shall — I shall expect you to look after me well."

"You can depend on me, Father."

"Augustine."

"Yes, Father."

"The mind is the finest gift bestowed upon us by the gods or by God, if Monica is right in her monotheism. You have an exceptional mind. Cherish it as you would a beautiful woman. Court it. Nourish it. Soothe it. Cultivate it. Discipline it. In the end it will yield you rich fruit. It will bring you fame. It will bring you wealth. It may even bring you happiness." His laugh was mirthless. "At least you will not end up a miserable broken-down apology of a man with a paltry estate, a disease and a bad conscience."

"Father, do not be bitter. You have done well. You —"

"Enough." Patricius pointed downward. "Get my sandals."

Augustine knelt before him. From under the couch he drew a pair of leather sandals studded with brass moons, and slipped them on his father's bare feet.

"I am off to town on business," Patricius said, and stood up.

"Business at midnight?" Augustine said to himself, and knew it was a lie. He straightened and said, "Yes, sir."

Patricius walked toward the doorway, moving with the queer hunching motion of a giraffe. He jerked aside the strands of esparto grass and was about to step outside. He changed his mind, turned around and regarded his boy.

"With your mind," he leveled an index finger at Augustine, "with your mind there is no reason why you should not become a second Victorinus or a second Fronto." The two men had gone from North Africa to Rome, where they had distinguished themselves as brilliant scholars. "Do you agree?"

"Yes, sir."

"Good," Patricius growled. "Now go to bed." He hunched out into the night and headed for the home of his mistress.

Augustine ignored his father's order. He gave a muffled whoop and went whirling around the room like a dancing girl. "Carthage!" he cried. "Music! Plays! Shows!" He struck a theatrical pose, and curled his left arm over his head. "Oratorical contests!" He held his arm straight out and threw his head back, as he had seen public speakers do. "Parades, women, new friends, new books, a whole new life! Ah-h-h-h!"

He stopped before Monica's spindle. He lifted glazed eyes to the ceiling, and spread both his arms aloft. He closed his fingers tight, as though clasping an article of great price. "Ah, Carthage, Carthage!" he exulted.

Then he was aware of a presence in the room. He turned toward the hall entrance. It was Monica. She was hovering inside the curtained doorway, watching him intently. Her hands were folded over her breast, her lips curled in an other-worldly smile.

"Mother!"

"Aurelius!" Augustine's full name was Aurelius Augustine. His mother always called him Aurelius.

They rushed into each other's arms. Monica's tears flowed unchecked as she pressed her lips against Augustine's neck and cheek and hair.

"You know, then?" he said.

"I know."

"Is it not wonderful?"

She fondled his head without replying.

"Mother."

"Yes, my son," she whispered.

"You are glad?"

"I am happy for you."

The restraint in her tone left him perplexed. His face clouded. He forced himself away from her and examined her. "You are not pleased."

She dabbed at her eyes with the sleeve of her robe. "I am both pleased and concerned. Pleased because you are to continue your studies, and that is good; concerned because you will be exposed to the corruptions of Babylon."

"Babylon had cultural value."

"So had Sodom no doubt. And yet if Lot, dwelling there, tormented his righteous soul from day to day and nearly destroyed himself, what will become of my Aurelius in modern Sodom?"

Augustine tossed his head proudly. "I survived the thorns and briars of Madaura's evils."

"Ah, yes, but meanwhile you have entered into manhood."

"I cannot deny it."

She took him by the hand and led him to the couch They sat so close, Monica's breath fanned her son's cheek. She kept her hold on his hand.

"You say you survived Madaura's evils," she said, "but did you? Since your year at Madaura you have shown no interest in the Church. I talk to you of Christ. You grow cold. I plead with you to read the Bible. You begin to chafe. I beg you to pray. You fume like a caged beast. Do you wonder that I am anxious about your soul?"

Augustine said impatiently, "Oh, Mother, I only want a good time."

"So did Lot. He never obtained it. Why? He tried to find it apart from God. If a man desires what is good and has it, he is happy; if evil, though he have it, he is wretched."

Augustine frowned.

"Aurelius, I am persuaded God has predestined you to be a burning and shining lamp for him. When you were an infant I had you enrolled as a catechumen. I had the bishop make the sign of the cross over your forehead and apply the salt of the covenant to your lips. Do you think God would suffer these tokens of grace to be given and leave you in a state of sin? That would be mockery. No, they should remind you constantly that you are not your own, that you have been bought with a price."

"Why did you not go a step further and have me baptized?"

"Only because the Church teaches that sins committed after baptism are more deadly than those done before. Seven years ago you fell ill of rheumatic fever. You begged to be baptized, and I called in the bishop. Just before he was to baptize you, you recovered. Again, you should be able to see the arm of God stretched out for your preservation."

"Sometimes I wish the bishop had baptized me."

"But you must remember that failure to receive baptism in no way gives you license to pursue your sins."

Augustine wriggled and stared at the floor. He decided it was time to make a break with the subject of sin. He said, "You chide me for not praying. Why should I pray? When I went to grammar school here I used to pray."

"You did?"

"Many times. My teachers threatened to flog me because I was lazy, they said. I prayed and asked God not to let them flog me. What good was it? You remember how I would come home from school with stripes all over my back and arms and legs, and you and father would laugh at me! I used to wonder if God was laughing too."

Monica took his head in her hands and smiled into his eyes. "My precious boy," she said, "we merely wanted to impress upon you the lesson you needed so much to learn: that there is no excuse for neglecting duty, even the duty of studying hard. Will you deny it?"

"Well — no."

"The floggings you were given were a form of chastening. 'It is good for a man that he bear the yoke in his youth.' Aurelius, you were lazy and you were an idler. All you wanted to do was play." She dropped her hands to his shoulders.

"I admit I liked to play," he said, frowning. "I still like to. Everyone who is honest with himself ought to admit he likes to play too. Tell me, why is it adults punish young people for doing the very things they themselves do? Only in our case they call it 'play'; in their case it is 'business'; I call it 'trifling occupation.' If there is any qualitative difference, I fail to see what it is."

Monica was conciliatory. "How analytical you are!" she said, trying without success to keep the pride out of her voice. "The answer is: it is all a matter of how much time should be spent at play, and how much time should be spent at work. 'There is a time for every purpose under heaven.' It is not play that is wrong, it is excessive play. Your mistake was not that you wished to play, but that you wanted to do nothing else."

Augustine sighed, and felt his loose tooth once more. "You may be right."

"The past is past," Monica said. "What matters now is your future."

Augustine released himself from her hands and rose. "Father told me to go to bed."

"Of course. It is very late."

"Good night."

"Aurelius, wait."

She rose and put her arms around him again, holding him close. He could feel his heart beating against his own.

"Are you in love?" she asked.

"No."

Her cheek was against his, so he could not see the look of profound relief that came over her face.

"Some of your friends are planning to be married, are they not?"

"Yes," he said.

"But you have no such ideas?"

"Well someday, maybe."

"You must be on your guard against women. Especially married women. Remember what Horace warned: 'Love is like the sea, as bright and tempting, and as treacherous.' My son, keep yourself unspotted from the world. Buy virtue. Cleave to chastity. Postpone thoughts of love and thoughts of marriage. All this will come later. Concentrate on your studies. Busy yourself with your work; it will be your salvation."

"I will remember."

She patted his arm affectionately. "I shall be interceding for you night and day with tears. Good night."

"Good night, little Mother."

He disengaged himself from her and stole away to his bed-chamber.

Monica crossed the room to the table containing the clay lamp. She leaned over and blew out the flame. Then, standing erect as the ilex tree before the house, she tilted back her head much as Augustine had done a few minutes before.

"O my Father," she breathed. "O my Father, grant him the washing of regeneration, and keep him from the corruption that is in the world through lust."

Chapter 4

*I was the ablest student in the school of rhetoric
(Confessions III, 3, 6).*

The week after Patricius told Monica that their son seemed to have attained manhood, he gave a banquet to celebrate the event and the donning of the *toga viriles*. Not that he could afford an expensive dinner, but local tradition called for it. To keep face, Patricius borrowed money for the occasion, rented the necessary dining equipment, and invited his friends to his home.

The banquet was held at eventide in the peristyle, the court in the rear of the house. Most of the guests, all male, were Patricius' fellow councilmen, one exception being the affluent Romanianus. They came draped in light, airy mantles of green, blue, and crimson. They also came bringing raucous congratulations, voracious appetites, and gifts for Augustine.

In placing his guests, Patricius followed the street rules of etiquette. The dining table was surrounded on three sides by one-armed couches, the fourth side remaining open for convenience of service. Patricius assigned Romanianus, the most prominent of the guests, to the *manius*, the seat of honor, the couch opposite the open side. Romanianus was a little man with yellow

hair, a trim yellow beard, and a courtly manner. People
in the community knew him as a paragon of kindness.

Patricius assumed the first couch to the left of the
opening, the seat of humility.

Monica directed the serving of the meal with effi-
ciency and quiet dignity. Two household slaves did the
work, noiselessly carrying the dishes out from the
kitchen to the peristyle. The children stayed out of
sight.

The dining table was made of mottled wood from
the citron tree. Monica had decorated it with red can-
dles set in tortoise-shell holders. In the center of the
board stood a massive silver saltcellar containing not
only a supply of salt for seasoning meats but also a
batch of sacrificial cakes to be offered to the *lares*, the
household gods, later in the meal. It was a sly compromise on the part of Patricius, whose guests were high-
placed pagans. Monica detested the gesture with all the
vigor of her enlightened soul but she was powerless to
prevent it.

The dinner was served in three courses. First came a
variety of pickled vegetables, salted fish, mushrooms
and melons.

"Excellent fish," said a councilman named Firmus,
over a piece of herring. "By the way, have you heard
that our noble emperor nearly lost his head?"

"How was that?" someone asked.

"You know how Valentinian loves to fight. It seems he
was chasing those upstart Alemanni back into Germany
after they were checked near Rome. A troop of them
ambushed him near the Rhine — almost lifted his
head. They say he had to leave his helmet and his armor-bearer behind and ride for his life."

"It must have pleased him to lose his armor-bearer,"
Patricius said, passing a platter of vegetables to his
neighbor.

"Why do you say that?" Firmus asked.

"Surely you have heard what a cruel man our emperor is. Why, they say he keeps two lions chained to his bed, and when some wretched subject offends him he simply sends for the poor fellow and feeds him to the lions."

"Lion," Firmus corrected him.

"Lion?" said Patricius, raising bushy eyebrows.

"He did have two," Firmus explained. "Innocence and Mica Aurea. Innocence performed such a thorough piece of work on a captured enemy that our emperor let him go as a reward for merit. A considerate soul, you must grant."

"And yet is it not strange?" said Romanianus, always quick to look on the best side of people. "No emperor has done more for education than Valentinian."

The servants brought the second course: fresh and salt water fish, rice, pheasant, peacock, and wild turkey smothered in truffles.

"Whatever you may think of our emperor," said Romanianus, "you must admit we owe him a great debt. It is reported that he has signed an edict of toleration that will give non-Christians the right to worship their gods in their own way."

"Bravo!" several of the guests shouted.

"That means," said Firmus, "that we can offer our sacrifices in public and stop offering them behind our barns."

Romanianus helped himself to a breast of peacock. "Only during the day. Night sacrifices are to be prohibited."

"Are you sure that applies to Africa too?" asked a man with a flaming red face.

"Indubitably," Romanianus said. "Why should it not?"

The red-faced guest sat upright, pointed a finger at Romanianus, and said angrily, "It should. But if some of our high-flown Roman friends had their will they would

take all our freedoms away." He glanced at the other
guests belligerently. "What are we to them? Barbarians.
Some of their writers say we are headless men. We are
monsters. We are horned and cloven-footed satyrs. We
are hideous centaurs. We are pygmies who fight against
cranes, no less. We are demons straight from hell."

"Now, now," Romanianus said mildly, "do not be upset by what one or two writers say. We may be sure that
Valentinian will see to it the edict is carried out here as
well as in Europe."

A warm debate followed. It ended only when Patricius ordered the third and final course served: a des-
sert of pastry, confectionery and fresh fruit.

At last the meal was over. The guests pulled themselves up from reclining positions and sat with lowered
heads while Patricius took the sacrificial cakes, broke
them and spread the crumbs on the table, and called
upon the *lares* to accept his humble offering. Monica
had discreetly withdrawn before the ceremony started.
At its conclusion, Patricius wiped his hands on a napkin
and bellowed, "Monica, send out the wine!"

The slaves appeared, bearing vases of Numidian
wine. They filled the goblets on the table while the banqueters stretched out on their couches and settled
down to the real business of the evening. The affair
slipped into a drinking marathon. There was coarse
laughter and coarser language as man after man became tipsy and hilarious.

Monica came to the peristyle for one more look. The
lounger on Patricius' left, more intoxicated than the
others, leered at her and said, "Come, Monica, drink
with us."

She ignored the invitation. The man repeated it. Patricius caught her eye and with a slight motion of the
head signaled for her to leave.

She obeyed.

"Why," the inebriate shrieked, pounding the table with his fist, "she insulted me!"

"No," Patricius answered, calming him. "You see, when she was a girl she used to taste the wine in her father's cellar. One day she drank too much and it went to her head. A slave girl saw her stagger out of the cellar and called her a drunkard. She was heartily ashamed and she has never drunk since then."

A guest across the table giggled foolishly. "Your Monica is good," he said to Patricius. "My wife told me some of her friends were complaining to Monica because their husbands beat them. 'What shall we do about it?' they asked Monica. 'Nothing,' Monica said. 'Do not forget what was read in your ears on your wedding day. You were informed that you were to be handmaids of your husbands,' she said, 'therefore they are your masters. Do not rebel against your masters.'"

"Well said, Monica!" another guest roared. "Ah, this is rich. I must remember to tell my wife about it the next time I give her a slap."

It was time for Augustine to make his debut in the new garment. Patricius, not without difficulty, succeeded in quieting the company. He clapped his hands three times and looked toward the house. Augustine, who was waiting in the kitchen for the signal, came out arrayed in his *toga viriles*. He wore it proudly.

Monica had woven the toga. It was pure white wool, full and flowing, arranged in a series of graceful folds. Its material was three times his body length. One end was flung over his left shoulder and fell to his feet; the remainder was brought around under his right shoulder, leaving it exposed, then circled his torso and dangled elliptically to a point below his knees.

Despite his nervousness, Augustine enjoyed the drama of the moment. The men were staring at him with admiration. He moved out to the peristyle and halted ten paces from the open side of the dining table.

Standing easily in the mellow night, he flung his most captivating smile at the banqueters. Flickering candle-light flooded his face. The low-slung stars, glittering like the points of silver spires, seemed to be winking at him and whispering, "Tonight is yours."

Augustine could not be called handsome. Even Monica admitted that to herself. He was hawk-nosed and his cheekbones stood out too prominently. His mouth had an almost feminine softness, as well as a disarming innocence. His forehead was high and broad, out of proportion to the rest of his features. Nevertheless most people found him strikingly attractive. His buoyant personality overcame any physical handicaps. He always brought with him a subtle excitement that pervaded a room like rare perfume, appealing and haunting.

That was especially true tonight. The wine in the drinking vessels did not sparkle more brightly than his eyes. The snowy whiteness of the new toga accentuated the fine duskiness of his skin. His hair, in true Roman style, was cut short. He dominated the scene as the moon overhead dominated the heavens.

The visitors at the table, never sorry for an excuse to down one more drink, seized their goblets and drained them heartily. They cheered, hiccupped, burbled, laughed, and hurled joyous felicitations at Augustine for his graduation from the school of boyhood to the college of manhood. Many were the vulgar quips injected into these congratulations. Augustine took them all in stride, tucking them away in the arsenal of his memory to pass on to his own friends on the morrow.

And back in the kitchen Monica, heartsick, watched and listened.

Eventually the confusion died down. Patricius nodded to his son. Augustine stepped backward two paces, cleared his throat, and proceeded to recite one of the *Eclogues* of Virgil. He loved Virgil with a passion that bordered on fanaticism. He devoured everything the

Roman poet had ever written, and memorized long passages from his works. More than once Monica had to take the *Aeneid* from his unwilling hands and hustle him off to bed. Often he wept over Dido's death. It was with love in his heart and with genuine feeling that he recited the *Eclogue* for his father's guests.

And the drunken crowd was moved. They applauded boisterously to show their appreciation.

Romanianus struggled to his feet, deep emotion on his face. He called for silence. Addressing Augustine, he said, "My young friend, that was tremendous. I have heard poorer reading from the lips of professionals in Carthage. I predict that one day you will be a truly great orator."

He fell back on his couch, and the guests cried wildly, "Bravo! Bravo!"

Patricius looked pleased. Beckoning to the slaves to fill the goblets again, he said to Augustine, "Now let us have one of your original poems."

"Yes, yes!" the others clamored. "A poem of your own."

Augustine gave in. He waited briefly, and then recited:

"All things grow not old;
But all perish.
In truth, when they are arising
And beginning to be,
The more they speed to grow into being
The more they speed toward ceasing to be.
This is the law of them. . . .
Even thus our speech completed
By means of syllables of sound.
And they rend her with pestilent regrets,
Because she desires that they may continue to be.
And loves to repose in what she loves. . . ."

He finished, waited an instant, and bowed. But the response was disappointing. Most of the guests were

too drunk to understand him. Some had dropped off
to sleep. One asked, "Eh? What's he talking about?"
and buried his nose in his goblet.

Patricius had trouble hiding his chagrin. Augustine's
eyes, as he turned away, were moist with bitter tears.

"Augustine!"

He brushed his eyes with the back of his hand and
looked around. Romanianus was motioning him to return. Slowly he walked back, stood at the table opening
and waited.

"My son," Romanianus said softly, "do not be discouraged. You were superb."

Augustine bowed in acknowledgment.

"You will be traveling to Carthage in the fall," Romanianus went on.

"Thanks to your goodness, I will."

"I want you to live at my winter home there until you
get your bearings."

Augustine's face was radiant. "Oh, thank you, sir!" he
cried. "Thank you!"

Romanianus glanced down the table at Patricius who
had been listening to the conversation. He raised his
goblet and smiled warmly. Patricius smiled in answer,
reached out a shaking hand and clasped his own goblet.

Augustine said good night and hurried to the house
and to Monica

"What did Romanianus want?" she asked, almost
fiercely.

"Mother!" Augustine said. "Oh, Mother, he's wonderful! He asked me to live at his home in Carthage."

She shivered with pure delight, then dropped her
head, closed her eyes and murmured, "Thanks be to
God. He has given my son a guardian."

Chapter 5

She informed her son of the servants'
meddling tongues (Confessions IX, 9, 20).

For Augustine the months that separated him from
Carthage dragged like camels straggling across the desert. Life was an unorganized boredom. He lounged in
the yard with Navigius and Junia, and debated with
them on every conceivable subject. He played pranks
on the household slaves until they were almost ready to
run away. He rode horseback and went on fishing trips
with Alypius and Evodius. Or he simply lay for hours on
his bed and deeded over his mind to the business of
daydreaming of the excitement that awaited him in
Carthage.

As a rule he passed his evenings at the Hollow, loitering with other young idlers. He loved dice throwing,
and when he had money he would gamble like a man
of substance. He worked tricks of magic with walnut
shells and dried peas. Sometimes he and his companions would sprawl on the grass under the porphyry
lamps and study the antics of the quail, blackbirds, and
redwings they had captured and clapped into reed
cages.

Then, of course, there had to flare up the regular
feuds between dissident cliques. Many were the summer nights when Augustine, more frail than his fellows,
crept home, groggy, weary, and bleeding. Monica never
failed to be there waiting to gather him into loving
arms. She would chide him for behaving like a wildcat
cub, anoint him with tears and unguents, and put him
tenderly to bed.

One bright summer morning Augustine summoned
Alypius and Evodius and led them to the Hollow for a
game of *trigon,* played with a cork ball.

The day was sultry. By midmorning the players were
hot and thirsty and ready to call a halt. They drifted to
the fountain for a drink.

Augustine drank first. "What water!" he said. "What
water! I shall miss it when I leave Thagaste. The nectar
of Olympus —" He stopped and scowled. "Olympus!"
he snorted.

Alypius, in the act of drinking, raised his head. He
swallowed and said, "What is wrong with Olympus?"

"Nothing except that it is in Greece."

"And what is so bad about Greece?" said Evodius, a
tall boy with the bearing of a soldier.

"I hate Greece." Augustine, who was left-handed, was
holding the cork ball. He slammed it into the palm of
his right hand. "I hate everything about Greece. I hate
everything that comes out of Greece."

"I cannot understand you," Alypius said, his great
owl eyes more serious than ever. "To me the Greeks are
a fine, cultured race."

A thick hedge ran along the parkway near the fountain. At Augustine's suggestion they walked around to
the far side and threw themselves on the ground. The
shadow of the hedge shielded their bodies from the
blazing sun.

"Why do you hate Greece?" Evodius asked.

"I am a Roman first and last," Augustine said proudly.

"But the Romans owe the Greeks a heavy debt," Alypius said.

"What debt?"

"Would we not be poorer without Homer, for instance?"

"Homer!" Augustine turned up his nose disdainfully. "What do we owe Homer? Give me a single line of Virgil or Horace to ten thousand *Illiads* and *Odysseys.*"

"You are getting yourself involved," Evodius said. "Remember what your beloved Horace said: 'My glory is that you should rank me with the lyric poets of Greece.'"

"An extravagance," said Augustine. "He was being modest."

"Then what about Virgil?" Alypius said. "He was forever writing about Helen and Achilles, and —"

"Not forever," Augustine interrupted. He spoke rapidly. To the annoyance of his friends, his alert mind would often race ahead of theirs, anticipate forthcoming statements and formulate replies before they could get their words out. "Not forever. You are thinking of that passage in the fourth *Eclogue.* What is Virgil getting at there? Very simple. He is contrasting the character of four Greeks with a coming deliverer:

"Another Tiphys shall new seas explore;

Another Argo laid the chiefs upon the Iberian shore,

Another Helen other wars create,

And great Achilles urges the Trojan fate;

And when to ripen he shall grow —"

A burst of feminine laughter broke in on the boys. A company of housewives, having finished their marketing, had begun to assemble at the fountain to rest, and to tell and hear the latest gossip.

Augustine frowned. "Look, you two," he said, changing subjects, "why not come to Carthage with me? You must be as tired of this place as I am."

Evodius turned over on his back. He reached up, tore a leaf from the hedge, and picked at it. "I am going to stay here for a few more years and then go into the Army."

"What about you, Alypius?"

"I would like that."

"Why not ask your father to send you?"

"I will," Alypius said. "I will ask him tonight. What—"

"Sh-h —" Augustine laid a finger on his lips and cocked his head to one side. From the buzz of voices at the fountain his ear had picked up the mention of his mother's name.

Augustine was still. Gradually he was able to put together the fragments of conversation. They made his heart sink.

By vicious innuendo, the gossipmongers at the fountain linked the name of Monica with the names of men she was supposed to be meeting at the *agapae*.

The *agapae* were love feasts held in cemeteries where Christian martyrs lay buried. In the church a custom had sprung up that encouraged the gathering together of the living pious about the tombs of the noble dead, there to eat and drink in their honor. Community skeptics whispered that the *agapae* were well named: on occasion things got out of hand and the love feasts served as a cover for lewdness.

The significance of the gossipers' comments filled Augustine with rage. He jumped to his feet and dashed around the hedge. The women were too occupied with their scandalizing to notice him.

He shook his fists at them. "You old crones!" He advanced on them like an infuriated bull. "You ragweeds! You daughters of mongrels! You filthy sows! You clots of vermin!"

Behind him Alypius and Evodius were on their feet peering over the parapet of the hedge. They listened to their friend's tirade with profound admiration of Augustine's juggling of invectives as he cursed, reviled, and consigned the offenders to the lowest balcony of the lowest pit of the lowest hell for time and for eternity.

The women heard him with open amusement. They looked at each other and smiled. Speaking in sharp Punic phrases, they told each other the boy's sanity was to be questioned. To dramatize the idea, they made circling motions with their hands.

This was like throwing oil on flames. Augustine's wrath mounted to the point of explosion. His voice, normally high and piping, rose to a crescendo of wild shrieks — then cracked.

The women cackled with delight.

Even Augustine felt the absurdity of the situation. His arms fell weakly to his sides. He spun around and ran away as fast as he could, boiling with shame and indignation.

A chorus of jeers followed him out of the Hollow.

Fifteen minutes later he stormed into his father's house, the tears trickling down his cheeks. He was in time to witness the unfolding of a strange drama.

Patricius stood in the center of the front room, clutching a long birch rod in his right hand. Before him cowered the two household slaves, and across the room Monica stood with Junia, Patricius' mother. Neither appeared upset over the violence of the scene.

For the moment Augustine forgot his own grief.

Patricius raised his rod and brought it down on the backs of the servants. "You *will* peddle lies about my wife!" he roared. "By Pollux, I will teach you!"

The slaves howled with pain and rolled on the floor. "Mercy!" they begged. "Have mercy, master!"

Patricius' face was black as a thunderhead. "Mercy?" He kicked at them furiously. "How much mercy did you have for your mistress when you spread those lies about her?"

"Forgive us, master! Forgive us, mistress!"

Patricius delivered a final kick on the hip of the slave nearest him. "Go to your quarters. And if I ever catch you lying about your mistress again, I swear I will cut off your ears and feed them to the pigs. Be off now."

Whimpering, the slaves crept out of the room.

"I will teach them to lie about my wife." Patricius tossed the rod away and went toward the jar of honey water. "The miserable dogs. I ought to get rid of them."

"Thank you, my husband," Monica said to him. She turned to her mother-in-law. "And thank you, dear Junia, for believing me innocent. I am so happy Patricius and I have a daughter named in your honor. May she always be a credit to you."

"May she indeed," said Junia. She detached herself from Monica and went to join Patricius.

Monica took Augustine aside and said, "You are in trouble, my son?"

"Not in trouble. I do not understand —"

"Let me explain." She ran soothing hands over his cheeks, still damp from weeping. "You see, someone who despises me started an ugly rumor. Our servants picked it up and told it to your grandmother. She felt that it was her duty to report it to your father."

"Yes, but — "

"How did I convince my family I was wronged? I called on Junia and dispelled her fears, and she came to us this morning to assure your father there was nothing to the rumor. You saw the outcome."

"But, Mother," Augustine said, "do you know that people in town are talking?"

"I am sure of it. I'm not disturbed at all."

"I am," he said.

She cupped his chin in her hand and smiled into his eyes. "You need not be," she said. "When one is right, one can afford to be patient. Water will not stay long in a leaky pail. Brush fires quickly burn themselves out. Falsehood has a way of wearing away — unless we keep it stirred up."

"I hope you are right."

"Besides," Monica said, "God ponders all the ways of His children. He knows that in the integrity of my heart and the innocence of my hands I conduct myself virtuously at the *agapae*. In His own time He will bring forth my righteousness as the light and my judgment as the noonday. Do you believe me?"

"Yes, little Mother," he said worshipfully. "I believe you."

Chapter 6

*So I arrived at Carthage, where the din of scandalous
love-affairs rage cauldron-like around me
(Confessions III, 1, 1).*

Beautiful in its location, the joy of the whole North
African world, was Carthage, mistress of the Mediterranean. Her poets praised her in lavish terms. She was
splendid. She was august. She was sublime. Thrust out
on a peninsula stretching into a blue bay, she sat astride
green hills and flaxen plains like an equestrienne of
rank, haughtily surveying the earth.

Carthage had staged the most remarkable recovery
of any ruined city in ancient history. As a climax to the
Punic Wars, the Roman general Scipio had leveled and
plowed under Rome's hated rival. It was assumed that
he had administered the deathblow. Then, like the
seven-headed beast described in the Apocalypse, her
deadly wound was healed and all the world wondered.
Shortly before the dawn of the Christian era, Octavius
Augustus undertook the task of reconstruction — and
with incredible success. He made the glory of Roman
Carthage surpass the glory of Punic Carthage.

In the year 369, Augustine had his first view of the
enchanted city. Like the Queen of Sheba beholding the

empire of Solomon, he found that the half had not been told. Elated, he rubbed his eyes, felt his heart soar, and fell in love with the city.

Carthage had followed the Roman pattern in building her Palatine, her Capitol, her Forum, her Odeum. The Colosseum rivaled Rome's Colosseum in splendor and size. Pagan temples rose all over the city, temples dedicated to Jupiter, to Juno, to Tanit, the favorite goddess of the Carthaginians, to Isis, the cow-headed Egyptian goddess, and to Saturn, formerly the Phoenician god Moloch. Basilicas also checkered the streets of the city, as did Christian cemeteries. Hardly a day in the calendar year passed that did not mark the martyrdom of some gallant Christian.

Nature smiled brightly on the Mediterranean port. She was blessed with liquid sunshine in abundance. In the spring, filmy showers fell. All the year round vapors swirled up from the sea like rosy wraiths to moisten the landscape and keep it perennially green.

Augustine arrived from Thagaste in the middle of September. He had come to Carthage early to adjust himself to cosmopolitan life, for the university would not begin its winter term until October. Alypius was to join him then.

He traveled by Imperial Post. In his baggage nestled Romanianus' formal invitation to be his guest, and in his head dreams of romance and adventure.

Romanianus' winter home perched on a cliff overlooking the Mediterranean. Located in Medara, the choicest of the suburbs, it was half encircled by other mansions with golden roofs gleaming in the sunlight like burnished shields. On the bluff before the house ran the famous forty-five-mile aqueduct that channeled the waters of the Zaghouan River into the reservoirs of Medara. Its series of fifteen arches loomed at regular intervals like the segments of a huge caterpillar. Lions' heads festooned it at the summit and gilded buttresses at the base.

The slender boy from Thagaste stood on the wide porch of the mansion, no longer filled with bravado. Under his tunic, his limbs shook like the boughs of a tree in a gale. With no little awe, he knocked on the door of the mansion. A Negro slave appeared.

Augustine handed the man Romanianus' invitation. "I am Augustine," he said.

"Yes, sir. Come in, sir."

The slave bowed and stepped aside, and Augustine crossed the threshold. He found himself in a spacious room ornamented with gold vases and censers. Silver candelabra hanging from the ceiling dazzled him. He eyed with wonder the ivory conches covered with lynx skins, birds and fish of black onyx, statues of tigers balancing crystal globes on their heads, and numberless other antiques. In the wall, narrow black discs, transparent as glass, admitted a diffused light.

The slave bowed again and went away. Augustine was engrossed in an admiring inspection of the room when a young man entered, foppishly gowned.

"I am Marcus," he said. "Romanianus is my uncle. He is in Utica on business, but he is expecting you."

"He has been marvelous to me," Augustine said.

"He is marvelous to everyone. Come with me to your room."

Augustine followed Marcus through a labyrinth of rooms to one of the guest chambers in the east wing. It was furnished with a couch of cedar, chairs and chests of cedar; along the wall stretched a bas-relief.

"Have you been to Carthage before?" Marcus asked.

"No, this is my first time," Augustine said. "What a fascinating city it is!"

"It is a great city. Would you like to see some of it after dinner?"

"I would like nothing better."

The slave brought in the small hickory chest containing Augustine's belongings, deposited it on the floor and bowed himself out of the room.

"Tonight will be a good time for you to see the city," Marcus said. "We are having the Autumn Festival in honor of Emperor Valentinian. It will be fun celebrating together."

Augustine agreed.

"Are you married?" Marcus said.

"No."

"Good."

Something about the way he said it stirred Augustine's curiosity. "Why?"

Marcus smiled mysteriously. "Wait and see."

At the sumptuous dinner that evening, Marcus presented Augustine to Romanianus' family and relatives. After the dinner, he pried himself and Augustine loose from the household, and the two set out for their evening of revelry.

Their sortie took them to Harbor Square, where they joined the throng of merrymakers. In the center of the square towered the sciapodes, an umbrella-shaped canopy of marble supported by the upraised legs of headless men stretched out on their backs. Harbor Square corresponded to the Aeropagus of Athens. Here idlers spent their time in hearing and telling any new thing.

The people of Carthage were in their festive mood. They kept up a torrent of good-natured banter, some of which Augustine took in, much of which he did not. A mixed multitude surged around him. Carthaginians predominated, arrayed in colorful togas bearing designs of animals, birds, and flowers. Greeks were there, notable for their clean-shaven faces and slim, graceful figures. Augustine saw swarthy Egyptians swinging massive square shoulders as they walked, and Gauls with long hair fastidiously coiffured and coiled on the tops of their heads like shiny serpents. Romans strutted about, easily identified by their statuesque forms or by Latin emblems pinned to their togas. Negroes from the desert and brown-skinned Numidians from coastal providences mingled with the revelers. The whole spelled out a kind of secular Pentecost that had gathered together men out of every nation under heaven.

The babel of voices that came from hundreds of throats amazed Augustine and amused him. Broad Latin, guttural Punic and staccato Celtic syllables blended with the harsh desert dialects, and sent up a cacophony of weird sounds. It reminded Augustine of the noises he had heard in the zoological gardens in Madaura. Everything fascinated him. He rocked along at Marcus' elbow, geared to the excitement of the festival and exulting in the free confusion and disorder. Eagerly he drank in the sights and sounds. His senses thrilled to the enchantment of the hour, and he felt sorry for Alypius, Evodius, and his other friends in Thagaste, because they couldn't be here to share his happiness.

"Shall we have something to drink?" Marcus said.

"Yes," said Augustine.

Marcus led him to a booth where a bald-headed man was dispensing wines.

"I would like cinnamon wine," said Marcus.

"I too."

The wine was highly spiced and Augustine didn't relish it. In Madaura he had tried intoxicants. He had never cultivated much of a taste for them. Then, too, he could not forget his mother's experience with wine. She had seen to that. So while Marcus drank greedily from his cup, Augustine sipped his with indifference.

"The parade, the parade!" someone shouted.

At once the crowd began to flow like water out of the square.

"Come!" Marcus set his cup down. "We must not miss the parade."

Augustine put down his cup. It was two-thirds full.

Marcus tucked a hand under the arm of his new companion and piloted him through the noisy mob, explaining points of interest as they went.

"Over there —" he pointed to a stone building with graceful arcades in the front — "are the Baths of Maximinianus. We must go there later tonight."

"Good."

"This street we are on now is the Street of the Jewelers. You cannot name a gem you cannot buy here."

"If you have the money."

"Yonder is the Temple of Tanit." Marcus made a lewd motion. An immense statue of the goddess standing with bared breasts on a marble mound drew wanton glances and wanton remarks from the men on the street. "I must bring you here to see the dancing girls some evening. What a sight that is!"

They swung from the Street of the Jewelers and found themselves on a broad cobblestone causeway over which the parade was moving.

"Now we are on the Via Coelestis," Marcus said, above the din. "It is the longest street in the city."

Knots of shrill observers lined the sides of the causeway to view the procession. Augustine had to stand on tiptoe and peer over people's shoulders to see the paraders.

Roman soldiers in armor rode in the battle chariots drawn by caparisoned horses. In other chariots Cappadocian archers with drawn bows and Balearic slingers stood at attention like frozen figures. Behind the chariots marched the Ligurian and Lusitanian wrestlers. Near-naked and flexing their muscles, they grimaced horribly at one another, beat their breasts like tom-toms, and screamed challenges at the spectators. After them came flotillas of caged animals taken from the African bush — lions, wild boar, snarling leopards, giraffes with necks smeared a hideous scarlet, wild dogs, zebras, anteaters, aerdwolves, and gazelles.

Back of the flotillas frolicked a hundred dancing girls, devotees of Tanit. Violet dust powdered their hair, which streamed loosely behind them. They had painted their cheeks with vermilion, and lengthened their eyelashes by applying a mixture of gum, ebony, and crushed flies' feet. They wore revealing silk dancing costumes studded with jewels that caught the light from torches and sent out prismatic rays in every direction. The girls turned and pirouetted with voluptuous grace, shamelessly calculated to incite the passions of men. Shamelessly and successfully. Marcus nudged Augustine. "There they are, the dancers I told you about back there. Quite a spectacle, is it not?"

"Quite a spectacle," said Augustine, breathing with difficulty.

After a break in the procession, a double line of elephants lumbered forward, their tusks gilded, their ears painted blue. A leather tower was attached to the back of each elephant, and every tower held a quartet of clowns. They grinned, laughed, shouted greetings from the emperor, and tossed handfuls of sesterces to the crowds. This was Valentinian's gesture of good will to Carthage.

A sextet of consuls from North African provinces brought up the rear of the procession. They sat in silver-crested chariots, and were uniformly clad in purple silk robes adorned with gold and gems. Always the politicians, they managed from time to time to marshal their blandest smiles for the people. When a round of applause would break out, there would be a lifting of fat, jeweled hands and a flashing of toothy smiles.

Then it was over. The last chariot rolled by, and the crowds became fluid once more.

Augustine sighed.

"Like it?" Marcus said.

"Enormously."

"And now what would you like to do?"

"You decide," Augustine said.

"Very well. Come with me."

Marcus led the way to the Mallapian district, where unctuous young men loitered before the doors of gambling dens, ringing bells to attract attention. Customers jammed into wine shops to quench their thirst, and crowded into restaurants to relax, dine, and engage in small talk. An air of licentiousness hung like a tainted breath over the district, and seemed to touch every phase of activity. Augustine felt it keenly, and it pleased him and frightened him. He wondered what other form of recreation Marcus had in mind.

He had not long to speculate.

Marcus turned from the main street into a dimly lighted alley. He drew up before a shadowy T-shaped building set back some distance from the alley. Two broken lines of men trickled in and out. Augustine saw a plaque fastened to a signboard near him. At the top of the plaque was spelled out in sprawling letters the word *Hostesses,* and underneath was a list of women's names.

Augustine stared at the plaque incredulously. A wave of guilty joy poured over him. "Why, this is a brothel."

"What else?" Marcus said with a mocking smile.

"Have you been here before?"

"Been here? It is my favorite haunt."

"Oh."

"Would you like to come in with me?"

Augustine hesitated, torn between natural impulse and a numb fear. If he yielded, Monica's God might rain down retribution on him. He recalled her warnings and admonitions, and trembled. Yet here beside him was Marcus, normal in mind and limb. He had broken over, and nothing had happened to him. What about his own father? As long as he could remember,

Patricius had flaunted God's laws. But God had not struck him down. Besides, in this vast licentious city, who other than Marcus would know of his misdeed?

For the past half year he had been building up to this moment. Now that it was on him, he was behaving like a silly schoolboy, not a resolute university man. Why?

He balanced the problem on the scales of his mind, while curious chills throbbed through him like shooting pains, enervating his whole body.

The door of the building opened to admit two men. A young woman came out. She advanced toward Augustine and Marcus, walking with a studied sensuality. She had on a dark, loose-fitting robe that was open at the throat and pulled far back over her shoulders in a way that left them bare. Her hair was piled high on her head in the form of a tower. Her mouth was a blob of crimson, and as she drew near the two youths it twisted into a bold smile.

Augustine thought she was going to stop and speak to them, but she merely nodded and moved on. It was then that he noticed something strange. From the lobes of her ears two white balls dangled. Simulated pearls, doubtless. They must have been perforated at the base, for out of them slowly oozed tiny drops of perfume that fell upon her shoulders. After she had passed, a penetrating fragrance assailed Augustine's senses with the violence of a blow.

The sardonic smirk still on his face, Marcus put out a hand to steady him "Is she not beautiful?"

Augustine was silent. He watched the woman walk away, unable to wrench his eyes from her earrings.

Then, as though by a miracle, she was no longer there. She vanished like a bolt of lightning. In her place was Monica. Yet, oddly, the drops continued to fall, though they were no longer perfume. They were tears, scalding, anguished tears. Tears in the dear, familiar eyes of Monica, tears that pleaded wordlessly. "Ah, my precious son," they seemed to say, "by the body and blood of the Savior, do not this wicked thing. Do not, I beseech you —"

"Well!" Marcus said impatiently, shuffling his feet. "What do you say? Are you coming in with me or not?"

Augustine ran a hand over his eyes as though to blot out an unpleasant memory.

"Yes," he said hoarsely. "Why not?"

Chapter 7

What apter name could be found for such people than "wreckers"? They are first wrecked and twisted themselves (Confessions III, 3, 6).

Alypius joined Augustine three weeks after his arrival in Carthage. They enrolled at the university and plunged into their undergraduate studies with the enthusiasm of novices.

Rhetoric ruled the world of higher education as queen of the arts and sciences. Dialectic, geometry, music, logic, philosophy — all were subsumed under the head of rhetoric.

The professors met their classes in a dreary, castlelike building in the heart of the city. Wooden benches made up the equipment in the lecture halls, and not a single hall was properly illuminated or ventilated. Moreover, the buzz of city life kept breaking in on the lectures. Chariot and carriage wheels could be heard clattering over the streets. Hawkers called out their wares raucously. Workmen sang at their tasks, and children at play chattered shrilly, making concentration a hard business.

One day Augustine asked a professor why the university did not move to some quiet zone in the suburbs.

"I suppose it has never occurred to the authorities," the professor said laconically.

If the material side of university life was disappointing, the intellectual side more than made up for it. Under the touch of the masters, Augustine's mind opened to the light of learning as the convolvulus opens its petals to catch the rays of the sun. The magic of classical learning entranced him and stirred his intellect more than he had ever before known. Fervently he worshiped at the altar of Virgil. He reveled in the anthologies of Propertius, Ovid, and Tibullus, melted before the blazing lines of Catullus, and stabilized his thinking in the more restrained orations and letters of Cicero.

The university provided no dormitories for its students. Augustine moved out of Romanianus' home into a boarding house in the student quarter of the city, where with Alypius he settled down to a steady routine.

One day soon after classes had begun, a young man knocked at the door of their room and was admitted.

"My name is Nebridius," he said. "I am from Curubis, and I am late enrolling. As you know, it is almost impossible to get lodging in the city. Somebody told me I might be able to persuade you two to let me come in with you."

"We would be glad to have you," Augustine said. He liked Nebridius' noble bearing, and more than that, the addition of another sharer would cut down the cost of lodging for himself and Alypius. "When can you move in?"

"Now."

"Excellent!" Augustine said.

"Agreed," Alypius said.

So Nebridius joined the Thagasteans and at once became a devoted friend.

Their quarters were surrounded by other boarding houses and apartments occupied by students. Augustine, who would never lose his zest for developing friendships, quickly acquainted himself with scores of fellow collegians. He loved nothing more than to come together with a roomful of these and pass away an hour or two discussing poetry, or debating a proposition in philosophy or any other topic that was introduced.

One evening half a dozen students living in or near the boarding house drifted into the boys' room to chat. They sat on beds, chairs, and the floor, and before long the discussion had swung around to the subject of memory.

"This is what I want to know," Augustine said. "How do I keep in my mind the images of sounds?"

"I think the vibrations make an impression on your brain," said a student named Honoratus.

"Yes, but the vibrations float through the air and then are lost. Take sounds of music, for example. They do not reach me in any bodily sense, and I have not seen them anywhere beyond my mind."

"True," Nebridius said. "Yet your memory has stored away their images."

"How can sounds have images?" Augustine asked. Seated in a corner of the room, he threw up his hands inquiringly. "And how do they get into my memory? Through the senses? How can that be? My eyes might say, 'If they are colored, we ushered them in.' The ears might say, 'If they are heard, they were declared by us.' The nostrils might say, 'If they have any smell, they passed in through us.' The sense of taste might say, 'If they have no flavor, ask me nothing about them.' My hands could say, 'If they have no bulk, I have not handled them.' When and how, then, did those sounds find their way into my memory?"

Honoratus had thick curling hair, a glowing complexion, and fine teeth. Alypius remarked later in the evening he had never seen a more handsome face. Honoratus accepted Augustine's challenge. "You have answered your own question," he said. "Your ears pick up the musical notes and carry them to your brain. Certainly they are not carried there by your eyes or hands."

"Wait a minute." Augustine's eyes sparkled and his cheeks flushed as he warmed to the subject. "When and how did they find entrance to my *memory?* You see, when I learned the notes, I did not believe them to be in another's mind but I recognized them in my own mind. I proved their truth and entrusted them to my mind, as if I were putting them away somewhere, where I could call them out when I chose. They were there, therefore, even before I had learned them, but they were not in my memory. Where were they, then? And why did I assent to them when they were sounded, and why did I say, 'It is true, it is true,' unless they were already in my memory? And if they were in my memory, they were so far off and so concealed as to be in the very secret corners, so that unless they were dragged out by the suggestion of another I could not even think of them by chance."

"Well!" Alypius shrugged futilely. "Maybe you fellows know what he is talking about. As for me, I have not the faintest idea."

Honoratus leaned forward and said, "Let me try to follow you. Do I understand —?"

He was interrupted by a sharp knock on the door.

"Come in," Augustine called out, thinking it was another student who wished to join them.

The door swung back and into the room burst a dozen young men, led by an upperclassman named Octatus. Augustine knew him slightly. Powerful, arching shoulders bulged under his tunic, and he exuded an air of recklessness, as did his comrades.

"Welcome," Augustine said, rising. "Will you sit down? That is," he added quickly, "if you do not mind sitting on the floor."

Octatus ignored the invitation. He put his hands on his hips and said, "You have heard of the Eversores?"

"The what?"

"The wreckers. The subverters."

"I have heard a little about them," Augustine said.

"Would you like to have some fun?"

"Everybody likes to have fun."

"Good. Then come with us." He glanced at the other students. "Anybody else want some fun?"

Most of the boys stood up. Only Nebridius and Alypius remained seated.

"You do not want fun?" Octatus said, scowling at them.

"I have other things to do," Nebridius said quietly.

"I have to study," Alypius said.

Octatus waved his arm, like a general ordering an advance. "Come on, then," he said. "Follow me."

They milled out of the room, leaving Nebridius and Alypius to their duties. They swarmed out of the boarding house and marched exuberantly up the street.

"Where are we going?" Augustine asked one of the band.

The young man leered at him. "You will see."

Three blocks away, Octatus turned in at a large stucco-finished building. The Eversores trooped in after him.

Octatus signaled for silence and tiptoed down the long hall. The boys waited at the end of the hall. They saw him pause before a certain room and place his ear against the door. He tapped gently. There was no response.

He motioned for them to come on. They obeyed.

Octatus opened the door and stepped inside. No one was there.

"Who lives here?" Augustine asked.

"Mensurius," said one of the subverters.

Mensurius was a professor of geometry at the university. Augustine had learned that the students did not like him though he himself felt sorry for the man. Mensurius was timid, unobtrusive, and lacking in self-confidence. Like so many brilliant teachers, he had no discipline in his classes.

"Now, shall we go to work?" Octatus said.

While Augustine and Honoratus looked on in amazement, the wreckers went to work. They seized the only bed in the room, turned it upside down and proceeded to empty a jar of water on the mattress of straw. They rifled Mensurius' writing table, ripped his lecture notes to shreds and sprinkled the bits of papyrus on the tile floor. Piece by piece, they took apart all the ornaments in sight.

On the walls of the room an artist had painted landscape scenes in rich pastel colors. To Augustine's horror, Octatus picked up a horn of ink and hurled it against the walls until they were splotched of shiny black liquid.

Meanwhile, two of the wreckers had spied a sea chest standing in a corner. They climbed up on it and jumped up and down until they had reduced it to a mass of splinters. They grabbed the articles of clothing that had been inside and tossed them about the room.

Several brazenly voided on the floor.

As this went on, they roared with laughter and cursed Mensurius.

Augustine's thoughts went back to the pear orchard at Thagaste, and, for the first time since that incident, he experienced a pang of remorse.

The damage done, the Eversores helped themselves to whatever pieces of jewelry they could find and swept out of the room, leaving it a shambles. They shouted gleefully as they spilled out on the street and started for the home of a second victim Octatus had marked out for a target.

Augustine lagged behind. The antics of the subverters had disgusted and disheartened him. He did not understand why this should be. How was it that he himself could lead a foray on a pear orchard with an untroubled conscience, and now feel vile to be a mere bystander in this escapade? It was altogether illogical. It was as senseless as suicide. What a mysterious power the conscience was!

Honoratus fell in step with him, his handsome face troubled.

"You do not like it either?" Augustine said.

"I loathe it. I loathe myself."

"You have had enough?"

"More than enough," Honoratus said.

They were falling farther and farther behind the wreckers.

"Shall we go for a walk?" Augustine said.

"I wish we could."

"What about Byrsa?'

"Excellent," said Honoratus.

The wreckers were paying no attention to them. At the first opportunity the two darted down a side street and set out for Mount Byrsa.

The night was fine and mild. An onshore breeze fanned the peninsula and filled the air with fragrant odors from the lemon groves.

The two students reached the foot of Mount Byrsa and trudged up the path that spiraled to the top. They passed the Temple of Juno and, further up the hill, the Temple of Aesculapius, the god of medicine. On the summit they saw the palace of Vindicianus, the Proconsul. It was a villa of white marble that glistened in the moonlight like snow.

The city of Carthage looked eastward over the Bay of Carthage. Augustine and Honoratus stood on the brow of Mount Byrsa and absorbed the witchery of the scene spread out like a dream world before them. To the north, the open Mediterranean rolled out from them, a dark liquid prairie. On their right, the bay shimmered under the stars like a chest of black ice. At their left sprawled the city, her streets cut into blocks after the pattern of a checkerboard, and tonight flocked with torchlight that flickered like fireflies. In the harbor a fleet of fishing boats rode restlessly, as though straining to put out to sea. Far across the bay at the tip of the Curubis Peninsula, they could make out a blob of light flashing from the lighthouse there, pinpointing the darkness.

Augustine looked down at the city, and he thought of Virgil's description in the *Aeneid:*

> There was a city of old time where Tyrean folk did well,
>
> Called Carthage, facing far away the shores of Italy
>
> And Tiber-mouth; fulfilled of wealth and fierce in arms was she,
>
> And men say Juno loved her well o'er every other land.

"Honoratus," Augustine said, "do you know what I believe?"

"No."

He raised an arm and pointed to the harbor. "I believe that Dido must have stood where we are standing when she watched Aeneas and his men set sail down there."

"What makes you think that?" Honoratus said.

"Remember what Virgil says:

> "Ah Dido, when you saw'st all, what heart in thee abode!
>
> What groans you gavest when you saw'st from the tower-top the long strand
>
> Aboil with men all up and down!"

"But, my friend," Honoratus said, "you are surely not serious. Everybody knows that is a fable."

Augustine wheeled on him angrily. "How dare you say that?" he cried. "Dido *did* live! She was a woman, a queen, a great and worthy queen, and when Aeneas sailed away, she *did* take her life by her own hand."

"Why, Augustine!"

Honoratus gazed at his new friend in surprise, for Augustine's eyes were brimming with tears. He could never think of the tragedy without being moved. Mortified at his outbreak, he dashed the tears away with the back of his hand. "Shall we go?"

"Must we hurry away? It is so beautiful here. What a difference between the atmosphere of Byrsa and that of Mensurius' room!"

Augustine was glad of a shift in the conversation. "Why," he said, regaining self-composure, "will people do devilish things? Why do we steal fruit? Why do we haunt brothels? Why do we destroy property not our own?"

"To gratify an impulse, I guess," Honoratus said.

"What impulse? Ambition? But ambition seeks honor and glory. What glory is there in destruction? Covetousness?" He shook his head. "Covetousness wants to possess, not despoil. Envy? Not envy. Envy quarrels about excellency. There is no excellency in lust, or in creating havoc. Anger? No. Anger seeks vengeance, and Mensurius never harmed a beetle, poor fellow. Fear? Impossible. Fear trembles at sudden adversities that endanger things loved, and takes precautions for their safety. What, then, is back of our misdeeds?"

Honoratus was studying Augustine with shining eyes. "Why," he said, "you are a philosopher. You talk like a man of forty."

"You do not answer my question."

"I have no answer. Have you?"

"I am sorry to say I have no answer either. It is like this." He drew a fingernail hard against the back of his hand. "See, I make a mark on my flesh. What happens? Inflammation sets in. Swelling. Corruption. A sore is raised." His voice was flat. "So it is with life. Yes, but is it life?"

Honoratus had nothing to say.

Augustine dropped his hands to his sides. For some moments he stared moodily at the city lights, his face a turmoil. Then without another word he turned away and started for the path that led down the slope of Mount Byrsa.

Honoratus followed him. He thought he had never in his seventeen years met so strange a personality, or one so complex.

Chapter 8

I was held spellbound by theatrical shows full of images that mirrored my own wretched plight and further fueled the fire within me (Confessions III, 2, 2).

Augustine wrote Monica:

"I am intrigued with everything about Carthage. It is a Malian fountain bubbling forth streams of exciting energy and activity. Its boom and surge get in one's blood; rather, I should say, in one's mind. It is strange: I have been here only a short time, yet already the pressure of duties has washed out so much of my past life. How is this, Mother? The floggings I received in school at Thagaste, my quarrels with Junia and Navigius, my wild boyhood pranks, those battles at the Hollow, my inane prattlings around home, all seem to lie buried; or have they glided back into secret crannies of my memory and must, as though new, be thought out again to be known? Why? I wish I could tell. Sometimes I seem to be two personalities, one apart from the other but fusing into the other. Which is the real Augustine?

"But enough of this.

"You would love Carthage. Even the weather has a soothing effect. On clear nights you feel yourself transported out of world up to the 'celestial globe, spangled with refulgent stars.' On clear days you can find yourself walking as in a dream through shining fields of white camomile. . . .

"From my room I can look out on the Mediterranean. Its changes are startling. It puts on fluctuating shades like veils of a thousand colors: sometimes green, a green of infinite tints; sometimes purple; blue sometimes. What lies below all this opalescent wealth? Who can say? Deadly currents. Undiscovered shoals. Sunken ships, no doubt. Hanno's triremes. Scipio's navy, in part. Fabulous treasures, forever lost. Dead men's bones. How like the sea the human heart! It is full of unseen motion, seething mystery, restlessness. It reminds me of Virgil's description — forgive me — of a woman: 'Whatever by her you have sense of, is in part; and the whole whereof these are the parts, you know not; and yet they delight you.'

"I am reveling in my studies. You will be proud to learn that I am at the head of my class. My professors drop flattering comments toward my bench. I have delivered one practice oration. It was well received.

"A boy named Honoratus has moved in with Alypius, Nebridius and me. He is a thoughtful one. The four of us get along well with one another.

"Greet Father for me. Also Junia and Navigius.

"I miss you constantly."

A letter from Monica crossed Augustine's letter to her. It was largely a monograph of gentle exhortations urging him to apply to Christ for salvation. She warned him of the pitfalls of city life, of the perils of fraternizing with false friends, especially female ones, of the crafty nature of the attacks of the Evil One, of the awful doom that awaits the impenitent on the day of God's judgment. She called on him to flee youthful lusts. She begged him to attend church services. She wanted to know if he ever read the portion of the Scripture she had given him when he had left Thagaste. He discarded the letter with a sigh. "If I had only received baptismal grace as a child," he thought ruefully, "I would probably have been insulated against these youthful lusts." He turned up the palms of his hands in resignation. "But what can I do about it now? Anyway," he concluded, brightening, "it's probably more fun unconverted."

Nevertheless an immediate reaction set in, and for hours after reading the letter he was downcast. When his roommates came in after classes that afternoon, Augustine said to them, "What about going to a play tonight?"

"Good," they said. "Where?"

"I know," said Nebridius. "They are giving Terence's *The Brothers* at the Odeum."

Augustine was fanatically devoted to the stage. "Good," he said. *"The Brothers* it will be."

It happened to be a Saturday afternoon. The students were ready to play after a busy week at the university, and endorsed the plan spiritedly.

They went to the Baths of Gargilius and enjoyed luxurious ablutions. Afterward they dined in a restaurant, then hurried to the Odeum.

Ordinarily plays were given in the Carthage Theater, but at the time the theater was being remodeled by order of the proconsul. Therefore the Odeum, where concerts were held, had been requisitioned for the staging of dramas. Unaccountably, the builders had placed the music hall in the heart of a cemetery. It was reached by underground passages. Columns of Simmitthu marble, spirally veined, guarded the entrances to the tunnels. A sloping tiled roof with overhanging eaves covered the building.

The four students joined the crowds flowing through the tunnels, and emerged in a hall equipped with graduated tiers of some benches arranged in a semicircle. The small stage at the front was out of proportion to the dimensions of the hall. A pair of nude black statues of Tanit flanked the wings of the stage, evincing the mighty influence the Goddess of Heaven exercised over the city. The young men marched as far to the front as they could, found an empty section of bench, and squeezed in between two other parties.

From an attendant they bought the thin sheets of lead listing the names of the cast, together with the order of scenes and acts. In accordance with local tradition, the management had inserted obscene jokes to fill the rest of the space. Carthage prided herself on the salacious brand of her humor. The playhouse prided itself as the spawning ground of much of that humor.

After a long delay the play opened. The players were a traveling troupe of somewhat more than usual ability. They carried off the roles of Terence's characters with drollery and subtle shading. In good North African fashion, interruptions from the audience often delayed the movement of the play. Rounds of applause dragged out too long, clearly annoying the cast. At one moment a self-appointed critic sprang up from his bench and began to censure one of the players. A man seated behind him bowled him over with a blow on the back. At another moment an inebriate burst into hysterical laughter and held up action until a brawny Libyan theater attendant ejected him.

Despite the interruptions, Augustine and his friends enjoyed the performance, and were sorry when it ended. They followed the throng out of the Odeum. A fine mist was drifting in from the sea, chilling the air. The boys pulled their tunics around their throats and headed for their boarding house.

"How did you like *The Brothers*?" Augustine asked.

"Demea," Honoratus said, "reminded me of my father. He has always been severe with his family."

"Not mine," Augustine said with a touch of pride. "Mine is like Miceo. He leaves it to me to tell right from wrong."

It was then that Honoratus first noted an interesting feature of Augustine: that in a group he was a different personality than when alone with a single friend.

"You say your father lets you decide what is right and what is wrong," Nebridius said slyly. "How are you doing?"

Augustine caught the point and chuckled.

"May I point out," said Alypius, in his serious way, "that Demea and Miceo were not too pleased with the way their sons turned out."

"Your analogy is plain," Augustine said. "Honoratus and I are speckled birds."

"Oh, I never meant," Alypius began.

"We shall try not to disappoint you," Augustine said, grinning at him.

"Augustine, I swear —"

"Do not swear, my lad." Augustine slapped the younger boy's back. "It is improper. It is also indecorous. You must leave that sin to us profligates to commit."

Nebridius decided it was time to raise the tone of the conversation. "I want to know what the appeal of the theater is," he said. "We all know we are watching something artificial when we see a play. Why do we pay to see professionals act out a story that never happened?"

"I think," said Augustine, without wasting a second, "that it is because of the vicarious element in the play."

"The vicarious element?" Nebridius said. "Please explain."

"When I know that lovers are taking their fill of love, even though it is imaginary in the play, then I am happy. Why am I happy? Because that actor up there is not another man. He is Augustine. When the lovers lose each other, I am unhappy. Why? Because that frustrated player on the stage is not another man. He is Augustine."

"What you mean is that the stage is a looking glass," Honoratus said.

"In a way it is a looking glass and in a way it is not."

"Please clarify that," said Nebridius.

"The stage is a looking glass in the sense that I see myself in the action. It is more than a looking glass because it carries me beyond myself. To illustrate, if I suffer in my own person I feel misery. If I suffer in the person of another, let us say the man on the stage, then I do not feel misery, I feel pity. Why? Because pity stems from sympathy, while misery stems from pain."

"And pity has more virtue than misery," Nebridius said.

"Exactly," said Augustine. "And in true pity, grief is without delight."

Alypius sighed. "I wish I knew what you are talking about," he said.

Augustine and the other two laughed. "There are times," Augustine said lightly, "when I wish that myself."

They had come to the Via Coelestis. Traffic was heavy as usual, and pleasure-bound pedestrians surged up and down the causeway, even at the midnight hour.

"Suddenly I am hungry," Alypius said. "I think I would like a dish of lentils."

"I too," Nebridius said.

"And I," said Honoratus. "Here is a restaurant. Shall we go in?"

"Spare me," Augustine said. "I am not the least hungry. You three go in. I need sleep more than food."

"Well then, we shall see you soon at the room," Alypius said.

"Very well."

The trio left him and walked into the restaurant at hand.

Augustine was wistful as he parted from them. He was famished, but ashamed to tell his companions that a deeper, more demanding drive than hunger was crying out fiercely for gratification.

He turned away, his pulse pounding, and struck out for the Mallapian district and the brothel.

Chapter 9

Even with the walls of your church, during the celebration of your sacred mysteries, I once made bold to indulge in carnal desire (Confessions III, 3, 5).

Early Sunday morning following his night of debauchery, Augustine awoke with a violent headache. The few hours of broken sleep he had salvaged had been anything but refreshing.

"Ah," he moaned, pressing his hands to his temples, "Whoever said that grief had a measure of delight lied. I wish I could die!"

In the uncertain morning light he could see Alypius and Honoratus and Nebridius sleeping heavily. How he envied them!

"I wish," he sighed, "that I had gone with them instead of to that pit of hell."

He rolled over on his stomach, buried his face in his pallet, and courted sleep without success. The wheels of his mind refused to stop whirring.

He recalled the events of Saturday evening. Now that he looked back, they seemed frightfully bleak, even repugnant. The thrills he had felt in his first visits to the brothel were missing. Why? Either the novelty was wearing off or the flames of passion had burned out, leaving his senses charred and smoldering, like reeds after a brushwood fire.

Suddenly, and for the first time since coming to Carthage, he had an impulse to attend a church service. He beat the idea down and trampled on it. How could he think of such a thing? It was a sign of effeminacy. Besides, what if university students should see him go into a church and should laugh at him? He couldn't stand that.

He tried to force his thoughts back to Terence's play. The effort failed. A whispered voice—was it Monica's? — said to him, "Go to the house of worship. Go to the house of God."

He smothered a feeling of shame, gave up the struggle, and crawled out of bed. He dressed quietly, crept out of the room and out of the house.

The fog that had rolled in the evening before clung to the city. Over the Bay of Carthage, the sun was fighting to send its rays through the damp gray covering. The December air was penetrating, and Augustine shivered as he set out briskly for the nearest church.

Already the streets were beginning to teem with life. Hard-eyed money changers took down the weatherboards from their shops in preparation for a busy day. Singing merchants stocked their stalls with fruit and vegetables. Butchers were hanging on outside hooks a variety of fowl, choice cuts of beef, mutton, veal, pork, and the flesh of reptiles.

Augustine had not gone far when he met a column of sacred courtesans of Tanit. Even at this early hour they were out urging the adherents of the Goddess of Heaven to go to morning worship! Clad in red robes and trailing blue and white veils, they clacked castanets and drummed on tambourines. Some of them tried to catch Augustine's eye, but he looked the other way and walked on.

Eventually he reached the Basilica of Felicitas. The Christians of Carthage had erected the church in memory of a faithful virgin gored to death by wild bulls during the reign of Septimus Severus. A grove of myrtle trees surrounded the grounds.

Augustine stopped outside the Byzantine enclosure and lifted reverent eyes to the rugged stone turrets ridging the facade. Ribbons of fog laced a formation of gray network around the turrets, as though the air were trying to slip fleecy haloes over them.

At that moment Augustine was glad that he was the son of a Christian mother, and, in a sense, a son of the Church, although a wayward son. He remembered with a little thrill of pleasure that he was still a catechumen.

"There it is," he said to himself proudly. "A great fortress of righteousness standing out of a backwash of corruption, offering salvation to ruined souls like mine."

Two women brushed past him, entered the enclosure, and disappeared in the church. A moment later an elderly man, leading a small boy by the hand, went in also. Augustine hesitated, divided between a yearning to follow them and an unwholesome fear. Again the still small voice whispered to him, "Do go in, my precious one."

He went in and found himself in the narthex, now empty. A staircase led up to the second floor. A man's voice drifted down. Augustine mounted the stairs.

The interior of the basilica was so planned as to accommodate three classes of worshipers. An unwritten law barred catechumens from the main nave; they had to remain standing in the atrium, the wide chamber at the head of the stairway, adjoining the nave. The custom was for men to occupy one side of the atrium, women the other.

Only baptized members were admitted to the rectangular sanctuary. They also had to stand, again the sexes being divided.

The clergy officiated from the chancel. In Carthage the arrangement of the chancel was unique. It was located squarely in the middle of the nave and not, as in other cities, in front of the congregation. An aisle, interrupted by the chancel, ran between the two sections of the sanctuary and separated the men's area from the women's.

Augustine reached the top of the stairway. Some sixty or more men and boys were at his right with their backs to him, and at his left perhaps a hundred women and girls. They faced the chancel and listened more or less indifferently to the preacher, a balding priest robed in a long black gown.

The last step squeaked under Augustine's foot. A number of people turned. Abashed, he stepped to the men's section and attached himself to the group. He studied the priest narrowly and, after a brief appraisal, disapproved. The man was short, stubby, over-sanctimonious. He rambled in a low metallic tone, and ended each sentence with a whine. He spoke "from the rails," from the steps under the pulpit. His hands folded behind his back, he turned his head this way and that, now addressing the men, now the women. Augustine thought the arrangement impracticable, for the priest could face only half his congregation at a time. At intervals he would leave the rails on one side of the chancel and step to the rails on the opposite side.

The sermon was based on one of the Psalms.

"I would remind you, dear people," the priest intoned, "that David calls God's way a perfect way. Why is God's way a perfect way? I will tell you. God's way is a perfect way because it is God's way, and not man's way. God's way —"

Augustine was certain that if the speaker repeated "way" once again, he would shout. He was tempted to stop his ears. At that moment one of the men near the chancel called out, "Your Reverence, if God's way is perfect, why does he allow holy souls like Felicitas to be done to death?"

"My answer," the priest said resentfully, "is that He wanted Felicitas with Him in heaven. Please allow me to continue with my sermon."

He droned on while listeners yawned, whispered, and stirred uneasily. Augustine did not lose interest in the message, for he had none to lose. Wearily he turned from the priest and inspected the worshipers around him. For the most part they were poor people, with an unvarnished simplicity of dress and mien. They did, however, radiate a glow that Augustine would forever associate with his mother, a nameless glory reflecting inner peace. He never found this in pagans. He wondered whether it would ever find lodgment in himself. Probably not, he thought sadly. Was he not beyond redemption?

The preacher went on and on, his voice rising and falling like the tides of the Mediterranean. Augustine toyed with the idea of leaving.

Behind him he heard a soft rustling sound. He glanced toward it. A figure was moving slowly up the stairway, a girl with a clear olive complexion and hair like the night.

Years later Augustine was to put in writing his ideas of art. In them he would reveal how he despised the ugly, whether in music, sculpture, or painting. An art object or a musical score had no beauty, he would insist, unless it showed harmony that expressed itself in unity and equality. In his mind he would inevitably go back to this, his first sight of the dark-haired girl.

He stared at her, scarcely breathing. Here was unity: the face and form were a blend of perfect line and contour. Here, too, was equality: the features were exquisitely proportioned, modeled as no sculptor could model them. Their oval outline followed the pattern of an Egyptian vase, framing eyebrows arched like rainbows, a straight nose, full lips that made Augustine think of the wings of a dove in flight, and a sensitive chin.

For the first time since entering the basilica, Augustine thought of God. He admired the creation of such perfection. If, as he believed, harmony must give each of its works unity and equality to produce beauty, then before him was a living emblem of harmony, and so of beauty.

The girl wore a purple robe, slightly faded, and frayed at the hemline and sleeves. A white rose was tucked in her hair, which was long and flowing. She put her foot down on the last step on the stairway. The step squeaked, as it had under Augustine's foot.

Those in the atrium turned their heads in annoyance. The eyes of the women scolded the latecomer. The men smiled. Color flooded her cheeks. Shyly, awkwardly, she joined the women, standing behind the last row to give the preacher her full attention.

Augustine could not keep his eyes from the girl. Drained of strength as he was from his night of debauchery, he could still know the sweet anguish of desire. A resolution, soon to flower into flaming passion, formed in his brain.

"I must have her," he told himself. "I must have her for my own. I shall die if I cannot have her."

The preacher ended his sermon. It was a tradition to conclude that part of the service with prayer, then dismiss the catechumens and visitors while the church members celebrated the Lord's Supper.

The priest lifted up his voice in the closing petition. Augustine saw the girl drop to her knees with the other worshipers. Afraid of appearing conspicuous, he also knelt and closed his eyes. Not a word of the prayer did he hear. His mind was on the girl in the purple robe.

The prayer seemed interminable. Augustine suffered agonies waiting for the priest to finish. He could stand it no longer. He opened his eyes and looked across the atrium.

The girl was gone!

Frantic, he jumped to his feet, ran to the stairway and hurled himself down, three steps at a time. He burst out of the narthex and dashed into the street. He glanced feverishly up and down. The fog had lifted, but it made no difference. She was nowhere in sight.

Augustine leaned against the Byzantine gate, numb with grief. Great swelling tremors convulsed him, but no tears came. The spring had dried up.

Chapter 10

I blundered head long into the love which I hoped would hold me captive (Confessions III, 1, 1).

Monica dispatched a letter to her son, pathetic in its terseness:

Your father has been struck down with a critical illness. Our physician holds out little hope for his recovery. My hope is that he will submit to baptism while it is still the accepted time.

Three days later a second letter came:

Your father left his earthly home. He was not a bad man. You must realize that, dear son. He sacrificed much to give you an education. He loved his family sincerely, if not demonstrably. Thagaste held him in high esteem, otherwise why would he have been elected to the curia these many years?

I rejoice to be able to write you that he allowed our bishop to come in and baptize him the day before his passing. I was confident that he would yield his soul to his Maker, as I am confident that you will do so one day. Again I would plead with

you, my own dear son, to remember now your
Creator in the days of your youth, before the evil
days come, and the years draw on when you will
have no pleasure in things of everlasting worth. . . .

Augustine received the word with little emotion. He
had liked his father. He had enjoyed his company,
when Patricius was feeling jovial. He had admired his
political sagacity, and appreciated the sacrifices his
mother had referred to. Yet he was not able to mourn
him sincerely. The truth was, all his filial affection he
had reserved for Monica.

One feature of his father's death made him uneasy.
He foresaw that unless Patricius had provided for the
financing of his education, his university days were
numbered. He could hardly endure the thought. For
him the lecture hall held a tremendous appeal. For
that matter, so did Carthage, with its sensuous charm,
its Roman flavor, the friends it had given him. Most important of all, there was the dark-haired girl who had
infatuated him with her beauty. He vowed he would
rather throw himself into the sea than return to Thagaste and forfeit the chance of possessing her.

He wrote a letter of consolation to his mother, then
fumed through a week of waiting to learn of his future.

Monica's reply came at last:

You are doubtless wondering about plans for
completing your education. You are to keep on
with your studies. Romanianus, our generous
friend, has written that he will continue your support. I cannot but thank God upon every remembrance of him. . . .

The pressure off his mind, Augustine settled down to
his winter schedule. Learning came so readily that he
did not have to study hard. By this time he had forged
far ahead of his class, leaving all competition behind.

He did expand his reading, however, and became as much at home in the classics as a bird is in the air. The faculty came to regard him as a prodigy. Students lauded him overtly, though some envied him. As for his friends, they lionized him.

"That Augustine!" they would say, sometimes in his presence. "He knows more than the professors."

"No, no," he would protest. "You overrate me." But secretly he believed them."

During the winter, he rarely played. He broke off his visits to the Mallapian brothel, determining never to go there again.

With the passing of time, the girl in the purple robe had become an obsession. She haunted him night and day.

Often after retiring, he would lie awake and try to recall every detail of her form and face.

"I must find her," he would whisper again and again. "I have got to find her."

He used his leisure hours roaming the streets and squares of the city in search of her. It was tedious business. After several hours, he would tramp back to his room, weary and depressed.

He said nothing to his companions about the girl. He continued to visit the Basilica of Felicitas every Sunday, hoping she might come back. He did not enter the church, but walked up and down outside. Or if he were late he would station himself across the street and wait for the service to end, then eagerly scan the faces of the women, hoping each one would be his love.

He never saw her.

That winter was more rigid and more prolonged than usual, Carthaginians said. When at last spring was ushered in, it came with the pageantry of a Roman festival. Beds of damask roses budded joyously. Hedges of geraniums, masses of purple iris, lilac and hibiscus bushes, and sprays of black fennel bloomed in profusion. A friendly sun kissed the almond buds into clouds of bluish-pink blossoms. The lemon and orange groves were transformed into a checkerboard of yellow and gold.

Augustine was glad to watch winter die, for spring revived fresh hopes of finding the girl who was playing such havoc with his emotions.

One sabbath morning in May he happened to oversleep. He dressed swiftly and hurried to the basilica. It was very late, and he judged that the service must be almost over. He took up his vigil across the street, and to pass the time studied cloud formations.

His face was averted when the girl in purple glided from the church narthex. She came down the walk to the gate, rounded the corner and started up the street. He chanced to look her way just as a group of pedestrians was about to block her from view. In that moment he spied her. His heart seemed to burst. There she was, after these terrible months! Instinctively, a prayer of thankfulness shot up within him, he knew not to whom. A floodtide of tenderness flowed over him. He longed to run to her, take her in his arms, and pour out his love. Yet she did not even know him. He would have to move cautiously. He would follow her.

He let her proceed until she was about a hundred paces from him, then crossed the street and struck out after her. Delirious with happiness, he pinched himself on the thigh to prove he was not dreaming. The long search was over, and he had to restrain himself from crying out for joy.

His eyes riveted upon her, he studied her movements, noting the light step, the full free swing of her limbs under the robe, the way her arms hung straight at her sides, making neither forward nor backward motions as she progressed. It pleased him that she carried her head in a lowered position, a hint of innate modesty, certainly. He was especially delighted that when bold men tried to attract her as they passed, she ignored them.

"What a splendid virgin!" he murmured. "What a magnificent woman!"

He drew a mental sketch of her. She would be poor, virtuous, retiring, not very clever. She would contain a hidden fire. She would respond to overtures of love warily, but if true love flowered in her heart she would be vibrant. He wondered how close he had come to her true character.

She led Augustine past the city cisterns, eighteen mammoth pools of water. She crossed the Via Coelestis, pausing momentarily at the water clock on its east side, then passed through the arcade leading to Malqua, the district lying along the fishermen's wharf. In Malqua the streets narrowed down to lanes and alleys. The residents of the district were raggedly dressed. Pinch-faced children romped in the mud and filth of the lanes. Scraggy mongrels and mangy-looking cats infested nooks and corners. The mud-walled houses were mere hovels, and seemed ready to fall apart if a hard wind blew against them. The air was pungent with the odor of drying fish and decaying clams and oysters.

Augustine threaded his way through knots of children and tangles of animals, still keeping a hundred paces behind the girl. A stone's throw from the wharf she turned in at a small white cottage with red windows and a red door. A sprig of arbutus was nailed to the door. In the small front garden clumps of larkspur, scoglia, marigold, cassia and aromatic bushes rose in plaintive protest against the squalor of the surroundings.

The girl, still unaware that she was being followed, entered the cottage. Augustine slowed his pace and strolled past the house, wondering what to do now. Should he go to the door and knock, introduce himself to the girl and her family, and explain his position? Or should he invent a mission? Should he pretend that he had lost his way and needed information? Should he leave and come back another day? His morning had been a success. The important and marvelous thing was that he had at last found her home.

He reached the wharf, reversed his steps and walked back to the cottage, debating the matter. He stood beside an aromatic bush and inhaled the spicy scent. He must decide now whether to go to the door or go away. He was torn between the longing to see the girl again and fear that her family might be offended at his insolence.

Quite unexpectedly, the problem solved itself. A clammy hand seized the back of his neck in an iron grasp, frightening the ardent young lover half to death. A male voice growled, "What are you doing here?"

With difficulty Augustine twisted his head around, and looked up into the leathery face of a giant whose blue eyes blazed with anger as they squinted into his.

"I — I was taking a walk," he said lamely.

"You lie!" the man thundered. "You were chasing my daughter!"

Augustine made a lightning decision. He would be honest and cast himself on the mercy of the father.

"I will be truthful with you," he said. "I am interested in your daughter." He tried to squirm loose, but failed. "Uh, sir, will you please release my neck?"

"Not till you tell me what I want to know."

"Yes, sir. What would you like to know?"

"I want to know who you are," said the giant. The smell of fish on his clothes and hands was impressive. "I want to know what you want with Melanie."

"Melanie?" said Augustine, still squirming.

"My daughter."

"Oh yes. Melanie." He liked the name, even under these adverse conditions. "Well, sir, you see, I am a student at the university "

"Oh." Melanie's father released the hold on his captive and rubbed his jaw. A crafty glint shone in his eye. "I see," he said, turning toward the cottage. "In that case — well, come in. I am Leporius. Come in, and you may have a talk with Melanie."

"Yes, sir," Augustine said gleefully, brushing imaginary specks of dust from his tunic. "Thank you, sir."

Chapter 11

What is it that entices and attracts us in the things we love? Surely if beauty and loveliness of form were not present in them, they could not possible appeal to us (Confessions IV, 13, 20).

Leporius led Augustine into a low-ceilinged room. It was dingy and drab, and reminded him of the cabin of a creaking old ship. There was no furniture in sight. Several piles of untanned sheepskins were strewn on the earthen floor, substituting for chairs. A galley-shaped lamp hung from a nail sticking out of the wall. Bouquets of arbutus, honeysuckle and hibiscus blossoms were arranged in flagons here and there on the floor. They gave out a pleasant fragrance and helped to neutralize the odor of sheepskin.

Leporius sank down on a heap of the skins and motioned his guest to another. "You can see that we are poor people." Augustine thought he detected self-pity in his tone. "I am a fisherman."

"It is no disgrace to be poor. My father was not a rich man, but I have never held that against him. Livy said once that of all kinds of shame, the worst is the shame of frugality or poverty. I often think of that."

"You say your father was not a rich man," Leporius said, rubbing his powerful hands against his thighs. "Is he not living?"

"He died this winter."

"So?" Leporius looked toward the door leading to the adjoining room. "Melanie!" he bellowed.

Augustine's heart pounded.

"Yes, Father," a voice called.

"Fetch us wine!"

Leporius discarded his crude wooden sandals. He lay back on the sheepskins, yawned, extended his long legs and twitched his toes. "Where are you from?"

"Thagaste, sir."

"Thagaste. I have never been there. We are from Syracuse."

"Indeed?"

"Melanie's mother was a Sicilian. She died four years ago."

"I see." Augustine was absorbing every bit of information avidly.

"She was beautiful. Everybody says Melanie is her image."

"Horace had a perfect description of Melanie: 'Distinguished, with black hair and black eyes.'"

"She has had many offers of marriage."

"She has?" Augustine burned with jealousy.

Just then Melanie stepped in from the other room. She carried a porcelain jar in one hand and a pair of wooden mugs in the other. Since coming into the house, she had tucked a lilac bloom behind her left ear. Augustine saw that her hair had been arranged over the forehead so as to form five black points, like the points of a star, directed toward the center of the forehead.

"I do not know your name," Leporius said, watching the student closely.

"Augustine."

"Melanie, our new friend Augustine."

She bowed. Augustine beamed at her and nodded.

Her eyes were downcast as she approached him and handed him one of the mugs. She bent over and poured jujube wine into it.

Augustine tingled with excitement. A tumultuous hammering went on inside him, like that of a carpenter pounding a nail. He could feel the blood racing through his veins. Somewhere in the vaults of his memory a passage from the psalms flashed back to him. He had heard his mother repeat it times without number. What was it? Something like: "My soul longs — my heart and my flesh cry out for —" The rest of the passage did not matter. Howsoever the writer of the words meant them and howsoever Monica applied them, her son applied them to himself. It was almost as though they had been written for him.

Close at hand, Melanie was lovelier than he had dreamed. How deliciously feminine and provocative she was! What thick lashes screened the heavy-lidded eyes! What incomparable blending of form and color in those divine features!

She must have been agitated, for in pouring the wine into Augustine's mug she poured too much and it spilled on his tunic.

His own reaction was one of delight that he could so affect her.

"Oh!" she cried, blushing. "I did not mean —"

"Melanie!" Leporius shouted. "By Serapis, you get clumsier every day!"

Vexed, Melanie bit her lip and shrank back. "Forgive me," she faltered.

Augustine passed it off with a laugh. "Oh, it is nothing," he said cheerfully. "Nothing at all. Has it never occurred to you that our clothing as well as ourselves might be thirsty?"

He set the mug on the floor and made a show of brushing the wine from the tunic, an impossible performance.

She gave a low, musical laugh. He looked up and their eyes met for the first time. "How can I thank you?" hers seemed to say.

Augustine half closed his own understandingly. He saw that her body shielded him from Leporius' range of vision. Borrowing the gesture used by the worshipers of Venus, he kissed his thumbs and raised them to her in a salute of adoration.

"Melanie!" Leporius growled.

"Yes, Father."

"Fetch another mug, and this time be more careful how you pour."

"Yes, Father."

She left the room.

"I shall be glad when she marries," Leporius muttered.

"Is she betrothed to anyone?" Augustine said anxiously.

"No, but she will be soon, by Tanit."

"Have you anyone picked out?"

"Not yet."

Melanie returned, served Augustine and her father, and slipped out again.

Leporius quaffed his wine petulantly. "You told me out there you were interested in her. Are you interested enough to take her for your wife?"

Augustine had been afraid of that question. He sipped the jujube wine, not relishing it. "I am only a poor student," he said. "Remember?"

Again the crafty gleam in the eye of the fisherman. "Does it not take money to attend the university?"

"Yes, but in my case it happens to be borrowed money. Besides, I am sure my mother would oppose my marrying while I am still in school."

Leporius drained his mug and flung it on the floor. Frowning, he wiped his mouth with a gnarled hand. Augustine knew he was displeased with the way the conversation was going.

"So," Leporius said, "you live by your mother's will, do you?"

"No, sir." Augustine rolled the mug between his palms. "But at the moment I am not in a position to displease her. She has secured the loan for me, and if I marry I may be cut off."

He did not believe this, but he knew Monica well enough to know that a marriage with a fisherman's daughter would break her heart. Also, he had another plan.

Leporius shrugged. "You are the one who said you were interested. If you are not interested enough to marry her, then—"

"Leporius!"

It was a man's voice calling to him from the lane.

"Coming!" he called back. "I must go and check my nets," he said to Augustine. He sat up, put his sandals on, and rose. "I am told that many of you students take mistresses. Is that so?"

"Some of them do."

"But you are a moralist."

It was a sly parting bolt. It was also a tacit endorsement of the very plan Augustine had worked out. For a Roman citizen, the courts would sanction a mistress, though she did not have the rights of a wife. Leporius seemed willing. Augustine told himself that only one hurdle now stood m the way of fulfillment: Melanie's consent.

Leporius said goodbye and left the cottage.

Augustine was rising to his feet when Melanie reappeared. She faced him with a troubled look. "You must excuse him," she said, twisting her fingers nervously. "He is like that."

Her voice cast the same spell over Augustine as her dark beauty. Her words were musical; they flowed from her lips like mellow notes from a lute. Augustine was keenly aware of the limitations of his own voice, and equally so of the good tone quality in others.

"You heard what he said, then?"

She nodded.

"Melanie."

"Yes." Again the downcast eyes.

"May I tell you I love you?"

Her cheeks glowed like hot coals. "You — you do not even know me," she whispered.

"But I do. Nearly half a year ago I saw you in church. I loved you the minute I saw you come up those stairs to the atrium. There has not been a single hour of a single day since then that you have been out of my mind."

But as he spoke, she was shaking her head.

"You do not believe me?" he said.

"It is madness."

He held out his left arm. "I am the one who is mad," He said, the words rushing down his mouth. "Sometimes at night when I lie thinking about you, I swear to you I lose all reason." He advanced a few steps toward her. "I have spent hours and hours combing this city for you. I have been to the basilica every Sunday since the morning I saw you there. You must believe me."

She stooped over, plucked a hibiscus blossom from the flagon at her feet, and began to pick at its red petals. "It is hopeless and useless," she said.

He let out a sigh. "Why? Tell me."

She said nothing, merely shook her head.

"Melanie, hear me." He spoke with deadly earnestness. "I have no money. I cannot offer you marriage. I am not good. I have a vile temper. There are times when I shall make you unhappy. What can I offer you then, my love? I swear to you by the great God of

Heaven that no man ever loved a woman as I love you. This is the one reason I want you to come to me."

She lifted her head and the jet-black eyes looked into Augustine's long and searchingly. "I must say no to you," she answered. "Not because you have no money. Look at — at this." She waved her arm in a circling motion around the room. "And not because you are bad, and not because you lose your temper, and not because you will make me unhappy. I am used to all that."

"Why then?"

"There are reasons I cannot tell you."

"I see. You think it would be wrong to come to me."

She crushed the hibiscus blossom in her hand. "Please go now."

"May I see you again?"

"No."

He moved closer to her.

"No, please go," she said. "If you love me as you say, please go."

Slowly and with his head down he walked to the front door. His despair at her refusal was greater than his elation at finding her. At the door he turned, intending to make one more plea. She stood watching him, her expression inscrutable. He changed his mind, gave her a final lingering look, thrust open the door, and stumbled out into the yard.

A western breeze had cleared the fog away, and a shower of sunshine was bursting in golden torrents over the peninsula. For Augustine, it might better have been rain. In his heart was a cloudburst.

Chapter 12

In love with loving, I was casting about for something to love (Confessions III, 1, 1).

Augustine resolved not to accept Melanie's refusal as final.

He let three days pass, three days during which he bore his burden of misery with bitter sighs and, when he was alone, tears. By the fourth day the burden had become intolerable. Unable to concentrate on his lessons, he abandoned his morning classes and started for the little white cottage in Malqua.

It was a mild morning. He arrayed himself in a new sleeveless tunic of white linen, girt with a scarlet sash. In the market place along the Via Coelestis he bought a chaplet of rose leaves for his head, and a gilded sparrow in a wicker cage for Melanie. He arrived at the house. His throat was dry and his nerves taut as he stood before the red door and knocked.

There was no response.

He knocked again, louder this time. Still no response.

"Melanie!" he called.

No answer.

He set the birdcage on the ground near the cottage and ran down to the wharf. The fleet of fishing boats was at sea. A few corn ships from Alexandria rode at anchor in the harbor. Small boys were wading in the shallow water under the wharf, trying to net crabs and small fish.

Impatiently, Augustine walked up and down the wharf. Sea gulls soared screaming overhead, or flew over the harbor, frequently pausing to dive into the water for fish. Once an aged sailor out for a stroll tried to engage him in conversation, but his brain was too occupied with thoughts of Melanie to think of others.

He returned to the cottage to find out if she had come home. She was still not there.

A strolling barber ambled down the lane. His equipment, consisting of a portable stool, a bronze razor, and iron scissors, was secured by leather thongs and slung over his shoulder. He banged on cymbals and shouted, "Haircuts, sirs! Shaves, gentlemen! Haircut or shave, gentlemen!" He spotted the dapper youth loitering before the little white house, and called to him, "Haircut, young sir?"

"Why yes, I think I need one."

The barber sprang into action. He slipped his equipment from his shoulder, set the portable stool on the ground near the flower bed, and seated his customer.

"Yes, sir," he said, as he began the cutting process. "Nice morning, young sir. I said to my wife when I left my home this morning — I said; 'Modesta,' I said, Modesta, I have an idea this is going to be a big morning for my business.' You know" — he stopped work and peered at Augustine — "you know, I can always tell when I am going to have a good day or when I am going to have a bad day, because something in my bones — "

"My good fellow," Augustine said irately, "Plato once went to a barber shop to have his hair cut, and the barber said to him, 'How would you like it cut?' Plato said, 'In silence.'"

The barber looked crestfallen. He resumed the operation, and finished it without another word. Nevertheless his injured air did not dissipate, even when Augustine gave him an extra denarius for good service. Augustine felt a trifle guilty when the barber had taken off. He wished he had not cut short the garrulous one.

He checked the position of the sun and decided it must be nearly noon. "Where is she?" he asked himself. "Why does she not come?"

He walked to the wharf again. He was on his way back when he saw Melanie coming toward home with a basket on her arm. Overjoyed, he hurried to meet her.

"Melanie!"

They met directly in front of the cottage. The basket, Augustine noticed, was stocked with fresh fruit and vegetables.

"Good morning." She said it softly, uncertainly.

Like Augustine, she was in white. Her simple cotton robe, splashed with designs in red caltrop, made a perfect foil for the ebony tones of her hair and her dusky complexion, and for a moment Augustine held his breath. The hair was swept back from her ears and arranged in a fall. A blood-red rose was caught on the left side.

"You have been marketing," he said.

"Yes."

"Are you angry at me?"

She tipped her head to one side prettily, but did not answer. She started up the path toward the cottage, with Augustine at her elbow.

"Please do not be angry with me," he said.

She caught sight of the canary in the cage, and her face lighted up.

"For you," Augustine said.

"Truly?" She put the basket on the ground and knelt before the cage. The gilded bird fluttered in terror.

"Forgive me, little one," she said, withdrawing. "I have frightened you."

"And you have destroyed me," Augustine said, unable to take his eyes from her.

She lowered her head, folding and unfolding her hands.

"Will you let me talk to you?" he said.

She looked at her hands but said nothing. Her silence lent boldness to her visitor.

"Come over here with me." He moved over to the aromatic bush and sat down on the grass beside it.

Melanie waited a full minute, then followed him diffidently. She let herself down on the ground and folded her robe over her legs and feet.

"On Sunday you told me you have reasons why you will not come to me," he said. "Have I not a right to hear them?"

Her fingers caressed a tuft of grass in her shadow. "I will tell you," she said, not looking at him. "My father and mother were slaves."

"Oh!" He tried to hide his surprise, but the effort failed. "Did Leporius purchase his freedom?"

"Yes."

"So now you are free."

She acknowledged it.

"Melanie, love sees beyond such differences. I have faults, but I do not have a false pride."

"It would always be a shadow over us."

"Never! I swear it! Have you no better reasons than this?"

"I am older than you," she said.

"How old are you?"

"Nineteen."

"I shall be twenty this summer," he lied, adding two years to his age. "What else?"

"You told my father that your mother would not approve of your marrying," Melanie said. "Would she approve of your taking — a companion? Especially the daughter of a fisherman?"

"What makes you think she would find out?" he said.

"Women have a way of finding out secrets."

"Melanie, hear me," he said passionately. "Nothing matters in the world except my love for you. Nothing." He laid a hand over his heart. "Since that day I saw you at the basilica, a terrible famine has been destroying me in here. I cannot tell whether my existence is a dying life or a living death. This I know: I need you. I have no incentive for going on breathing and learning unless I can have you."

She picked a blade of grass and used it to draw imaginary pictures on the back of her hand. "And what about my own mother?" she said.

He flung up his hands in amazement. "Your mother? But Leporius told me your mother was dead."

"She is dead. But if she could talk with me I know what she would say."

"Not to come with me?"

She nodded.

"Was she a Christian?" Augustine asked.

"Yes. She became a Christian when she was a slave. Three months before her mistress died, she converted my mother to the true religion."

"And you?"

"Mother enrolled me as a catechumen."

"So living with me is against your principles?"

She nodded again.

"But the state allows this sort of union," he said.

"The state does not own my conscience."

Augustine realized that if he was going to win this prize, he must use every weapon in the arsenal of logic.

"I have not seen you in church for months. A catechumen ought to attend services regularly." The inconsistency of the statement coming from one who was himself a catechumen did not occur to him at the moment. "Would you not say so?"

Her head went up and down. "My father sees to that," she said. "I have to slip out when I go."

A sea gull winged its way over the cottage, cawing harshly. Augustine threw an annoyed glance at the bird and pursed his lips. When it had gone, he said, "Tell me, why has not Leporius married you off?"

She let her eyes rest on his face finally, and Augustine felt his heart step up its beat.

"He had tried six times to marry me," she said. "Oh, you should see the men he picked out. They were monstrous. I told him I would take my life if he forced me into marriage."

"That stopped him?"

"Yes. He is a strange man, but he does have a conscience."

"Why is he so anxious to have you off his hands?" Augustine said.

"He is homesick for Syracuse. He used to be a sailor before he took up fishing. His ship stopped at Syracuse, and ever since he has wanted to go back."

"Were you born there?"

"Yes."

"What about you? Do you ever get homesick for the place?"

Again she bent her head to one side, and Augustine loved the gesture. "What does it matter?" she said dolefully. "I am a woman."

"It matters to me. Tell me about your mother."

Melanie changed her position. She spread both arms behind her body with her hands on the ground, and leaned back. She looked up and stared dreamily at the chiffon clouds that drifted over the harbor.

"My mother was more angel than mortal."

"So are you," he said impulsively, and watched for her reaction.

She blushed, and said, "She was the slave of a great Christian lady who taught her to read and lent us books. My mother read them to me, and before she died she taught me to read too."

"What did you read?"

"Homer, Socrates, Pindar —"

"Greeks!" Augustine sniffed.

"You do not like Greeks?"

"I am a Roman. Well, never mind that. Tell me about Syracuse."

"There is no place in the universe like Syracuse," she said, her eyes starry. "Cicero called it the fairest of all cities, remember?"

"Of course you have seen the Fountain of Cyane?"

"Oh yes! And the Ear of Dionysius."

"The Fortress of Euralys?"

"And the Temple of Minerva," she said.

"I understand the Theater of Syracuse presents free plays."

"It does. You know, Aeschylus directed his own plays when he visited the city."

"Plato also was there."

"And Pindar. And Plutarch. Oh, it is majestic, Syracuse! Its flowers are so fragrant they say hounds cannot follow a scent for their perfume."

Half an hour slipped by. Melanie talked of Sicily, while Augustine fed her questions and listened to her replies with rapt attention. He delighted in the throbs and sighs that punctuated her flow of words. In that hour, a force as subtle and inexorable as a current of the sea drew them together. At points in their conversation, Augustine's heart was so full he had to repress the impulse to shout for happiness.

The sun crept past the meridian. Melanie began to cast glances in the direction of the wharf, and

Augustine was aware of her former restraint coming back.

"I must go," he said reluctantly, scrambling to his feet.

Melanie stood up too.

"May I come back?" he said.

"If you wish," she said shyly.

"You are sweet. Let me take your basket in."

"No. I will."

They edged toward the cottage without speaking. Their silence seemed to forge another link in the chain binding them together.

They came to where the basket lay beside the bird cage.

"Thank you for the canary," she said.

Simultaneously, they bent over the cage to pick it up. The action brought them into bodily contact. Augustine's shoulder brushed against the girl's arm. Each gave a start, and strength went out of their bodies. They hovered over the cage like two paralyzed people, both conscious of a current passing between them, uniting them in a covenant of love as vital as life and as inevitable as death.

The canary had resumed its fluttering.

Melanie was the first to stir. "Oh-h-h," she breathed, taking the cage by the handle. She straightened up and stood holding the cage, with her back toward Augustine, her head elevated.

Still shaken, Augustine forced himself up. He put his hand to his head, jerked off the chaplet, and hurled it at Melanie's feet. Then with unsteady steps he stalked out of the yard and up the lane toward the Via Coelestis.

All he could think of was a line from Catullus. Dazed, he said it over and over, as a priest of Jupiter would repeat an incantation:

"Great the bliss that awaits your future day."

Chapter 13

*Laying myself open to the iron rods and burning
scourges of jealousy (Confessions III, 1, 1).*

Long after his talk with Melanie, Catullus' line re-
volved in Augustine's brain. He told himself that his victory was assured, that Melanie must capitulate under
the pressure of his love. How could it be otherwise? Perhaps she had not yet come to love him with the deep
womanly devotion a lover had the right to expect. Still
from the beginning she had revealed by her conduct
that physically, at least, she was drawn by his magne-
tism. It would be only a matter of time before she would
give in. So, with the verve of Tanit's dancing girls, he
pressed his courtship, and yearned and hoped.

To his infinite disgust, he soon found out that the
campaign was not going to be so simple. He confided
the truth to Alypius one evening when they were alone
in their room.

"Alypius," he said, "have you ever been in love?"

Alypius was reclining on his bed, involved with a
book on mathematics. He laid the book aside and fastened his great solemn eyes on his friend. "Why do you
ask?"

"I happen to be in love."

"You? With whom, pray?"

Augustine told him everything.

Alypius whistled. "But," he said with a worried frown, "surely you cannot bring the girl here, even if you do get her consent to come to you."

"Naturally, not in this room with you three. Still, there must be another place for rent somewhere in the neighborhood."

"You mean you are willing to break your bond with us?"

"Of course not," Augustine said irritably. "I can be with you a good deal. It is only in the matter of living together. How will that affect our friendship?"

"It is bound to make a difference. I do hope you will not form any alliance like this."

"Well," Augustine said sarcastically, "I never knew I had such an innocent companion. I can see you never loved any woman."

"Wrong. I had an experience a few years ago."

"You did?" said Augustine, grinning. "In Thagaste?"

"In Thagaste. While you were at Madaura, studying."

Augustine crossed the room and threw himself down on Alypius' bed. "How was it?"

"I have forgotten."

"Forgotten?" Augustine exploded. "What a naive lover you are!"

"Naïve enough to tell you that your plan will never bring what you expect."

"Well, Alypius is turning soothsayer, is he?" Augustine rose and flounced out of the room, leaving behind him a disturbed Alypius.

The next Sunday morning Augustine went to the Basilica of Felicitas. He did not go to worship but, in accord with previous arrangements with Melanie, to meet her there.

He waited for her near the entrance. Crowds of Christian worshipers filed past him and entered the church. The service started but Melanie failed to appear. Moodily, Augustine paced the street in front of the basilica.

Half an hour passed.

A shaggy mongrel ambled up and snapped playfully at his heels. Augustine whirled, let out a curse, and kicked the animal in the stomach. Howling with pain, it scampered away.

He was all repentance. "I have got to get away from here," he mumbled. "Why does that girl put me on edge like this?"

He hurried to Malqua to learn why.

There was a shock in store for him. Coming in view of Leporius' home, he saw Melanie, dressed in white, dallying with a burly Roman soldier near the flower bed. They were standing close together. Too close, Augustine thought. The soldier's brass helmet was perched at a cocky angle on the side of his head, and he seemed to be doing the talking. Melanie faced him, but her head was bent over some sort of flower from which she was plucking petals. The soldier must be saying something amusing, for a smile played on her features.

Augustine stopped, furious and hurt. His heart breathed slaughter. Why, the miserable jackal! What right had he to be so possessive? And where was her shame, letting him woo her out there in sight of her neighbors?

He sprang forward and charged down the lane, a thoroughly aroused suitor, propelled by jealousy and made doubly strong by rage.

The soldier's back was toward him. Melanie lifted her head and saw Augustine closing in for the assault. She screamed. Augustine grabbed the intruder by the shoulder and swung him around. He let go a stinging blow to the jaw. The force of the blow sent the soldier's helmet down over his forehead and eyes.

"You keep away from her!" Augustine bellowed. "Keep away from her, do you hear?"

"Augustine, stop!" Melanie cried, stamping her foot.

The astonished soldier tipped his helmet back in place in time to ward off a second blow. "You little whelp!" he said between clenched teeth. He doubled a powerful fist and sent it crashing into Augustine's chin. It landed with a thud. "You—!"

Augustine did not hear the second epithet. Flailing the air with both arms, he staggered backward and slumped to the lane like a sacrificial ram going down under the hammer.

When he recovered consciousness he heard the hum of voices, but he could not put the sounds together to make sense. They might as well have been the bleatings of sheep.

One eye fluttered open. Then the other. A ring of faces hung over his. He put out a hand with the palm down. Grass. So he was on the ground. How did he get there?

He brought up his hand and touched his cheek. It hurt.

The faces above him showed relief.

Melanie said, "Please go away, everyone. I think he will be all right now."

The faces withdrew.

He was lying under the hibiscus bush with the late morning sunlight sifting through its leafy cracks. He recalled his brief but disastrous bout with the Roman soldier.

"Where is he?" Augustine groaned.

Melanie sat down on the ground and leaned over him, filling his horizon. "Who?"

"The soldier."

"I sent him away."

"How did I get here?"

"I had my neighbors carry you here."

"Oh, my jaw!"

"You know," Melanie said, and her face was imperturbable, "you have the mind of a man and the emotions of a child."

He raised his head, felt dizzy, and let it fall back on the grass. "Who is the soldier?"

"One of my cousins. He has just been assigned to Carthage."

"I want to know the truth. Who is he?"

Her black eyes were troubled. She turned away and started to rise.

He put out a detaining hand. "Please stay with me."

She hesitated.

"I believe you," he said. "If you say he is your cousin, I believe you."

She relented and sat back again.

"I am an imbecile and a jealous fool," Augustine said. "And can you not see the reason? Jealousy is the fruit of love. My mother used to say that jealousy is as cruel as the grave, and burns like coals of fire."

"Is that why you cannot marry?"

"What do you mean?" he said.

"Is it that she wants all your love for herself?"

"No, no, no. She thinks I should not consider marriage until I finish my education."

Disconsolately, Melanie regarded the hibiscus bush spreading over them.

Augustine raised his head again. There was no dizziness now, so he sat up. "Would it be wrong for me to ask if you have any feeling of jealousy?" he asked pointedly.

Her olive complexion turned crimson.

The man living next door put in his appearance. "How is the young man?" he said. "Better?"

"Thank you," Augustine said pleasantly. "Am I obliged to you for pulling me off the lane?"

"I helped carry you over here."

"It was good of you, and I am grateful."

The man bowed and moved on.

Augustine addressed Melanie again. "Tell me, fair one, do you love me?"

"What is love?"

For a moment he said nothing, deliberating.

"You must have an opinion on love," Melanie said.

"I have an opinion on everything."

"What is love?" she repeated.

"Love," he said thoughtfully, "is light, the prince of colors. It suffuses all you see. Even when you are concentrating on other things, it charms you with its varied play."

"Is that original?"

"Yes."

"I never knew you were a poet," she said.

"Who can define the indefinable?" He rolled over on his side. "One can only try. I wake up in the morning, and the light of the sun filters into my eyes. This sweetens my whole day, for light is sweet. Love for you shines in my heart and love is sweet. Your beautiful face comes before me, and my day is sweet."

She was listening to him with parted lips.

"If the love one gives is not returned," he went on, "there is a sting to that love. The sweet becomes bitter-sweet."

"You are saying that if I do not return your love, you are —"

"I am wrapped in a flame."

She laid a finger on his lips. For a moment he thought she was going to confess her love. Instead, she murmured, "You are a strange boy."

He captured her hand and held it tight. "Can you not love me, Melanie?"

She shivered, although the day was warm.

"Melanie, my beloved, why not be honest with your heart?"

"I am afraid."

"Why?"

She inclined her head to one side.

"Why, Melanie?"

"I am afraid because — because if I fall in love once, I shall not fall in love again."

"My beloved, there will never be any love but yours," he said desperately.

"When the time came for you to put me away, as it would when you grew famous," she said in a flat voice, "you would smash this heart in a thousand pieces."

"Never! I promise it."

"You would."

"My sweet-voiced lark, let me tell you this: you are a lonely, lonely person. I have been studying you, as you have been studying me. Do you realize that you are troubled with doubts?"

She dug her teeth into her full lower lip.

"And do you not know I can give you surety?"

She was close to tears.

"Melanie, believe me, I can and will."

She disengaged her hand from his and started to rise.

"Come with me, Melanie. Nothing stands between you and surety, and happiness, and my protecting love — nothing but your will."

"And my conscience." She looked away. "It is wrong, Augustine, wrong. And since it is wrong, there cannot be happiness and there cannot be surety for either of us — for either of us." Her voice trailed away.

"I need you," he said.

She rose, trembling, and hurried toward the cottage.

"Melanie, wait!"

It was no use. She disappeared through the red door.

A moment later Leporius came up the lane from the wharf in time to see the figure of a young man leaving his premises. The young man's head was on his breast. He made his way along the lane slowly, as a mourner walks in a funeral procession. The fisherman's eyes were shot through with malice and cunning as they rested on the slender back. . . .

Two nights afterward, Augustine was seated at a table writing a letter to Monica when Nebridius burst in, waving a sheet of wax. "I met a man outside," he said. "He had this letter for you, so I told him I would be glad to deliver it."

Augustine dropped his pen and seized the letter.

It read:

> Melanie to Augustine: "My father has sold the house and sailed for Syracuse."

That was all.

Augustine dropped the wax sheet on the table, jumped up and dashed out of the room. Before Nebridius could ask a question, he was on his way to Malqua.

Twenty minutes later, out of breath from running, he staggered up the path to the little white cottage. A slight form huddled forlornly at the door.

"Melanie!"

"Augustine!"

He gathered her in his arms, and she offered no resistance. Her body trembled as she clung to him. Her cheek against his was warm and wet.

A moment slipped by while Augustine regained his breath.

"Oh, Augustine, what shall I do?"

"My little nightingale," he said, not too excited to be gallant, "your battle with yourself is over."

Her hands slid up to his temples and caressed them.

"You are mine!" He made no attempt to keep the exultation out of his voice.

She did not deny it.

He speared a quotation from the shelf of his memory, forgetting that he had inherited it from Monica.

"'Many waters cannot quench love, neither can floods drown it.' This is true, my heavenly one. You are coming to me through waters and through floods. Ah, but you are coming to me. Does it matter what you have been through?" She drew back her head, raised her face to his, and their eyes locked. Tears glistened on her cheeks. The scent of lilacs was subtly present. The glow from a flesh-colored moon bathed her finely carved ivory features, accentuating their perfection.

"You were never more lovely," he said.

"Augustine, I do love you, I do love you!"

He leaned toward her and their lips met in their first kiss. For both, time and space curled away like the ripples of a broken wave washing back to sea.

Chapter 14

I was loved, and I secretly entered into an enjoyable liaison, but I was also trammeling myself with fetters of distress, laying myself open to the iron rods and burning scourges of jealousy and suspicion, of fear, anger, and quarrels (Confessions III, 1, 1).

"Melanie!"

Melanie slipped through the curtained doorway leading to the bedchamber. "Yes, my dearest," she said, rearranging the sprig of yellow fennel behind her left ear.

"I want to ask you about the two hundred sesterces I gave you yesterday." Augustine looked up with tired eyes from a table littered with scraps of parchment on which were embossed columns of figures.

"I spent most of it on food." She came and stood behind him, and ran her arm around his neck. The air about her was redolent of the lemonlike scent of fennel. "Why do you ask?"

"Because we have got to save our money." He fussed with the pen in his hand. "I find I am going deeper and deeper into debt."

"You think I'm wasteful, don't you?"

He said nothing, but returned to his calculations.

"Don't you?" she insisted.

He grunted an assent.

She withdrew her arm and moved around to his side. She stood there meekly, and behind her back her fingers twisted nervously. "Augustine," she said.

"What is it?"

"This is the only garment I have bought in my two years with you." She fingered the simar she was wearing. It was a hyacinth robe with flowing sleeves, gathered at the waist with a ribbon of blue fleece.

The pen continued to scratch across the parchment.

Melanie was about to speak again. She changed her mind, shrugged, and started for the bedchamber.

Augustine threw down the pen, stretched out his arm and flexed his fingers to unlimber them. He called to her, "Wait!"

Melanie drew up, but kept an uncompromising back toward him. Her head was lifted defiantly. Through the west window of the room she watched the rays of the afternoon sun wash the headlands of the Curubis Peninsula, across the bay.

"I understand," he rasped, "that you had an escort when you came back from market this morning.'

Her head went still higher.

"You do not deny it, then."

"I never realized you had spies working for you."

"I also understand that a man has come to the house three times inquiring for you."

"Which one is the spy — Alypius, or Honoratus, or Nebridius?"

"Virgil was right when he said that woman is a fickle creature, and always changeable."

"Is a woman to blame because men find her attractive?"

Augustine's cheeks reddened. He leaped to his feet, knocking over his chair. "You are a whore!"

She turned around slowly. The color had drained from her face, leaving it a grayish white. A terrible serenity furrowed her brow, her hands hung limply at her sides, her eyes were as calm as pools of black water. "You are right." She articulated every word. "I am your whore."

She spun on her heel and rushed into the bedchamber.

Snatching at any excuse to justify his volcanic temper, Augustine surveyed the room with disgust. It was in the same building in which he had lived with Alypius, Honoratus and Nebridius prior to Melanie's coming to him. Melanie, by her own admission, was not a good housekeeper. Indeed, in the falling gloom of late afternoon, the room looked as though the rascally Eversores might have torn through it. Cushions were strewn here and there on the stone floor. A chest of acacia wood stood open, half its contents spilling out. Smudges marred the light plaster walls, and curlicues of dust spiraled under the single couch along one wall. A cracked amphora on the east window sill held a few stalks of wilted goldenrod.

"Look at this place!" Augustine roared, working himself into a frenzy. "The swine in a filthy sty could not put up with it ten minutes. How I have put up with it two years I will never know."

The silence that followed his diatribe was penetrating.

"Why could I not have been satisfied to stay with my friends?" He roved about the room, kicking chairs and table legs. "At least we had some kind of order." He stood still, deliberately faced the bedchamber, and shouted, "And I had to play the fool and give that up!"

The sound of weeping floated out to him.

Augustine shook with fury. He jammed his fingers in his ears and lunged out of the room and out of the house into the cool of the Numidian dusk.

The Mediterranean breathed a soft wind into his face. The clean white streets, lined with cedar and eucalyptus trees, offered welcome relief from the drabness of his quarters.

In the twilight he climbed Mount Byrsa. Poised above the busy city, he spread his legs, folded his arms, and gazed across the Bay of Carthage. He let his mind drift like a sea mist.

It had been a tempestuous period, his two years with Melanie. After their first six months together, months of unbelievable passion, a gradual change had affected their union. Augustine tried to analyze the change, but it was a vain effort. He swore to Melanie and to himself that he loved her no less than at the beginning. Somehow the avowals seemed to have a hollow, almost a mocking, ring. He was at a loss to understand what was happening, and in mind and body he reached out frantically for the answer. He compared himself with Tantalus standing in a pool of water, putting his head down to drink only to watch the waters recede, leaving him parched with thirst.

It was curious that the change physically coincided with a change in his mental state. For no reason he knew, Augustine found that his intellectual passion was becoming blunted. His interest in the classics waned. Even Virgil bored him. His professors and friends noted a listlessness in his attitude, and wondered what had brought it about. Was he, perhaps, sated because there were no more worlds to conquer?

By sheer will power, he recovered from his inertia. Outwardly, everything was the same — his appearance, his friendliness, his dynamic way with people. Only Melanie and he knew that an inner tension, perplexing and unreasonable, continued to hold its grip on him. Financial strain, personal jealousies, and ordinary domestic friction added coals to the fire, it was true. Deeper than all this — and both had a sense of it — was the pull of a force as mysterious as the tides, and as powerful.

This Augustine reviewed as the sepia shadows of evening stretched out over the coastline. Lights flared in the city under the hill, and dimly the murmur of voices reached him. The wind blew harder now, and churned the waters of the bay into swirling white foam that made the lonely watcher on Byrsa think of the turbulence in his own heart.

All at once he was back, in his imagination, in the whitewalled room in Patricius' farmhouse in Thagaste. He was a child again, and it was night. He, Navigius, and Junia were seated on the floor at their mother's feet. Monica was reading the Bible to them, this night from the book of Proverbs, her favorite Old Testament book. "The heart," she read, "knows its own bitterness—."

Augustine interrupted the reading. "What does that mean, Mother?"

He would never forget her reply. It seemed that just as he asked the question, they heard Patricius' footsteps outside the house. He was coming back from what he had announced was a business call in town.

Monica reached out and laid a hand on Augustine's head. "My dear, dear boy," she said gently, "you will not have lived out many years before you will know what it means."

How right she had been!

When he returned to their rooms, Melanie was not there. "Maybe she has gone to one of her lovers," he said to himself bitterly.

He lighted an oil lamp and prepared a meal of herring and steamed bread. It was tasteless.

He tried to read. It was no use. His mind was on Melanie.

Later in the evening, Alypius and Honoratus dropped in for a chat. Honoratus' probing mind divined trouble. "Is something wrong?" he asked.

"Nothing serious," Augustine said distantly. "A little financial pinch."

Alypius glanced around the room. "Where is Melanie?"

"Oh — out somewhere."

"This late?"

"This late," Augustine said.

Honoratus saw that he wanted to be alone. "Come, Alypius," he said. "We should be at our books."

After they had gone, Augustine went to the bedchamber and lay down, without removing his tunic. For hours he tossed and rolled fitfully. Resentment against Melanie, and at the same time concern for her safety, filled his mind and ruled out sleep.

"I hate her," he muttered. "I hate her and I love her. I know how Catullus felt about Lesbia, and like Catullus, I am in torment."

The first amber strands of dawn had begun to thread the eastern horizon when he fell into an uneasy sleep.

He did not know how long he slept. It could not have been long because the sun had barely come up. The sound of objects moving across the floor in the next room awakened him. Startled, he tumbled out of bed and dashed to the door. There in the early morning light was Melanie, exactly as he had last seen her, except that shadows lay under her eyes and there was grief in them. She was cleaning the room.

"Melanie, what are you doing?"

She would not look at him. "I am going to be a better housekeeper."

He was about to ask if this was her sacrificial offering to cover her sin of infidelity, but checked himself. He said nothing, hoping she would interpret his silence as an unspoken inquiry. He had not long to wait.

Melanie held a damp dust cloth in her hand and was about to kneel and wipe the floor under the couch. Passing the cloth from one hand to another, she said, "You are wrong in what you think. I have not once been unfaithful to you."

His heart sang.

"The man who brought me home from the market — he was a sailor. A drunken man insulted me on the street, and this sailor was going by and heard him. He knocked the drunken man down and walked home with me to protect me."

"What about the other fellow?"

"You mean the man who has been here to ask for me?"

"Yes."

"I do not know. He may be a relative,"

"Like the Roman soldier I found you with that day in Malqua?"

"My mother had a large fam —"

"It appears they have all converged on Carthage."

Her face showed suffering. "Do not hurt me anymore. I cannot stand it."

He wanted to go to her and ask for forgiveness, but there was still the matter of her absence.

She seemed to be reading his thoughts. "I tried to leave you tonight," she said, so softly he heard her with difficulty. "When I went away, I was never coming back." She shook her head sorrowfully. "It was no use."

"Melanie!"

In three bounds he closed the gap that separated them. He pulled her to the couch, threw his arms around her, and kissed her with a ferocity that hurt.

She drew a long quivering sigh. "I love you, and only you," she choked.

"Can you ever forgive me?"

She pressed her lips against his cheek. "I wish I could make you happy," she said. "Why are you not happy?"

"I wish I knew."

"I was right, was I not? I came to you wanting to bring you happiness. I have not brought you happiness."

"And I promised to give you surety," he said. "I have failed dismally."

"We have both failed. Why?"

"I blame myself. You are everything a man could desire. And Melanie —" he pressed her to his heart — "I love you now as I loved you that first day I saw you."

They kissed again, and in spite of their exhaustion, the contact fired each with intense longing. Lovingly, Augustine gathered her in his arms and carried her into the bedchamber.

Why was it that at the most unexpected times, passages of scripture he had heard Monica quote flowed back to him? He was at a loss to understand it. As he bore Melanie through the doorway, like a bridegroom with his bride on their wedding night, a passage from Paul came to his aroused mind: *For two, saith he, shall be one flesh.* Surely this would seem to be God's endorsement of the union with his beloved, otherwise why should he be recalling the passage now?

What he did not know, or had forgotten, was that the words were written to condemn, not condone, his own liaison.

In Augustine's arms. Melanie placed her lips to his ear and whispered, "Dearest, would you like to know a secret?"

"I know. You love me."

"Yes, but it is not that."

"Stop being mysterious and tell me," he said.

"Are you ready for a shock?"

"With you next to my heart, I am ready for anything."

She kissed the lobe of his ear. "I think you are going to be a father."

Chapter 15

*How ardently I longed, O my God, how ardently I
longed to fly to you away from earthly things
(Confessions III, 4, 8).*

For fully a minute after Melanie's announcement,
Augustine stared at her with stunned incredulity.

"You are not pleased." She turned away from him.

"Should I be pleased?"

"Some men would be."

Outside a curlew lifted its strange plaint to the morning sun. Rich saffron sunshine poured into the bedchamber. A group of four Roman soldiers clattered by
the lodging house, exchanging loud and ribald quips.

"You are worried," Melanie said. "It means another
mouth to feed."

"It is not that."

"It is because the child will keep reminding you of —
our relations."

"You are wrong."

"You are worried that sooner or later your mother
will find out about us."

After a pause, he said, "In her last letter she hinted
that she might come to Carthage for a visit."

"Why do you not tell her the truth before she comes?"

"I dare not," he said, squinting up at the ceiling.

"My darling, you cannot keep it a secret forever."

"I cannot tell her," he said.

"Poor Augustine. I have given you only trouble."

He denied it vigorously.

"Of course," she said, "I could be wrong. It may be something I have been eating that has me upset."

He saw through her tremulous evasion, and derived no comfort from it.

For days after that, Augustine prayed that she had been mistaken, that she might not be with child. A month later he learned that his prayers had not been answered. Melanie was definitely pregnant.

The dreaded word sent Augustine spinning into a whirlpool of nervous agitation. Melanie feared he would never be the same to her again.

In the weeks that followed, they lived under a perpetual cloud. Melanie was ill much of the time. Their tempers flared, they quarreled incessantly. Anxiety plowed furrows in Augustine's forehead. He was seldom without a frown. His disposition became so unpleasant that most of his friends avoided him as they would an outcast.

It was while he walked the valley of deep shadow that he came across a passage in Cicero that was to alter the direction of his life.

One night after Melanie had retired, he was doing an assigned reading in an essay, "Hortensius." Unexpectedly the words at the conclusion seemed to leap from the page like a flurry of arrows and fasten themselves in his brain:

If, as pretend the philosophers of old who are also the greatest and most illustrious, we have a soul immortal and divine, it behooves us to think that the more it has persevered in its way, that is to say, in reason, in love, and the pursuit of truth, and the less it has intermingled and been stained in human error and passion, the easier it will be for it to raise itself and soar again to the skies.

A tremor of joy shot through Augustine! He read the statement a second time, letting the book fall to the desk and sitting with his chin in his hand, digesting Cicero's words. In two readings the sentence was engraved in his mind. He returned to it again with the deep pleasure of a jeweler examining a gem of great price. He repeated it and with each repetition the words took on fresh beauty and power.

With the essay spread before him under the oil lamp and a warm glow bathing his soul. Augustine took personal inventory. "Let me see. He says the philosophers teach us wisdom, a wisdom that can put us in touch with heaven, if we apply it. This is magnificent! But then, why is it that I, who am steeped in their learning, am still earthbound? The philosophers say that one must persevere in reason, and in love, and in the pursuit of truth. I have a mind that is supposed to be able to reason, I know something of love, and no one could search for truth more eagerly than I have done. They have promised exaltation. Is it because I am, as they say, 'stained in human error and passion' that I do not raise myself and soar upward? No more than other men, certainly. Then why is there a gap between the promise and the fulfillment? Some key piece is missing. What is that piece?"

Instinctively his thoughts flew back to his mother. Monica had so often said to her children, "Christ only can make you wise unto salvation. Never forget, my precious children, that in Him are stored up all of the treasures of wisdom and knowledge. Only sit down under His shadow with great delight and you will find his fruit sweet to your taste."

Augustine pounded his knee. "Why, that is it, of course," he said aloud. "Christ is the key piece. That is the thing wrong with Cicero. He has no Christ in his thinking, and neither have the philosophers."

The inconsistency of his conclusion did not occur to him — that he, freethinker and proud young rationalist, should himself exclude Christ from his own system and yet grieve that philosophers should be guilty of the same omission.

Having analyzed Cicero, he jumped to his feet, nearly upsetting the oil lamp at his elbow, and crossed the room. He knelt before the small chest of acacia wood and lifted the lid. With nervous fingers he rifled through its contents until he found a book Monica had given him years before. It was a copy of the New Testament.

He took it back to the desk, unrolled the vellum leaves, and began to read. He read avidly, like a starving person devouring a meal. He read until his eyes smarted and his head ached. He read himself to sleep.

Next morning, when Melanie emerged from the bedchamber dewy fresh and lovely, she saw him slumped over his desk, fast asleep. The oil lamp at his elbow was still burning.

"Augustine!" she called.

He did not stir.

She shook him until he was awake. "You should be getting ready for your classes."

"Oh," he yawned, rubbing his eyes. "I must have slept."

"A brilliant comment." She glanced at the scroll. "You have been reading the Bible?"

"Is it a crime?"

"I think it is good. Have you found help?"

"Help?" He rose and stretched. "Who needs help?"

"We all do."

"Not I."

"You especially."

"Look here." He snatched up the New Testament and slammed it to the floor. "This bores me like Greek myths. It has neither the depth of Virgil nor the dignity of Cicero. For simple souls it may do, but not for scholars. Now may I have something to eat? Alypius will be stopping for me any minute."

Women understood Augustine better than he understood himself. Melanie was aware of the fact that, for all her lover's superior airs, something had happened to turn his thoughts to higher flights of learning. She watched him go back to his classical studies with new ardor. She also watched carefully to see if this burst of interest would calm his brooding restiveness.

It failed to do so. At the center of his personality, Melanie sensed, there still existed a vacuum. He might feign self-sufficiency before her and before others. It failed to fill the vacuum. It also failed to deceive Melanie, and she waited to see what door he would next enter in his search for satisfaction.

One afternoon Augustine was browsing in a bookstall in Harbor Square when two men standing near the sciapodes not far from him became involved in an argument. At first Augustine paid no attention. The argument became violent. He tried to seal off his mind and concentrate on his reading. It was no use, and finally he gave up and turned to listen to the debate.

"You hear me, old man." The speaker was a pimply-faced youth in a white robe. His manner was blustering, his voice harsh. "We Donatists have the true faith and you know it. Your trouble is you are too damn stubborn to admit it." Augustine knew of Donatism as one of the offshoots of the orthodox Christian religion. "Why will you not admit what every thinking person comes to recognize, that there is only one religion and that is ours?"

"I admit nothing," said his opponent, an ascetic–looking man of perhaps sixty. He mopped his brow with a sleeve of his black tunic. "Tell me this, if yours is the true religion, where did evil come from?"

Augustine's interest in the controversy sharpened. He had often pondered the same problem himself but had never been able to reach a satisfactory conclusion.

"Where did evil come from?" The young man with the pimples scuffed at a broken block in the pavement and looked surly. "I suppose Adam introduced it."

"Then," retorted the other, "where, pray, did Adam get the power to sin?"

"Who knows?"

"You see." The ascetic's eyes gleamed exultantly. "Mani alone has explained the origin of evil."

"Who is Mani?"

"A Persian philosopher. He taught that there are two kingdoms, the kingdom of light and the kingdom of darkness. Out of the kingdom of darkness Satan came. He declared war on the kingdom of light. From this conflict our sinful world developed. It contains detached portions of light imprisoned in darkness. I suppose you Donatists think Adam was created in the image of God, don't you?"

"Certainly."

"Wrong. Adam was created in the image of Satan. So was Eve, only with a smaller spark of life. She is the principle of seductive sensuousness. You probably believe that Cain and Abel were sons of Adam and Eve."

"I do."

"Wrong again. Cain and Abel were the sons of Satan and Eve. Seth was the son of Adam and Eve."

"But the Old Testament says —"

"The Old Testament!" said the ascetic acidly. "The Old Testament was inspired by Satan and his false prophets."

"You lie!" The younger man doubled his fist and advanced on his antagonist darkly. "What kind of religion are you peddling?"

"The true faith. The faith of the Manicheans."

"Manichaeism is heresy."

"Heresy?" The ascetic smiled disdainfully. "What is heresy? Heresy is the self-appointed authority you claim for yourself in order to anathematize me. You cannot meet my arguments, so you threaten to use force. Go ahead —"

The stout youth struck the older man a terrific blow in the stomach, causing him to double over. Thereupon he delivered another blow on the man's mouth, knocking him to the pavement. The assailant calmly pivoted and walked away, muttering imprecations into the breeze.

Shocked at this exhibition of brutality, Augustine hurried to the prostrate ascetic and bent over him. The man's lips were bleeding. His hands clutched his stomach; he moaned, rolling his eyes.

No other person in the square paid the slightest attention to him.

"Here, let me help you." Augustine slipped an arm under the Manichean's head. He produced a handkerchief and wiped the blood from his lips. "Are you hurt badly?"

"I cannot tell," the man answered, regarding Augustine with glassy eyes. "You are a kind young man."

"May I take you to a physician?"

"No, no. I am feeling better."

"The fellow who hit you is a wretch."

"You — you saw it happen?"

"Yes."

"Who are you?"

"My name is Augustine. I am a student at the university."

"Augustine, you are an intelligent young m-man. I am Marius. Will you help me up now?"

"Yes, sir."

Augustine took Marius by the arm and brought him slowly to his feet. "Where is your home?" he asked.

"Some distance from here. Before we part, I would like to invite you to have some refreshment with me. I know a fine eating house nearby."

"I would like that," Augustine said, brightening. "As a matter of fact, I want to ask you some questions about your faith. I am interested."

"Excellent," said Marius, patting him on the arm paternally. "We Manicheans have all the answers to all c-c-conceivable questions. Let us go."

Chapter 16

I fell among a set of proud madmen
(Confessions III, 6, 10).

Marius led Augustine to an eating place in a cellar off the Via Coelestis. A half-naked Indian slave, with a ring in his nose, escorted them to a booth with a wooden table and divans covered with alligator leather. He brought in porphyry basins containing perfumed water. They washed their hands, drying them on napkins, and Marius ordered black olives, barley rolls, dates, and a bitter tea unfamiliar to Augustine. Over this light repast he proceeded to unfold the tenets of Mani.

"You observed," he said fixing burning eyes on Augustine, "that our D-D-Donatist friend had no answer to my qu-questions about the beginning of evil."

Augustine nodded, munching a date.

"Do you know where evil originates?"

"You tell me."

"It is like this." Marius raised himself on his elbow, pushed aside the bowl of olives, and with a bony finger drew two intersecting circles on the surface of the table. "Man enters the world with a compound of good and evil in his nature. This circle here is his body; this circle is his soul. This first circle, his body, is sinful: this circle, his soul, is pure. For example, you — " shaking his head at Augustine "excellent young man that you are, you have in you a mixture of good and bad impulses. True?"

"No argument."

Marius was speaking earnestly. This lent fluency to his words, practically eliminating his tendency to stuttering. Augustine noted the improvement and marveled.

Marius took a sip of tea and continued, "Where do our evil impulses spring from?"

"From a deceitful heart, I have been told."

"Not so!" Marius thumped the table so hard that the olives, dates, and barley rolls jumped in their dishes. "Passions, appetites, and d-desires are rooted in the body. On the other hand, good intentions, k-kindness, benevolence, pure thoughts and generous motives have their origin in the soul. That explains the dualism in our nature. Does it not sound reasonable? Does it not commend itself to your fine mind?"

"It could," said Augustine cautiously, weighing the thought. "Is it proper to ask how Christ fits into your system?"

"A good and welcome question." Marius took an olive from the bowl and chewed on it. "Olives," he said, "are the food of foods. Their oil is charged with light particles — but more of that later. By the way, are you from a Christian background?"

"I am."

"I suspected it. Well you must first of all cleanse your mind of the Christian notion of incarnation. You should know that God had always had hands, hair, eyes, ears, and feet — in short, corporeal substance. What would be the point of his assuming a second bodily form?"

Augustine shook his head.

"I see you are puzzled," Marius rushed on. "That is natural, for I have not yet answered your question. You asked how Christ fits into our system. We believe that Christ is the Sun Spirit. As the Sun Spirit, He attracts light forces from the physical world. The devil and his evil spirits, who are locked up in the stars, try to keep him from doing this. But the Sun Spirit does not fight alone. He is aided by the Holy Spirit, who dwells in ether. He is also aided by the sun and the moon, those bright, shiny ships which convey cargoes of light from realms of darkness into the eternal kingdom of light. The twelve signs of the zodiac are other agents which assist in the operation."

"Yes, but how is salvation worked out?" asked Augustine, bewildered by this mass of absurdity.

"Salvation is a process of physical refinement," Marius said, his gaunt face animated. "It is a mystery forever identified with light. The suffering Jesus, writhing on the cross, symbolized the world soul still unfettered in matter. That suffering is repeated every time a flower pushes its head up through the dark soil of earth, struggling for light and freedom. It is repeated in each step of redemption the great Mani has outlined for us, his enlightened disciples."

"But where do you get this information? I have never read it in the Bible."

"The Bible indeed!" sneered Marius, spearing an olive. "Do you not know that the teachings of Jesus were corrupted by Paul and the other so-called apostles? It remained for Maru, the promised Paraclete, or Advocate, to clarify the teachings of Jesus. Without Mani's explanations there is not the slightest hope of deliverance from the chains of darkness that bind humanity."

For hours Marius continued his dissertation on the doctrines of the Manichean faith. Augustine often interrupted with pointed questions. Marius' answers perplexed him but he did manage to draw at least one clear, satisfying conclusion from the interview: although the elect, or "perfect," of the Manichean sect were supposed to pursue a life of rigid asceticism and self-abnegation, the catechumens or "hearers" were merely exposed to a flexible set of rules of conduct, none of which enjoined separation from evil. The religion of Mani, like every cult, placed salvation within easy reach of its adherents and at the same time permitted the practice of sinning. This feature pleased Augustine enormously. It was exactly the kind of religion he was looking for. He could join the movement, receive salvation as a reward, and at the same time maintain his relationship with Melanie. Manicheanism, like a sentinel, would patrol the outer walls of the bastion of the heart without interfering with activities within.

The mask of evening had began to spread itself over the face of Carthage when Marius and his new acquaintance got up to leave the table.

"I can see that you are interested in the truth," Marius said on the way up from the cellar. "Shall I enroll you as an inquirer?"

"What does it involve?"

They emerged from the building and stood on the Via Coelestis, where an early evening throng swept up and down the causeway in quest of entertainment.

"You should attend our lectures regularly. That is all for this time."

"Very well. You may enroll me."

"Good. You will not be sorry. And this, I may tell you, is our signal." Marius stepped back a pace and extended his right arm. He turned up his hand and drew the thumb across the open palm, holding the four fingers straight up.

Augustine imitated the gesture.

"Goodbye, my young comrade."

"Goodbye," said Augustine.

A few days after his meeting with Marius, Augustine graduated from the university with the highest honors ever accorded a student. The Proconsul delivered the commencement oration. In his opening remarks he paid tribute to Augustine's scholarship. After the exercises, professors and classmates were lavish in their praise of the Thagastean's achievements. He passed off the honors with a show of modesty, but inwardly he was as puffed up as the bladders of swine suspended by local butchers in front of their meat shops.

Romanianus, who had gone to Thagaste for the summer, sent him for a graduation gift a marble bust of Apuleius, the sage of Madaura. Monica wrote tender, loving congratulations. She had hoped, she explained, to come for the exercises but finances had not allowed it. Could he not come to Thagaste for a visit? They could discuss his future plans together.

He talked over her suggestion with Melanie.

"Oh, you must go," Melanie said brightly. "You must go."

"Perhaps I should."

"Of course you should. And you must tell her about me."

He winced. "I should go next week," he said, shrugging off her remark.

Before he left, he attended three lectures at the Manichean lecture hall. Marius and the other Manichean teachers, very much aware of their inquirer's growing reputation among the intellectuals of Carthage, were the heart of solicitude and the soul of flattery. They pressed attentions upon him profusely. When they learned of his forthcoming journey to Thagaste they presented him with a handsome purse. It would, they said, help defray his traveling expenses. And it might help to remind him who his true friends were, they added.

The result of these contacts was that when Augustine set out for his home in Thagaste, he was like a youth in the flush of his first love. He had embraced the rudiments of the Manichean religion with all the zest of his spirit. Fortified with what he thought was the answer to his search for reality, he had become a swaggering, exuberant personal worker for the principles of Mani.

In a single exchange he had converted Alypius. His steady barrage of propaganda had began to impress even Melanie.

As he moved south toward Thagaste, traveling by Imperial Mail carriage, he daringly conceived the thought of trying to win Monica over to the cause. The more he toyed with the idea the more he liked it.

Chapter 17

*What I thought of was not you at all; an empty
fantasy and my own error were my God
(Confessions IV, 7, 12).*

"Dear, dear son, I perceive that you are in the gall
of bitterness and the bond of iniquity."

Monica sat on a bench of hickory wood under a fig
tree in the yard of her estate. Augustine, sprawled out
on the grass at her feet, broke twigs into pieces and
flipped them away.

"Surely Satan has taken you captive at his will. Why
have you gone into this deadly error? What evil men
have persuaded you to forsake the truth?"

"The truth, Mother? Why, it is the Manicheans who
have the truth."

"Manicheanism is the synagogue of Satan." Her
voice crackled with anger. "It is the great Babylon. It is
the habitation of demons. It is the cell of every foul
spirit and the cage of every unclean and hateful bird. It
— "

"Why, Mother!" Augustine was outwardly calm but
inwardly boiling. "Does not your own Bible say something about which of the prophets have not the fathers

persecuted? It might have added 'and the mothers too.'"

"Ah, how wicked you are to use the blessed Word of God to support your damnable heresy! God pardon His handmaiden that such an evil should be spawned under my roof. What a failure I have been as a mother in Israel!"

Monica had aged ten years in the three she had been separated from Augustine. Lines of suffering grooved her cheeks. A brooding sadness marked her features and there was a stoop to her shoulders as though an unseen burden were pressing down on her. Nevertheless, all the passion and vibrancy of youth showed in her voice and gestures and warned Augustine that here was still an impregnable fortress of faith. He realized that to convert his mother he must apply every ounce of his resourcefulness.

He turned on his side and with his hand shielded his eyes from the glare of he morning sunlight that streamed through the bower of fig leaves. "Mother, you taught me to believe in miracles, did you not?"

"I hope that I did."

"So my confidence in the tenets of Mani is verified by miracles."

"What are you saying?"

"I am saying that there was once a fig tree just like this fig tree you and I are under, and it was uprooted by a supernatural power."

"Go on," she said defiantly.

"When that happened the tree shed tears of milk."

"Sheer folly. Are you not confounding a counterfeit miracle with Christ's cursing of the fig tree?"

"No, Mother, you are the one who is mistaken. Not only did that fig tree weep but also a Manichean saint ate some of its fruit which mingled with his entrails. The result was that he breathed out angels. Yes, in his prayers he groaned and sighed forth particles of Deity.

Those very particles would have remained bound in the fig unless the man of God had used his belly and teeth to free them. Furthermore —"

A bitter sob broke from Monica's lips and stopped Augustine from going on. She was bending forward, her face buried in her hands. Tears trickled through her fingers and fell on the grass, where they glistened like dew.

Irritated, Augustine pursed his lips and changed his position. He dug his fingers into the soil and worked them in and out impatiently. "I must be patient," he thought. "This is all a shock to her. I must win her by patience and sympathy."

He rose and stood beside her. He put his arm over her shoulders and patted her tenderly. "Do not cry, little Mother. I love you very much, truly I do. I am only trying to help you to see the truth."

She kept her head in her hands. Gradually her sobs subsided.

"Come," he said, forcing himself to be cheerful. "Let us talk about my future." He sat down on the ground beside her and took her hands in his. "You know I plan to open my own school of rhetoric this fall when I go back to Carthage."

"I thought perhaps you would settle down in Tagaste to teach."

"The opportunities are greater in Carthage. Besides, I have managed to build something of a reputation for scholarship in Carthage. The Proconsul has promised to recommend me to the public."

"How splendid!" She leaned back and looked at him with a glow of pride, her eyes still moist. "Of course Carthage is the place for you. If my finances improve I may be able to visit you this winter."

She saw the merest flicker of dismay steal into his eyes. It passed immediately but Monica caught its significance.

"You do not want me to go to Carthage," she said.

He was silent, realizing how futile it would be to attempt deception.

"Why? Is it that you are ashamed of me?"

"No, Mother." His hands tightened on hers.

"Why, then?"

He decided that the time had come to tell her about Melanie. He drew a long breath, as a diver does when he prepares to plunge. He looked away to Mount Atlas towering in the distance. Then he told her the story. He told it from the beginning. He told it simply and honestly. He told it with emotion, sometimes with a catch in his voice, feeling deep compassion for Melanie and for himself.

"As I look back now," he concluded, "I think my love for Melanie was as inevitable as the creation. It was something I had no more power over than I had over my birth. Well, what do you think of me?"

"You have done wrong," she said, after a pause. "I cannot excuse you as you excuse yourself. My standards forbid the forming of such a contract. But I am glad you have not married. You must not marry. It would spoil your future. Promise you will not marry."

"I promise," he said, immensely relieved that she was taking the news so philosophically. "And now that you know the truth, I do want you to come to Carthage."

"Are you sure?"

"I am sure."

"Mother!" It was Junia, sixteen, slim, attractive, calling to Monica from the door of their house.

"Yes, Junia?"

"Romanianus is here to see you."

"Very well," said Monica, rising. "We are coming."

"Romanianus," said Augustine with pleasure. "It will be wonderful to see him."

The long summer days and evenings witnessed an odd blend of fellowship and conflict between Monica and Augustine. Common ties bound them close to-gether. For a woman of their time, Augustine had always found Monica extraordinarily well-read and well-bal-anced. Mother and son held lengthy and exhilarating discussions on politics, current history, the classics. But whenever the talk veered to the subject of religion, the atmosphere grew tense and both of them were un-happy.

One evening in August there was a violent eruption.

"You keep talking about the light, the light!" Monica said. "You seem to forget that God is our sun. When we find the sun we do not need to go prowling about look-ing for fireflies."

"I resent your insinuation," said Augustine, who was in particularly bad humor that evening. "My religion is not a firefly religion. And anyway, I never did get any comfort out of your stuffy creed."

"Naturally. Sin and conscience cannot lie on the same couch and be comfortable."

They were in the front room of their home. Monica was at the spinning wheel. Augustine was lying on the couch Patricius had so often occupied. At this point he sprang up and stalked across the room.

"Sin, sin, sin!" he bellowed. "Am I to blame that the cause of my sin is in the sky? Besides, I am sick of the word, sick of it! Why are you orthodox people so con-sistently morbid?"

"We are not morbid, we are realistic. We know that the heart is deceitful above all things, and desperately wicked."

"Nonsense!" Pausing at the front door, he seized the strands of esparto grass that hung in the doorway and gave them a pull. "Why am I forever being told that I am a moral leper?"

"Aurelius, listen to me." Monica stopped her spin-ning and turned to face him. "Last night I had a dream which I believe God sent me. In the dream I saw myself standing on a wooden platform alone. Suddenly a young man appeared and came to me. He was cheerful and smiling. I, on the other hand, was overcome with grief for his condition. He asked me why I was sad. I said I was sad because he was a doomed soul. He consoled me with a message. 'You must be at rest,' he said. 'For where you are, there I will be also.'"

Augustine's scowl gave way to a smile. "Excellent," he said, rubbing his hands and continuing to pace the floor. "I understand the dream perfectly. It is a parable and it tells me that you and I will not be separated long. Do you not see? God has promised that one day you shall be with me where I am?"

"No, no," said Monica, piercing his sophistry. "You forget that the message was '*where* you are, *there* will I be also,' and not '*where* I am *there* will you be.' God has prophesied that you shall accept my faith, not I yours."

"Nonsense!" Augustine shouted again. "I have had enough of this eternal preaching. Romanianus has invited me to his summer home any time I want to move in. If I cannot convert you, I am sure I can convert him, because he has an *open* mind. Tomorrow I am leaving you. Good night."

He turned and rushed out of the room to his bedchamber.

Silent and hurt, Monica slipped from her chair, knelt beside the spinning wheel and lifted up her voice in supplication. "Father in heaven," she breathed, "O my Father, my Father — perfect that which concerns him."

The next day, when Augustine had left for Romanianus' summer home, Monica called on the bishop of the parish and explained her situation to him tearfully.

"Can you not deal with my son?" she pleaded. "Can you not refute his errors, instruct him in the way of righteousness, try to snatch his soul as a brand from the burning?"

The bishop was a hulk of a man with a leonine head and a loving heart. "Monica," he said gently, "your boy at this stage is altogether unteachable. He is puffed up with the novelty of his heresy. He would not listen to me. I want to tell you something. My mother was a poor, misguided Manichean, and I embraced Manichaeism as a young man. I not only read their writings, I also copied and memorized them."

"Who converted you?"

"No one. I read the Bible and came out of the pit with no human help. The grace of God alone did it. Not even the Church lifted a finger."

"Then you think we should not try to win him back to the faith?"

"Let him alone for a while. Pray God that he will of himself find what the error is, and how great is its impiety."

"But it is such a desperate state he is in," said Monica. "Is there nothing I can do? Nothing?"

"Yes," said the bishop, and his smile was luminous. "Yes, Monica, you can trust God. Go your way and God be with you. It is not possible — *it is not possible that the son of these tears should perish.*"

Chapter 18

This man was intellectually astray along with me,
and my soul could not bear to be without him
(Confessions IV, 4, 7).

Forty stadia from Thagaste stood Romanianus' summer villa. He had personally supervised its construction and made sure that it was the ultimate in magnificence. The villa rose sheer from the Plain of Medjerda like a mountain out of a field. A network of black-sanded footpaths ribboned the estate, and cypress trees, imported from Utica, shaded the paths and studded the lawns. A diamond-shaped pool of water, paved with turquoise tiling and stocked with eelpouts, sparkled on the west lawn like a fine jewel.

A legion of relatives and friends lived with the indulgent Romanianus. With an expansive hand, the patrician provided for one and all. He made it a principle, he said, that since first the gods had begun to smile on him brightly and broadly, he had never once turned away from his doors friend or enemy.

He welcomed Augustine with quiet cordiality. "I am glad to see you," he said. "And I have a proposal for you. Instead of returning to Carthage to open a school of rhetoric, why not open one here at the villa?"

"Here?" said Augustine, surprised.

"Yes. There are at least thirty children on the premises. I have seven of my own. Until a month ago we had an instructor. He was hopelessly stupid and I had to dismiss him. Will you take his place?"

"Yes," said Augustine, without any hesitation. "When shall I begin?"

"At once."

The assignment did much for Augustine's morale. Such a boost he sorely needed, for his dispute with Monica had upset him badly. Also, he was insolvent. Further, the position would open up a field in which to plant the seeds of Manichean doctrine, for as a private tutor his standing in the community would be greatly elevated. It was small wonder that he attacked his duties with elation and pride.

In leisure hours he engaged in personal evangelism. The young people at the villa proved to be excellent subjects for his technique, so that within the course of a week after he had moved in he had made converts and was holding evening classes to instruct converts and inquirers. The class grew in number from three to five, from five to nine, from nine to fourteen. Some of the children brought their parents to him. Romanianus himself became interested.

One afternoon early in the fall Augustine sprawled on the lawn under a cypress tree, reading a book on advanced Manichean thought. He was so engrossed in the treatise that he failed to notice another young man approaching.

"Hello, Augustine," the young man said.

Augustine looked up. "Oh, hello, Spendius," he said warmly. "Will you join me?"

Spendius lowered himself to the turf. He was a native of Thagaste, and had gone to school with Augustine, although at that time they had not known each other too well.

"I understand you have taken up the Manichean religion," he said — somewhat testily, Augustine thought.

"Rather it has taken me up," Augustine said, smiling. He noted with favor that Spendius clipped his hair in conventional Roman style and wore a sleeveless Roman toga. "Are you interested?"

Instead of answering the question, Spendius said, "My younger sister is studying under you. That is good. You are trying to influence her toward the Manichean cult. That is bad. I want it stopped."

Augustine, who was lying on his stomach and balanced on his elbows, juggled the book briefly, then passed it from one hand to the other. "Why?" he said.

Spendius frowned. Curiously, the frown made his face attractive and gave it character. Augustine was aware of a certain noble bearing in the boy. His brooding eyes, jutting jaw and serious expression interested him. "I like this man," he thought. "He will be worth winning to the truth."

"I have no use for cults, that is why," Spendius said.

"Romanianus is your uncle?" Augustine's voice was pleasantly disarming.

"Second cousin."

"Oh, yes. Tell me, Spendius, are you a Christian?"

"I am a catechumen, yes."

"And you do not like Manicheans?"

"No."

"You know, one of the tragedies of modern intellectual life is that we do not realize that Manichaeism is the ripest expression of the true Christian faith."

"How can that be," Spendius said with considerable heat, "when it is all mixed up with Judaism and with Persian heathenism?"

Augustine checked a rising flood of indignation. He smiled again and said, "What you do not see is the truth —"

He had to stop as Spendius broke into a spasm of violent coughing. Augustine could tell from his thin frame and pale complexion that he was far from well.

While Spendius was getting his breath Augustine changed his position. Discarding his book, he sat cross-legged on the grass like a desert Bedouin and folded his hands. "Truth, my Spendius," he said presently, "is like a lodestone, which has a wonderful power of attracting iron. Take an iron ring and put it near a lodestone. The lodestone pulls the ring to itself. Take a second ring and put it near the first ring. The first ring attracts the second because the lodestone had communicated its own property to the ring. And so it goes." He illustrated the process with gestures. "Thus it is with truth. It communicates drawing power to its disciples. In the present instance Mani's formulations attracted a Carthaginian named Marius. Marius won me over. I, in turn, experience a terrific inner compulsion to draw others to the lodestone. Am I to blame for that compulsion?"

Spendius coughed again, this time until he was purple. Augustine always carried with him a bag of lozenges a Carthage physician had prescribed for his own chronic throat irritation. He reached inside his toga, pulled out the package and offered it to Spendius.

"Thank you." Spendius took a lozenge and chewed it slowly. "Your talk is convincing," he said. "But there is a need for orthodoxy. It is solid and permanent. Why should Mani or anyone else take the truth of God and mix it with the religion of Zoroaster?"

"But you must remember that we live in a changing world. Truth, like a brook, is fluid. Remember what Lucretius said:

"No single thing abides, but all things flow,
Fragment to fragment clings — the things thus grow
Until we know and name them. By degrees
They melt, and are no more the things we know."

"Ah, yes, but Lucretius was a pagan."

"A pagan? What is a pagan? My good mother thinks I am a pagan. 'Paganism' is a tag we tie on people who do not agree with us. Listen, Spendius, I quite sympathize with your wish to hold on to your traditional creed. We always hold on to the good until the better comes along. 'The fresh cask long keeps its first tang.' The glory of my faith is that it allows me to retain the tang of my mother's religion. It merely adds another and more bracing one."

"Then," Spendius began, looking bewildered, "you do not think there is a conflict between —?"

"Between your faith and mine?" Augustine flourished a hand. "Not at all. I too believe the Bible."

"You do?"

"Of course. It is all a matter of interpretation."

For hours Augustine expounded his rationalism, interrupted only by Spendius' coughing spells. It was late in the afternoon when a slave came out to summon them to dinner.

"I cannot say that I believe as you do," Spendius said as they stood up to go, "but I confess I cannot answer you."

"All I ask is an open mind," said Augustine, throwing a friendly arm around him. "An open mind is a cleansed mind."

From that afternoon the two were the closest of friends. They delighted in each other's company. They went for long walks in the desert. They rode horseback, wrote poetry, fished in mountain streams, went to the theater together, were seldom apart except during morning classes. Spendius attended the evening classes in Manichaeism and before long professed to embrace the doctrine.

Yet in spite of his profession Augustine entertained an uneasy doubt about the genuineness of his friend's conversion. "I am afraid it is more his affection for me than anything," he told himself more than once.

Nevertheless he was flushed with the success of his evangelistic efforts at the villa, and wrote Marius a glowing report of his activities.

He also wrote Melanie long love letters. He sent her money from his salary. He promised to come to her before the birth of their child. He assured her that only the chance to make money and so whittle down his debt to Romanianus kept him away from her.

Twice he called upon Monica, once taking Spendius with him. The visits were failures. Both Monica and he were conscious of the wall that separated them. They talked in generalities, fidgeted, and tried too hard to cover their nervousness. After the second time, Augustine resolved not to see his mother again until he was ready to go back to Carthage.

The rift between them disturbed him emotionally far more than he suspected. That, with his absence from Melanie, reacted on his soul like the damming of a river. It clamored for another outlet. Deep called out to deep. The turgid, pent-up waters bowled over boundaries imposed by circumstances and rushed toward another object. The object in this case was Spendius.

Spendius grew to be his life. In his own romantic mind Augustine compared their attachment to that of Pylades and Orestes. The pungent line Horace had used, "One soul in two bodies," found fulfillment, he was certain, in Spendius and himself. Never had he dreamed that such close communion could exist in human friendship.

Then disaster struck.

A mysterious fever prostrated Spendius, wrenching him from Augustine's side. No one but the physician was permitted to see him. For days Spendius hovered between life and death, insensible in a heavy sweat. The physician held out no hope for his recovery.

His mother, a frail widow, was a member of the local church. Promptly she sent for the bishop who, with the consent of the physician, entered the bedchamber and baptized the young man. While the mother prayed and Augustine agonized, Spendius recovered consciousness. Almost miraculously he began to mend. The whole villa fervently rejoiced, for Spendius had endeared himself to everyone.

At last the physician gave his consent for Augustine to visit him. Spendius lay on a couch under a coverlet of brocaded gold silk. He was white and wasted, and on seeing him, Augustine's heart dropped. Spendius smiled wanly.

"Spendius, my beloved fellow." Augustine grasped his hand. "I am overjoyed that you are getting well."

"I have missed you," Spendius whispered, staring at him with frank devotion.

"And I you, dear friend. For a while you nearly broke me down. But you will be up soon. The physician says you will be up soon."

"Yes."

"Did you know that while you were unconscious they baptized you?"

"Mother told me so."

"It is, of course, ridiculous. When you are yourself you will repudiate the sacrament. Now that you are a Manichean —"

Spendius shook his head. "No, Augustine," he said. "I am not, really."

"What?"

"To be honest, I never was. In my heart I believe in Jesus Christ and His Gospel, not in Manichean doctrine. Do you hate me for telling you?"

The physician touched Augustine. "You must go now."

"Do you hate me?"

"Hate you? How could I hate you?" Augustine wrung his hand. "When I walk through that doorway," he pointed back of him, "I leave my heart behind."

"Goodbye, sweet friend," Spendius said, the tears rolling down his cheeks.

"Goodbye, Spendius. Goodbye."

Augustine left the room, grieved and disappointed. Spendius' return to his mother's faith was unsettling. He had hoped to convert the lad soundly to Manichaeism, perhaps even turn over his class in instruction to him before going back to Carthage. Now that was finished.

For two days he brooded over the blow. He did not try to see Spendius again. The residents of the villa observed that their young rhetoric teacher was strangely detached. Knowing his great love for Spendius, they considerately avoided him.

On the morning of the third day Romanianus came to Augustine's bedchamber while he was dressing. "I have bad news for you," he said soberly.

"Yes?" said Augustine, premonition assailing him.

"Spendius had a relapse in the night. He died a few minutes ago."

Chapter 19

Within me I was carrying a tattered, bleeding soul
(Confessions IV, 7, 12).

The passing of Spendius plunged Augustine into a vortex of grief which, like a fall into cold water, first numbed, then sharpened, then struck all his sensibilities until they throbbed with dull pain. He could not contain himself. In the privacy of his bedroom he writhed on the marble floor and beat on it frantically with clenched fists.

"No, no, no, no!" he cried. "I cannot see him! I cannot lose him!" He groaned, and raved.

There were moments when shadows hung over his mind so heavily they almost eclipsed his reason. At other times his grief became so poignant he had physical pain in his heart.

He tried to pray. "God, why must I suffer like this?" he would demand of the Almighty. "My soul is torn and bleeding. I need you, O my God, I need you. Why wilt you not come to me now that I need you? Is it my sin that keeps you from me —?"

His prayer rebounded from the ceiling, hollow as an echo. The corporeal Deity of Manichaeism was absurdly unreal, and as unrelated to his sorrow as the moon. For the first time, even in this elementary stage of his faith, Augustine entertained secret doubts about his religion.

He sought relief in sports, songs, elaborate banquets given by Romanianus and his friends. The experience was torture. He tried to find comfort in the old haunts he and Spendius had frequented, the desert, the hills around Thagaste, the pleasant lemon groves where they had enjoyed intimate communion. Everywhere the ghost of Spendius rose to haunt him. He tried writing poetry. It reopened the wound.

Once he set out for his home, burning for Monica's sympathy. He remembered their quarrel and turned back.

He grew to hate the light of day. A ghastly purple pall shrouded his world, colored every action and every desire. More than once the thought battled its way into his mind, "Why do you not take your life and join Spendius out there?"

It always left him weak and terrified. He feared death, and hated it too, in proportion as he loved Spendius. He had not thought too much about death up to the present, not even when his father had passed away. Now that death had overcome Spendius, he pictured the event as a black phantom falling with dizzy speed on all men, devouring the whole world. He marveled that others should be alive, and that he should be alive, since the one he had loved with a deathless love — "half of my soul" — was gone forever.

Then Augustine stumbled upon an odd discovery. He found that he could have solace in tears. Not in prayer was there relief, not in revelings or banquetings, not in the classics, not in writing poetry or teaching rhetoric, but in the ministry of weeping. He wondered why this should be.

Almost every evening that autumn witnessed the son of Monica lying face down on his couch, sobbing in the dark like a broken-hearted child. Often between sobs he would murmur a requiem borrowed from Monica's Bible: "your love to me was wonderful, passing the love of women."

The old year was drawing to a close when Romanianus approached his guest one evening. "Augustine," he said, "I can see that you are not happy here. Do you wish to go back to Carthage?"

A great yearning for Melanie swept Augustine. The past few days had driven her from his mind. "Yes," he said. "But I must stay until I am able to pay off my debt to you. You have been good to me."

"Consider the debt paid off."

"But, sir —"

"I insist," said the patrician, waving a hand.

"What about a rhetoric teacher for the children?"

"I shall secure one in Carthage. I leave for Carthage the day after tomorrow. Would you like to travel with me in my carriage?"

"Indeed, yes," said Augustine. "How can I thank you for your generosity?"

"By visiting me at my Carthage home."

"You may be sure I will."

The next day Augustine called on Monica to say goodbye. The parting took place outside the farmhouse. It was terse, awkward.

"Will you come to Carthage in the spring?" Augustine asked, glancing up at a swallow skimming the olive trees.

"Perhaps." Her eyes never left his face. "Do you wish it?"

"Of course. Why not?"

"I was not sure."

Augustine rubbed his chin and turned his attention to the ground. "By the way," he said, "Romanianus has canceled my debt to him."

"What a friend he has been!"

"He is taking me to Carthage in his carriage."

"God reward him," Monica said.

"I shall write to you."

"I shall be waiting to hear from you."

"Well." Augustine looked at her and forced a smile. "I have to go. Goodbye."

He leaned forward and his lips brushed her cheek. She choked off a rushing impulse to fold him to her breast and remained quietly poised.

"Goodbye," she said softly.

He hurried down the path winding toward town. Monica's eyes stayed on him while he was in sight. Her lips continued to move in prayer long after he had gone.

Melanie noted a profound change in her lover upon his return. He was moodier than ever, more reserved, yet considerably more thoughtful than he had been before his journey to Thagaste. He seldom smiled and never jested. His colossal pride, too, had leveled off, and his cocksureness had vanished. He treated her tenderly.

"I have been faithful to you, my love," he told her. "The fairest rose that blooms in Thagaste is a desert reed beside by beloved."

"How can that be? I am round and ugly, like a Malqua fish cask."

"You are lovelier than a star." He embraced her with a warm tenderness. "And I love you with my whole heart."

"Did you tell your mother about me?"

"I did."

"What did she say?"

"I did not expect her blessing, of course," Augustine said. "But my mother is a surprising woman. When I told her, she was as calm as the Bay of Carthage on a windless day. You would almost think she had known."

"Perhaps she did know."

Augustine shook his head. "I doubt it seriously. And you, my lark, did you miss me?"

"Dreadfully."

"You seem worried over something."

It was true. Melanie's eyes kept darting apprehensively from Augustine to various articles in the room and back to him. Her elegantly formed mouth curved at the corners like the ends of a Roman bow.

"Is it the child?" Augustine said. "Are you afraid you will not have strength —?"

"No, it is not that."

"What, then?"

"Oh, Augustine!" Her head was tilted to one side. "Oh, my dearest, my coming to you was wrong. Our living together these years has been so wrong, and our having a child out of wedlock is sinful."

"Nonsense." He stood behind her with his hands on her shoulders. "Have you forgotten that our religion teaches us this disorder of conscience is all a fiction?"

"I have not forgotten. But how do you explain away these stabbing pains here?" Her hands came together over her breast. "What does Mani say to do about them?"

He wheeled her about. Her eyes were brimming with tears. Augustine kissed them away, holding her close.

"My nightingale, listen to me," he said. "I have been sorry about many things I have done and have not done in my fickle adolescence. I can tell you now by all the sacred writings of Mani that I do not regret my great love for you. If I have one regret, it is that I cannot give you what you pine for. My own heart, let me be your stability."

Melanie crushed her lips to his and held them there passionately as though to draw from Augustine's body the steadfastness she needed. When she forced herself away from him, she said, "I tried to leave you again while you were away, my beloved."

"If you had, I would have died."

"My love has chained me to you."

"Glorious, golden chain, how I adore you!" He traced her lips with his forefinger.

"And now," she said, brightening, "have you chosen a name for your daughter?"

"Daughter? I am going to have a son."

"Have you been to an oracle?"

"No, but I shall have a son," he said. "Yes, I have a name."

"Tell me."

"Not now."

"Please tell me," she begged.

"Later."

Three days later their son was born. Melanie was in labor twenty-three hours, and nearly died. Augustine thought he would die too. While Melanie moaned and gasped and finally delivered the child with a piercing, agonizing wail, he stood outside the door of their bedchamber, paralyzed with horror. Twenty minutes later — he swore it was hours — the midwife opened the door and signaled for him to enter.

Scarcely breathing, he tiptoed in. Melanie lay on the bed, white and motionless in a dead faint. Beside her, wrapped in a brown blanket, nestled a tiny form with a thatch of wet brown hair and a face as wrinkled as a dried pomegranate.

Augustine moved to the bed like a man walking in his sleep. He shook his head to insure sensibility. He stared at the child in dismay. "He looks like an old man," he gasped.

The midwife stood at the head of the bed and wiped the perspiration from Melanie's brow. "They all look like old men," she said in a matter-of-fact voice. "You looked like an old man when you were born."

"Is it a boy?"

"It is a boy."

"A boy!" He threw up his arms excitedly. "A boy!"

Charmed with the word, he repeated it a dozen times.

Melanie stirred. "How is she?" Augustine asked the midwife.

"Sick. Very sick," said the woman. "She can never have more babies."

"But she will live?"

"She will live. You must give her the best of care."

"I shall."

Melanie's eyelids fluttered.

Augustine leaned over her. "My precious one, it is all over. I was right. I have a son."

Her breathing was irregular. She tried to speak.

Augustine laid a finger on her lips. "Do not talk," he said. "Rest. Rest and sleep. Everything is wonderful."

She smiled wanly and closed her eyes.

"You must go now," the midwife said.

"Yes, of course. I must go and tell my friends the marvelous news. Goodbye, Melanie, my sweetheart. And goodbye, my dear son."

Without opening her eyes, Melanie whispered, "What?" and inclined her head toward the child, who was now screwing his face into all sorts of comical shapes.

"What am I going to call him?" Augustine said.

She nodded.

"I shall call him Adeodatus."

"Adeo — datus?"

"Adeodatus — the City of God."

Chapter 20

*I made no move whatever to break off my habit of
consulting those charlatans whom people call
"mathematicians" (Confessions IV, 2, 3).*

Augustine opened his own school for boys. He
rented a hall not far from the university and nailed a
sign over it: *Augustine's School of Rhetoric*. At once, largely
through the influence of Romanianus, a dozen pupils
registered. Augustine settled down to a routine that
yielded rich satisfaction and enough revenue to support his little family.

He was a natural teacher. He lectured with clarity
and force, and had no trouble holding the attention of
his pupils. His reputation as a lecturer spread with the
happy result that more pupils enrolled. This he
counted a major victory, for numerous educators had
established private schools in Carthage and competition was keen.

Gradually he recovered from the shock of losing
Spendius. Alypius, Nebridius, and Honoratus were
quick to observe that his waspish temper had lost much
of its old sting, that suffering had mellowed him They
rejoiced in the change and gladly went back to him.
They played and sang, read together, studied and ar-

gued, hunted and fished with youthful zest and carefree abandon. These diversions, Augustine told Melanie, were "so much fuel to melt our souls, and out of many make one."

Melanie was a long time regaining her strength. She did not regret the slow convalescence. It had this excellent compensation: Augustine waited on her with patience and amazing consideration. Her response was pathetic. Once, when he brought home a bouquet of musk roses, white as light and fragrant as spice, she cried, "Oh, I do not deserve this!"

"My beloved deserves the choicest," Augustine said. "Has she not given me the smartest lad in the Roman Empire?"

He picked up Adeodatus and held him aloft at arms' length. "Ho, my son, what a princeling you are! We shall make you into the most polished orator since Cicero. We shall indeed."

"You are a mysterious person." Reclining on the couch, Melanie buried her face in the roses and inhaled their perfume. She had twisted her ebony hair into coils and piled them like a plaited wreath on her head.

"In what way?" Augustine said, and clucked at his son.

"Remember how angry you were when you knew you were going to be a father?"

"I was not well." He lowered the child, who had begun to take on a strong resemblance to Melanie. "Ah, but this bundle of life is a treasure! Are you not, my tiny one?"

Adeodatus repaid him with a cheerful toothless grin.

"You are happy, then?" Melanie murmured as she plucked a rose from the bouquet and placed it in her hair.

"I am living in the suburbs of paradise. And you?"

Augustine was so taken up with his son he did not notice that Melanie made no reply.

He crossed the room and kissed her. "You are as beautiful as you are sweet," he said. "Here, will you take the treasure? I must get ready for the Bema. I promised to take Honoratus with me tonight."

The Bema, which the Manicheans celebrated every March, was their most important festival.

"Is Honoratus still not converted?" Melanie said, cradling the baby in one arm and the roses in the other.

"Yes. Strange, is it not? I had no trouble converting Alypius and Nebridius. Like you, they were impressionable as wax. Honoratus is of another stripe. He is bound to see the truth soon, though."

"There are so many things in the doctrine that I cannot seem to understand."

"Do not worry about it. The light process had been going on in me for a year and I have questions too. They tell me at the lecture hall that our greatest living authority on Mani's doctrine, a Doctor Faustus, is coming to Carthage some day. He will explain everything, they say."

Late that evening Augustine exploded into the apartment, jubilant. "I am a prophet!" he exclaimed. "I told you Honoratus would be convinced."

Melanie was stitching a little cotton robe for Adeodatus. "So?" she said. "And is he enjoying his conver —?"

As so often, his words raced ahead with his mind. "Not exactly. He looked a bit ill when I left him. He was pale and peaked — you know, as if he had had a battle inside. But then, he is better off now that he has come to see the truth."

"Is he?" Melanie said.

Augustine stared at her. "Certainly." He frowned. "You and I are, are we not?"

She concentrated on her sewing. "Are we?"

"You are a foolish girl. Of course we are." Augustine scooped an apple from a brass bowl on the table and bit into it defensively. "Why should we not be?"

"Then," said Melanie, "why does that look stay in your eyes?"

"What look?"

"That gleam. You seem to keep searching for something you have not found yet."

Augustine dropped the apple back on the table. He moved over to Melanie and gripped her arms. "My heart," he said softly. "My very life, that gleam is my love for you, can you not tell? You round out everything I have ever wanted in the world. You have made me content, divinely, supremely content. If I were asked to exchange places with the emperor, I would say no. Do you believe me?"

For an answer, Melanie sprang up, threw her arms around him and kissed him as though it were their last kiss.

In spite of his protestations of contentment, within a week Augustine was indulging in a new fad. He boasted to his friends that he was getting interested in the liberal arts. But the liberal arts turned out to be nothing more than ancient astrology. He consulted a school of soothsayers who posed as mathematicians. He studied his connection with planets and stars to determine his destiny. He bought books on the zodiac, and investigated the meaning of dreams; he read about how to gain insight into the future by peering into the entrails of slaughtered animals, and crowded his mind with all manner of chimeras.

Nebridius scoffed at his new interests. "I go along with you on Manichean doctrine," he said. "But I stop at astrology."

"Why?" Augustine said, chewing on a piece of galbanum that was supposed to bring good fortune.

"I too have had some experience with the stuff. It is the essence of pseudo-science."

"It helps me understand certain mysteries." Augustine swallowed the bitter resin. His eyes watered, his lips puckered. "Whew!" he said, wiping his mouth on a sleeve.

"What mysteries, for example?"

"Well, is it not true that our lives are affected by outside influences, mystic influences?"

"I agree."

"Could not these influences proceed from Mars and Saturn and Venus?"

"There is not the slightest evidence that they do."

"I like to think so."

Nebridius, aware of the workings of Augustine's mind, asked slyly, "Is it perhaps because it helps smooth out the wrinkles in your conscience?"

Augustine laughed and shrugged the question off.

Circumstances contrived to raise up a second antagonist to his last venture. Each spring Carthage sponsored a poetry contest. Ambitious poets were given a chance to recite an original poem for a prize. The contest was held at the Odeum.

Augustine's companions urged him to enter. He consented, and won honors.

The judge was Vindicianus, the Proconsul. When it was over, he said privately to Augustine, "Will you call on me some evening? I would like to know you better."

Augustine flushed with pleasure. "I consider your invitation a higher honor than taking the prize," he said.

A week later he received a note written on a sheet of ivory inviting him to Vindicianus' home the next evening.

The Proconsul lived in a mansion a stone's throw from the Acropolis, on the summit of Mount Byrsa. A slave met Augustine at the door. He took the invitation, ushered Augustine into a spacious drawing room, and slipped away to summon his master.

Augustine, sleek in a new scarlet-and-gray robe he had bought for the contest, with wrist amulets to ward off evil spirits, surveyed the drawing room with awe. Low-stemmed golden candelabra furnished both illumination and ornamentation. Elephants' tusks formed arches over all the doorways, and a pair of silver Roman eagles on long standards faced each other from opposite sides of the room. A circular mosaic inlaid with an intricate oriental dragon design graced the stone floor. Four lacquered calabashes hung at the ends of chains suspended from the ceiling.

"Good evening, my young friend," said Vindicianus, appearing suddenly.

"Oh, good evening, Proconsul."

Vindicianus subsided on a dais decked with richly embroidered silk cushions. He signaled for Augustine to take another one.

He wore a purple silk toga that was slit at the sides, exposing gold lacing around his legs and ankles. He was sad-looking, austere, and overserious, Augustine thought. He had silver hair, long, tapering fingers that constantly toyed with a string of fat beads, and cheeks that puffed like the pouches of a squirrel.

"I understand you turned down the offer of one of our augurs before the contest," he said.

He referred to an incident that had taken place the previous week. As Augustine was entering the Odeum, a soothsayer of unsavory reputation had intercepted him.

"What will you give me to insure your winning the prize?" he has asked.

"Do you mean you will offer a sacrifice to the spirits?" Augustine had said.

"Yes."

"Look here, you scorpion's egg!" Augustine had stormed. "I want to win the garland, but I would not give you a denarius to sacrifice a fly for me, even if the garland were made of gold."

Reclining on the dais, Augustine lowered his eyes modestly. "I would not say there was much virtue in turning down that kind of proposition," he said.

"You are modest as well as bright. I also understand you mastered the Ten Categories of Aristotle with no help from our philosophers."

Augustine nodded.

"Astonishing!" Vindicianus twirled the string of beads around a finger. "Our very ablest scholars scarcely follow Aristotle, even those who have studied in Greece."

"Would you care to examine me, Proconsul?"

"By the gods, no! I am a scientist, not a philosopher. I practiced medicine before I entered politics. Philosophy is a riddle to me. But what truly puzzles me about you, Augustine, is this: how can a youth of your power to pierce the subtleties of mighty Aristotle, how can you entangle your mind with the astrological absurdities of soothsayers?"

Augustine squirmed. "Why is it such a problem?"

"It is utterly inconsistent." Vindicianus rang a bell and a slave appeared. Vindicianus ordered wine. "When I was in the university I planned to take up astrology as a profession."

"Your father forbade it?"

"No. Fortunately the gods have endowed me with two gifts, a clear mind and a conscience. My mind would not permit me to embrace a speculative scheme such as the astrologers have worked out."

Augustine's face clouded.

"You are angry," Vindicianus went on. "Do not be angry at honesty. My mind was not as nimble as yours. It was able, however, to lay hold of the axioms of Hippocrates. Only when I began to study Hippocrates did I become conscious of the senselessness of astrology."

The slave brought in goblets of wine and served guest and host.

"In the second place," Vindicianus said, "my conscience refused to let me embrace a gigantic hoax."

"But, sir," Augustine said, struggling to keep calm, "how is it that so many predictions of the astrologers come to pass?"

"The force of chance," said Vindicianus, sipping his wine. "To illustrate: My first name is Pollio, it happens. It also happens that I have a son who hopes to be assigned to the office of Proconsul. Confidentially, I have the promise of our emperor that he will be appointed some day. Now in Virgil's fourth *Eclogue*, you recall, he makes a prophecy:

> "The lovely boy, with his auspicious face,
> Shall Pollio's consulship and triumph grace."

"Oh, but he was prophesying of the Messiah, not your son."

"Precisely," said Vindicianus. "You see, using the method of the astrologers, I can pick that couplet out of the context, carry it over and make it apply to my son. But it is dishonest. Virgil did not have my son in mind at all as you point out."

"But what of their other powers?" Augustine said with some heat. "A pupil of mine tells me that he asked the astrologer, Albicerius, what he — that is, my pupil — was thinking of. Albicerius answered, 'A verse from Virgil.' 'Correct,' said my pupil. 'What verse?' Albicenus, who was not an educated man, immediately quoted the verse."

"I know, I know." Vindicianus nodded grimly. "The men who used to teach me cited similar cases."

"How do you explain them?"

"I have no explanation. I am a scientist. Augustine, I urge you to give up this silly trickery and stick to your rhetoric. You are far too useful to society as a rhetorician."

In vain the Proconsul argued with his visitor. Augustine remained adamant in his determination to press on with his astrological experiments.

It was late when they parted at the door. Augustine thanked the Proconsul for his interest.

"What it is in astrology that fascinates you I shall never know," said Vindicianus glumly. "There must be a drive in you somewhere that clamors for a goal you have not yet attained. I cannot show you where to find it, for I have no notion what that goal is. But I can assure you of one thing — if you are seeking reality in astrology, you are foredoomed to failure." A wistful note had crept into his voice. "I wish I could tell you where to look. I wish I could tell myself."

Chapter 21

You were straight ahead of me, but I had roamed away from myself and could not find even myself, let alone you! (Confessions V, 2, 2)

For Augustine, the years scudded by like ships before a wind. Nine years. Nine years crammed with sharp, sometimes delirious joys alternating with biting disillusionment. Years of intellectual triumphs, broken by lapses into despondency and frustration. Seasons of self-examination and self-delusion, of tortuous efforts to mold a pattern of life out of clay.

"How like the apples of Sodom are pleasures!" he would complain to Melanie. "Delightful to behold, only to crumble to dust when touched."

He had purchased a tan stucco house in a district of Carthage called Agaro. There he passed the years, earning his living as a rhetoric teacher. He cherished Melanie as a faithful husband would his wife. He nurtured Adeodatus on the cream and honey of classical learning, so that by the time the boy approached ten he had the mental development of a youth of fifteen. No child could possibly have exerted a greater influence for harmony in the home than Augustine's son. His sweet disposition and winsome ways kept friction to a minimum, and peace ruled in the home, if not in the hearts of the parents.

Augustine loved his mistress with a constancy that stood out as the unique feature of his ever changing career. He longed to marry her, and thought about it hard and long. Always a shadow, falling across the plan, caused him to hesitate. And always, even when he made love to Melanie, an enigmatic breach divided them, so that when there should have been an exalted blending of spirit with spirit, there was no such union. Each was conscious of the barrier, but each would have died rather than speak of it.

Augustine had given up dabbling in astrology. Once he had had his fill it no longer seemed colorful or interesting to him. Finally, he burned his charts and his books on astrology, and threw away his amulets.

At twenty-nine Augustine had put on weight and a mature dignity. His school was doing well. His circle of friends and acquaintances had expanded to include some of the prominent figures in the city's political life. Carthage had come to regard the rhetorician as one of his foremost intellectuals.

Alypius had gone to Rome to enter the diplomatic service. Honoratus and Nebridius were budding local lawyers, just commencing to enjoy a degree of prosperity after years of apprenticeship.

Late one afternoon in midsummer the three were swimming in a pool of scalding water in the Baths of Gargilius. The pools were in the *caldarium*, the rectangular room where the series of steps in public bathing began. Deliciously relaxed after a day of great heat, they languished on their stomachs on the stone ramp that slanted up from the water, their bodies submerged up to their necks. Private parties had engaged most of the other pools indenting the *caldarium*, for Carthage had absorbed Rome's passion for bathing.

They were discussing Manicheism. Nebridius wiggled over on his back and watched the hot water spurt from the pipe connected with the metal heater and fall into the pool. "You know," he said, "I am wondering how much longer I can stay with the movement."

His words startled Augustine. For months he himself had been pondering the same thought. His discovery of the charlatanry in astrology had filled his mind with doubts about the genuineness of all systems of thought. "What has brought you to question the truth?" he asked, glancing at Nebridius out of the edge of his eye. Habit had made him refer thus to the Manichean faith.

"For one thing, I find too much secrecy in the higher orders," said Nebridius. "We three are inquirers. All right. What do we know about the mysteries our elders are always bragging about? No more than we knew nine years ago."

"You have been reading Epiphanius." Augustine cupped a handful of water and let it trickle over his face.

"No," said Nebridius. "But I have heard a lot about his exposure to the corruption of our teachers. Plenty of men are agreeing with him, too."

"Have you seen any of this corruption firsthand either of you?" asked Honoratus.

"I have," said Augustine. "A few nights ago I was walking home from a meeting. Three of our so-called elect were walking in front of me. I could not help overhearing their talk. Obscene? It was worse than any language you hear from pagans. Not only that, their gestures were as obscene as their language. I am not posing as a saint, but I tell you I was ashamed that I was in the same movement with them."

"Is it not your duty to report them to the brotherhood?" Honoratus said.

"I did m-mention it to Marius," said Augustine, imitating the evangelist. "He passed it off with a l-laugh."

Nebridius splashed water in Augustine's face. "Perhaps Marius was afraid of opening up more scandal."

Augustine pulled himself out of the water and stretched. "Shall we go to the *frigidarium*?"

The adjoining room contained a large cold-water plunge where bathers cooled off before their rub-down. Presently the three were swimming about while slaves watched them from a bench. They waited, with towels in hand, to escort them into the unctorium for massage.

"Another thing that arouses questions in me," said Nebridius, swimming on his side, "is that incident that happened at our last Bema."

"What incident was that?" Honoratus asked.

"Did you not hear? While our elders were holding their vigil one night, the lights went out. And stayed out, they tell me. What went on — well, you can only guess. It must have been pretty shocking."

They had reached the far end of the pool. They stopped swimming and floated listlessly on the surface of the waters, enjoying comparative privacy.

"Alypius wrote me an interesting letter last week," Augustine said. "He told me about a well-to-do Roman hearer by name of Constantius who set up a monastery in Rome for the elect. When Constantius invited the elect into the monastery he assumed they would live under the rules of the Mani. Alypius said in no time they were denouncing each other for stealing and gluttony and immorality and what-not. He said the men went to Constantius and complained about the strictness of the rules. 'Then,' Constantius told them, 'the rules must either be capable of being kept or our founder was a fool.' That broke up the project, and the men stormed out of the monastery in a temper. Not only that, Alypius said, but the bishop, of all people, ran away with a bag of Constantius' money. Nice situation, is it not?"

Honoratus looked stunned. "You got us into this religion. What are you trying to do now, get us out?"

Augustine ducked his head under water. When he came up, he said, "The learned Doctor Faustus is finally coming to the city. Marius has promised us an interview with him. I intend to pepper him with a thousand questions, and if he cannot answer me, I shall be ready to break."

"And I," said Nebridius. "Only I am not waiting for Faustus to come before I start my campaign."

That evening Nebridius went to the lecture hall and surprised the Manichean leaders with a pointed query. "What would the powers of evil have done to God if he had not struggled against them?" he asked.

The elect tried to hide their embarrassment. One of them said weakly, "They might have overcome Him."

"In that case, then," Nebridius retorted, "God must be violable and corruptible."

"Oh, no," the men said. They looked at one another, obviously confused.

"But if he is incorruptible and beyond their power," Nebridius continued, "why should he have mixed a portion of himself with matter, as you claim he did?"

"Wait until Doctor Faustus comes," Marius said, dropping a hand on Nebridius' shoulder. "He will resolve all your difficulties."

"I have been hearing that for years," Nebridius said shortly.

"You must be patient. He is coming soon. Very soon. He will vindicate our position and make everything clear."

Marius was partly right. Ten days later Doctor Faustus did arrive in Carthage to deliver a series of lectures on Manichean theology. But Marius was wrong in that Faustus did not vindicate the Manichean position and make everything clear — at least, not to the three anxious inquirers.

Chapter 22

*All through that period of nine years, during which
I was spiritually adrift as a hearer of the Manichees,
I had been waiting the arrival of Faustus
(Confessions V, 6, 10).*

Augustine listened to the renowned Faustus lecture with mixed feelings. As a rhetorician himself, he admired the doctor's glib tongue. As a seeker after truth, he was disappointed in the content of the lecture. Faustus had not spoken ten minutes before Augustine's inner ear caught the ring of superficiality.

"With a modicum of intelligence, any mortal can perceive that our twelve aeons correspond to the twelve signs of the zodiac and to the twelve stages of the world, as well." The lecturer was portly, with the innocent eyes of a baby and three receding chins that put Augustine in mind of the three decks of a trireme, the Roman galley ship. He wore a creamy toga with cerise borders, adorned at the hem with small bronze bells that tinkled merrily when he stirred. He declaimed in a loud voice and drove home his points with studied gesticulations. "These aeons emanate from primeval light, whence

wander the gleaming stars in their boundless pastures
and the full-orbed moon in her lost refulgence."

"The clever thief," Augustine said to himself. "He
picked that phrasing out of Seneca's *Oedipus.*"

"While this process was going on," Faustus continued pompously, "darkness, all wrapped in murky
clouds, filled with the plethora of eternal fire, burned
in his cerulean ocean but shone not, while hosts of demons within his Stygian precincts battled for supe-
riority among their own legions. Nor swerved they from
their purposed course until they had laid hold of one
ray of paling light that had escaped the bright mansions of celestial glory: the primeval man, Christ."

Faustus rested his hands on his hips, threw back his
head and held it arched, like the head of a camel. He
beamed at his audience genially, inviting applause. The
feeble round he drew died out instantly, and with it his
smile.

Augustine glanced at Honoratus and Nebridius,
seated next to him on the bench. He could tell they
were disappointed too. "This old fool is bluffing," he
whispered to Honoratus. "He is no scholar, he merely
sprinkles that drivel with quotations from Seneca and
Tully."

Honoratus nodded mournfully.

The lecture over, the three friends jockeyed Faustus
into a corner and were about to ask for an appointment
when Marius bustled up. "Now see here, young men,"
he said, "the great doctor is tired after his lecture. You
must not trouble him, you know." And he whisked the
great doctor away with the finesse of a magician.

The trio went home, thwarted.

It was a week before they managed to secure the interview. Even then, they had to use force to keep
Marius from repeating the vanishing act.

At the end of the final lecture they swarmed reso-
lutely to the front of the lecture hall. Honoratus and

Nebridius sealed off Marius, while Augustine marched straight to Faustus. "Doctor," he said, "my friends and I wish to ask you some questions relative to your lectures. May we?"

Faustus owned one of the few pairs of spectacles in Africa — two squares of glass linked by a nosepiece and held to the eyes by hand. When Augustine addressed him, he lifted the spectacles, peered at his inquirer, and asked coolly, "Who are you?"

"My name is Augustine. I am a rhetoric teacher."

"Augustine?" Faustus lowered the spectacles and tapped them against his wrist. "Hm. Ah, yes, Marius has spoken of you. You also write, do you not?"

He referred to a book Augustine had recently published, entitled *On the Fair and Fit.* In it he set forth his theories of beauty. Literary men had ridiculed his effort in the most scathing terms, thus puncturing the rhetorician's illusions of literary greatness.

Augustine covered his embarrassment as he replied to Faustus, "Oh, in an amateurish way. Sir, if my friends and I might borrow a few moments of your valuable time, we would like you to clarify certain problems that perplex us."

"Why not?" Faustus said affably, spreading his arms.

Augustine looked over his shoulder. Across the hall Nebridius and Honoratus were busy fending off Marius, who puffed and fumed like an offended lover as he tried to break through and rescue Faustus.

"Your henchman over there might tell you why not." Augustine rolled his head in Marius' direction. "For some reason he does not want us to come together."

"Marius!" Faustus called to him. "Desist!"

Marius desisted. Honoratus and Nebridius rearranged their tunics, and with an air of triumph hastened to Augustine's side. He presented them to Faustus.

"Shall we sit here?" the Manichean leader said.

He seated them on the front bench and, to the music of the tinkling bells, lowered himself into a chair before the bench. The hall was practically empty. Only three or four of the elect lingered at the door to discuss the lecture. A slave was putting out the oiled torches in the rear. Marius was nowhere in sight.

"Now, young gentlemen," Faustus said, "what, pray, is the nature of your interrogation?"

"My question," said Augustine, "has to do with origins."

"Yes, yes."

"As I understand our position, we maintain that two eternal principles coexist, light and matter. Light is good, matter is evil. The universe had emerged from their union. Is that right?"

"Precisely." Faustus' moonlike face moved up and down, like that of a happy harlequin. "Light impregnated matter. Out of the womb of matter issued the starry glory of the lofty firmament."

Augustine recognized another of Seneca's phrases.

"Very good." Augustine jammed an index finger into his open palm. "Now I would like to get back to causality. You remember that Aristotle says we can never really know anything until we know the why of it. He says there must be a first and moving cause, that the idea of an infinite series is absurd. He claims that flesh comes from the earth, earth comes from air, and air from fire. But the series cannot be endless. Thus he contradicts our premise that light and matter are eternal. It strikes me that he is far more logical than we are. Do you not agree?"

Faustus made no attempt to hide his boredom. He yawned. "I honestly have not a scintilla of knowledge of metaphysics."

Augustine puckered his lips in exasperation. "But do you not think there has to be a first cause? What I am trying to find out is this: if there is a first cause, what is it?"

Faustus toyed with his spectacles and shook his head. "Ask me questions about theology and I shall be glad to enlighten you."

"Look," said Nebridius with considerable choler, "you bishops are always accusing Christian teachers of demanding raw faith in place of reason. You keep saying, 'We Manicheans invite you to lay hold of truths which we can "explain and enable you to grasp perfectly.' Well then, why, if you have exhaustive knowledge, do you not answer Augustine's question?"

"I have already disclaimed the ability to solve abstractions," said Faustus patiently. "I do not pose as a philosopher. Let us confine our discussion to doctrine."

"Fine," Nebridius said, leaning toward him. "Not long ago an orthodox scholar, one Helpidius, came to Carthage to lecture. He challenged the Manicheans to produce one bit of evidence to support our charge that the text of the New Testament is spurious."

"Well?"

"So why did we not answer the man? Not a Manichean stood up to answer Helpidius."

"Certainly not," said Faustus uneasily. "Why should we cast pearls before swine?"

"Pearls before swine!" Nebridius leaped to his feet, his face scarlet. "Why, that —"

"Sit down, Nebridius," Augustine said calmly, laying a hand on his friend's arm.

Nebridius slumped back on the bench, still ruffled.

"Doctor," said Honoratus, breaking his silence, "I want to ask you something. Our elect are bound to absolute purity by the three seals of mouth, hand, and breast. Why is it that some of our most prominent leaders are foulmouthed and immoral?"

Faustus shrugged. "You know how it is," he said with a sigh. "What Seneca calls 'mischief's fatal power' assaults us all. Was it not ever so? Drunken Lot fathered children by his own daughters. Samson succumbed to the charms of Delilah. David yielded to the blandishments of the flesh. Which of us is perf — ?"

"But you yourself have written a book against the Old Testament!" cried Augustine. "Is it not morally inconsistent to defend our actions on the basis of bad ethics such as you accuse the Old Testament of teaching?"

"I wrote against the God of the Old Testament," said Faustus, squirming. "The Jewish concept of monism which finds expression in the Jehovah of their sacred Scriptures is utterly repugnant to thoughtful minds. Now, we Manicheans, for our part, derive profound intellectual satisfaction in dualism." And he launched into a wordy dissertation on Mani's views of Deity which the three had been exposed to for years.

Toward midnight, Marius appeared and broke up the interview. "It is late," he said. "The holy bishop is weary after a strenuous day of work. I must ask you to postpone further deliberation."

Augustine and his companions said good night and withdrew. As they strolled down the deserted street leading from the lecture hall, Nebridius said: "It is perfectly clear we are not getting any help from Old Moonface. Think of it. Marius used to tell us the Holy Spirit had vested him with plenary authority. Hah!"

"Do not be bitter," said Augustine. "In a way I like the old boy. He at least had some measure of honesty. He admitted there are some things he did not know. You must agree it is a concession most of our elect refuse to grant."

"I cannot get over it," said Honoratus sorrowfully. "You would think the leading bishop of our movement could furnish more light than he gave us."

"I cannot share Augustine's sympathy for his obese reverence," Nebridius said. "In our law courts we expect shilly-shallying, but not in temples dedicated to the propagation of truth. As far as I am concerned, this is the climax. I am out of the movement and I feel good all over."

"Augustine, what about you?" said Honoratus.

Augustine did not answer at once. He moved along for a moment, then said, "Like both of you, I am discouraged."

"But are you going to break, like Nebridius?"

"I must give it more thought." He would not commit himself further.

Sometime after he parted from the two, he arrived home and announced to Melanie, "I am going to leave Carthage."

Melanie had retired. Augustine did not light a lamp. He sat on the edge of the bed while they talked in the dark.

"Why, my beloved?" she said.

"I have got to get away."

"Where will you go?"

"Rome," he said.

"But why? What made you decide this?"

"Several considerations. I am not feeling too well."

"Your throat?"

"Yes. Also the Eversores are on the prowl again. They raided my school today. I am told the schools in Rome have no such outbursts."

"And what of Doctor Faustus?" she asked.

"A quack, if I ever heard one."

"I see."

Augustine bent over her and kissed her forehead. "My adorable nightingale, as soon as I settle I shall send for you and Adeodatus. Alypius will no doubt help me get students for a new school in Rome. It will be the best thing for everyone, for you and the boy too. Think of his growing up in that magic city."

"It will be wonderful." She sat up and her arms slid around his neck. Had there been light in the room, he would have seen fear in her eyes. "It will be wonderful."

The way she said it troubled him. "Melanie, what is it? Is anything wrong?"

"Oh, my darling, there is something I have not told you."

Alarmed, he said, "You mean you are going to have another —?"

"Oh, no, no."

"What then?"

"Augustine — your mother is in Carthage."

Chapter 23

*Matters are so arranged at your command that every
disordered soul is its own punishment
(Confessions I, 12, 19).*

Shortly after Augustine had set out for the
Manichean lecture hall that evening, a woman
knocked on the leaved doors of the tan house in Agaro.
She was stooped, and her face was shrouded in a black
veil. Melanie went to the doors, humming a bright Sicilian tune she had learned from her mother. She drew
the doors apart a few inches and peered through the
opening. A shaft of light from the oil lamp slanted
across Monica's veil. Without being able to see the face.
Melanie knew instinctively who was before her. The
music died in her throat.

"Oh," she said, her heart beating fast, "you are his
mother."

"Yes, I am," Monica said.

Melanie forced the doors open and stepped aside.
"Come — come in, please."

Monica crossed the threshold and, standing there,
gave the room a swift inspection. Melanie was glad she
had cleaned house that morning.

Adeodatus sat at a table in the center of the room, reading a book. When Monica entered, he struggled to his feet and bowed low.

Melanie said, "Adeodatus, you have never seen your grandmother." She turned to Monica. "He knows you because his father has talked of you so much."

Monica drew her veil aside and regarded her grandson with smiling eyes. "Adeodatus." She enunciated every syllable lovingly. "How I do rejoice to see you!"

"And I to see you," he said formally, and bowed again.

"Adeodatus, Gift of God," Monica murmured.

The boy's glance shot past her and rested on Melanie. She hovered with her back to the door and rubbed her hands together in agitation. The color had drained from her face, and young as Adeodatus was, he knew his mother was terrified.

"Your father is not at home?" Monica asked.

"No, Grandmother," Adeodatus said, standing straight as a soldier.

"He is attending a lecture," Melanie explained. "Please sit down."

Monica walked to the couch. "Come, my grandson," she said, beckoning to him. "Sit with me."

He obeyed without any hesitation.

Melanie tore herself from the door and started for the cubbyhole that functioned as a kitchen. "You will have some refreshment?" she said. "Wafers, or barley water, or —?"

"I dined at the home of Romanianus," Monica answered pleasantly. Her eyes were on Adeodatus, but somehow Melanie had the impression that it was she Monica was studying.

"Oh." She halted at the door of the cubbyhole, still fighting to hide her excitement. "You are stopping there?"

"Yes. Romanianus has repeatedly invited me to share his winter home with his family."

"Romanianus is fine man."

"When do you expect Aurelius home?" Monica said, caressing her grandson.

"He said that he may be late tonight," Melanie said. "He will be glad to see you."

"The way opened suddenly for me to come to Carthage," Monica said. "I had no time to send him word."

"Did you have a comfortable trip?"

"Very comfortable."

Melanie remembered Augustine's words, "My mother is a surprising woman." She thought he could have added, "And strong too."

Nine years had not dulled the power of Monica's character. If anything, widowhood, financial responsibilities, and the care of the estate had made her more self-reliant than ever. The quick, sure movements of her body, the forward thrust of the chin, the fire in her eye, and especially the set of her mouth stamped her as a woman of indomitable will. "She is too strong for me," Melanie told herself in a flutter of agony. "She will be my undoing. Unless Augustine shields me, she will be my undoing."

Yet Melanie was fair enough not to confuse strength with cruelty. She knew that Monica's firmness did not cancel out her kindness. She felt that under different conditions, she and the older woman might have developed a warm friendship, a mutual devotion that could have been a strengthening influence in her own uncertain life.

"Adeodatus is an apt pupil, Aurelius writes me." Monica took his hands in hers. "He must have his father's capacity for learning."

"He has," said Melanie.

"He is your image, Melanie."

There, I was right, Melanie thought hopefully. She is kind.

"How is Aurelius?"

"Not too well." Melanie sat down on the edge of a chair. "His throat has bothered him lately."

"Has he ever mentioned moving back to Thagaste?"

"I have not heard him."

Augustine's mother noted the musical cadence in Melanie's voice, and her pliant beauty, and understood why her son had fallen in love.

"When does Adeodatus go to bed?" She might as well have said, "I want to be alone with you, Melanie."

"It is time now," Melanie said.

The lad stood up without a word and bowed to Monica.

He kissed his mother and clung to her briefly, then left the room. Melanie watched him go as one watches the last prop withdrawn before a plunge into the unknown. A nameless dread gnawed at her as she waited timorously. She folded her hands as though to discipline them, and sat with downcast eyes.

"He is a dear boy," Monica said. "You must be proud of him."

"I am. That is — we both are," Melanie stammered.

"Melanie." Monica fell back on the couch and brushed the veil farther back from her face. "Sooner or later we must come to this point, and I propose that we discuss it now. Tell me, do you not think Aurelius would enhance his prestige if he —?" She broke off, unable to finish what she wanted to say.

Melanie's hand flew to her breast to quiet the tumult there. Her cheeks blazed. "If he were free?"

Monica eyed her compassionately. Her nod was barely perceptible.

"Who am I to — to oppose his seeking freedom?" Melanie could hardly speak for the ache in her throat and in her heart.

"I was certain you would say that. You and I both love him. This we have in common. We want done only what is best for him, is it not so?"

"Yes, of course," Melanie whispered, and covered her face with her hands.

"You favor such a course, then?"

Melanie waited a long time before trusting her voice. "I favor — whatever Augustine favors."

"Melanie, my dear." The voice was genuinely sympathetic. "Can you see ten or twelve years into the future and perceive your own boy as an adult. He is a young man of great promise; possibly he will become a great man. Now ask yourself this question: do I wish the son of my love to be involved in concubinage?"

A pitiful cry burst from Melanie's lips. She sprang up, her face still covered, and fled into Adeodatus' bedchamber. She flung herself across the bed where he lay wide awake, and gave herself up to her grief. Terrible, convulsive sobs racked her body. She thought she was going to faint. "God, God, God," she prayed, "please help me! Please help me!"

Adeodatus crept out from under his coverlet and lay down beside her. Their arms entwined. Their tears merged and splattered on the cotton coverlet like drops of rain "Ah, Mother!" was all he could say. "Mother, Mother; Mother, Mother . . . !"

"My boy, my heart, my very life!"

They were too grief-stricken to hear the leaved doors in the adjoining room open and close.

Suffering bound them together. The son's precocious mind had grasped the implications of what he had overheard from his bedchamber. His mother was aware of this, and she loved him with a new, sublime love that was ointment to her wound. They lay on the bed, heart pounding against heart, cheek welded to cheek, voiceless, understanding. After the tears came quivering sighs. Then silence, a long, healing silence that for the moment quelled the fears that haunted the mother's breast.

Adeodatus broke the stillness. "Mother."

"Yes, my beloved son?"

"Why does God let this happen to you? Why does God let you suffer?"

"It is not God's fault, it is my sin that has brought it on."

"Does Grandmother think that?"

"Your grandmother is right," Melanie said, her hands running over his cheeks tenderly. "When you are older, you will know she is right. She is a great and good woman."

"Mother."

"What is it, dearest one?"

"Nothing will come between you and Father. I will not let anything come between you and Father."

She seized his hands and held them to her cheeks. "Of course you will not," she said fiercely.

"And God will not," he said. "Will He?"

'No, little one." From her heart a prayer of penitence winged heavenward: O God, forgive this lie — this lie, with all my other black, black sins.

Her effort to allay his anxiety could not have been convincing, for she felt a tear splash on the back of her hand. She clutched his head to her breast and stroked it with fingers that communicated messages of love.

Gradually the tense little body relaxed, and the breathing slowed down. At last, like the disciples in ancient Gethsemane, the child slept for sorrow.

Chapter 24

When she had finished blaming my deception and
cruelty, she resumed her entreaties for me, and
returned to her accustomed haunts, while I went
to Rome (Confessions V, 8, 15).

O n the quay at Malqua Augustine chafed, waiting
to board an Egyptian corn ship in the harbor.

It was the fifth night after Monica's sudden appearance in Carthage. In the intervening days her son had
devoted every moment of his spare time to her. He had
escorted her on tours of the city, taken Adeodatus to
call on her, entertained her in the finest inns on the Via
Coelestis. He had even accompanied her to a basilica
and gone through the motions of worship.

Their last conversation, which had taken place that
afternoon in the home of Romanianus, had turned out
to be explosive.

"Have you considered coming back to Thagaste and
opening a rhetoric school?" she asked.

"Mother, Thagaste has no need of another school,"
he protested.

"Your health would be so much better in a dry climate."

He laughed at her. "Every mother in the world thinks her son's health suffers when he is not near. Why is that?"

"I should think," she said, paying no attention to his question, "that you would consider Adeodatus, if not yourself. This — this Babylon you are raising him in, is it the proper atmosphere for an impressionable boy, do you think?"

"You believe Thagaste provides a purer atmosphere?" he said.

"I do."

"One of my closest friends went astray in Thagaste."

She refused to give up. She became mysterious. "Melanie and I have had a talk."

He looked worried. "You have?"

"We have. She is an excellent young woman. She has agreed to give you your freedom."

"Freedom!" he exploded. "What am I, a slave?"

"Aurelius," she said calmly, "you will not deny that your relationship with Melanie is bound to be a fetter. Your influence cannot but be hurt by such a connection. It is not worthy of you."

"Very well, Mother. I have the solution. I shall marry her."

"No!" Monica's eyes seemed to shoot forth jets. "Aurelius, you cannot do this to yourself!" Her voice was threaded with undertones he recognized as dangerous. "I forbid it, do you hear?"

"Mother, listen to me." He was pleading now. "Melanie is a rare and gracious woman, and I am in love with her. Does it mean nothing to you?"

"What it means to me has no relation to the situation. It is you I am thinking of. It is time for you to think of breaking this illicit union."

Augustine had choked down his rage and charged out of Romanianus' house, fully determined to effect his break, not with Melanie, but with Carthage.

He had to steel himself for his parting with Melanie. Without hesitation he returned home to reveal to Melanie his plan, drawing her aside to their room for a last word.

"Sweet love," he said, embracing her, "we will not be separated long. I hope I may start a rhetoric school at once in Rome. If I can make a success of it, I shall send for you and Adeodatus the day I have saved enough money."

Their son lay asleep in his room. Augustine did not awaken him to tell him of his plans, leaving that task for Melanie.

"Are you well enough? What of your throat trouble?" Melanie nestled in his arms and stroked his cheek fondly. "Promise me you will take the best care of yourself until we join you."

"I promise." He drew away and regarded her with loving eyes. "I do not know what you may say to my mother, when I have gone."

"You should tell her."

"No. You know I cannot do that now."

She threw herself into his arms again. "I am sure you are right," she cried. "I am sure."

"Until we meet in Rome then —" He kissed her long and tenderly. Then he took up his bundle of personal effects, and went out into the night.

On the quay, he brooded over the quarrel of the afternoon, kicked at the wooden planks underfoot, and wished he were on his way to Rome.

Lack of wind was causing the delay in sailing. Out in the harbor the vessels, becalmed, sat like a fleet of ghost ships, motionless. On the pier, threescore or more passengers walked back and forth, abusing the gods for holding back the winds. The dank, pungent odors of wet cordage, dried lobsters and crabs, and decaying oysters made breathing unpleasant.

"Good evening, Augustine." It was Philologus, a young Greek instructor at the university. Augustine was not happy to see him, simply because he had never overcome his dislike for Greeks.

"Good evening," he said, not too cordially.

"Are you waiting to sail too?"

"Yes."

"How good it would be if we could import a breeze!" Augustine agreed.

"Shall we take a stroll?" said Philologus.

The rhetorician could think of no excuse to refuse. They started for the far end of the quay.

"I judge you are going to Rome too," the instructor said.

"Yes. And you?"

"I have been transferred to the university there."

"I see. Have you been in Rome before?" Augustine said.

"Oh yes, I studied there several years ago."

"Do you like the city?"

"No," said Philologus.

"Why not?"

"It lacks the cleanliness of Carthage. It is constantly being racked with some serious epidemic. It is anti-foreign. It thinks of nothing but food, and sooner or later everyone who lives in Rome becomes a glutton. Never have I seen such a city of gourmands."

"Truly?"

"It is also a city of rolling heads," Philologus went on. "Some of its prefects suspend baskets from the windows of the Praetorium. Roman citizens are urged to turn informers, make denunciations against their fellows and drop them in the baskets. This goes on morning, noon, and night, and as you would surmise, the city executioner is an overworked official."

Augustine had heard these rumors before, but in laying his plans to flee to Rome he had forgotten them.

Had he made a grave mistake in judgment? Was he really going to improve his lot by cutting all links with Carthage? It was still not too late to change his mind and go back to Agaro. Ah yes, but there was Monica to reckon with, should he return. He must count on increasing pressure from her to put Melanie away, whereas in Rome Melanie and Adeodatus could join him soon. No, he must not think of turning back now.

"If Rome is so bad," he said to Philologus, "what is it that takes you back?"

Philologus' smile was wise. "The answer is a substantial raise in salary."

They reached the end of the pier. A lighted torch on the top of a pole had attracted swarms of moths. The unfortunate insects flew into the flame, singed their wings, and dropped by the score into the waters of the harbor, where a large school of fish vied to devour them. The two now watched the destruction until they tired of it, then turned and retraced their steps.

Augustine found himself dissatisfied with Philologus' comments on Rome. After all, the man was a Greek, and Greeks still smarted over the Roman conquest of their nation.

"Are you sure conditions are as bad as you make out?" he asked.

"Worse," said Philologus. "You will see."

Augustine shook his head. "Then if they are, it would take more than money to make me go back."

"Perhaps I should say there is a secondary motive. Perhaps I should look upon myself as a missionary."

"A missionary?" Augustine echoed.

"Precisely. Who can tell? If enough Greeks infiltrate Rome, there may be another revival of learning."

"What are you talking about?" Augustine's patriotic blood was stirring. "When did Greece ever bring a revival of learning to Rome?"

"My dear fellow," said Philologus in a needling tone, "you have forgotten what Horace wrote:

"Greece conquered Greece, her conqueror subdued,
And Rome grew polished, who till then was rude."

Augustine was about to make an indignant reply when suddenly, to his dismay, a familiar form materialized. It was Monica in a flowing black mantle and black veil.

"Mother!" he cried.

She stood before him, a stricken look upon her face. "How can you do this wicked thing? Have you no heart, no soul? Are you without natural affection?"

Augustine feigned innocence. "I do not understand you. Why, my friend Philologus here is sailing for Italy, and I came to see him off."

She faced the Greek. "Is he telling the truth?"

Philologus took his cue from Augustine. "Of course he is telling the truth."

Augustine's alert mind was working fast. What had happened? Had Monica's intuition ferreted out his plan? Had she pried information from Melanie?

"How did you learn I had come to the pier?" he said.

"I went to Agaro to see you. I wanted to tell you that Romanianus had agreed to take you back to his villa at Thagaste as the teacher of rhetoric."

"Was it Romanianus' idea?"

Her head went up defensively. "No, it was my idea, but it met with his approval."

"Tell me, did Melanie tell you I had come to the quay?"

"I found it out, yes."

"Did she tell you about Philologus?"

"No," Monica said. "As soon as I heard the word 'quay' I had a sickening premonition. I was sure you were going to leave, so I hired a carriage and drove here."

From somewhere in the harbor a sailor called out the time of the night watch.

"Ten o'clock," Philologus fretted. "Already we are two hours late."

"May we sit down somewhere?" Monica said. In spite of the covering of the veil, she gave every evidence of fatigue.

Her question nudged Augustine's brain into action. With startling suddenness it conceived a scheme that would solve his dilemma.

"Mother, listen to me. There is a basilica less than a five-minute walk from here. Let me take you there until Philologus' ship sails, then I shall take you home."

"Are you sure it will be all right?"

"It is perfectly in order. It is by far the most comfortable place." He extended an arm and waved it about. "You can see there is no place here to rest."

Carthaginian Christians had erected the Basilica of Saint Cyprian in memory of Cyprian Thascius Caecillius, a stalwart third-century presbyter who had sacrificed his life for the cause of Christ. The building stood in a flower garden protected by a high wall. Though it was dark there so late at night, the garden offered ample refuge for sojourners.

Augustine led his mother through the arcade into the churchyard. Here the air, heavy with the scent of jasmine, was blessedly pure after the odors of the quay. Olive trees tapered up from the ground, pointing like stubby fingers to the stars.

They discovered a long stone bench beside the footpath, and Augustine helped his mother stretch out on it. He loosened the folds of the mantle about her throat and patted her cheek. "Rest well, little Mother," he said. "You will be safe here until I come for you."

"Aurelius."

"Yes, Mother?"

"You will come for me? Do you swear you will come!"

He smiled reassuringly. "Why not?"

She was lying on her side with her head cradled on an arm. She did not answer but searched his face with loving eyes.

He bent and kissed her. "Sleep well, dear heart," he whispered. "I shall come back as soon as I can."

Long after he had faded into the night Monica remained prostrate, her eyes closed, her breathing heavy.

The moon vaulted over the rim of the wall and spun a gossamer web of gold across the garden. Monica roused herself and rubbed her eyes. "I must rise and pray," she murmured. "He needs my prayers."

She forced herself from the bench and knelt on the warm earth beside it. She folded her hands, raised her head and prayed. "Lord Jesus, Lord Jesus," she said, "You who frustrates the tokens of liars and turn wise men backward and make their knowledge foolish, keep him on these shares. O my Savior, keep him here. Do not let him go, for the glory of your name and the salvation of his helpless, distracted soul."

For two hours she fought off the onslaughts of slumber to pray. But the powers of the flesh have limitations, and at last, worn out by her long vigil, she surrendered. She slipped to the ground as sleep, like a gentle nurse, took over her senses and soothed the ache in her heart.

No sooner had she succumbed than a soft breeze began to puff in from the east. On board ship the sailors greeted their tardy guest with lusty shouts, while passengers on the quay jammed into the dinghies and put out for the corn ship, still complaining of the indifference of the gods. Augustine and Philologus moved quickly to the first dinghy.

Other passengers started a running stream of comments on the allurements of Rome. Augustine stood in silence in the prow of the dinghy and grasped its sides with tense hands. He had at the moment not the slightest interest in Rome. Deep in the matrix of his memory two images were struggling to fuse. One was the outline of an olive grove, the other a traitorous kiss. They nearly touched, swam apart, then came together and impregnated in his mind a thought that weakened and sickened him: he had become the incarnation of Judas Iscariot!

He started in terror. He wanted to cry out to the sailor at the oars to put back to the dock so that he could fly to Monica and sue for forgiveness. Pride rose and sealed his lips. He turned his face to catch the cooling drafts of wind sweeping in from his right.

Beautiful breeze, he thought, I would give my life if only you could cleanse the dust and rust from my vile, vile conscience.

Chapter 25

I am concerned with the immorality, at first seeping in little by little, then like a torrent, making a ruin of the republic (The City of God II, 22).

Augustine arrived in Rome in the autumn of 383, and settled in the home of a Manichean friend. He lost no time exploring the fantastic city, which, like a great vortex, had drawn its resources from all the provinces of the empire to beautify itself. He visited the Forum, the Pantheon, the Palatine, the Colosseum, the Capitol the Odeum, the Temple of Saturn, the Gardens of Sallust, and the Circus Maximus where chariot races were staged. Full of curiosity, he inspected basilicas, baths, temples, theaters, and libraries. He stood on the highest point on the Quirinal Hills and looked over the pulsing scene below. The former capital expanded at his feet like a great golden bubble, flecked with a hundred shades of color. Augustine thought of what Monica had once remarked to her children: "The first city was built by Cain, a murderer, and murderers have been building cities ever since. The one city God is interested in founding is the New Jerusalem."

Augustine had been in Rome only a few days when he decided he did not like his new home. Everything

Philologus had told him of the city was true and more.
It was a seething pit of political unrest. Rumors of barbarian invasions from the East circulated among the
citizens, and everywhere fear tugged at the hearts of
men. Moral decay was eating like leprosy into the fabric
of social life. The patricians had accumulated vast sums
of money, and the plebeians resented their wealth and
their snobbish ways. Magicians and soothsayers by the
hundreds took advantage of the confused state of
thinking, brazenly exploiting the public for the sake of
gain. The masses sacrificed almost every personal pos-
session for money to seek pleasure in the circus, the
theater, horse races, chariot races, gladiatorial com-
bats.

This Augustine found wherever he went, and his
heart raged. Then on the seventh day of his wander-
ings, misfortune struck. In the home of his friend, he
awoke with a deadly fever. Desperate as his condition
was, he would not call upon the God of Monica, as he
had done in his childhood. As the days passed and he
grew no better, he despaired of life, and resigned himself to dying, although the prospect filled him with terror. Yet at the moment he was certain death was closing
in, he began to mend. It seemed then that he heard the
prayers of his mother.

He regained his strength slowly. As soon as he was
able, he left his friend's home and rented a room in the
Velabrum district. He set about establishing a thetoric
school, hoping to make enough money to send for
Melanie and Adeodatus. Alypius helped him secure a
few students as a nucleus.

Late one rainy afternoon, several weeks after he had
launched his new project, Alypius called on him. He
found his friend hunched over a portable charcoal-
burning stove in the middle of his room, reading Juvenal.

"Dear fellow, how are you feeling?" Alypius shook the drops from his toga, removed the garment, and threw it across a dilapidated couch near the room's lone window. "You look somewhat fatigued."

"I have been better off." At thirty, Augustine was prematurely gray at the temples. The illness had left him quite wan. His cheeks were sunken, and his eyes, formerly aglow with a remarkable brilliance, had become lackluster and brooding. "How are you?"

"Never better." Alypius went to him and dropped a hand on his shoulder. "You must not be discouraged. Tell me about the school."

Alypius was doing well in the emperor's service. He wore a blue silk tunic with a garnet hem. The pair of garnet stripes that fringed his collar indicated his position as assessor in the office of Treasurer General. His silk-bandaged legs were a further sign that he had adopted Rome's fondness for silk. He had also yielded to the city's passion for food, as the bulge in the middle of his tunic revealed.

"It is a relief not to have our friends the Eversores rush in on my classes," Augustine said, putting Juvenal aside. "There is one bad feature of Roman schools, however."

"What is that?"

"The students come to you for a while and then move on to another school without paying their tuition. How does one make a living in a situation like this?"

Alypius was all sympathy. He patted Augustine's shoulder, helped himself to a quince from a fruit bowl on the table, and sat down on a stool opposite the rhetoric teacher.

"What you need to do is relax." Alypius took a bite of the quince. "Why not begin to enjoy some of the good things of Aurata Roma?"

"Golden Rome!" Augustine said sarcastically. "As far as I can see, the only golden feature of this city is the lining of the politicians' togas."

"Why not come with me to the Colisseum tomorrow afternoon?"

"You mean that you are going in for gladiatorial games?" Augustine said severely.

Alypius was impassive. "What is bad about gladiatorial games?" he asked, eating the quince with relish.

"How could you ever have gone in the first place?"

"You see, it was like this." Alypius finished the quince and dropped the core into the stove. "Some of my friends at the office wanted me to go to the Colisseum with them. I held out for some time. Then one day I decided I would go, but only to keep them company, not to watch the swordplay.

"While the games were going on, I kept my toga over my eyes. Of a sudden I heard the crowds shout, so I lowered the toga and looked at the fight. To my surprise I liked it, and I confess I have been attached to the sport ever since then."

"You are as naive as you were in Carthage," Augustine said, smiling in spite of himself.

"And what of you?" Alypius said, not at all offended. "I can see you are homesick for Carthage and Melanie and the boy. I know what it means to be homesick. The first year I was here I died three hundred deaths, but then I stopped feeling sorry for myself. I learned to find amusement — music, banquets, the circus, the races, the Colisseum "

"Is that life?" Augustine said, and quoted: " 'How differs unrecorded life from death.'"

"All right, Juvenal," Alypius said.

"Silius."

"Silius, then. Where do you get your pleasure, may I ask? From Manicheism?"

"No more," Augustine said.

Alypius stood up and walked over to the table. "Do you mind if I have some more fruit?"

"Help yourself."

Alypius selected a bunch of Tuscany grapes and returned to his stool. "Is it possible that you have broken with the truth?" he asked, eating one grape after another with obvious enjoyment.

Augustine told him of the latest developments in Carthage, and of his dissatisfaction with the Manichean faith. Alypius listened wide-eyed to the story.

"What about Honoratus and Nebridius?" he said when Augustine had finished.

"They feel exactly as I do. All three of us have secretly broken with the movement."

"What a coincidence!" Alypius said. "I have been ready to leave it for the past two years."

"Good."

"Now the next question is, what do we tie ourselves to next? Orthodoxy?"

Night was settling over the city like a black shroud. It was raining harder than when Alypius had come in. Augustine rose and lighted the grease-burning lamp on the table. While Alypius continued to devour grapes, he paced the floor.

"You are not going to answer my question?" Alypius said.

"Yes. I will tell you this, my friend, and do not be shocked. The Academics have convinced me of one thing, and that is, no truth can ever be comprehended by man."

"You mean you do not even believe in God?" said Alypius, bewildered.

"At this point I believe in nothing."

Alypius stopped eating grapes. "Do the Manicheans know?"

"I have told no one but you."

"And now that you are a full-fledged skeptic, how do you feel?"

Augustine drifted to the window and gazed out over the dreary Velabrum. Rows of wooden buildings filed away to where the Tiber twisted southward like an enormous yellow serpent, swollen with the current rains. The graduated causeways below him had been converted into a skein of cascades, the unpaved alleys into churning quagmires. Oriental porters and roustabouts floundered through the mud on their way home after a killing day's work. Their wide-brimmed straw hats moved up and down like umbrellas, and their weird chanting floated up to Augustine and Alypius like funeral dirges.

"How do I feel?" Augustine said. "I feel as though I had lost touch with reality. I am like a character in a fable or a man walking in a dream. The people around me, including you, my dear Alypius, are like shadows on the wall in Plato's cave, without substance, illusionary, fictitious."

"But your soul, man!" Alypius cried. "What about your soul?"

"My soul?" Augustine doubled his fist and struck the plaster wall. "I question the existence of the soul. I have come to accept the proposition of Lucretius:

". . . here we reach the goal
Of science, and in little have the whole —
Even as the redness and the rose are one,
So with the body one thing is the soul."

Chapter 26

A message had been sent from Milan to Rome,
addressed to the prefect of the city, asking for a
master of rhetoric (Confessions V, 13, 23).

Not long after Alypius had called on Augustine,
he sent him a brief note. "Meet me at seven o'clock this
evening at the Baths of Caracalla," he wrote.

The Romans had come to look upon bathing as a
fine art. Emperors from Nero to Diocletian had erected
elaborate *thermae,* which they threw open to the public
free of charge. These buildings were more than bathing houses. They contained the various pools the baths
of Carthage had, but, in addition, gymnasia, museums,
libraries, terraced lawns filled with statues, rooms and
covered colonnades where people might loiter and
converse. The *thermae* served almost as clubhouses, and
Rome would sooner have gone into captivity than give
them up.

Caracalla's Baths was one of the favorites. Alypius
and Augustine liked it best because its chambers, some
of them solid silver, were lined with green marble
panelings from Numidia, and the granite that had
gone into the pillars had been imported from Egypt.
They liked it too because it was never crowded; more

than sixteen hundred marble seats surrounded the pools.

Alypius was late for their appointment. Augustine waited for him in the hall of entrance, a rotunda almost as large as the Pantheon, and resembling it in form. A great concrete dome vaulted the interior, with its fluted columns and tiled floor. In the front a portico, reached by steps, ran the width of the building proper.

While Augustine fretted in the hall, his attention was drawn to a couple of men near him. One was considerably older than the other. Both wore costly togas, and were engaged in earnest conversation. Augustine could not help overhearing them.

"No one is more sorry than I that your summer home burned down," the younger man said. He held a scroll before the older one. "To show you how sorry I am, I have taken the liberty to solicit subscriptions from your friends and associates so that you may begin to think about building a new home. This gives you a record of the amount I have managed to collect, with the signers."

"Why did you do it?" The older man, nonetheless, appeared grateful. "You know that I have the resources to build a replacement without help."

"I want you to realize who your best friend is." The younger man's mouth all but dropped oil. "It is these crises in life that show us who our true friends are, you know."

Augustine listened in disgust to this self-recommendation. He was able to see perfectly through the younger man's motive. The clever talker was one of the contemptible class of Roman swindlers known as legacy hunters. These men would go to any length to curry favor with childless patricians in order to cut themselves in on the inheritance. Thoroughly ruthless, they made it a practice to shower gifts on the wealthy who had no heirs, loudly pray for them when they fell sick, resort to flattery on every occasion, and even draw up false wills for display, naming the patricians as heirs. The newest practice was the one being employed in Augustine's presence. Free from the love of money himself, the Thagastean harbored a violent loathing for anyone guilty of covetousness. He thought seriously of going to the older man to expose the scheme, but at that moment Alypius rushed up to him.

"My dear fellow, I am sorry to be late," he said, nibbling a honey cake he had bought from a street vendor. "Shall we sit down? I have important news for you."

"Very well," Augustine said.

They found a place on a marble bench near the entrance to the baths. Groups of citizens were beginning to arrive for their evening amusement.

Alypius disposed of his cake, and said, "The Senate is holding an oratorical contest next month, and it is to be open to the public. Would you like me to enter your name?"

"Tell me more about it."

"The prize will be an appointment to the office of rhetoric professorship in Milan under our system of public education. It means that the one who wins may have a permanent position with the state."

Augustine's eyes lighted with a flash of their former brilliance but instantly grew listless again. "Everybody in Rome knows that unless a contestant is lucky enough to have a contact with our prefect he may as well save his breath."

"Spoken like a true augur. You see, that is where our Manichean brothers come out on the stage."

"Symmachus is not a Manichean."

"True again. Our esteemed prefect is a heathen of the heathen, and a clever one. He despises Christianity. At the same time he is enough of a politician to see that Manichaeism is his best buffer against the Christian faith. Why should he not award the prize to a Manichean? And

why not to Augustine, therefore? You have never made
an open break with them."

Augustine had anticipated the idea and was already
turning it over in his mind.

Alypius imitated a motion he had often seen
Augustine make. He extended his left arm dramati-
cally, and said, "I can hear Symmachus at the close of
the contest: 'I take supreme delight in bestowing upon
our honey-lipped orator of the classroom the honors of
the evening and may all the gods smile upon him.
Augustine, my gifted young man, come forward and receive this certificate in the name of our great Emperor
Valentinian.' Well, how does it sound?"

Augustine looked down at his leather sandals, which
were almost worn out. He shook his head uncertainly.

"The fact is, the Manicheans are this very moment
putting pressure on Symmachus," Alypius said. "That,
plus a few pieces of gold in his nervous palm, should
get you his vote and the award."

Out of the edge of his eye he studied his companion.
Before the poetry contest in Carthage, Augustine had
recoiled in horror at the suggestion of bribery. What
would be his reaction now?

"You are wondering if I will go along with the bribe."
Augustine placed the tips of his fingers together and
tapped them pensively.

"It is not a matter of going along with anyone. It is a
matter of sitting still while our Manichean comrades
manipulate the strings."

"Alypius, old friend —" impulsively Augustine's arm
went round him — "how do you explain yourself? I
have heard the story of how you turned down a bribe
from one of our most powerful senators, that you jeop-
ardized your post rather than compromise. Yet you are
willing to do this for me. Why?"

Alypius' wide eyes did not blink. "Who could refuse
a favor to a brother in need?"

"Plautus had someone like you in his mind when he had one of his characters tell another, 'There never was and never will be, and I do not think there is now, any man on earth whose faith and fidelity to a friend can equal yours.'"

Alypius' normally placid expression gave way to a broad smile. "You agree to the plan, then?"

"Had you brought it up ten years ago I would probably have knocked you down." Augustine's sigh was audible above the shuffling of the sandals on the tiles. "How I have deteriorated! Of course I shall go along with the plan. What else can I do?"

Alypius ran an arm under Augustine's elbow and helped him to his feet. "Shall we bathe now?"

"Why not?" Augustine said tonelessly.

They joined the line of prospective bathers drifting toward the pools.

"Are you making expenses?" Alypius asked. "Because if not, I should be glad to lend —"

"Thank you, no. I can meet my debts."

"And Melanie's as well?"

"And Melanie's."

"When you win the contest and go to Milan, you will be able to send for her and the boy."

Augustine felt his heart palpitate. "So I must win that contest," he said grimly. "I simply must win it."

Chapter 27

*The beggar was undeniably happy while I was
full of foreboding; he was carefree, I apprehensive
(Confessions VI, 6, 9).*

V alentinian II had been ruling as emperor from
Milan, capital of the Eastern Empire, for two years
when Augustine moved there. Strongly influenced by
Ambrose, the Bishop of Milan, Valentinian did not
hesitate to exert his power and energy in the overthrow
of paganism. He refused to allow the Roman Senate to
give the Altar of Victoria, goddess of victory, a place in
the Senate building. He prohibited public assemblies
of the Manicheans and other heretics. True, he did tol-
erate the offering of heathen sacrifices and the celebration of heathen festivals, but only because he realized
how hopeless it would be to stamp out such activities.
Also he saw that in time these would die a natural
death.

That was the situation when Augustine arrived in Milan, fresh from his victory in the Roman oratorical contest. Success had restored his self-confidence. As public
rhetorician and municipal orator, he would rub shoulders with aristocrats and intellectuals, lecture at the
university, and deliver orations at the court of the em-

peror. He would be in a position to match wits with the wisest. Certainly Monica's ambitions for her son seemed to be reaching fulfillment.

He told himself he was the happiest man in the empire. Not in his wildest dreams had he expected to be projected to such heights of prosperity. His years of drudgery were past, and the future unfolded before him like a splendid vista, promising fame and glory.

Actually, he was not happy at all. An ulcerous growth continued to plague him and keep him in a state of misery. He tried to rationalize his way out of his condition. He had no soul. Soul and body were identical as Lucretius taught. Any other notion was an illusion.

This line of argument afforded him no relief whatever.

The first thing he did when he got to Milan was to call on Ambrose. An acquaintance told him that the bishop was as accessible as sunlight. Strangers and friends, old and young, patrician and plebeian, all were permitted to walk straight into his study any hour of the day and speak with him.

The ecclesiastical palace adjoined the basilica where Ambrose preached. Augustine, attired in a new toga of brown silk, located the building, where he found a double line of men and women going and coming like a two-way parade of ants. He took his place in the entering line, and at the end of half an hour had inched his way to the door of the study. By craning his neck, he had his first view of the illustrious Bishop of Milan.

Ambrose was seated before a wide table stacked with books, scrolls, and tablets. He wore a pallium of lamb's cloth that fitted his shoulders like the ephod of a Jewish priest. The garment was in-wrought with four black crosses. A crosier, formed exactly like a shepherd's staff, inclined against the table.

Augustine saw a man with a gaunt, gray face. It was rumored that Ambrose spent most of his nights in prayer. Snowy hair fell shoulder-length to create a proper framework for the delicate features. The bishop had the eyes of a patriarch. Over quarter-moon shadows they shifted like discs of mercury, absorbing everything with swift, stabbing glances. They scanned the book he was holding. They rested compassionately on the care-creased face of the widow who stood beside him, unburdening her soul. They slid down the line to Augustine, poised on the tips of his toes in the study doorway. They darted back to the book. When he spoke, his words were gentle and sparing.

Ambrose was known to have had a remarkable career. His father had served as the Prefect of Gaul. The son had followed him in the service of the state, officiating as Imperial Praetor of Upper Italy for a time. His name soon became a synonym for justice. Later he was transferred to Milan.

The Bishop of Milan, an Arian, passed away shortly after Ambrose's arrival in the capital. While the orthodox party and the Arians were battling over a successor, a child's voice suddenly rang out in the basilica, "Let Ambrose be bishop!" The Church interpreted this message as the voice of God. Catholics and Arians united in demanding that he be installed as bishop. So it was decided.

At the time he was a mere catechumen, not yet having received baptism. He fought hard to free himself of the forced responsibility, but to no avail. An archbishop baptized him, and eight days later he was consecrated as bishop of Milan.

Immediately, he sold his estates and gave the money to the Church. He cut off all social contacts and devoted himself to study, preaching, and hymn writing. He exercised a tremendous influence over the minds of the people of Milan, and also the emperor.

At last Augustine's turn came to talk with the great man. He bowed to the white head. "I am Augustine, Your Holiness."

"Ah, yes. How are you, Augustine?" Ambrose's eyes stayed on the book before him. Augustine noticed that it was a commentary on the Psalms.

"Well, thank you, sir."

"You are from Carthage." It was a statement rather than a question.

"Yes, sir." Augustine marveled at the prodigious memory.

Ambrose went on reading. "You are interested in the cult of Mani, are you not?" His voice was sweetly pleasant.

"No longer, sir."

"When did you give it up?"

"Well, sir, it has been a gradual process."

"I see. You are a Catholic?"

"A catechumen." Augustine noticed tiny canals running across the distinguished forehead. He knew Ambrose to be a scholar, and almost prayed that the scholar would inquire into the health of his soul, forgetting for the moment he was supposed to have no soul.

"Good. You must attend our services on the Lord's Day."

"Oh, I shall."

"What is your problem, Augustine?" The question was impersonal, businesslike. Ambrose had not yet looked up from his book.

"Well, sir, I wish to pay my respects."

"So good of you. I shall look for you on the Lord's Day."

It was tantamount to a dismissal. Stung and angry, Augustine jerked his head down and up, spun on his heel and stalked away. He could not know that the shrewd, patriarchal eyes followed his figure with a gleam of amused pity. The bishop's favorite Old Testament incident was that of the prophet Elisha's sly snubbing of leprous but arrogant Naaman. Ambrose understood the psychology of the snub, and often chuckled over it.

Augustine flung himself out of the palace, seething inwardly. "He might at least have been courteous!" he raged. "I shall die before I go to hear him preach!"

He did go to hear Ambrose preach and had had not died.

He stood with the catechumens in the atrium of the basilica and hung on the words of the preacher with the eagerness of a boy witnessing the circus. Ambrose's message was lost to him. All his attention was focused on the bishop's style. What mannerisms! he thought. A ritual of unsullied grace. And what would I not give for his voice? Such resonance, such richness and power! Is it possible that it belongs to the same retiring man of the study? How I envy him!

When the catechumens had been dismissed and Augustine was leaving the church, he could not but compare Ambrose with Faustus. There was no question about it; as an orator Ambrose was infinitely the superior of the two.

Augustine rented a spacious and comfortable house on the outskirts of Milan. It was quadrangular in shape, and enclosed a garden of plants and shrubs, overlooked by four porches. On one side a canal flowed peacefully by, and on another a grove of fig tress broke the view of the Lombardy plain.

He sent for Melanie, urging her to come to Milan with Adeodatus as quickly as possible.

A week after he had taken up his work he came home one day and was met by Alypius, whom a slave had admitted to the house.

"Alypius!" he cried, throwing his arms around his friend. "My dear, dear fellow, I have no words to tell you how thrilled I am you are here! Have you left Rome for good? Can you live with me?"

"Easy, easy," Alypius laughed, grateful for the warmth of the reception. "Yes, I have left Rome for good."

"Excellent, excellent. Sit down, good fellow."

Alypius sat down in a *cathedra,* an armless chair, while Augustine remained standing and called for the slave to bring in food.

"I decided I would rather be with you than live in Rome," Alypius said. "I gave up my office the day you left for Milan."

"You never made a wiser decision. What will you do here?"

"I think I would like to take up law."

"Good. I shall be one of your lecturers at the university."

The slave brought in a basket of fruit and a platter of nuts, and Alypius set about demolishing the fruit without inhibitions.

"Of course you will live with me," Augustine said.

"Until I get my bearings, if —"

"Nonsense. You are now in your permanent home."

Alypius paused to look around. "This is a fine residence you have. What about Melanie and Adeodatus?"

"I have sent for them."

"And your mother? What of her?"

"She is in Thagaste. I am glad to say she has finally granted me amnesty. She was quite upset when I left Carthage for Rome."

"How do you like Milan?" Alypius munched an apricot happily. "Better than Rome?"

"So far much better. I shall never be able to repay you for getting me this position."

The two adjusted themselves to their new relationship, Augustine in the role of professor, Alypius as a law student.

Melanie wrote that Honoratus was having some difficulty disposing of the house in Agaro, so she and Adeodatus must wait until it could be sold before joining him in Milan. Augustine swallowed his disappointment and, to keep his mind occupied, applied himself to his teaching with all possible diligence.

The old year wore on, and Milan prepared to celebrate New Year's Day. At this season it was an annual custom for the city rhetorician to deliver an oration honoring the emperor. Augustine put an uncommon amount of thought into the preparation of the speech.

On the last afternoon of the old year, Alypius came home and found him slouched on a sofa before a brazier, the embodiment of dejection. One hand gripped the manuscript of his oration, the other a tuft of hair.

"My hapless Charon, what is it?" Alypius asked playfully. "No traffic on the Styx?"

Augustine waved the manuscript in a flourish of despair. "I wish I had stayed in Carthage."

"Tell Alypius all about it." The law student threw his textbooks on the table and lifted a chestnut from a bowl.

"Skeptic that I am, I do not know how to cool an overheated conscience."

Alypius cracked the chestnut and scooped out the meat. "No problem," he said, tossing it into his mouth. "Either you put out the fire or you lull the conscience to sleep at the circus or gladiatorial com — what are you saying? I thought you had disposed of that bothersome faculty. I thought you said conscience was a phantom that had no real existence."

"You are right," Augustine replied disconsolately. "But I suppose my early training refuses to let it die."

"What brings on this melancholy mood?"

"My oration." Augustine let the manuscript fall to the floor. "It is a nest of lies. It is one flattering platitude after another, a screen of smoke and a camouflage. I shall deceive nobody, Valentinian included. Even the court fools will blush when they hear it."

Alypius chewed reflectively on both the chestnut and the confession. "Why not throw it away and write another?"

"By evening?" Augustine said impatiently. "I have to deliver it tonight."

"Well, is it not your duty to soap the emperor's ego?"

"But not drown it in lather." Augustine stood up and walked about the room with his hands behind his back. "You know, while I was on my way home from class this afternoon I met a beggar."

"I pass beggars every d —"

"Not like this one. Most beggars you see on the street are sad, are they not?"

"Yes."

"This fellow was happy. He whooped and sang and danced like a professional clown."

"Maybe he was drunk," Alypius ventured.

"Precisely the point," Augustine said. "He was drunk, like a magistrate at a banquet."

"You call that being happy?" Alypius took another chestnut from the bowl and broke it open. "It is not my idea of happiness."

Augustine leveled an accusing finger at him. "You miss the contrast," he said. "Look at me. I am a successful rhetorician hunting for unanxious joy. Where to find it I have no idea." He swung his arm around and pointed outside. "Out there is a filthy social outcast who has found what I want — what I need. Do you not see that the whole picture is distorted, paradoxical, upside down, insane?"

Alypius went on eating. "Then," he said, "what is the problem? Go out and get drunk like the beggar."

"You think I have not pondered it?"

"Why not do it? I will be glad to go with you."

Augustine seemed to forget that Alypius was there, and paced the floor, folding and unfolding his arms. "The beggar will digest his intoxication while he sleeps." He went on, thinking aloud, as though he were composing his oration. "Me, I shall sleep and tomorrow I shall wake with mine still upon me. Also the next day and the day after, all through the mist we call life." He stopped and addressed Alypius savagely. "Behold the modern Sisyphus!" he crackled, pounding both fists on his chest. "I roll my stone to the top of the hill of ambition. It should stay there, by all the laws of the Medes and Persians, which alter not. Does it stay there? No, it falls off. I push it back again and again, and still an unknown force dislodges it and hurls it down at me. Such, my unruffled Alypius, is my life, and such is my fate. What am I going to do?"

Alypius could only shake his head futilely, and go on eating.

Augustine calmed himself, stepped to the brazier, and stood looking into the fire. "Since watching that drunken beggar do his act, one thing has been bombarding my brain. I am absolutely sure there must be more to life than you and I have found. Do you agree?"

"Yes."

"But where to find it?" His voice sank to a whisper "Where to find it?"

Chapter 28

*Look upon my heart, O my God, look deep within it
(Confessions IV, 6, 11).*

Four weeks after the New Year season had passed,
Melanie and Adeodatus arrived in Milan.

Melanie had slipped into the stage of maturity
marked by a color and richness of character turbulent
youth never attains. A subtle depth of sympathy and understanding matched her eternal beauty, and Augustine
was amazed and enthralled. It was as though a new di-
mension had been added to her personality.

"My incomparable songbird, you make me forget the
torment of separation," he said when they were alone
that night. "I remembered that you were beautiful, but
how beautiful I could not remember. Since I have last
seen you, your loveliness has distributed itself to every
part of you as a rose saturates a room with its fragrance."

"You have not been out of my thoughts one hour,"
she said shyly.

Augustine continued, "Every night I would lie awake
and try to call back everything about you. Long since
have I come to the conclusion that the mind is a treasure house of unnumbered impressions of all kinds,

kept in store by the senses. My will is the monitor of the mind, and whenever I desire I bid hidden images to come forth from the treasure house. Sometimes unwanted thoughts break in. I brush them from the face of my recollection until what I wish looks out from the clouds. So, dear heart, it has been with you. Many unbearable hours were made joyous and exciting because I could dwell on you, being absent from you. Just as in my imagination I can distinguish the scent of lilies from that of violets, though actually receiving no impression of sense, so I was able to see your cheeks, your eyes, your chin, your sweet mouth, separating these from the features of ten thousand other women."

"And were you faithful to me, my beloved?"

"I swear it by all that is sacred," he said fervently, and imparadised himself in her arms.

Adeodatus had turned the corner of boyhood. He was an ungainly adolescent, all hands, feet, and craning neck, but his father overlooked his awkwardness and said he was a prodigy. He enrolled him in the best rhetoric school in Milan, displayed him proudly to his colleagues, and loaded the lad with costly gifts. Miraculously, Adeodatus remained unspoiled.

About the time of the reunion, Augustine was reminded of his physical weakness. The weather, which had been fairly mild until February, changed abruptly. Winter unleashed her full fury on Milan. Biting winds swept down from the Alps and chilled the city rhetorician to the marrow. On windless days, thick fogs billowed up from the canals like wreaths of smoke to provoke his old throat trouble and chest pains. Melanie ministered to him day and night like an experienced nurse, loving the service.

In March a thornier problem struck.

People had always gravitated to Augustine. It was a mark of leadership, Monica used to say. In Milan he was not long to enjoy the life of privacy with his family and

Alypius. One day Nebridius put in an appearance, bringing with him his bride of a month.

"Life was empty without you," he told Augustine. "Honoratus had to give up the plan because of business involvements."

"You are more than welcome," Augustine said cordially. "I am sorry Honoratus could not have come too."

"I hope to get a position with a friend of mine in Milan. He has a law office. My wife and I wanted to rent a house near yours so that we may be with you as much as we can."

"I have a better idea. This house is much too big for four people. I suggest that you two cast your lot with us."

Romanianus was the next addition. A lawsuit necessitated his presence in Milan. He came, accompanied by his wife and oldest son, a young man named Licentius. Augustine opened the home to the three, as he had to Nebridius and his bride.

Evodius, his boyhood friend, had been discharged from the Army and gone back to Thagaste. Overcome by an irresistible longing to see Augustine, he too traveled to Milan, and was prevailed upon to join the group.

Finally, in early summer, Monica and Navigius descended upon the expanding household.

"Mother! Navigius!" Augustine cried, embracing them. "It is so wonderful to have you here. Where is Junia?"

"She has entered a convent, as she has always wanted to do," Monica said.

"I have a family of nine," he laughed. "With you two it comes to eleven. Mother, you can take over the management of the house, if you like. It is going to be too much of a burden for me."

"I would be happy to help in any way possible," she said, immensely pleased.

By now the sometime quiet house had been transformed to a sort of hostel or caravansary with a split personality. On the one hand it overflowed with good will, good fellowship, and highly geared cultural discourse, and on the other generated a current of friction that was felt by all the residents but never discussed.

From the day Monica appeared, Melanie went into semi-retirement. People saw her at meals, and rarely elsewhere. Augustine observed her restraint, and one evening when they were together in their room he mentioned it.

"You are displeased with me," she said, bending her head to one side.

"Can you blame me for wishing you to be more congenial?" he asked.

She wrung her hands. "Augustine dearest, surely you should understand my position. I am a mistress — your mistress, living with families who have normal and proper relations with each other."

"Some of the most prominent men in Rome and Milan have mistresses. What we have is not so different from legal marriage. Why, the law allows and recognizes people of our situation."

"What about a higher law?" she said, looking straight at him.

"What?"

"The law of God. Also the law of conscience."

"Oh, that," he said lightly.

She buried her face in her hands. Augustine went to her and slipped his arms around her. "What is it, my sweet nightingale? What can I do for you?"

"Oh Augustine!" Her lips were against his. She put her whole heart into the kiss. "Beloved, take me away from — from them!" she said passionately. "Take me away, please!"

"Are they not good to you?"

"Outwardly, yes. But oh, I know they resent me. They are not at fault. I would too, were I where they are."

"Melanie sweet, listen to me." He cupped her chin in his hand. "I am the host here. How can I possibly go away?"

She flung herself against him. "No, no, you cannot go away. Forgive me, dear heart, forgive my weakness. I am such a coward — such a dreadful coward."

"Let my love give you strength."

"I will! Oh, I will!"

"You are life to me," he said. "You are melody and the breath of flowers, you are spice and honey, you are my present and my future, you are my very soul. Apart from you, I have no soul."

"I adore you."

He kissed her again. "Wait here, and I shall be back. I have one interview before I can retire."

"Do hurry." She smiled wanly. "I shall postpone living until you come to me."

Augustine left the room, fully intending to go to Monica and say once more that he was going to marry Melanie, no matter what Monica thought. But once outside the room, he wavered. He knew his mother well enough to know the futility of the mission. Tormented and rocked with uncertainty, he plunged out into the night to meditate.

In the bedchamber, Melanie heard his footsteps in the garden, heard his low agonized moan, and guessed what had happened. She wanted to rush out to him, press him to her heart, and cry, "Ah, my beloved one, you wanted me to take strength from your love! I beg of you, dearest, I beg of you now to let my love give you the strength you need for this ordeal!"

She must not do this, she told herself, it would only embarrass him. No, there must be some other course.

She sat down on the edge of the bed, suddenly faint. There was another course! She folded her hands and clenched them until the tips of her fingers showed red. "I have to do it," she whispered, staring dully into space. "There is no other answer to this terrible thing. He must not suffer so. . . . Dear God, please give me the strength to do what I have to do. . . ."

Chapter 29

The woman with whom I have been cohabiting was ripped from my side, being regarded as an obstacle to my marriage. So deeply was she engrafted into my heart that it was left torn and wounded and trailing blood (Confessions VI, 15, 25).

It was a Sunday afternoon. The men of the house were together listening to a project being sponsored by Romanianus.

"My thought is that we withdraw to some rural community, purchase property and set up a hermitage," the patrician said. "Personally, I am growing tired of the complexities of modern life. My affairs are in litigation, and promise to stay there indefinitely. Would not this be the answer, not only to my difficulties but to yours also?"

"How would this be financed?" Nebridius asked.

"I shall assume the full responsibility for the establishment of the original building. After that, we may have a common treasury and run the house on a communal basis. There will be no such thing as private interests, for each of us will contribute all his resources to the treasury."

"Who will act as steward?" Augustine said.

"I have thought of that, too. My idea is for us to elect two of our number annually. The two shall be entrusted with the oversight of the finances, goods, and all that pertains to our living. How does the notion strike you?"

All present endorsed it enthusiastically.

At that point the women, who had been inspecting the flower beds in the garden, walked into the house and demanded to know what was going on that produced such open pleasure. Romanianus explained the action taken by the men.

Romanianus' wife, a mountain of flesh in a silk brocaded mantle, folded her arms like a man and said, "And what about your women?"

The men looked at each other in consternation. They had forgotten to take account of this angle.

Romanianus cleared his throat. "Well," he said feebly, "you see, my darling, we thought perhaps you would be willing to stay here in the city while we —"

"No!"

"But why not?"

"No! And again no! And lest there be any doubt in your minds — *never!*"

"Oh," Romanianus said, passing a sleeve over his brow. For emphasis he added, "Oh."

"Do you agree?" His wife turned to the other women for support.

"We agree," they said simultaneously.

It was the end of a splendid dream.

Every Sunday Monica went to the basilica to hear Ambrose preach. Sometimes Augustine slipped away and took his place in the atrium, but he did not tell Monica or anyone else. He suspected that Melanie attended too. She was mysteriously absent from home during the hours of worship. Whenever he was in the atrium, he sought to spy her out in the women's section, but a multitude of catechumens and inquirers was there, and she could easily shield herself from view.

Late in the summer, Melanie was putting Adeodatus to bed one night when unexpectedly he said to her, "Mother dearest, why are you sad?"

"Oh," she said, taken by surprise, "am I sad?"

"Yes. What can I do for you?"

She tucked the coverlet around his chin and said quietly, "Nothing, precious treasure. There is nothing anyone can do — but Christ."

"You believe in Christ, Mother?"

"Yes, with all my heart."

"Does Father?"

She caressed his temples. "Your father is not sure about his faith."

"Grandmother says she wants to take me to the church next Sunday."

"I am glad. I pray that our Lord will make you to grow to be a great and holy man, like Ambrose."

"Mother."

"Yes, dear son?"

"Sometimes I have a feeling," he said slowly and thoughtfully, "a strange feeling that I shall not live to be a man."

She caught his head to her bosom and said frantically, "Never say that, dearest dear! Never even think it!"

"I shall try not to." A moment later he said, "How beautiful you are, Mother!"

"What is beauty, Adeodatus?"

"Beauty is the outshining of a light inside you."

She smiled into his eyes. "You sound just like your father." She kissed his cheek. "Sleep well, precious one."

"Good night, Mother."

Without warning, a premonition, dark and ominous as a shadow, fell across the heart of Melanie, filling her with fear. A muffled voice seemed to say, "You will not see him again."

She started. "Adeodatus!"

"Yes, Mother?"

"Did you say something?"

"No, Mother."

"Are you sure?"

"I am sure."

"Oh — good night then, my son. I love you very much."

"I love you, Mother."

She held his head against her heart once more, then kissed him on the forehead which was a perfect replica of her own. She wrenched herself from him, put out the oil lamp, and crept away to her room. She fell on the bed and lay there writhing, too numb to feel or think or weep. . . .

Sometime later she heard Augustine coughing violently in the next room. Oh dear, he is catching cold, she thought. He stopped coughing and began to speak. Melanie was certain she heard him mention her name.

She told herself she should not do it, but she had not the power to resist. She got up, tiptoed out of the bedchamber into the hall, and stood in the dark, listening.

"I tell you Melanie is standing in your way," Monica was saying. "You must do something about it."

Augustine coughed again, and when he answered his mother, his voice was so low that Melanie caught only the word "marriage."

"I have told you many times that will not do," Monica said firmly. "Whether you and I like it or not, we are a learned family. Melanie is a fine woman — there I have no argument with you. Unfortunately, and through no fault of her own, she does come from a different kind."

In the dark, Melanie blanched.

"I love her, different or not," Augustine said.

"Aurelius, listen to me. You are a man of culture and intelligence. They tell me that Manlius Theodorus believes you to be one of the outstanding thinkers in Milan."

Manlius Theodorus had once been Proconsul of Carthage. He had retired from office and was now living in Milan, where he studied philosophy, entertained civil authorities with a lavish hand, and generally promoted the intellectual life of the upper classes.

"That is all very well," Augustine said. "But remember that he who is praised by men when he is successful will seldom be defended by men when he fails."

"Apart from worldly success," Monica said, and Melanie was aware of a gentleness in her tone, "there is the far more important matter of your relationship with God."

"What about it?" Augustine asked defensively.

"I have always believed that you are predestined to be a prince and a prophet in Israel. I never was more convinced of it than now."

"Because you have seen me in church?"

"That is only one sign."

"I see. And you think Melanie is the one factor keeping me out of the Kingdom?"

"I am sure of it."

Melanie put her hand on her heart to still its wild beating.

"I wonder if a mother lives in all the world who believes there is a single woman good enough for her son," Augustine said, and coughed once more.

"You are wrong, Aurelius."

"I wonder if I am."

"I shall prove that you are wrong."

"How?"

"Because," Monica said, taking a long breath, "I have made arrangements for you to marry."

Melanie felt herself slowly dying.

"You what?" Augustine cried hoarsely.

"This girl is from one of the noblest families in Milan. She is fresh and vivacious, and has the dew of youth. She has culture and wit and beauty. She will be a perfect mate."

"But, Mother —"

"I know I am right, my son. Everything has been arranged."

Melanie heard Augustine break into a racking cough. She put a hand over her mouth to stifle a cry. Trembling, she groped her way back to her room, and crumpled to the floor in a dead faint.

Toward midnight, Augustine entered the bedchamber, weak from coughing and sick at heart. He burned with shame at the prospect of having to face Melanie with the pain that others had already designed.

The lamp on the lampstand was beginning to flicker, its supply of oil almost used up. Augustine drew back in amazement. The bed was empty.

"Melanie!" he called out.

Everything was quiet. Then he noticed a parchment scroll curled up on the coverlet. He picked it up and carried it to the lampstand. He held it up to the feeble light and blinked at it unbelievingly. It read:

Melanie to Augustine:

At last I have been given strength to do what I ought to have done years ago. I am leaving you, my beloved. Do not try to find me. It would do no good, for I am going to enter a convent and give my poor sinful life to the service of my Lord.

I leave Adeodatus with you. He says he does not think he will live long. He may be right. God struck the child of David's son. Will he strike the child of my son? I have returned to the Christ I once knew and trusted and loved. I have the sweet assurance that He has forgiven my iniquity.

I shall never stop loving you, and I shall never stop praying for you. We may not meet again on earth. This I can endure. But oh, how I long that we shall meet above in the glory of our Savior's house!

Chapter 30

You have made us and drawn us to yourself, and our heart is restless until it rests in you (Confessions I, 1, 1).

A month after Melanie's disappearance from Milan, Monica intercepted Alypius one afternoon as he strolled into the house. "Alypius, may I speak with you?" she asked.

"Yes, indeed," he said cheerily.

They sat down, and Monica promptly said, "I want the truth. Has Aurelius taken a second mistress?"

Alypius glanced out the window at a group of boys wading in the waters of the canal. It was late summer, and Milan sweltered in a heat wave.

"I am afraid he has," Alypius said.

Monica's features were twisted with pain and vexation. "Who is she, and where is she?"

"I do not know her name. She lives on the other side of the city."

Two weeks before, Augustine, unsettled by grief and detesting himself for his weariness, had commenced a round of nocturnal sallies that had aroused apprehension in Monica's heart. She fought it until she could stand it no longer. She felt that she must appeal to Alypius. Now she had the truth.

Ironically, this was the day she had arranged for his marriage to the daughter of the Milanese nobleman. In shaping her plans, she had overlooked one detail. It came to light that the girl was too young to marry; according to Roman law she would have to wait two more years. The disappointment was particularly galling to Monica, who had assured herself that all she hoped for her beloved son would fall into place.

"How can he do this terrible, terrible thing?" She swayed from side to side in her chair and uttered low moans. "And just when I thought him not far from the Kingdom of God."

"He is not far from the Kingdom of God," Alypius said.

Monica sat still and looked at him skeptically. "I always knew you were unimaginative," she said, "but this sounds like the statement of one who dreams."

"You wish me to give you proof?"

"You are a lawyer. Yes, I would appreciate proof."

Alypius had finished his schooling and had began his own practice. He was by no means overworked, as the capital was oversupplied with lawyers, but he hoped for success.

"Very well. Reason one, your son is no longer interested in fame or prestige. He speaks of them as 'the baggage of the world.'"

"Ah, bless you, Alypius," Monica said, her worn face brightening.

"Reason two, Ambrose's preaching is surely getting through to him. He is seeing that his old prejudices are not so much against what the Church truly holds as they are against what he wrongly *thought* the Church held. Also I often come across him reading Scripture. He seems to be intrigued with Paul."

"God be praised! Go on, sweet Alypius!"

"Reason three, the conversion of Victorinus has made a powerful impact on his thinking. If a famous scholar like Victorinus, a man whose statue is in the Senate, will renounce his paganism and confess the Christian faith publicly — well, Augustine says, there must be more to Christianity than pious fiction."

"Yes, yes." Unconsciously, Monica folded her hands and lifted them thankfully to heaven. "I bless God for the boldness of Victorinus. Go on, go on!"

"Reason four, the case of Anthony. If a rich man like Anthony is willing to sell three hundred *ingera* of land as well as all his personal goods for the benefit of the poor, and then go out in the Egyptian desert to live, there must be a divine power behind such a sacrifice, Augustine says. Only yesterday, upon hearing the story, he said to me, 'Oh, how I pant to be touched by such power!'"

"But answer this, Alypius. If Aurelius is as close to the Kingdom of God as you say he is, why does he keep indulging in his licentiousness?"

Alypius turned up the palms of his hands. "Who can say why we do certain things and we do not do certain things?"

"Are you a Christian, Alypius?"

"No," he said wistfully.

"If Aurelius becomes a Christian, will you?"

"Probably. He converted most of his friends to Manicheism. He should certainly be able to lead us to—"

"Alypius!" It was Augustine, calling to him from the garden.

"Yes!" he answered. "Coming!"

He sprang up and dashed from the room as Monica bowed her head and prayed.

The shock of losing Melanie had driven Augustine almost to the breaking point. "Why should I go on living?" he asked himself. He had no answer. He would have taken his life but for the awful fear of what lay beyond the last breath.

He had ranged the gamut of human experience. He had drunk from all the cisterns of the world. He knew the scorching thrill of sensuality, the pathetic quality of cultism, the mocking ring of rationalism, the barrenness of atheism, the mirage of materialism. The wit and wisdom of the ages lay compressed in the core of his brain. And what does it all mean? he mused bitterly. What does it come to?

In a conversation with Alypius and Nebridius, he said, "I maintain that the most satisfying system of philosophy was worked out by Epicurus."

"You mean," Alypius said, "let us eat, drink and be merry —?"

"Exactly. Why not? If we were immortal, and allowed to live in perpetual bodily pleasure without fear of losing it, why should we not be happy, or what else should we seek?"

"Then you admit Epicurus had one fatal flaw in his system," Nebridius said. "For you qualified your statement with, 'if we were immortal.'"

"Alas, yes," Augustine answered morosely. "It is that terrifying word *if* that becomes the wall between happiness and misery. For if Epicurus is wrong in his denial of a future destiny, then *how* wrong is he! And what tribulation awaits us who are to be citizens of the nation of darkness!"

Yet for all his discouragement, Augustine was not willing to give up altogether his search for reality. His unquenchable intellectual yearning drove him on and on, as physical thirst sends a man in the desert staggering over burning sands. He turned to the writings of the Platonists. From them — strange paradox — the son of Monica rediscovered that the Deity was not a glorified man with hands, feet, hair, and nails, as the Manicheans had taught him. No, God was a spiritual

Being, incorporeal substance, infinite, boundless, and unchangeable.

The effect of this knowledge on the unpredictable rhetorician was that he became bloated with pride, as though his own cleverness had brought him the discovery. The male peacock strutted and preened himself before his friends with the aplomb of the finest bird in the Milanese Zoo.

Years later he would confess to his flock in Hippo, "My cheeks were so puffed up with pride that my eyes were closed to the Light. I tell you, my beloved friends" — and he would say it with a twinkle — "I tell you that knowledge divorced from the Word of God makes a windbag out of a man."

The Platonists, notwithstanding their erudition, were powerless to bring him to fellowship with the deity they set forth.

Hungering and thirsting, he went back to the Scriptures of Monica. To his delight, he began to perceive in them both a purity and a unity he had not known existed. Contrary to what the Manicheans had argued, he found that Paul contradicted neither himself, nor the doctrines of Christ, nor the prophecies of the Old Testament, as he had thought. Moreover, he learned that the Bible presented Christ as the living Word made flesh, co-eternal with the Father, coming to earth to die for the ungodly and to rise on the third day.

"Ah, what a fool — what a fool I have been!" he said to Alypius brokenly. "All these years I have been lifted up upon the stilts of a more elevated teaching, all the time hearing not him who said, 'Learn of me, for I am meek and lowly in heart, and ye shall find rest unto your souls.'"

The preaching of Ambrose confirmed what he read. In spite of the bishop's tendency to allegorize Scripture, enough life-giving doctrine flowed from the pulpit to enlighten inquiring minds. Platonism had served as a signpost, vaguely pointing Augustine toward a higher plateau. Now Ambrose was to show him Immannel's country, bathed in the supernal glory of the King of kings. "For one thing it is," he would write in his *Confessions*, "from the wooded hilltop to gaze upon the land of Peace and find no way to it, and in vain while all around deserting fugitives lay siege and ambush, with their prince, the lion and the dragon; but another, to hold the way that leades thither, beneath the strongholds built by the heavenly commander."

Now a single obstacle barred his way to these heavenly strongholds: his own enchaining will. He had the intellectual honesty to admit it. "Of a forward will," he told himself, "is a lust made, and a lust served, and a habit formed; and a habit not resisted is a necessity. A hard slavery has me bound. I long to be delivered from its chain, but not now — but not now."

"And why not?" his conscience demanded.

The voices of sensuality answered conscience, "Think you that he can do without us? How can he abandon us, who have given him so much gratification?"

Memory rushed to the support of conscience. "Think of the multitudes who have found continence through Christ's power. Why not Augustine?"

The enemy counterattacked, "Yes, but what of the delights of the flesh? Why surrender these delights for a life of celibacy, a life devoid of sensation and natural pleasures?"

The struggle was to reach its climax on the afternoon of Monica's talk with Alypius. Augustine came home from a long walk in the country, weary without and wearier still within. He heard voices in the house. A longing for the companionship of faithful Alypius overcame him. He called his friend's name.

Alypius hurried out to him. He was alarmed at the look of suffering on Augustine's face, the deep pallor of his complexion. "Man, you are sick!" he cried.

"I am sick," Augustine said woodenly. He touched his breast. "I am sick to death in here. Will you bring me the New Testament?"

"Of course."

Alypius stepped into the house, and in a moment came back carrying the sacred volume. He handed it to Augustine and together they sat down on a stone bench. Twice Augustine opened his mouth to speak and both times changed his mind.

Alypius took his hand and pressed it, conveying a mute message of sympathy. Augustine was looking at him helplessly.

"Listen," Alypius said at last, "you need to be alone. Let me go away for a while."

"No, I will go."

Augustine laid the Bible on the bench, rose and turned into the grove of fig trees bordering the garden. Alypius' eyes gleamed with pity as he watched him disappear.

In the center of the orchard Augustine stopped, drew a tremulous breath, and fell on the ground. He prostrated himself, face down, and let the pent-up tempest break. Powerful sobs shook his body as though trying to wrest the principle of life from it. Two colossal, almost superhuman forces seemed to be converging on him as two ocean currents come together in a boiling maelstrom. He recalled Jude's strange reference to Michael the Archangel and Satan contending over the body of Moses, and he wondered if the same two opponents could be contending over his poor soul. If so, how would the battle end?

He beat the ground in anguish. "How long, Lord?" he cried. "How long, how long?" A mockingbird perched on a limb of the fig tree and derided him. He stopped his ears. "How long? How long?" he choked. "Tomorrow and tomorrow? But why not now? Why not this hour make an end of my uncleanness? Why not?"

Never had the chaste life been so desperately desirable or more unattainable.

"How long, my God? How long?"

Exhausted, he took his hands from his ears and rolled over on his back, too weak to cry anymore. A numbness like paralysis crept over him, stifling his thinking and feeling. He lay with arms outstretched, his eyes closed, inert, insensible to the stimulus of the world around him.

How long he lay thus he could not tell.

The murmuring of a cicada came to him with soothing gentleness. The mockingbird had flown away. He passed a hand over his forehead. It was wet with perspiration.

Dimly at first, then more distinctly, he was conscious of a new sound. For a while he paid no attention to it. But its very persistence arrested him.

"Take, read," it buzzed. "Take, read."

The words drifted in from the edge of the orchard. Was it the voice of a boy or that of a girl? He could not decide.

"Take, read. Take, read. Take, read."

The oddity of the order set in motion the machinery of his mind. "Whatever is this?" he asked himself. "A game some children are playing? Certainly none that I know."

"Take, read. Take, read." The voice rose and fell with the monotony of lapping waves. "Take, read. Take, read. Take, read."

He started up in amazement as an idea struck him. "Why, it must be the voice of an angel! Of course. It is God commanding me to take His Word and read it."

With the thought, strength poured back into his body. Aroused and invigorated, he sprang up, dashed through the grove with the speed of an emperor's courier, and burst into the flower garden. Alypius was still in his same position on the bench, staring into space. He looked up and cried, "Augustine!"

Augustine sat down beside him, out of breath and trembling with excitement. He picked up the Bible and opened it at random. His eye fell on a passage in the Epistle to the Romans. He read it in silence:

> Not in rioting and drunkenness, not in chambering and wantonness, not in strife and envying. But put ye on the Lord Jesus Christ, and make not provision for the flesh to fulfill the lusts thereof.

He read no further. The words were as surely a communication from Heaven as though God had spoken vocally. What a perfect answer to my need! he thought. As I don my tunic and it protects my nakedness from outside forces, so I am to put on the blessed Son of God and He will block off every evil influence — even my lust.

He shut his eyes and prayed, while Alypius waited reverently by his side.

"Oh, my King and my Savior," he said in his heart, "I come to you, affrighted with my sins and the burden of my misery. Many and great are these infirmities of mine — many are they and great, but your medicine is greater. Be you the Conqueror, and I the conquered. Be you the Victor, and I your willing victim. Be you the Reconciler, I the reconciled. Be you the Monarch, I the subject. O my great high Priest and Healer, graciously unite my heart — this poor, foul, diseased, broken member — unite this heart to fear your name, O my Lord and my God. . . ."

A deep-lodged peace, sweet as the music of the nightingale, stole over the son of Monica. He opened his eyes.

"Alypius," he said, laying a hand on the lawyer's knee.

"Yes, Augustine."

"I have been regenerated," he said joyfully.

"I am glad. Tell me, what passage was it that struck you with such force?"

Augustine pointed to Romans 12:13-14. Alypius read the section very slowly, even went on to the next verse.

"Look, my dear fellow," he said spiritedly. "There must be hope for me too, for Paul goes on to say: 'Him that is weak in the faith receive. . . .' No one could be more weak in faith than I."

Augustine laughed and threw his arm around his closest friend. "Of course there is hope for you! Together we must study the Word for more light, we must pray, we must receive instruction from Ambrose." He stood up and raised his arms to the sky exultantly. "You know, dear fellow, it is as though a great torrent of water has poured over my soul and washed it clean."

"It must be wonderful," Alypius sighed.

"It is indescribably wonderful. And now let us go into the house. I must tell my mother what happened. She will be mad with joy."

Arm in arm, they started for the room where Monica waited and prayed. At the door, Augustine paused.

"Shall I go in?" Alypius said.

"Please do. I want just a moment before I tell her."

Alypius disappeared into the house. Augustine looked back at the grove of fruit trees with moist eyes. To him the very ground of the orchard would be forever sacred. The fig tree was to be virtually a symbol of the tree of life. The words, "Take, read," would reverberate in the halls of his memory as long as God allowed him to think.

Monica's prayer had been heard. And Melanie's. *Melanie's.* He caught his breath, and felt his heart leap. He would see Melanie again!

Chapter 31

*At Cassiciacum . . . we found rest in you from the
hurly-burly of the world (Confessions IX, 12, 35).*

Soon after his translation from darkness to light,
Augustine made an important decision. He turned in
his resignation as imperial rhetorician.

Two factors contributed to this move. His health
broke; a severe attack of bronchitis, combined with a
throat disorder, made public speaking an impossible assignment. Then, too, he realized that, as a spiritual
counterpart of Lazarus, he had been called out of the
tomb but was still wearing grave clothes of which he
had to rid himself. The grave clothes stood for the trap-
pings of the unregenerate life. Now that grace had begun its cleansing operation in him the old order must
give way to the new. Had not Paul declared in the inspired script that, recreated in Christ, old things passed
away and all things became new?

The time for taking the step seemed favorable.
Three weeks after his experience in the orchard, a na-
tional holiday known as the Vintage Festival was sched-
uled. It put into Augustine's hands the weapon he
needed to cut his connection with the secular world.

He resigned. The court authorities approved his resignation with regret.

The action coincided with an invitation of a colleague, a Milanese grammarian, to use his summer home at Cassiciacum, not far from Milan. "You and yours," the invitation read, "are welcome to live in my villa as long as you wish."

Joyfully Augustine accepted the offer. He and the members of his household, Monica, Adeodatus and all his friends, transferred their residence to Cassiciacum and settled down to a manner of life framed in a holiday climate.

Cassiciacum was a rural community nestling in terraced foothills, and, like the Plain of the Jordan in Abraham's day, was well watered everywhere. Ribboned by brooks, hedged in by balsam and fir trees, its resinous air bracing as champagne, the village presented itself to visitors with jaded nerves as an open sanatorium, a hiding place from the wind, a cover from the tempest, the shadow of a great rock in a weary land. The canticles of songbirds pierced the air. In full view, a chain of lakes shimmered like sapphires in the sun. Off in the distance the profile of the Alps, like the teeth of a mighty saw, cleaved clouds that swept down in white bodies as though anxious to be cut to pieces.

Augustine cast one look at the setting and said with glistening eyes, "This will be to us all a sojourn to the mountains of myrrh and the hills of frankincense." And remembering the goodness of his benefactor, he prayed, "Reward him, O Lord, in the resurrection of the just."

So began the vacation of the overworked rhetorician. Yet it was not a vacation altogether. Anyone with a temperament like Augustine's could no more relax than mercury. There was still work to be done. He must give attention to the culture of his own soul, preparatory to receiving baptism; Ambrose had advised him to study the Book of Isaiah. He must instruct his first convert to the Gospel, Adeodatus, in the truths of the holy oracles. In addition, the oversight of the affairs of the villa fell to his lot. Finally, a pair of his students, Licentius, the son of Romanianus, together with a friend, had insisted on following their professor to Cassiciacum, there to continue their studies in rhetoric. Augustine welcomed these diversions as a fisherman welcomes the sight of water, nets, and bait. He moved into a daily routine.

Now Licentius posed a jagged problem. His disposition contrasted as vividly with the disposition of Adeodatus as shadings of color in Italian art. Licentius was fickle as a weather vane; Adeodatus, in adolescence, had the firm convictions of an adult. From morning to night Licentius bragged of his intellectual powers; the far more brilliant Adeodatus preserved a modesty that was at times painful. Licentius loved to point to himself as a gourmand and a wine drinker, and complained loudly of the simple fare Monica set forth; Adeodatus ate and drank as sparingly as a monk. Licentius delighted himself with Greek tragedy, Adeodatus had inherited his father's prejudice for Roman drama. Licentius had a fine tenor voice and wanted everybody to know it; Adeodatus was soft-spoken and practically tone-deaf.

Besides all this, Licentius gloried in his paganism. The fact that he was such an unlikely candidate for the Kingdom of God challenged Augustine all the more to convert him. Having in a few weeks won over to the faith of his mother some of his closest friends as well as his own son, he was encouraged to expand his evangelistic efforts.

"Licentius," he said one morning as they were reclining on marble benches on the front lawn of the villa, "how is it you fail to see that it is not through vanity but through verity that man is made happy?"

They were studying the *Eclogues* of Virgil and had been discussing a line dealing with the theme of happiness.

"Happiness," Licentius said with an impudent smirk, "is a relative state. Take me. When I am full of good wine, I am happy. When the effect wears off I am unhappy. What has verity to do with either state of mind?"

Augustine said patiently, "But the same argument might apply to the animal kingdom. Take a cow and fill her stomach with fodder and she is content. Take away her feed and she is miserable."

"Exactly." Licentius waved his hands in a flourish of triumph. "Man is merely an animal with refined impulses."

"No." Augustine pushed aside his copy of the *Eclogues* and gave his full attention to Licentius while the second student looked on with interest. "God has given the irrational soul memory, sense and appetite, that is true, but to the rational soul, that is man, He has given intelligence and will and the power to worship. Have you ever seen a sheep at prayer?"

"I admit I have not. But as far as I can see the same thing happens to man that happens to beast, ultimately. Both die. Both dissolve and decay, and so have a common end."

"Not at all. Christ painted pictures of Heaven in strokes that glitter. 'In my Father's house are many mansions.' 'The beggar died, and was carried by the angels into Abraham's bosom.' 'Come, ye blessed of my Father, inherit the kingdom prepared for you from the foundation of the world.' Nor must you neglect His warnings about hell. 'Fear him,' He said, 'who is able to destroy both soul and body in hell.' He defined hell as a place 'where the worm dies not, and the fire is not quenched.' Remember that."

Licentius squirmed on his bench and glanced up at a squirrel hopping from branch to branch on a fir tree. "How can that be? Fire destroys whatever it —"

"Not so," Augustine said. "Certain mountains in Sicily have been on fire from the earliest point of antiquity until now. Why should it be thought a thing incredible to you that the great God who performs wonders in the empire of nature here and now should be unable to project His powers into the future life?"

"For example?"

"I have cited one example. Take some others. Is it not strange that fire, although it is bright, blackens everything it comes in contact with?

"Or consider the wonderful properties of charcoal. It is so brittle that a light tap breaks it and slight pressure pulverizes it, and yet it is so strong that no moisture rots it, nor any time causes it to decay.

"Or consider the diamond, a stone so hard it can be wrought neither by iron nor fire, nor, they say, by anything at all except goat's blood.

"Or what about the salt of Agrigentem in Sicily? When thrown into the fire it becomes fluid as if it were water, but in water it crackles as if it were in the fire.

"The Garamantae have a fountain so cold by day that no one can drink it, so hot by night no one can touch it.

"There is a stone found in Arcadia, and called asbestos, because once lit it cannot be put out.

"The wood of a certain kind of Egyptian fig tree sinks in water, and does not float like other wood; and stranger still, when it has been sunk to the bottom for some time, it rises again to the surface, though nature requires that when soaked in water it should be heavier than ever.

"Moreover — " But Licentius had had enough. "Excuse me," he said, pulling himself up. "I really must have a drink." He started toward the vialla.

But a few minutes later Augustine and the second student heard him blithely chanting a hymn in the pine grove behind the villa. In spite of Licentius' lyrical piety, Augustine had to confess that the boy turned out to be one of the few subjects his apologetics had no impression on.

The autumn days flew by with incredible speed. In his latter years Augustine would look back on them and call them days of heaven on earth. Sweet indeed proved the companionship of Monica, Adeodatus, Alypius, his brother Navigius and others; rich the periods of early morning meditations on the Psalms when the dew of grace distilled on his soul as the dew of heaven on the tender grass. Tuned to the voices of nature about him — the song of the thrush, the whisper of the brook, the crowing of the cock, the murmur of field insects — Augustine's poetic heart responded as face answers to face in water. And under their spell he made progress, as had the young Jesus, in wisdom, and stature, and in favor with God and man.

The vacation, however, was not all pleasure. There was discipline too. Augustine suffered from insomnia — suffered, oddly enough, in proportion as his bronchitis and throat trouble improved. Long after the other residents of the villa had dropped off to sleep he would lie awake on his bed, fingers of moonlight sneaking in through his window, and wait for sleep to melt away his thoughts.

Sometimes he prayed. Sometimes he repeated portions of the Psalms. Other times he thought of Melanie, wondered where she was, and how she was, wondered if she might be thinking of him, wondered if she were as beautiful as when he had seen her last in Milan. Then his throat would ache and his conscience would ache, and he would whisper, "My beloved one, can you forgive me, ever?"

Often, by applying all the power of his will, he would clear his brain, summon his reason into action, and carry on a dialogue. To a dialectic machine like Augustine's mind there wasn't anything strange about this. He would mentally record the dialogue and the next morning put it down in writing, later to publish the series under the title, *Soliloquies.*

So, by transcription, men have heard echoes from Cassiciacum:

Reason: But why, I ask, do you wish your friends to live, and to live with you?

Answer: That with one mind we may together seek knowledge of our souls and God. For in this way, if one makes a discovery he can without trouble bring the others to see it.

Reason: But if they are unwilling to inquire?

Answer: I shall persuade them to be willing.

Reason: But what if you cannot persuade them, because they think they have discovered the truth already, or that it cannot be discovered, or are hindered by other cares or longings?

Answer: We shall do the best we can.

Reason: But if their presence hinders you from inquiry, will you not wish and strive, if their attitude cannot be changed, not to have them with you?

Answer: I confess that this is so.

Reason: Then you desire their life and presence not for its own sake but in order to find out wisdom.

Answer: I agree without hesitation.

Reason: If your own life was a hindrance to the obtaining of wisdom, would you want it to continue?

Answer: No; I should flee from it.

Reason: If you learned that you could reach wisdom equally by continuing in the body or by leaving it, would you greatly care whether you enjoyed what you love in this life or in another?

Answer: If I knew that I should encounter nothing that would drive me back from the point to which I have already progressed, I should not care.

Reason: Your reason, then, for fearing death now is lest you be involved in some evil which would rob you of the knowledge of God.

Answer: Not only lest I should be robbed of such understanding as I have reached, but also lest, retaining what I myself possess, I should be precluded from the society of those with whom I eagerly share it.

Reason: So you do not wish for continued life on its own account but on account of wisdom.

Answer: That is so.

Upon this, sleep, like a gentle physician, would break off the dialogue, administer its anesthetic, and begin its renewing therapy in the brain and body of Monica's son.

Chapter 32

*In the fifty-sixth year of her age, in my thirty-third
year, that religious and godly soul was set free from
her body (Confessions IX, 11, 28).*

At the mouth of the Tiber River, crossroads of
maritime traffic, sprawled Ostia, the port of Rome. Into
the port flowed merchandise of gold, ivory, oil, grain,
marble, fine linen, silk and scarlet, brass and iron,
spices and perfumes from the Orient; immigrants and
slaves from all parts of the world. Not to be compared
with Rome, Ostia nevertheless boasted her Forum, temples, theaters, baths, warehouses, statues and crowded
shops.

It was summer of the year following the vacation at
Cassiciacum and a brief stop at Milan when Augustine
and his party arrived in Ostia. Now, by the hand of Ambrose a baptized Christian, as well as Adeodatus and
Alypius, he came with his head full of plans to return to
Thagaste, found a monastery there and take up the life
of contemplation away from the dizzy world. His
months of retirement at Cassiciacum had convinced
him that monasticism was really the only life worth living. His glimpse of the monastery Ambrose had established near Milan had inspired him to want to follow

the bishop's example and set up the same type of order
in his own community. A piece of property his parents
had bequeathed him made this experiment possible.

Weather conditions delayed their sailing. Disappointed, the company engaged rooms in a hostel as far
from the center of the city as possible — Ostia had
earned a name for its din, odors, and loose morals —
and waited impatiently for their date of embarkation.

Toward sundown on the evening of the second day
the company left Monica and Augustine and set out for
a stroll. Mother and son stood leaning on the casement
of a window in Monica's bedchamber and talked of
plans for the monastery.

After the journey across the Apennines by caravan
both were tired, especially Monica. From time to time
Augustine would steal a worried glance at her. He could
tell that the trip had caused too much strain on the frail
body. She had lost weight so that the black robe she
wore hung in folds about her. A pallor had whitened
her face, which like a relief map showed lines indented
by erosion — the erosion of care and anxiety. Only the
eyes remained bright, youthful as a schoolgirl's.

"You do not wish to retire, Mother?" Augustine asked.

"Not yet." The window before which they were stationed faced north. Below them a flower garden in full
bloom helped cancel out the depressing shabbiness of
the hostel's exterior. Beyond the garden, a stretch of
plain curled northeast with the Tiber, and spent itself
in a wood some distance up the river. Monica stared
dreamily at the scene. "I never stop marveling at the
infinite variety of articles in the house of nature . . .
which," she added, "is the house of God."

As usual, Augustine fell into her mood. "To think
that once I identified God with his house! I asked the
earth, 'Art you God?' and it said to me, 'I am not he.' I
asked the sea and the depth and the creeping things
with life, and they answered, 'We are not God; seek you

above us.' I asked the breezy gales and the airy universe, and all the denizens said, 'Anaximenes is mistaken. I am not God.' I said to all things that stood about the gateways of my flesh, 'Ye have told me of my God, that ye are not he; tell me something of him,' and they all cried with a loud voice, 'he made us!'"

"Your study of them was your question to them," Monica said. "Their beauty was their response to you."

"True. I questioned the whole fabric of the world about God, and it said to me, 'I am not he, but he made me.'"

The waning sun splashed its ray over the plain, turning it to a painted desert of pastel shades, lavender, violet, rose, turning to fire the evergreen shrubs that lined the Tiber, changing to silver the Tiber itself which, straining between its banks, looked like a thread being pulled through the eye of a needle. To the northwest, purple hills writhed in undulating rolls, like camel humps piled against the sky.

"The Master architect," Monica said, "hath made all beautiful in his time. Think — if all things appear so majestic now, with groaning and travailing in pain under the curse of God — think of the beauty that awaits us in the world to come."

Augustine shifted his eyes to the garden. A fountain bubbled in its center. Around the fountain, larkspur, camellias, indigo tuberoses, lobelias, marigold, pink hydrangeas burgeoning like balloons, put together a rainbow of rare delicacy. He could not but think of Melanie and her passion for flowers. He envisaged her gliding among the bushes down there, fondling each bud and blossom with the tenderness of a mother-nurse.

Monica read his thoughts. "My son," she said, "never forget that heaven is to be a garden, or rather a fountain of gardens, a well of living waters and flowing streams from Lebanon. Or better still, an orchard, an orchard of pomegranates, with pleasant fruits; camphire with spikenard, spikenard with saffron, calamus and cinnamon, with all trees of frankincense, myrrh and aloes, with all the chief spices." Her voice, at first quite faint, was taking on new strength, new vigor. Augustine noticed the change and was happy.

"Better than an orchard, a park," she went on presently. "A park watered by the water of life which shall spring from the throne of God and of the Lamb. And there shall grow the tree of life and it shall yield her fruit every month and the leaves of the tree shall be for the healing of the nations; and there shall be no more curse, but the throne of God and of the Lamb shall be in it; and his servants shall serve him and they shall see his face . . . his face. . . ."

Her voice rang now, not harshly, but with a vibration like the chords of a harp. With uplifted eyes and a radiance of face that could be mistaken for the reflection of the sun at noon, she breathed through burning lips words that enflamed Augustine with a holy blaze he had never known. His excitement mounted.

At this point her discourse changed to prayer.

She prayed, "How lovely are your tabernacles, O Lord of hosts! My soul longs, yes, even faints for your courts; my heart and my flesh cry out for the living God. When shall I come to you, O my God? When shall I come to you . . . and to Mount Zion . . . and to the city of the living God . . . to the heavenly Jerusalem . . . and to the innumerable company of angels . . . and to the general assembly and church of the firstborn? There are they with you, your God: these who have washed their robes and made them white in the blood of the Lamb, they stand before your throne, O my God — they serve you day and night in your holy temple, and you who sit on your throne do dwell among them . . . and you, Lamb of God, in the midst of them — you are leading them to fountains of living waters, O my Savior and my King. . . ."

She grew silent. And at that moment, just as the sun met the horizon, Ostia was silent. Entranced, Augustine felt earth fuse into heaven, sense into spirit, time into eternity. The tumult of his heartbeat was hushed. Images of earth faded, the river, the plain, the garden, the horizon. With Monica, he was walking through the heavens, planting his footsteps on the stars, treading on the moon and the clouds, soaring as on wings higher and higher until he drew near to the heart of God and rested, as had John at the Last Supper, on the bosom of the Savior. . . .

How long the ecstasy lasted he would never know. What he recalled later was that he passed beyond the realm of matter — then fell back to earth, panting, when he heard Monica say, "My son, as for myself, I delight no longer in anything in this life. What I may yet do here, and why I linger here I know not, now that the hope of this life has died within me."

"Ah, Mother —!"

"There was but one thing for which I longed to tarry: that I might see you a Catholic Christian before my death. And now that my God has given me so abundantly to see you become His servant, able to despise mere earthly happiness — tell me, what am I doing here?"

Shocked and grieved after his period of rapture, Augustine could only fold her to his breast and cry, "Mother! O little Mother . . . !"

Five days later a raging fever struck her down. Mercifully, she became unconscious.

Sons, grandson and every member of the party gathered around her bed, praying. Intermittently, they stayed there for the next four days.

On the fourth day she opened her eyes and said, "Where was I?"

"You have been very ill, Mother," Augustine said, taking her hand and rubbing it.

"Aurelius — "

"Yes, little Mother?" He bent over the bed, fearing lest he miss a word.

"Will you bury your mother here?"

To Augustine, as to most people of his time, the notion of burial in a foreign land was startling. Monica's request so surprised him that for the first time in years he had no answer to a question.

His brother came to his help. "But, Mother," Navigius said, "it is our wish that you may get well so that we may take you back to Thagaste."

She turned her head toward Augustine. "You heard him," she faltered. "You heard him. I care not where you bury this poor body. This only I ask of you: that you remember me at the altar of the Lord."

Augustine understood. It was her intention not that he should intercede for mercy at the altar, but rather that he should express thankfulness for blest memories of her.

"We shall indeed, little Mother," he said, fighting for self-control. "We shall indeed."

Monica half smiled. She put all her ebbing strength into the hand Augustine was holding. Her eyelids fluttered. She struggled for breath. The group surrounding her stood frozen in their places, aware that they were watching the passing of a holy woman.

She breathed her last and lay limp on the pillow. There was a moment of strained quietness; then Adeodatus burst into a bitter, racking sob, a sob that moved Augustine so deeply that for a moment he thought it was his own heart crying out.

Quickly Alypius and Navigius went to the boy and with caresses and words of comfort calmed him.

Augustine hovered over the deathbed, dry-eyed, his soul a barren wilderness.

At last he stirred himself, reached out a hand and drew Monica's eyelids down over the dear eyes, smiling in death.

Evodius sought out a Bible, turned to one of the Psalms and began to chant: "I will sing of mercy and judgment; unto you, O Lord, will I sing," and the entire company of mourners joined in the response.

The words of Ambrose's hymn came to Augustine in his bereavement and brought him peace:

> Creator God, O Lord of all,
> who rules the skies, you clothe the day
> in radiant color, bid the night
> in quietness serve the gracious sway
> of sleep, that weary limbs, restored
> to labor's use, may rise again,
> and jaded minds abate their feet,
> and mourners find release from pain.

Chapter 33

*Late have I loved you, Beauty so ancient and so new,
late have I loved you (Confessions X, 37, 38).*

Augustine built his monastery at the base of a hill near the gate of Thagaste. He would have preferred a less public location but the property he inherited was there and he had no choice. Patricius' original farmhouse had been sold and the money used to pay off his debts. Only the property near the city gate remained of a once moderate estate.

The rambling house in the center of the property Augustine and his friends converted into the monastery proper. They cleared it of all furniture except wooden benches, tables, bookshelves and beds. Simplicity must be maintained at all cost. Yet Augustine, as abbot of the new order, did not insist on cells. Rather, each monk was assigned a tiny chamber where he could pray and meditate in private.

They erected a small chapel next to their headquarters. They planted vegetable and flower gardens. Through the generosity of Romanianus, who, while continuing to reside in Milan, still followed the development with interest and sympathy, they obtained livestock and fowl. Thus they were able to make the enterprise practically self-supporting.

Mountain greenery, an apron of lush meadow, and a stream swishing down from the hills formed an idyllic setting for the new home. The blue mirror of sky overhead and the clean desert air around them left nothing to be desired.

What little money Augustine had left over after equipping the monastery he gave to the poor.

Thagasteans hailed the experiment — the first of its kind in that part of Africa — with the enthusiasm of schoolchildren. Augustine's fame as a rhetorician and scholar, as well as the news of his transformation, had preceded his return. Consequently many of his former friends and acquaintances flocked to the monastery to consult with him. Some begged to be admitted. Within a fortnight capacity was reached, and it became necessary to draw up a waiting list.

So at last, in his own province and allowed to live the life he had often prayed to live, he was content. True, his throat still troubled him — as it would all his years — but in general the improvement in health was so great that a hundred times a day he breathed little prayers of praise up to heaven.

He set himself to the study of scripture. Fortified by the commentaries available, he locked himself in his room and pored over the bible until his eyes ached. The obscure portions held a special charm. The penitential psalms, too, he fell in love with. Often as he dwelt on a favorite psalm with racing pulse he would stop and lift eyes to the hills and say, "All my hope is nowhere but in your exceeding mercy. Grant what you dost command and command what you wilt." Or, "Far too little doth he love you, who loves anything with you which he loves not for you." Or, "O love, who ever burnest but never consumest — O charity my God, enkindle me!" Or, "You hast called and cried aloud and broken through my deafness. You hast blazed forth and shone and scattered my blindness, for you are fragrant, and I draw in my breath and pant for you."

Sometimes as the blue haze of evening coiled about the meadows, he left the monastery and strayed up to the hills above Thagaste. Standing alone on a plateau in the twilight, he looked out over the city and reviewed his riotous youth: the evenings he had played and fought in the Hollow; the night he had led the band of youthful robbers to the pear orchard; the hours Monica had spent pouring out her heart like water before the face of her Lord, pleading for his salvation. He thought of Spendius, that cherished friend death had snatched away like a kidnapper, leaving him broken and bewildered.

"I entered into the recesses of my memory," he later wrote, "those manifold and spacious chambers, wonderfully furnished with innumerable stores; and I considered and was afraid, and could discern nothing of them without you."

For months he had been storing up polemics to hurl against his old friends, the Manicheans. In Africa, as in other parts of the Roman Empire, they were on the march. They did not hesitate to use the church as a recruiting station for their cause.

Augustine turned his hand to writing tracts exposing their errors. He was human enough to lose his temper as he wrote. The Manicheans were men "raving with pride . . . in whose mouths were the snares of the devil"; "a bird lime made up of a mixture of syllables"; "men of Sodom"; "depraved and crooked persons." At the thought of their follies he burst like a punctured wineskin. His reed pen spilled sarcasm. "What a confusion of ideas! What amazing fatuity! Admirable customs! Excellent morals! Notable temperance!"

At the same time he did distribute light as well as heat. Having studied their doctrine for nine years at close range, he was qualified to debate authoritatively as well as with skill.

He wrote to Nebridius, who had returned to Carthage: "I now know why the King suffered this burning branch to blaze his way through the tunnels and dungeons of Manichean treachery. It was to spy out the darkness of the land, that he might some day put to flight the armies of aliens with the Sword of the Spirit. . . ."

The Manicheans learned to fear him as much as they resented him.

In his leisure hours he exploited his hobbies. Here in the monastery the manifold facts of its abbot began to flash forth in full luster. He wrote essays on grammar, rhetoric, mathematics, and philosophy. He finished six books on music, five of which he had begun in Milan. He wrote on art and poetry. He wrote so many letters he used up all his ivory tablets and parchment.

The empire came to recognize him as an authority on civil law, and Africans constantly appealed to him for counsel. Throughout the Roman world the name of Augustine became synonymous with learning.

With his fame spreading like desert heat, he was still able to maintain a humble routine. Every morning at dawn he roused himself and his monks and called them together into the dining room, where they sang a Psalm or hymn of praise. Augustine or one of the others read a passage of Scripture and led in prayer. After a light breakfast, the monks filed out to the fields and orchard to do their work and Augustine retired to his room to study and write.

The day was checkered with sessions of prayer and relaxation at nine, twelve, and three. Dinner late in the afternoon consisted of a heartier meal than breakfast. Augustine left evenings open for leisure reading, walking, bathing, or discussion.

Problems of discipline seldom arose. On the whole, the prevailing mood was one of tranquillity.

One of Augustine's greatest joys was, of an afternoon, to detach himself and Adeodatus from their brother monks, wander away to a secluded spot by the stream or on a hilltop, and sit down for an hour of instruction.

Adeodatus would soon celebrate his seventeenth birthday. The younger monks idolized him. "That Adeodatus," they said. "Some day he will be a famous scholar like his father. And he is blest with such a sweet disposition too."

Augustine thought he was the image of Melanie as truly as the face on a Roman coin was the image of the emperor.

Then one day a mysterious African disease struck the boy down. The physicians of Thagaste could do nothing for him. They said they had never seen a sickness like it. They said they knew of no medicine in the world that could cure his trouble.

Augustine listened to their report, bowed down with grief.

A raging fever sapped Adeodatus' strength. He lapsed into a coma. On the thirty-fourth day of the illness, while his father and a few of the monks looked on, brokenhearted, he breathed away his life

Augustine groped his way to his chamber to pray, the hot tears coursing down his cheeks. He remembered Melanie's message to him, "Adeodatus says he does not think he will live long. He may be right. God struck the child of David's sin. Will He strike the child of my sin?"

Now at last the question was answered.

Chapter 34

I came to this city [Hippo] to see a friend whom
I thought I could gain for God, to join us
in the monastery (Sermon 355, 2).

Augustine spent three years at his monastery —
joyous years, dimmed only by the loss of Adeodatus,
and, later, Nebridius. Especially precious to him and
the other monks were the hours of fellowship when
they sat down together to talk of their redemption.
Then their hearts burned within them, as earth re-
ceded and heaven came near.

Augustine would have been as satisfied to stay at the
cloister as any anchorite. To study, to meditate, to write,
to debate points of theology and philosophy, to counsel
with inquirers — this, he felt, was to fulfill David's own
testimony, "My cup runneth over." He could not know
that this was but a brief time of inner strengthening.

Great events turn on small pivots.

A letter came to him from an acquaintance living in
the Mediterranean port of Hippo Regius. The man was
a clerk in the Office of the Interior of the imperial service.

I am beset with a growing desire to give up my worldly tasks and enter a monastery. I would gladly come to you for consultation, but at this time I cannot because of the pressure of my work. Forgive me for burdening you with this request, for I have no claim on you other than that you are the Lord's servant. Can you not come to Hippo to advise me about my future? I assure you I shall be grateful beyond words.

Augustine took the letter to Alypius, who was talking with a new arrival at the monastery, one Possidius. "What shall I do?" he asked, when they had read it. "Shall I go or say no?"

Much was involved in the decision. Augustine's reputation as a Christian leader had so flowered throughout the empire that ecclesiastics everywhere talked of drafting him into the service of the Church. Remembering Ambrose's experience, he grew increasingly wary of taking to the road for fear he be seized and pressed into the priesthood. He was firmly persuaded God had called him to serve as a lay scholar.

"What should you do?" Alypius said. "You have nothing to fear." The chemistry of grace had wrought a radical change in him too, had purged away his pleasure madness and begun its ennobling work within. "The church at Hippo is staffed with a bishop and a full corps of priests."

"Surely, then," said Possidius, who would one day write a biography of his abbot, "surely they will not make demands on you."

Augustine shrugged. "What you are saying is: Go. Very well. If you think it is my duty, I have no choice."

So he went to Hippo, though a presentiment haunted him. It was in the heart of the winter of 395. Augustine arrived to find the harbor cluttered with grain ships waiting to sail for Ostia. Crowds of sailors strolled the streets of the city, merging with the population of Numidians, Jews, Egyptians, and Greeks. A bitter wind blew in from the sea, cutting into Augustine's flesh.

Hippo held no attraction for the monk from Thagaste. He said to himself, "I hope I never have to live here."

His interviews with the clerk proved disappointing. Augustine detected a stratum of insincerity in the young man. If, as he had professed in his letter, there glowed in him a zeal for the monastic life, that zeal had faded. Normally expert in personal counseling, Augustine could not draw out the reason for the man's change, and after the third interview he gave up.

On Sunday he went to the Basilica of Peace to hear Bishop Valerius preach. In general the basilica was arranged in the usual plan of such centers of worship. At the rear, the atrium, reserved for inquirers and catechumens, was approached through a pair of doors. Three rows of marble columns split the basilica itself into four sections, two for men and two for women. A distinctive feature of the Basilica of Peace was its floor, a splendid golden mosaic, the pride of every member of the church. A baptismal font stood in front, before the apse or chancel. On the apse, the bishop's chair occupied the space directly behind the altar, which was a plain oblong table that served as the pulpit. Curiously, African bishops preached sitting down, while the congregation heard the sermon standing.

The basilica was only half filled when Valerius began his sermon. The congregation gave every sign of being in an unruly state. Worshipers chattered like jackdaws as they drifted in and out, as though attending a show or an athletic contest. Whenever a person felt so inclined he called out a question to a friend across the aisle, or even back in the atrium.

Valerius had sprung from Greek stock. He spoke Latin poorly — someone had told Augustine that he spoke no Punic at all. And though unquestionably earnest, the aging bishop was blest with few pulpit gifts. His delivery lacked fire, his manner lacked ease, and Augustine surmised that what he said had little relevance to the needs of laymen. His listeners seemed as bored as mutes.

For over an hour Valerius droned on while men and women came and went. Augustine himself was tempted to leave, when suddenly the speaker came to life. It was evident that a burden was weighing upon his mind. It put such urgency into his words that a change stole over the congregation. People stopped talking and moving about, and gave the bearded bishop their attention.

"My brethren," Valerius said, raising his voice, "I appeal to you. The harvest is great and the laborers are few. Why are the souls of men perishing? It is because you younger members of God's church are hiding yourselves — I do not hesitate to say it, you are shirking your spiritual responsibilities."

Augustine glanced about the basilica. The sermon seemed to be gathering power, for a number of the younger men about him shifted uncomfortably.

"Some of you out there besprinkled with the dew of youth — some of you are strong, and bright, and gifted, and qualified to labor in this corner of the Lord's vineyard . . . and what are you doing? You are saying to Christ, 'I pray you have me excused.' You are saying, 'I have bought a yoke of oxen and I go to prove them.' You are saying, 'I have bought a piece of ground and I must needs tend it.' Tell me — tell me one thing, I pray. Think you that your excuses will be endorsed by our Judge in the day when he shall bring to light the hidden things of darkness, and make manifest the counsels of the heart?"

As Valerius flung the challenge at his flock he stood up and leaned over the altar, pausing a moment before answering his own question. "No, my dear and beloved young brethren," he cried with flashing eyes, "your excuses will not stand in the day of judgment. What will you do when you face your God?"

Faulty as was his spoken Latin, the words tumbled from his lips. Augustine could not believe he was hearing the same preacher who a few minutes before had spoken with such lack of spirit. Silence had fallen over the basilica, the worshipers listening like a company of people hypnotized.

"Therefore, you of this diocese who are able and educated — you of whom it can be said, 'You are strong and the Word of God abides in you' — I appeal to you as in Christ's stead, my dear young brethren, come out and come forth and give yourselves as priests to the most high God. I implore you — nay, I charge you in the name of Jesus Christ so to do. . . . Amen."

Valerius ended his appeal, and bent his head over the altar, his lips moving in silent prayer. The pall that lay over the congregation was almost tangible.

Then there was a stirring. A middle-aged man standing behind Augustine had been studying him for some time.

Years before, the man had lived in Thagaste. As the sermon ended it had dawned on him who the monk in the coarse goatskin robe really was. Now he shot a fist into the air and shattered the spell of quietness with the shout, "Augustine is here! Augustine is here!"

The announcement rolled out like a clap of thunder. Church members craned their necks or jumped into the air to catch a glimpse of the Thagastean scholar.

Someone else took up the cry and bellowed it out: "Augustine is here! Augustine is here!" In a few seconds the whole congregation was echoing it until the basilica rang. The bishop stood helplessly behind the altar looking out over the scene of confusion, not knowing what to do.

Utterly dismayed, Augustine shook his head and tried to move away, but people surrounded him on every side, hemming him in. "Augustine is here!" they roared. "Augustine is here!"

The man who had done the first acclaiming was surprised at the tumult he had raised. But he was also delighted. Now another idea struck him, and he called out above the din: "Augustine a priest! Augustine a priest!"

Instantly this caught fire, as the other phrase had. "Yes, yes! Augustine a priest!" the congregation echoed. "Augustine a priest!"

"No, no!" Augustine stammered, but it was a futile protest. No one would listen to him.

A dozen men fell on him, and began to drag him up the aisle toward Valerius. "Augustine a priest! Augustine a priest!"

The practice of forced ordination, though rare, was not unknown. Both Ambrose and the eloquent Chrysostom had been subjects of mob pressure, had been thrust into the office of bishop by popular demand. Valerius saw that he had no choice but to yield to the voice of the church. Quickly he dispatched an altar boy to his study to procure the articles of the ordination rite; then he started down the stairway leading to the open space before the apse.

"Augustine a priest! Augustine a priest!"

Augustine wept as they pushed and pulled him down the aisle. The thing he dreaded most was happening to him. He remembered now the premonition that had been shadowing him. Why had he not heeded its voice and remained in Thagaste?

He doubted his readiness for the priesthood. Was he not a novice? Did he not need more study, more discipline, more months to rid his mind and soul of the cobwebs of paganism that still clung to him? Why could not this frantic mass give him a chance to speak for himself?

"Listen, good people —!" he cried out.

They were too intent on their objective. "Augustine a priest! Augustine a priest!" They chanted it as they drew him before Valerius, who stood waiting beside the font.

Augustine addressed Valerius with tears in his eyes "Your Reverence, am I not permitted to give reasons why I cannot be a priest?"

The venerable man shook his head. "My son, I am sorry," he said. "You and I have no choice. You see the temper of the congregation. Above all, remember that this must be God's will, otherwise it would not have taken place."

"Yes, yes," murmured the people, quieted now. "It is God's will."

What could one say to such belief? Augustine looked long and earnestly into the eyes of Valerius, reading in them a mute appeal. "We need you in our service," the old man seemed to say. "We need you sorely. Come, give your consent, will you not? For our sake, if not for your own."

Sorrowfully, Augustine bowed his head and knelt before the bishop. With a sigh of relief, Valerius took the cruet of anointing oil from the hand of the altar boy, dipped his fingers in the liquid and applied it to the head of the priest-elect. Then from a grateful heart he offered the ordination prayer. Beautiful in its simplicity, moving in fervor, Augustine felt it melt away his resentment, flooding his spirit with infinite sweetness.

" . . . make him, our Father, valiant for truth," Valerius was praying. "As we now anoint this your servant with material oil, do you graciously anoint him from heaven with your Spirit — that he, after the example of his Savior, may preach good tidings to the meek, that he may bind up the broken-hearted, that he may proclaim liberty to the captive, and the opening of the prison to them that are bound. . . ."

Chapter 35

*Be angry with wickedness, yet forget not
human considerations (Letter 133).*

It was a year after Bishop Valerius had ordained
Augustine to the priesthood that the old man summoned him one day and said gravely, "My son, I wish
you to preach in my stead until Easter. I am not well this
winter and feel that to serve my congregation well is
beyond my strength."

Augustine checked an exclamation of surprise. This
was something new — hitherto only bishops had held
forth at the altar.

"But Your Reverence," he protested, "I have no experience in developing or delivering a sermon."

Valerius regarded him sternly. "Remember what the
Lord said to Moses when he called upon him to spread
his Word — 'Who made your mouth?'"

"But, sir —"

The Bishop of Hippo dismissed any further argument with an impatient tug at his beard. "It is also my
wish that from now on you serve as my coadjutor. You
will preach whenever I am unable to do so, and you will
baptize catechumens."

A flutter of apprehension passed over the soul of the priest, and once again he deplored ever having left Thagaste.

Seeing his perturbation, Valerius mellowed. "You will do well, my son." He put his hand on Augustine's shoulder. "You will do well, have no fear of that. The King who touched Isaiah's lips with a coal from the heavenly altar will touch yours too."

His words were prophetic, for to his joy Augustine found that starting to preach was comparable to a plunge in the *frigidium:* once the initial shock wore off, the reaction was enormously invigorating. A trained orator, he already spoke with ease and fine fluency. Despite his chronic throat ailment, his diction had acquired a polish that was soon the envy of Hipponese rhetoricians, while his command of Latin, over against the halting speech of Valerius, drew admiration from the congregation. Crowds were soon flocking to the Basilica of Peace to hear the bishop's new coadjutor.

Toward the close of the Lenten season that year Alypius journeyed north to visit his friend. Meeting for the first time in many months, they shed ecclesiastical dignity like formal garments. They threw themselves into each other's arms, laughed, exchanged playful blows, and in general behaved like schoolboys.

"And to think I am to hear you preach tomorrow!"

Alypius, still guileless as a cherub, beamed affectionately. Augustine's features, although more worn, had lost none of their animation since his student days. He contorted them in a sudden frown. "I am afraid you will be exposing yourself to a sermon burdened with much negativism."

"Why is that?"

"You know what goes on at the *agapae* — the love feasts — around the tombs of the martyrs?"

"I do."

Augustine lowered his head. "Here in Hippo they are even worse than at Thagaste. What was once an innocent feast has deteriorated into an orgy. Tomorrow I must denounce the evils of Joy Day."

Ascension Sunday was to be followed by this yearly festival during which merrymaking would go far beyond the limits of decency. In the cemeteries, by the graves of the dead, there would be feasting and much drinking, followed by mass indulgence of sexual license. It was a holiday when many who professed the true faith joined hands with those outside the Church in an unbridled pagan celebration. From the day of his appointment to the office of coadjutor, Augustine had determined to do everything in his power to strike at its excesses.

Next day the basilica was crowded. Augustine chose his text from St. Paul: *Have ye not houses to eat and drink in? Or despise ye the church of God, and shame them that have not?* He recited the passage twice, then bade the congregation repeat it with him before he began to preach.

He spoke in the conversational style he had once used to lecture in the classroom, avoiding the rhetorical flourish of orators, and it was with a thrill of pride that Alypius stood with a company of local monks and studied his friend. He caught the deep note of sincerity in the warm voice that sounded from the apse, and was aware that it evoked immediate response.

Stealing a glance around the basilica, Alypius saw that Augustine was addressing a motley cross-section of citizens. Among the men were Roman officials in blue-and-garnet togas, listening respectfully with arms folded and heads erect. A dozen or so legionnaires in gleaming armor were present, and sailors in green, loose-fitting vests. Priests and laborers had come out, artisans and housewives: a composite of humanity from every occupation and social stratum. Beyond the marble column and to the far side of one of the women's sections, widows and consecrated virgins, motionless as statues, gazed up at the preacher from behind black veils. Between them and Alypius were a few painted faces with blood-red lips and eyebrows and lashes heavy with makeup. They brought to his mind Christ's words: *Publicans and harlots go into the Kingdom of God before you.*

Alypius marveled at Augustine's resourcefulness in trying to arouse the personal sympathies of his listeners before unleashing his denunciation. Augustine sat at the altar, his pale face etched against the dark silk tapestry that ornamented the wall of the apse, sharp eyes moving restlessly from the men's sections to the women's, thence to the atrium at the rear and back again. He chose simple words and delivered them with crisp directness, employing figures of speech familiar to the most illiterate, yet conjuring lively images in the minds of all as he reached the crux of his sermon.

"The camel goes forth without drink, yet some of you cannot cross the desert of this world without surfeiting yourselves. Ah, you disciples of Bacchus," he declaimed, his voice gathering force, "when will you learn that no drunkard has any inheritance in the Kingdom of God? You modern Cretans, when will you know that life is more than the food that sustains it, and the body more than its raiment of flesh? When will you stop to think that God will judge the adulterer according to the precept of divine justice?"

At once Alypius became conscious of a sudden surge of anger mounting among the people. Aware of the volatile temperament of the Hipponese, he was wondering how long it would be before the congregation protested, when an obese, ruddy-faced man standing nearby raised his right hand above his head and shouted: "Joy Day is observed at Saint Peter's in Rome. If it is evil, why is it allowed?"

Then a second man far in the rear stamped his foot for attention. "And why is it that the Church says nothing of the dances at Carthage, if they are as unholy as you say?"

"Yes, why is that?" the congregation shouted, voice after voice adding its protest. "Why, why?" Stamping of feet and the uplifting of clenched fists accompanied the swelling roar. "Why is that? Why is that?" The chant grew.

Alypius quivered with fear. Nothing like this ever disturbed the church at Thagaste. What could Augustine do to bring order out of chaos? Would he not have to end the service here and now?

Behind the altar, the bishop's coadjutor was a study in serenity. Whatever emotion was within him, outwardly he seemed the calmest person in the basilica. He looked out over the sea of angry faces as a general would inspect his legions, waiting unmoved until the uproar exhausted its fury. When quiet was restored, he sat another full minute before undertaking to speak.

Then he leaned over the altar, grasped its edges with both hands, and said evenly, "I want to tell you a story. Will you listen?"

There was resentful murmuring, but no one opposed him.

Augustine sat upright. "A certain public orator was once delivering a speech with great enthusiasm. During the oration, he allowed himself to be carried away by his subject. He became demonstrative, as have some of you here today. He stamped his feet. He hurled himself about the platform like a circus performer. He slammed his fists into the wall and cracked the plaster. He ranted until he — and his audience — were quite worn out."

Augustine paused. His dark eyes wandered over the congregation. Complete silence had fallen over the worshipers. He leaned forward again.

"At last an elderly gentleman in the audience stepped forward, and said to the orator what Saint Paul said to the Philippian jailer: *'Do thyself no harm; we are all here.'"*

The silence continued another moment. Then a peal of laughter rang out, followed by another and another. Never, Alypius told himself, had he witnessed such a lightning change of mood. In the twinkling of an eye, rancor gave way to good will, rage to hilarity. The worshipers applauded and gave vent to exclamations of approval. The virgins giggled behind their veils and the old men grinned toothlessly, while here and there a legionnaire or a sailor slapped his thighs, or an official wagged his head, smiling sardonically.

When the church was quiet again, Augustine went on to explain that the recognition of Joy Day by Christians in Rome and Carthage had been a temporary concession to paganism, but that the time had come for it to be abandoned. The true faith was strong enough now for compromise to become a thing of the past, and it should be Hippo's pride to be in the vanguard of reform.

Throughout the rest of his address there was no further heckling, and when Augustine had pronounced the Benediction the congregation filed out of the basilica subdued and thoughtful.

Alypius was in a fever to greet his friend. Outside the church, priests, monks and laity crowded around Augustine as soon as he came out, wringing his hands and babbling congratulations for his handling of the explosive situation. Then they fell back as Valerius appeared and went forward to embrace his coadjutor.

"I was listening to you from an anteroom, Augustine. God reward you, my son. No mistake was made when we ordained you to the priesthood."

At last Alypius seized his hands. "You were magnificent!"

Augustine smiled. "You are what is known in court as a biased witness, but I still like to hear it, old friend. Now let us eat. I am famished."

The monastery to which they went for a meal was a three-story building of quarry stone at the east end of the basilica grounds. Augustine had only recently founded it with the blessing of Valerius and, as in Thagaste, men from the locality were continually gravitating to it to enroll as monks in his new order.

"You have gained a great victory," Alypius declared as they walked together to the refectory.

"Alas, only a partial one, I fear," Augustine replied.

"Why do you say that?"

"Tomorrow many who are now full of good resolutions will be swept away by the excitement of the festival. There is an infectious quality to sin. Next year I shall be forced to denounce Joy Day all over again."

Priests and monks were strolling beneath the trees of the monastery grounds, discussing the dramatic scene in the basilica. But as great as was their interest, Alypius was quick to perceive that all was not well. While many of Augustine's fellow clerics greeted him cordially as he passed, others merely nodded and several pointedly looked the other way.

"I wonder if it is because they are jealous," Alypius mused.

They were nearing the refectory when the two friends heard footsteps behind them; then a feminine voice called to them timidly. They turned to see a girl in a lavender robe bound by a black sash. It was plain that she was deeply embarrassed. The blood rose into cheeks that were already russet red with youth and sunshine as she stood with downcast eyes, her fingers plucking at her sash.

"Lucilla," Augustine said gently. "What is it?"

The girl bit her lower lip and scuffed a tuft of grass with her sandal.

"What is it?" Augustine repeated. "What may I do for you?"

Still no answer. Then the girl's lips parted, and she forced out one whispered word: *"Eulogy."* Breaking into a sob, she buried her face in her hands and ran away.

Augustine stared at the retreating figure, his expression puzzled. *"Eulogy?"* he murmured.

It was some years before that a custom had been started in the Church; certain of its members had initiated the practice of giving and receiving the *eulogy,* a piece of love bread, as evidence of the good spirit of fellowship existing between them. Feeling that it smacked of the paganism he so detested, Augustine had never favored the custom, although he granted others the right to observe it if they so desired.

"Perhaps she wishes to exchange the *eulogy* with you," Alypius suggested. The mention of food invariably induced a pang of hunger in the monk from Thagaste. He veered toward the monastery. "Our meal is overdue."

Augustine swung into step with him, still puzzled. "That was strange. I wish I knew why she was so discomfited. Perhaps she remembered too late that I disapprove of the *eulogy* and do not partake of it."

"All feminine action is strange," Alypius rejoined.

Augustine chuckled. "You are right." Taking his friend by the arm, he broached an issue nearer his heart. "And when are you going to receive the laying on of hands?"

For a moment Alypius forgot his hunger. "During your sermon I felt a longing to follow you into the priesthood," he confessed gravely. "It came on me when you were first preaching. Could it have been the call of God?"

Augustine pressed his friend's arm fervently. "If it was, be sure of one thing, dear fellow. Be sure that you are not disobedient to the heavenly call."

Chapter 36

For me, good things were no longer outside, no longer quested for by fleshly eyes in this world's sunlight (Confessions IX, 4, 10).

"And how are things going at Thagaste?" Augustine addressed the question to Possidius, who had come to Hippo Regius not long after Alypius' visit. "Well, I trust, and flourishing."

"One could not ask for more of the blessing of heaven," Possidius said. "Everyone there misses you."

Augustine smiled. At forty-two his smile had lost none of its charm, although, his friends noted, it creased the tired face less often than in his youth. "Do not think for a minute I have forgotten Thagaste."

"Alypius says to greet you in the name of the Lord. So do all the monks."

"Bless them. I long to see them more than they know."

They were seated on wooden benches at a dining table in the refectory of his monastery. The monks had finished their evening meal and withdrawn, leaving him and Possidius to talk. "Alypius reports that you labor more than you should as coadjutor to the bishop."

"It imposes extra duties. I conduct classes in cate-chism, carry on correspondence for the bishop, call on the sick, and spend long days in court arbitrating civil cases. Not to mention preaching."

"I am anxious to hear you. Tell me, do you enjoy preaching?"

A servant emerged from the kitchen. With a good deal of clatter he cleared the dinner bowls and utensils from the tables. Augustine delayed his reply until the man had left.

"Always the Gospel terrifies me," he said solemnly. "It terrified Paul. Remember what he wrote to the Corin-thians? 'I was with you in weakness, and in fear, and in much trembling.' Yet in the same letter he wrote, 'I overflow with joy.'"

"I see what you mean. It is a paradox."

"It is. Yes, I love to watch people when I teach from the altar. Here are women of the street standing before me with hearts as empty as seashells, and lonely as a night sentinel. 'I have a Friend for you,' I tell them. Here are pagans submerged in their polytheism. They have come to hear me out of curiosity. No matter. I have a living and true God to present to them. He has told me His Word is like a fire, and like a hammer that breaks the rock in pieces. I cast the fire and wield the hammer, and I look for Him to do what He has said. And He does, He does."

Possidius found himself picturing the hearers in the congregation of the Basilica of Peace and was carried away by the enthusiasm of his friend.

"Here are Donatists, smug in their notion of their own superior holiness," Augustine went on. "And here are Manicheans, shackled in their dualism. I know what they believe and I have a message for them too: the Word made flesh, full of grace and truth. At least one Manichean was converted gloriously."

"It is good to hear," Possidius said.

"There are Roman officials, men of culture and breeding. I have an Aristocrat for them, the Lord of lords, the Prince of life. I tell them of Him, and like the Proconsul of Cyprus, Sergius Paulus, they send for me and ask to hear more about the Word of God."

"I am gladdened," said Possidius.

"And there are the common people, the kind of people who harkened to my Savior in the days of His flesh. I tell them of Him who was so poor He had no place to lay His head."

The rare smile played on Augustine's lips as he talked on. Possidius listened. In Thagaste, he had learned to admire the abbot. In the few hours he had been in Hippo, he had come to love the priest.

"And so you see," Augustine said, "I can summarize this engaging side of the priesthood in the words of Cicero, *'Doceat, delectet, flectat* — To teach is necessary, to delight pleasurable, to win victorious.'"

Suddenly an overwhelming urge to follow in his friend's footsteps took hold of Possidius. Years later he would say, "I was called to preach the Gospel my first night in Hippo Regius."

Controlling his emotion, he said, "They tell me that Valerius is grooming you for the office of bishop when he retires."

"I hear it too. I confess I dread the prospect as much as I used to dread the priesthood."

"With your gifts you have nothing to fear. What of the monastery here? And what kind of monks have you?"

Augustine leaned away from the table, pulled up the hem of his cotton byrrhus, crooked a knee in his hands and swayed back and forth. "I can tell you this, my friend, the best men in the world — and the worst — live in monasteries."

Possidius looked shocked.

Augustine tipped his head toward a strip of birch bark nailed to the refectory wall. "You see that motto?" Possidius read aloud the words burned into the bark:

Let those who like to slander the lives of the absent know that their own are not worthy of this table (Possidius, *Life of Augustine* 22, 6).

"I judge your monks are given to gossip," Possidius said

"Many a time have I threatened to walk out of the room unless the butchering of character stopped."

"It seems incredible." Possidius shook his head. "We have so little of it at Thagaste."

Augustine refrained from pointing out that the aging Valerius, not he, chose the monks that were admitted into the local order, and that the bishop's judgment had often been faulty. "The whole monastic movement needs reforming," he said. "I am glad the emperor is doing something about it. They tell me Ambrose supports his reforms."

"We have heard nothing about the reforms in Thagaste."

"Surely you know about the army of corrupt priests and monks swarming in from the East, to escape the barbarians," Augustine said, surprised.

"Vaguely."

"It is sad. Some of our little brothers under the cowl have watched wealthy widows come into the church with the desire to deed over estates and even large sums of money to the Lord's work. Shades of Balaam! The glitter of gold has gotten into their eyes — eyes that are supposed to be fixed on God. So what are these vultures doing? They are actually moving into the homes of some of these benefactresses. They are representing themselves as stewards of God's property, and you may be sure they plan to fatten their own purses at the expense of our generous Lydias and Dorcases. Not to speak of other excesses and indiscretions. Some of my brethren are enraged at me because I insist on turning down all legacies and bequests."

"Indeed, you have problems we have never had at Thagaste."

The servant came in again, and spoke to Augustine. "Sir, a woman wishes to see you."

"Did she say why?"

"She says she needs you to indemnify her son. It seems they have put him in jail."

Augustine heaved a sigh. "For stealing?"

"She did not say."

"I see. Tell her it is too late to do anything today. Tell her to come back in the morning."

"Yes, sir." The man bowed and went out.

Augustine eased his foot to the floor and rose. "It happens every hour of the day," he said. "Would you like to take a walk?"

Possidius followed him out of the refectory, and Augustine escorted his guest around the grounds of the basilica. He showed him the monastery and the convent, the chapel dedicated to martyred Christians, and the cemetery behind the chapel. Last, they went into the Basilica of Peace, where Augustine indicated the various points of interest. Monks turned to stare at them as they passed, for Possidius looked enough like Augustine to pass for a brother. "In my brother and colleague," Augustine once wrote of him to a churchman, "you will discover, in effect, my double."

From the basilica they sauntered down to a bay that nature had carved in the shape of a half-moon. They stood on the sand and gazed out to the sea, where a solitary ship broke the skyline. To the west the sun had just tipped the edge of the Mediterranean, a huge blood-red buoy, poised momentarily before plunging into the choppy waters. On the beach fishermen spread their nets to dry, after their day's toil. While they

worked they sang ballads of the sea, or boasted pro-
fanely of the lucky catch the gods had given them that
day.

Augustine and Possidius talked of Thagaste for a
while. Presently Possidius asked, "Do you like Hippo?"

"I do." Augustine folded his hands behind him and
planted his feet apart. Unlike Possidius he wore shoes,
not sandals. "I loathed the place at first."

"I know I sound like a curious woman, but I am interested in hearing whatever you talk about." At Thagaste,
Possidius had made up his mind to write Augustine's
biography. A life so full of dramatic power, he decided,
must be passed on. All the information he could marshal he filed away in the cabinet of his memory, later to
polish, and record in what would be a labor of love.

As the friends conversed, the sun dropped into the
Mediterranean. At the spot where it had rested a glow
lingered between sky and water. At last Augustine
ceased talking of his daily life. "We had better go," he
said, giving a last look at the sea. "We should not be late
for vespers."

They turned and plodded back along the beach.

Dusk had deepened to darkness as they entered the
city precincts. The two men threaded their way
through the crowded streets, Augustine exchanging
warm greetings with not a few of the citizens. Some,
however, glowered at him with heads lowered and eyes
spiked with malice.

A hulking fellow in a white robe spotted the priest
coming toward him. He halted in his tracks, snarling
like a dog. "Heretic! Heretic!" he shouted, and added a
curse.

Augustine walked by him without a word.

"Who was that?" Possidius asked.

"One of the Donatist leaders. This place is a Donatist
stronghold."

"Does the white robe stand for anything?"

"Purity."

"Purity?" Possidius raised his eyebrows. "With that language? What a travesty on the pure life!"

"They are as charitable as they are pure." Possidius caught the inflection of gentle irony. "Have you heard that the Donatist bishops have forbidden their bakers to sell bread to Catholics here?"

"They are wolves in sheep's clothing!" Possidius muttered. "How I wish Christ would send a spirit of confusion into their pack!"

"Let us ignore them. To go back to one of your questions," Augustine said, "you asked what I liked least about the priesthood."

"I am anxious to hear you out."

"To be truthful, what irks me most is the pettiness that stains human nature. Even regenerated nature."

"I am not surprised to hear you say it. You yourself have such an overflowing heart, it must be hard for you to endure bickering in any form."

"Yes, I confess it is — this, for example. You are aware of the Church's practice of exchanging *eulogies* — pieces of holy bread — among the members in token of mutual affection?"

"I am aware of it," Possidius said. "And as I recall, you never favored the idea too strongly."

"I could never see that it had much value. Well, last month a certain young woman in the congregation here started a rumor to the effect that I had hidden a love potion in her *eulogy.*"

Possidius laughed. "Why did she think you had done that?"

"For the purpose of seduction."

The smile faded. "That is beyond a jest."

"I am not exaggerating," Augustine said. "Whether she is a Donatist spy, or a weakling the Donatists bribed to help them in their campaign to dishonor me, I cannot say. I suspect it is the latter. At any rate, the damage has been done. The Donatist party has used the story to strike and strike hard. I marvel you have heard nothing of it in Thagaste. As a matter of fact, I was waiting for you to question me."

"The rumor was so incredible, I did not bother even to ask the details. What do you think will be the outcome?"

Augustine shrugged. "No one can tell yet. It has developed into a serious issue. The Donatists would love to have my head."

"It must harass you exceedingly."

"From my enemies I expect this kind of treatment. If men called Our Lord an agent of the Devil, and if Paul carried on his ministry despite evil report as well as good report, why should you and I expect something better? What pierces me to the heart is the realization that my own brethren — yes, and in some instances my own co-laborers in the priesthood — have added their voices to the chorus."

"'I was wounded in the house of my friends,'" Possidius quoted. "The motive is envy, is it not?"

Augustine shrugged. "It seems impossible for Christian men to forget my deplorable past."

"Why does not Valerius discipline the girl who has done the mischief?"

"She has gone away to visit relatives, her family says."

"How is Valerius reacting?" Possidius asked.

"He has stood behind me through the whole ordeal, good soul that he is. It has taken much from him. He is far from well, you know. His physician thinks he will not be with us much longer. Yet he is willing to invest his waning strength in the battle against the monstrous lie that is burning like straw all around me."

"I am sorrier than I can tell you." Possidius touched his friend's arm sympathetically.

"Thank you. The latest word is that our Primate of Numidia — "

"Megalius?"

" — that Megalius, too, has heard the scandal. Next week he is due in Hippo on church business. No doubt he will review my case."

"Yet you do not seem too perturbed over it."

"My mother used to tell her children that when one is in the right he can afford to shake off anxiety," Augustine said calmly. "Often she reminded us that our Heavenly Father will one day bring forth our righteousness as the light and our judgment as the noonday."

They had reached the grounds of the Basilica of Peace. Monks, nuns, and lay folk were converging on the chapel to attend vespers. Augustine and Possidius stepped up their pace in order to be on time.

"May I ask your permission to do something?" Possidius said.

Augustine regarded him quizzically. "If it is in the orbit of reason."

"May I send for Alypius? Surely he will want to be with you when Megalius comes to review your case."

One of Augustine's rare smiles played across his features. "Of course." He crooked an arm around Possidius and hugged him. "I shall need him, as I need you and my other faithful comrades. 'Ointment and perfume rejoice the heart: so doth the sweetness of a man's friend by hearty counsel.'"

Chapter 37

He who after the battle would receive the crown
ought not to be broken in spirit while the battle is on
(Letter 99 to Italica).

The African Church being so organized that every province was supervised by a primate, usually the oldest bishop, upon him was conferred the power to convene convocations and synods, and to ordain deacons, priests, and bishops. The Primate of Numidia, the venerable Megalius, also served as Bishop of Guelma, which lay a day's journey southwest of Hippo Regius. The city might be said to have formed one of the anchor points of a triangle, Hippo and Thagaste being the other two. Megalius had written to Valerius that he was traveling to Hippo to appoint and consecrate the aged Bishop of Hippo's successor. But Valerius and the other leaders of his diocese suspected that this was a secondary reason — that Megalius' real purpose in coming was to investigate the "love-potion scandal" that was rocking the Church in Africa.

As the day of Megalius' arrival drew near, excitement mounted among both clergy and laity. Augustine's enemies swelled with exultation. "Now we shall see that degenerate priest receive the reward of his iniquity," they said among themselves. His friends were proportionately depressed.

"How will he be able to clear himself?" they asked one another apprehensively. "What can he do against this broadside of slander?"

The evening meeting at which Megaliús was to announce his choice of Valerius' successor was held in the Basilica of Peace. A dozen bishops from neighboring cities were there to learn of the appointment, and later to assist in the consecration service. Present also were a number of monks, as well as citizens of Hippo.

Augustine stood in the men's section near the front of the basilica, flanked by Alypius and Possidius on his right, and on his left Evodius, who had lately come to Hippo to enroll as a monk. Megalius had not yet interviewed Augustine — probably, Alypius suggested, because he wanted first to finish the matter of consecrating a bishop.

The primate presided, occupying the vacant space before the chancel, and directly under the pulpit. He wore a pallium much like the one commonly worn by Ambrose. Well over seventy, small-boned, his face was as stern as the captain of a ship that had weathered the fiercest storms at sea and come through unscathed. The people of Guelma knew him for a strict disciplinarian — strict, yet eminently fair. Even those who disliked him respected him.

He opened the session with a lengthy prayer. Then, speaking in a remarkably clear, crisp voice, he stated the reason for his coming to Hippo. Some time before, he and Bishop Valerius had agreed that it was time to choose a priest to take the place of the bishop, whose days must, in God's will, now be numbered.

"I have had conferences with five candidates for the office," he said. "Each of these candidates has unique gifts. Each would make a worthy office bearer. But, alas, I can appoint only one man. Therefore —"

"Your Grace!"

Every head turned to the rear of the church. Valerius, his complexion as white as sun-bleached sand, was moving up the aisle on the arm of a gentle young monk named Heraclius, who attended him now. Enfeebled by illness, his frail figure contrasted vividly with that of Megalius, who stood as erect as a pillar.

"Your Grace," Valerius quivered, fixing his eyes on the primate as he stumbled forward, "Your Grace, I wish . . . to propose the name of Augustine . . . as Bishop of Hippo."

A gasp rose from hundreds of throats.

Megalius said nothing until the bishop and monk had come all the way down the aisle. That morning he had tried to call on Valertius in his sickroom, but the leader of the Hippo Church had been in such distress of body that his physician would permit no one to see him. Megalius was astonished, therefore, to see the dying man appear before him.

"Your Reverence," he said solicitously, "you should not have attempted to leave your bed."

Breathing heavily, Valerius seemed on the point of fainting. Megalius signaled an altar boy to fetch a chair, and with Heraclius' assistance helped the bishop into it.

A hush had fallen over the crowded basilica. People who had come out of curiosity found themselves present at the unfolding of a drama.

On Valerius' forehead lay a mass of beaded perspiration. With the sleeve of his robe he wiped it away, leaned forward, panting, and a moment later straightened up. His sunken eyes were glassy as they met those of Megalius.

"I pray you, Your Holiness," he said unsteadily, "consecrate Augustine . . . in my place."

Megalius faltered only an instant, then shook his head. "I cannot do it in good conscience."

"Why not?" Valerius spoke impatiently. "Why? Because of the lies . . . the lies the Donatists have spread? Is that why?"

"How can I bring myself to appoint as successor to Your Reverence a man who lives under a cloud of suspicion?"

Some Donatists in the basilica murmured openly, and Valerius' troubled eyes swept the church until they found Augustine. With a fluttering hand he beckoned him forward. Reluctantly, Augustine detached himself from his friends, stepped into the aisle, and joined the Bishop of Hippo before Megalius.

"My dear Augustine," Valerius began, "I want you to give . . . to give your . . . defense before . . . His —"

The strength ebbed from his body and he pitched forward in a dead faint. Only the intervention of Augustine and Heraclius kept him from crumpling to the floor. Evodius, used to emergencies from his army life, sprang forward like a soldier following orders. He gathered up the unconscious bishop in his great arms and carried him tenderly out of the church, as Heraclius bore his staff behind them.

A few of the women wept. The morbidly curious drew sighs of satisfaction. This was even better than they had anticipated.

Megalius faced Augustine. "I am a practical person," he said, not unkindly. "I had intended consulting you after the transaction of the business on hand, but since our beloved friend and bishop is so zealous to have you succeed him, I will postpone the announcement of my choice. I will grant you the privilege of making your defense. It is common knowledge that you have been accused of immoral conduct What have you to say?"

Without hesitation, Augustine stretched forth his hand and spoke up. "Your Grace," he declared in ringing tones, "with another of our Lord's servants, I may say that since my awakening to righteousness I have exercised myself always to have a conscience void of offense toward God and toward man."

Then he swung about and addressed the men and women staring at him. "Is there one in this sanctuary," he challenged them, "is there one who has the courage to charge me face to face with a misdemeanor?" His eyes were half-closed with anger. He waited a minute. No one stirred. "No!" he thundered. "Yet some of you — and not all Donatists, either — some of you have spewed the poison of asps among your friends and your neighbors. What are you?"

He swung back to Megalius, and regained his composure as quickly as he had exploded.

"Your Grace, a member of this congregation has accused me of inserting a love potion in a maiden's *eulogy* in the interest of enticement. May I ask if Your Grace is willing to listen to the testimony of those who know very well my manner of life?"

Megalius hesitated. Several men behind Augustine called out, "Let us hear witnesses!"

Augustine was at home in the role of counselor. Since his founding of the monastery in Thagaste, he had spent hundreds of hours in civil courts listening to counselors and judges argue the merits of cases. Often he himself received permission from the bench to defend monks or church members who he was persuaded were being indicted falsely. He was better versed in Roman jurisprudence than many judges and now he was fortunate in his knowledge of judicial matters.

Glancing over his shoulder, he said, "Alypius, please come here."

There was a shuffling of sandals and stretching of necks as Augustine's closest friend started up the aisle. Alypius would soon be a priest. The Bishop of Thagaste recognized him as a potential leader of men, and had already determined to ordain him.

"Now, Alypius," Augustine said briskly, when they stood together before Megalius, "you were with me when I established the monastery in Thagaste, were you not?"

"I was."

"Tell me, did I ever institute the practice of exchanging *eulogies*?"

"No," Alypius said.

"Did I ever explain why?"

"You did. You told us that you could not see any virtue in the custom. You said that there was no scriptural basis for it, and so abstaining from participation was not a violation of a Biblical principle. You said that it was like the eating of meat offered to idols in New Testament days. Paul's position on that was that if Christians ate, neither were they the better; if they did not eat, neither were they the worse."

"Did you ever see me give or receive the *eulogy* in the church where I worshiped at Thagaste?"

"Not once," Alypius said.

"Thank you." Augustine looked at Megalius. "Does Your Grace wish to ask anything of Alypius?"

Megalius shook his head.

Augustine motioned for Alypius to retire, and called out, "Will Possidius come to the front of the basilica?"

Possidius hurried to him, eager to make his contribution to the cause. He answered Augustine's questions in the manner Alypius had done.

At that point a monk tiptoed up the aisle and whispered in the ear of Heraclius, who had returned and was hovering at Augustine's elbow throughout the proceedings. Excitedly Heraclius gained the priest's attention, and murmured, "Lucilla is here."

Augustine remained impassive except for a flicker in his dark eyes.

Next, he summoned half a dozen local monks and priests, and asked each one the question, "Have you

ever known me to give or take the *eulogy* in any service
or ceremony, in public or private?" All gave an em-
phatic "No" in reply.

Once more he addressed the congregation. "Are
there any of you who will testify that you have seen me
distribute the *eulogy* in your presence?"

There was a stony silence.

"Now," he said, taking a deep breath, "I wish to request Lucilla to come to the front."

Augustine's words created a commotion in the rear
of the women's section. A plaintive cry burst out, followed by protests. "No, no, no, no!" a girl's voice
screamed. "Oh, please let me go!"

The wedge of humanity parted, and the young
woman, frantic with fear and blushing furiously, was
catapulted into the aisle.

"Ah, have pity!" she begged, trying to ward off feminine hands that pushed her toward the chancel.
"Please, for the love of —"

"You go up there!" A powerful woman seized her by
the arm and dragged her up the aisle. "You started this
ugly business; now finish it."

Megalius stood at the end of the aisle with folded
arms, his countenance severe. Augustine eyed the terrified maiden with compassion, almost regretting that he
had called upon her.

"Here she is, Your Grace," the large woman said to
Megalius. "Please God she may tell the truth at last."

The girl who had accosted Augustine that day was
the daughter of a farmer, a lovely young creature with
red provocative lips, and eyes like brown velvet. Now
Lucilla cowered before the primate, wringing her
hands and sobbing pitifully.

"My daughter," Megalius said, "you are here in the
interest of justice. I charge you before the Judge of the
whole earth to answer me truthfully. Did this priest give
you a love potion?"

"No, oh no!" she moaned.

"Then before God and these witnesses do you retract the sinful lie you circulated about him?"

"I do, I do!" she cried. "God forgive my wickedness."

"One more question," Megalius said. "Did you allow yourself to be used by the Donatists to start the report?"

The maiden nodded. "My uncle — " She stopped, too anguished to continue, and placed her hands over her tear-drenched face.

"We will investigate later." Megalius whispered to the woman who had brought her up the aisle, "You may take her away."

The woman led the trembling girl back up the aisle and out of the church. It was a fitting climax to the drama. The curious among the crowd congratulated themselves on having witnessed an excellent show; the orthodox rejoiced that their esteemed priest had been exonerated; meanwhile the Donatists slipped out of the building, singly or in groups, muttering of a miscarriage of justice.

Smiling, Megalius held up his hands. Gradually over the congregation fell quiet.

"Good citizens of Hippo," Megalius said, "this young priest — " he indicated Augustine, who stood with bowed head — "this man of ten talents has abundantly vindicated himself of the base falsehood his enemies have projected against his character. I am bound to say also that none will question his zeal for the cause of Christ and His Church or his scholarly attainments, or his ability to proclaim the counsel of God, or his administrative powers, or his love for people. I am prepared to declare that I do most sincerely and joyfully appoint him successor to holy Valerius. Tomorrow evening, here in the Basilica of Peace, Augustine shall be consecrated."

A glad shout from the congregation greeted the announcement. People laughed for joy and embraced each other. Alypius and Possidius went forward to their friend, clasped his hands, and offered him their felicitations.

More elated over the clearing of his name than over his naming, Augustine's eyes shone. "Brothers like you make me feel at times such as this that I am dwelling in the suburbs of Heaven."

It was a solemn moment when the Primate of Numidia consecrated Augustine to the sacred office of bishop. The anointing of the chrism, the investiture with the pallium the ring, the books, the shepherd's staff, the kiss of brotherhood — these offices were performed with the utmost gravity. Finally Augustine knelt for the laying on of hands, and Megalius, standing over him, lifted up his voice in the consecration prayer.

Augustine heard not a word of it, for as Megalius was interceding for him, in his heart he was beholding the face of Monica. She smiled at him through veils of clouds, as in an aura of supernal, mystic glory. The familiar voice broke through, winging its way into the vaults of his soul in muted notes of comfort and love. "My precious, precious boy, I was more sure than life that our God had predestined you to be a burning and shining lamp for him. Bless you, my son, and never forget that with the laying on of the hands of your brethren, there has been also the vastly more blessed laying on of the nail-pierced hands of your Elder Brother, whose you are and whom you serve."

Chapter 38

From this earthly city issue the enemies against whom the City of God must be defended (The City of God I, 1).

Augustine strode through middle age as he strode through the streets of Hippo, a slight figure with spring in his step and fire in his eye. A driving zest for life, for knowledge, for the interests of the Kingdom of God, and for the honor of the Roman Empire motivated all his actions. A non-conformist in dress, he discarded the pallium soon after his consecration to the office of bishop, and he wore instead the plainest black cotton robe he could persuade his tailor to make. The residents of the city grew accustomed to seeing him marching briskly to the law court to contest a case, to the hospital on a visit of mercy, or to a private home to call on a poor family. Invariably he would be accompanied by a group of priests or monks to whom he lectured enthusiastically on some point of doctrine as they walked — this in the interest of saving time.

The result of his rise to fame as a church leader was twofold. It called forth flattering tributes from admirers all over the empire, and it drew resentment from men of ill will, poisoned by jealousy. Hero worshipers overpraised him; his enemies misrepresented him, twisting the details of his early years into a portrait of monstrous distortion. Even Monica came in for her share of abuse. Out of this background of light and shadow was born his *Confessions*. The trenchantly honest autobiography failed to stop the tongue-wagging, but it succeeded in reducing it. To a friend in Italy Augustine explained:

> Therein you have to believe me — not other people — about myself; in that mirror you can see me, you can see what I was and through my own fault. If you find therein anything that pleases you, then in company with me praise Him whose praises for His work in me I would have men sing; but do not praise me. "He made us, not we ourselves"; rather had we made shipwreck of ourselves, had not He who made us, remade us. And when you discover me in that volume, then pray for me that I fail not but may be brought to perfection.

To the surprise of the people, Valerius rallied under young Heraclius' gentle care and his life was prolonged a full year after Megalius' visit to Hippo. True, he was bedridden much of the time; but, as Augustine told his friends, he was a constant source of inspiration to the younger bishop, encouraging him, counseling him, praying for him hour upon hour. His dying words were: "Put on the whole armor of God, my son Augustine. Endure hardness as a good soldier of Jesus Christ."

In the tempestuous years ahead as the Bishop of Hippo, Augustine had frequent occasion to remember the charge. For the new century brought down upon mankind the most violent social upheaval that had yet come.

Out of Moesia and Trace poured hordes of Visigoths, led by the crafty Alaric. They devastated Greece, were driven out, crossed the Julian Alps, and set about terrorizing Italy. Young Honorius, the emperor, dis-

patched Stilicho, his favorite general, to meet Alaric
with a veteran army. In the spring of 403, Stilicho
stopped the Visigoths at Verona, turning them back de-
cisively.

Early in the summer, he entered Rome at the head
of his victorious legions. He rode with Honorius himself in the emperor's chariot. The city went wild with
joy, and celebrated a Roman holiday such as had not
been staged since the capital had been transferred to
Milan.

But Alaric had withdrawn to the Alps only to reor-
ganize his troops. When the hysteria of the Roman
populace passed, he advanced to the gates of the city,
encamped on the banks of the Tiber, and proceeded to
cut off the food supply. The Senate paid him a huge
indemnity to leave.

A year later he repeated the move. A second indemnity was paid, and Rome awoke to Alaric's perfidy.
Many patricians, disheartened, fled the city, taking
their wealth and possessions with them.

Alaric was so flushed with the success of his first two
threats that he followed them up with a third. This time
the Senate refused to pay the price he demanded, and
he thereupon effected a siege that kept Rome contained for a whole summer. Finally, a traitor opened the
Salarian Gate and let the barbarians in. The weakened
defenders put up almost no resistance. Alaric's men
carried out a sack that was punctuated by wanton destruction of property, wholesale slaughter, torture,
rape, plundering.

The debacle of Rome's destruction came as a body
blow to the civilized world, which had come to think of
the Eternal City as an impregnable fortress that could
no more fall than could the stars from their courses.
The idea of a heathen army conquering the center of
religion and culture was preposterous. Yet it had happened, and all wondered why.

The pagans said, in effect, "The gods permitted the fall because the state forbade us to worship them." Christians said, "The Lord has brought judgment upon the empire for its idolatry and pleasure-madness. Let us search and try our ways and turn again to the living and true God."

Foreseeing the outcome, Augustine set about preparing Christendom for the dissolution of the Roman world, with all its implications. People must be made to understand the moral as well as the military reasons for such a social upheaval, and thus he began work on *The City of God.* Burdened as he was by countless duties and obligations, fellow churchmen never ceased to marvel that he mustered the time and strength necessary for the development of this massive compendium of theology, philosophy and history, though they had no way of knowing that this work would affect the thinking of generations unborn.

The vindication of Augustine's character before Megalius was a turning point in his struggle with the Donatists, but as with an earthquake, though the great shock came and went, tremors still jarred the ecclesiastical field for several years to come, and the seething resentment of his adversaries showed itself in covert attempts to gain final victory.

One autumn morning in the year 411, Augustine and young Heraclius, now a priest, were walking along the dusty highway to Hippo Regius, returning from a call on a rural church member who had fallen sick. It was a fine day, and the spirits of the two churchmen were high as they discussed a recent decision of the Council of Carthage, convened by the emperor for the purpose of resolving the issue that had for so long split the African Church between Catholic and Donatist.

"The Donatists, of course, are convinced the settlement was unfair," Augustine said. "They claim that since the tribune liIarcellinus who presided was my friend, it is small wonder the decision favored the orthodox wing."

"The fact that Marcellinus happens to be a friend of Your Reverence had nothing to do with the decision," Heraclius said loyally. "The picture ought to be clear to all who have an open mind. The Donatists accused two of our bishops of acting as traitors. The Council cleared them of the accusation. What else could it have done under the circumstances? The evidence for their innocence was as overwhelming as — as yours in the *eulogy* case."

"Truth is of little concern to our Donatist friends. What irks them almost to the point of madness is the Council's verdict that ours is the true church, and theirs a heretical movement."

At that moment a burly young farmer in a mottled tunic came up from the rear and fell into step with them. "Are you gentlemen going to Hippo? If so, may I go with you?"

Heraclius thought the request somewhat presumptuous, but said nothing.

"Hippo is our destination," Augustine said pleasantly, "and we shall be glad indeed to have you go with us. I am Augustine, and my friend here is Heraclius."

The intruder nodded, as though familiar with the names and neither surprised nor impressed. "I am Renatus. I believe I heard you talking about the Council of Carthage. And I am sure you were concerning yourselves with their decision. For my part, no matter what the Council decided, the Donatist Church is the only true Church. To begin with, have we not the largest membership?"

After an exchange of glances, Augustine chose to let the priest take up the argument. Heraclius, the bishop could tell, was trying to remain calm, remembering that in his lectures to his novices Augustine urged the cultivation of a meek and quiet spirit when in debate.

"What exquisite modulations," he had said, "what dulcet notes fill the air when the nightingale pours forth its song! Go, my future defenders of the faith, go and be your Lord's nightingales."

No one could have attempted to modulate his speech more sincerely than Heraclius now did. "Just a moment, my friend," the young priest began. "Let us keep the issue straight. Numbers have nothing to do with it. It is like this: you Donatists say 'We are the true Church because we are a holy society. A holy society can allow only holy people in its membership. . . .'"

As Heraclius threw his whole earnest soul into the wayside argument, Augustine noted his strengths and weaknesses, pleased to observe how rational the young man remained even when unfairly attacked by an unworthy opponent. But presently he interrupted.

"I beg your pardon, my young theologians." He halted at a point in the highway where a lane joined it. "It occurs to me that while I am here, I should visit another of our ailing members."

"But, Your Reverence," Renatus protested, his manner undergoing a curious change. "I — that is, we — had hoped to have the benefit of your learning in our controversy. Can Your Reverence not make this sick call some other day?"

"No, the man is one of our deacons. I should go to see him now."

"I will go with you," Heraclius said.

"I prefer that you go back to my house," Augustine said to him. "If there are any of our people waiting to consult with me, please tell them I expect to be home soon."

"But, Your Reverence — " Renatus broke in anxiously.

Augustine had already started down the lane. "Farewell, my brethren."

"How rude he is," Renatus mumbled resentfully, hesitating as if reluctant to go on without him.

"To get back to our discussion," Heraclius said, when they had resumed their journey toward Hippo, "let me give you Bishop Augustine's answer to the Donatist argument. He puts it this way: 'I derive my faith from Christ, not from the clergy. The clergy simply serves as his agents.'"

"You and your Augustine!" The farmer's lips curled contemptuously. "Who is Augustine, after all? An immoral heretic."

"He is no heretic," Heraclius countered, more warmly. And if he *was* immoral, he no longer is. Since his conversion he has led a blameless life."

"We are still not convinced about the philter he gave Lucilla."

"That was a miserable fabrication. You seem to forget that he was exonerated by the Primate of Numidia."

Renatus snorted. "Does that undo —?"

"What have you against him?" Heraclius cried. "What has he done to offend you people who hate him so?"

"He preaches and writes against us."

"Against your errors, not against you. And he began that only after he broke his heart trying to reconcile our two churches."

They were approaching a sharp curve in the highway where a thick growth of bushes stretched from a nearby meadow to the edge of the road. Suddenly out of the bushes sprang a quintet of rough-looking Numidians led by a red-bearded man in a white robe. They advanced on Heraclius and Renatus menacingly.

"Where is he?" the leader demanded of Renatus.

The farmer glanced uneasily at Heraclius, then stammered, "He — he left us back there on the road."

"So you let him get away!" The red-beard's voice rose to a roar.

"We lay a careful plan to take care of our enemy for good, and you let him get away!"

"I tried to make him stay with us," Renatus whimpered, falling back. "I tried —"

"So you tried!" In a fury the man raised his cudgel and brought it down on Renatus' back. "Next time we'll choose a guide we can depend upon." And with an oath he tossed the cudgel into the hedge, spat on the cowering farmer in disgust, and strode off down the road leading away from Hippo, the other four at his heels.

Heraclius regarded the discomfited Renatus in horror. "And you Donatists accuse our bishops of treachery! Only the providence of God thwarted your evil intention."

The peasant winced as he rubbed his bruised back. "Your Augustine deserves to die," he growled, and fell into step with the priest, who had swung off down the road.

"You do not know what you are saying!" Heraclius exclaimed. "Our Lord said that by this should all men know that we are His disciples, that we have love one for another. Have you Donatists fulfilled this tenet of Christianity? Let me remind you of what you did to Possidius, our Bishop of Guelma."

"What about him?"

"Donatists hounded him to his home, and when he refused to come out they set fire to the house. They would have beaten him to death had not your bishop stopped them."

They were approaching the outskirts of Hippo. Pedestrians, mule and donkey drivers, and carriages coming in from outlying hamlets began to obstruct the highway.

"And your so-called Athletes for Christ, your *Circoncelliones.*" Heraclius, himself slight of figure, waved his arms at the thought of these activists. "How do they show their love for their Catholic brethren? They plunder our houses and steal from our warehouses. They killed one of our priests, and cut off the tongue and hands of one of our bishops." Flushing with righteous wrath, he demanded: "What kind of Christianity is that? At Calvary, our Savior prayed for his enemies. What must he think of men who profess his sacred name and at the same time kill and destroy and spread hatred and bitterness?"

Renatus' scowl was ugly. "It is Augustine. He is the one who keeps our people stirred up — he and his ravings from the pulpit."

Heraclius held his peace, for they were in the suburbs of Hippo now, not far from the basilica. In a last burst of spleen, Renatus turned upon the priest. "I say he is a jackal and a son of Belial!" His face was contorted and his breathing came hard. "I say he should be excommunicated and sentenced tohHell!" With this the Donatist wheeled on the priest, doubled a fist and landed a blow on the side of his head, following it with a second to the jaw.

Heraclius reeled backward, and shook his head to clear it. He recovered quickly and eyed his assailant in astonishment, putting a hand to his jaw. "You are a defamer!"

Rage twisted Renatus' features as he closed in on the priest, his arms flailing. Passers-by, seeing a fight in the making, hurried to watch, and the two men were quickly surrounded by a circle of onlookers hoping for a free show. Heraclius put his hands up to defend himself as Renatus lunged at him. Then neatly he sidestepped, and as the farmer lurched past him, he sent a fist crashing into the unguarded chin. The spectators heard a sharp crack and the man in the mottled tunic went down like a falling tree. Suddenly he was lying motionless in the gutter.

An urchin in the crowd stared up at Heraclius in awe. "You put him to sleep," he breathed.

Ruefully the priest rubbed his knuckles. He bent over the prostrate body, picked it up, and, staggering under its weight, gestured to the crowd to make way. "I must take him to a physician."

The people stood aside respectfully as Heraclius, endowed with unaccustomed strength, bore the unconscious peasant down the street.

Two hours later he stood before the Bishop of Hippo in his study. Augustine was seated at a writing table, mounds of scrolls and parchments piled before him. Tired but sparkling eyes searched the face of the gentle young priest.

"Tell me about it, Heraclius," he said.

"About what, Your Reverence?"

"Come, Heraclius, the fight."

Heraclius shifted his weight from one sandaled foot to another. "Your Reverence has heard, then?"

"My son, there are thirty thousand citizens in Hippo. By now, twenty-nine thousand have heard that one of my priests has been playing the role of a boxer."

So Heraclius told his bishop the story.

"Is the man all right?"' Augustine asked, when he had heard him out.

"The physician says nothing is broken — it is merely a bad bruise on the chin. By now he has probably gone home."

"Did you pay the costs?"

"I promised I would."

"I see. You may tell them to send the reckoning to me."

"But, Your Reverence —"

Augustine held up a hand. "That is my order. Thank you for telling me all, Heraclius."

The priest turned to go.

"Wait, my son. I have one question before you leave."

Heraclius bowed. "Your Reverence?"

"Tell me, was it not hard to — shall we say, discipline the belligerent one?" A merry twinkle lighted up the black shadows of Augustine's eyes.

"No, Your Reverence."

"Why not?"

"Because I remembered something Your Reverence once told us in a lecture."

"Which was —?"

"Your Reverence said, 'It is perfectly proper to defend a person's honor, if necessary, provided you do it in a spirit of love and not in a spirit of revenge.' I think of the two, my love for you was greater than my anger at your defamer."

"Ah, thank you, Heraclius. You may go now."

The slim defender of ecclesiastical honor bowed and went out. No sooner had the door closed behind him than Augustine put his hands to his sides and rocked with quiet laughter. His eyes filled with tears, and happiness surged over his tired soul.

Chapter 39

*It is not the body, but the corruptibility of the body,
that is burdensome to the soul (The City of God XIII, 16).*

In the autumn of 413, Augustine's physician insisted
that he call a halt to his activities, leave Hippo Regius,
and withdraw to some quiet place for a complete rest.
"Your Reverence is killing himself with work," the doctor said. "If you do not follow my orders, you will suffer
a collapse from which you may never recover."

Instinct told Augustine that the physician was right.
An indescribable weariness possessed him day and
night. The pressure of his duties, combined with his
old throat trouble, a painful attack of lumbago, and violent headaches, drove sleep from his eyes and reduced
his appetite until the very sight of food nauseated him.

Two other deep apprehensions contributed to his
exhaustion. The fall of Rome in 410, momentous as it
was to the world at large, signified more to Augustine
than political and social reshuffling. To him the savage
Vandal wave engulfing the civilized nations was a threat
to the very life of the Church. That the wave would extend to the empire in Africa seemed inevitable. The un-
timely death of Alaric had not checked Gothic
ambitions. Sooner or later the invasion must come, and

Augustine fought to block from his imagination the staggering consequences when it did. After Rome's collapse, he sought earnestly to prepare the African Church for the shock he foresaw.

His other concern was more personal but no less pressing — his growing struggle with the doctrine of Pelagianism.

Almost single-handedly he had broken the backbones of Manicheism and Donatism. Those battles won, he longed to devote himself to a positive exposition of the historic Christian faith. But it was not to be. The growth of Pelagianism had sent him out on the ecclesiastical battlefield again.

Pelagius, the Achilles of the movement, was a devout monk. Born in Britain soon after Augustine's birth, he, like Augustine, had been nurtured on the classics. Unlike Augustine, he reveled in Greek culture, and had drunk deeply from the founts of Eastern learning, including its theology. To him Augustine's doctrine of human guilt and sovereign grace were anathema. He taught that since human nature was basically good, only a modified divine assistance was needed to perfect the character of man.

Pelagius had settled in Rome, but the threat of Alaric's assault on the city had caused him to flee to North Africa. From there he had gone to Jerusalem, leaving behind him at Carthage his friend and follower, Coelestius, to champion his doctrine in the African Empire. But it was a scholar-bishop from Campania, named Julian, who had become its most dangerous proponent. Gifted with quick dialectical wit and a clever wordsmith, Julian mounted a sustained attack against Augustine that kept him constantly on the alert.

His early skirmishes with the new enemy brought encouraging results. Pelagianism, with its denial of original sin, its optimistic view of human nature, and its rejection of man's absolute dependence on divine grace for redemption; received official condemnation at a series of councils called by the emperor. Yet the victory proved costly to the champion of orthodoxy. Augustine came out of the engagement like a soldier who has lost too much blood, battered and unnerved.

Nevertheless, when his physician counseled him to take a rest, he rebelled. "I cannot abandon my flock at this critical time," he said.

"Who will care for your flock if Your Reverence dies?" the physician asked pointedly.

"That will be faced when the time comes. I am not dead. I am still very much alive."

The physician pursed his lips. "I can promise Your Reverence that there will be new leadership in this diocese before Christmas if you are not realistic. The church has an able staff of priests. Let them bear your burdens for a few weeks."

"But where can I go?"

"I know an excellent place. One of my friends has a cottage on an oasis halfway between here and Zama. He will be honored to have Your Reverence there."

Grudgingly Augustine gave in, and two days later retired to the resort, taking with him a servant and Heraclius.

The oasis comprised a triangle of green surrounded by a strip of lonely desert, dotted with half a dozen cottages owned by professional men in Hippo, all of which were empty at that season of the year. Here Augustine could relax under the blazing sun by day and the bright stars by night, letting tensions run down in the first vacation he had taken since Cassiciacum. Yet though his mind assured him he was entitled to the breathing spell, the still small voice of conscience forever chided him for the neglect of his vineyard

One of many afternoons found him sprawled on a patch of grass under a tamarisk tree. The warm desert wind fanned its branches, ruffling Augustine's open-neck garment. Sunshine sifted through the tree's foliage over his wasted frame. He lay with his eyes closed, breathing great drafts of the pure air and trying to calm his mind with thoughts of boyhood days when he had roamed the desert near Thagaste and dreamed wild dreams. It was a vain attempt. The present darkness erased from his mind those dear memories, filling him with oppression.

Heraclius came to him from the spring at the heart of the oasis, carrying a gourd of water. He was stripped to the waist, having peeled off the upper part of his cassock and secured it to the cloth belt that encircled him. He loomed above Augustine, silent and awkward, concern for the sick man showing forth in his features.

Augustine opened his eyes, mustered a feeble greeting, and closed them again.

"Would Your Reverence care for a drink?"

"Thank you, no."

Heraclius set the gourd on the ground and quietly stretched out at Augustine's feet, understanding that the bishop had no wish to talk. The young man had learned this subtle fellowship of silence while Augustine was passing through the turbulent days of toil and conflict just past. He understood also that his bishop's illness was not so much of body as of spirit, and that the present withdrawal to this blessed retreat was merely a lull before Augustine must return to the storm center of his life.

An hour passed before the silence was broken. "Heraclius."

"Yes, Your Reverence?" The priest raised his head.

"May I have that drink now?"

Heraclius sprang up. "Let me fetch some fresh water."

Presently he was back from the spring. He placed an arm under the weary head and lifted it with the gentleness of a nurse. Augustine sipped slowly.

"Thank you, my friend." The sick man fell back on the grass. "It is living water that issues from a spring, Heraclius. Water that gathers in cisterns is not living water."

"That is so," Heraclius said eagerly, always overjoyed when the philosophical temper revealed itself.

"So it was with the downfall of Rome. She ceased to send forth living waters. She became, in Solomon's words, 'a spring shut up, a fountain sealed.' That is the tragedy. Rome was a city of rare privilege. She could have been the fountainhead of truth and knowledge. Instead she allowed greed and lust and unholy ambition to crowd out every virtue — and with devastating consequences to the world!"

"Your Reverence had a great love for Rome."

"And I still do." The dark eyes stared up through the bright green of the tamarisk. "And I still do," Augustine repeated. "Heraclius, may I open my heart to you?"

"I am here only to serve you in every way."

"As soon as I am granted the necessary strength, I mean to continue work on a book I am writing. I call it *The City of God.* In it, I hope to show that ultimately there are but two communities, two cities. Both are constituted by love."

"By love?" Heraclius propped his hand on his head and listened almost with reverence.

"By love," Augustine went on. "There is a community of which Rome is the symbol — that is, of the earth. And it is formed by love of self, even in contempt of God. But there is also a second city, one of heavenly origin, formed by love for God even in contempt of self. The one delights only in herself, the other in the Lord. The first seeks honor from men, the second the approval of God. In the one, the lust for power prevails, both among her own rulers and among the nations she rules; in the other, each serves his fellows in charity and subjects himself to the laws of the King."

Heraclius' eyes glistened. "One is the city of man, the other the city of God."

"Precisely."

Augustine winced as a dull pain shot through his back. Perceiving this, Heraclius rose to his knees.

"Let me give Your Reverence some relief." He helped Augustine roll over onto his stomach, and folded back his garment. "My father was a sailor. He learned some useful treatments — tricks, he called them — from physicians in other lands."

Augustine sighed as he felt the priest's thumbs pressing against the aching vertebrae. "How glad I am you came with me, Heraclitus!"

Anxious for the bishop to continue his dissertation, Heraclius prompted: "We are told that Rome is a city of sorrows."

"Probably no city on earth except Jerusalem has known the sorrow Rome has known, because it is a city of great and grievous sin. Had our friend Pelagius stayed there any length of time and experienced its horrible degeneracy, the pollution and the hideous cruelty, he would long since have given up his doctrine of man's innate goodness."

Somewhat emboldened, Heraclius interjected: "Is it not ironic that Pelagius fled from the very men whose morality he defended?"

"It is indeed. The manifold evils — murder, plunder, unbridled power-madness and licentiousness — that marked the fall of Rome, showing to all but the blind what Paul calls 'the exceeding infidelity of sin.'"

"And the crying need for divine grace, Your Reverence?"

"That too." Augustine put up his hands to signal his masseur that he had had enough. "Heraclius, how can I thank you? I am grateful beyond words. Your father bequeathed his son a useful inheritance indeed."

In the days that followed, Heraclius noted a slow improvement in his bishop's condition. Rambling walks over the desert, hours of luxuriating under the October sun, frequent massages by Heraclius beside the spring or under the tamarisk trees, hearty meals put up by the servant — all this could not but have its healing effect on the exhausted man. Soon a fine tan touched up his pallor. The throat disorder cleared; his headaches diminished; his spine no longer ached. The old vitality began to return, surging back like torrents over dry creek beds.

Little occurred to punctuate the tranquil routine of their days until the morning a messenger rode in from Hippo bearing a pouch of letters, some of them needing an immediate reply. Augustine had the servant transport a writing table to a shady spot under the tamarisk tree. Heraclius sat at the table with pen and rolls of parchment before him, while Augustine reclined upon the grass, leafing through the sheaf of papers.

The first letter he dictated was to the priests of his church at Hippo:

> I have been informed that you have forgotten your habit of clothing the poor; to that work of mercy I exhorted when I was with you, and I now exhort you not to be overcome and made slothful by the trials of this present world, which you now see visited by such calamities as our Lord and Redeemer, who cannot lie, foretold would come to pass. So far then from having any right to curtail your works of mercy, you ought to increase them beyond your usual measure. For just as they who see in the crumbling of its walls the impending downfall of their home hasten to remove themselves to places more secure, so ought Christian hearts, the more they feel by the increase of its

trials the approaching downfall of this present
world, to be the more prompt and active in trans-
ferring to the treasury of heaven those goods they
were proposing to store up on earth . . .

Augustine paused and, hardly noticing, regarded a
scrawny desert goat who had wandered up to nibble the
grass. Not for long, these days, could he keep his mind
from Rome. With a sigh, he continued his letters to the
end.

Then laying the answered epistle aside, he turned to
one from a Christian wife, Ecdicia, requesting counsel
on a delicate marital problem. She, having decided to
live a life of dedicated continence, had prevailed upon
her husband to do likewise. The husband, unable to
abide by his decision, had, by his own confession, involved himself in adultery. What was the good Ecdicia
to do?

Augustine reflected long before answering:

I have been greatly grieved that you chose to act
toward your husband so that the edifice of chastity which had already begun to be built up in
him has, through his failure to persevere, toppled
to the pitiful downfall of adultery. If, after making to God a vow of chastity and already undertaking its observance in deed and in disposition,
he had returned to his wife's body, his case would
have been deplorable enough; but how much
more deplorable is it now that he has plunged to
deeper destruction, with such precipitous collapse into adultery, furious toward you, injurious
to himself, as if his rage at you would be the more
violent if he accomplished his own ruin! This
great mischief has come about because you failed
to treat him with the moderation you ought, for
although by agreement you were no longer coming together in carnal intercourse, yet in all other

things you ought to have shown the subjection of
a wife to your husband in compliance with the
marriage bond, especially as you were both members of the body of Christ. Indeed, if you, a believer, had had a husband who was an unbeliever,
it would have been your duty to conduct yourself
with submissiveness, as the Apostles enjoined, so
as to win him to the Lord.

I leave out of account the fact that I know you
took this chastity upon yourself before he consented, which was not according to sound doctrine, for he should not have been defrauded of
the debt you owed him of your body, before his
will too joined with yours in seeking that good
which is above conjugal chastity. But perhaps you
had not read or heard or meditated upon the
apostle's words: "It is good for a man not to touch
a woman; nevertheless, to avoid fornication, let
every man have his own wife, and let every
woman have her own husband. Let the husband
render unto the wife due benevolence; and likewise also the husband hath not power over his
own body, but the wife. Defraud ye not one the
other, except it be with consent for a time, that ye
may give yourself to prayer; and come together
again that Satan tempt you not because of your
incontinency." According to these words of the
apostle, even if he had desired to practice chastity
and you had not, he would be bound to "render
you due benevolence," and God would give him
credit for chastity, since he would have been
granting you marital intercourse through regard
not for his own weakness but for yours, so as to
prevent you from falling into the damnable sin of
adultery. How much more fitting was it that you,
who ought to have been in greater subjection,

should give way to his desire in the rendering of
this benevolence, so that he might not be led by
the Devil's tempting into adultery, since your desire for chastity would have been acceptable to
God, as you were unable to carry it out for fear of
driving your husband to destruction . . .

Augustine laughed aloud. "Nor did I when I was ordained a priest," he replied. "Had I known, depend
upon it, I would have offered stiffer resistance."

Nearly two hours of fluent composition gone by,
Augustine looked up to see his scribe flushing. Repress-
ing a smile, he stretched himself.

"Well, my young friend," he said, "perhaps we have
had enough dictation for one morning."

Heraclius threw down his pen and limbered the fingers of his right hand. "I — I never realized before
what various matters Your Reverence has to deal with."

Chapter 40

If you love Pelagius, may he love you too,
or rather deceive himself and not you! (Letter 186)

On his return from the desert, Augustine well
knew that he would be contending with Pelagian opponents who had whittled their sophistry to a sharp point
of destructive penetration. "Do not imagine that here-
sies are the products of little minds," he wrote a friend.
"It takes a big mind to make a heresy."

The official condemnation of the Pelagian position
had also resulted in an endorsement of Augustine's formulations on guilt and grace. Then, in 418, word came
that some nineteen Pelagian bishops, including Julian,
had been expelled from Italy.

Augustine was exuberant. The fierce struggle had
obviously come to a happy conclusion. "Causa finita
est," he declared from his pulpit. "The matter is at an
end. May it be that God's workmen may now concentrate upon building the walls of Zion without distrac-
tion."

His hope was not realized. From his place of exile in
the East, Julian kept up his barrage against the Bishop
of Hippo, increasing, in fact, the intensity of his fire.
Augustine had no choice but to extend the controversy.

Two years passed. Then one day, a disturbing letter arrived from Alypius, who had since been consecrated Bishop of Thagaste. It seemed that the insidious heresy was to assail even the friends of Augustine's dearest friends.

"You will be grieved to learn that the Pelagian error has cast its shadow over the good Paulinus, who is here with me from Nola," Alypius wrote. "My own persuasions having failed, I can think of no recourse but to bring him to you. Perhaps you alone can dissipate his doubts and bring him back once more into the fold of the true faith."

A distant relative of Julian and a true aristocrat whom Augustine had known at Milan, Paulinus was a man of culture and a considerable poet. After his conversion, he had distributed his wealth among the poor, and it was indeed a cause of grief to Augustine that such a true follower of Christ should have been seduced by the heresy.

It was a rainy morning when the two men called on the Bishop of Hippo, who was at work on *The City of God*, now in its seventh year of composition. With an effort Augustine recalled himself from his abstraction, but as the servant withdrew he rose to greet his visitors with the utmost cordiality.

Austerely dressed, Paulinus wore a tunic of plain brown satin; there were no jewels in his hair, as he had had in Milan, and his fingers, once heavy with rings, were unadorned. Augustine noticed a wishbone of frown lines between his eyebrows, as though he had for long been perplexed by some insoluble riddle.

As if in embarrassment, Paulinus put a hand to his mouth. "Alypius will have told Your Reverence that I have been studying Pelagius," he began without preamble.

Augustine folded his hands upon the table. "We have that in common," he countered pleasantly. "I have recently reread his Defense of the Freedom of the Will."

"Then you will understand when I say that its author appears to me a clear thinker."

"Not only so," Augustine nodded, "but he is also a man of high morality."

Paulinus relaxed and glanced inquiringly at Alypius, who asked, "Augustine, you have met Pelagius, have you not?"

"I have never had that pleasure," Augustine replied. "He called on me once on his way through Hippo, but unfortunately I was away. However, we have exchanged letters, and his correspondence is the soul of courtesy. It is not with the man himself that I have any quarrel, but with his beliefs."

"His belief, Your Reverence," Paulinus interjected eagerly, "is that freedom of will is one of God's gifts to man. It must be so, since without evil to reject, it is meaningless if we choose good."

Augustine was immediately aware of the innate graciousness of his inquirer in choosing to quote Pelagius rather than his own kinsman Julian. In his disputation with the Bishop of Hippo, the now-exiled bishop had allowed anger to reduce him to the level of personal attack. "Augustine is the stupidest of men," he had written, adding that "his friend Alypius" was highly questionable. Remembering his response — "The very ink should have blushed when Julian penned that" — Augustine smiled at Paulinus.

"You have put it succinctly," he said. "And he goes to Nature for his illustration when he says that the root produces the flower. Man's will in this argument being the root, he declares it can produce of its own choice either a blossom or a thicket of vice."

Stimulated now, Paulinus took him up quickly. "And how would Your Reverence answer his argument?"

Without hesitation Augustine responded. "In the matter of contrary choice," he said, speaking rapidly, "how could this be so if we are to believe in the redeemed in heaven? And what of the angels? Are they not in a state of *non posse peccare*, inability to sin? Can they choose anything else but good?"

Paulinus faltered, and Augustine tempered his pace.

"Is then their choice without freedom?" he asked gently.

Paulinus lowered his eyes and the forked line between his brows deepened.

"As to Pelagius' contention that the root can produce both good and bad fruit," Augustine continued, "you will surely recognize that this contradicts our Lord's own teaching. Jesus said, you remember, 'Every good tree brings forth good fruit, but the corrupt tree brings forth evil fruit. A good tree cannot bring forth evil fruit, neither can a corrupt tree bring forth good fruit.'"

Paulinus clasped his hands between his knees. "But how does Your Reverence explain the fact that man does both good and evil, both right and wrong, since we are all children of God and sprung from one root?"

Augustine replied, "Whatever we do that is good, the grace of God disposes us to. Whatever we do that is evil, our own sinful hearts lead us to do."

Paulinus smiled sadly. "Then man is indeed sinful," he said. "Your Reverence holds a dark view of human nature."

"You are right, my dear brother." Augustine touched his own breast. "No one knows better than I what it is to wallow in fornication and lust."

"But does that not stem from the will?" Paulinus was earnest. "Pelagius teaches that we sin or not as the will decides. He likens it to the sense of smell — we can choose to smell a bad odor, or turn our nostrils away."

"But suppose someone ties our hands and places us somewhere with noxious fumes rising all around. What power have we then? We can only inhale the fumes."

Paulinus spread his hands. "Your Reverence is resourceful, but have you not placed us in an artificial position in order to prove your point?"

"I have merely used the instrument of parable. Our Lord used it Himself, continually. Scripture tells us that since the fall of Adam, every man born of woman comes into the world with a nature opposed to good. And if you think my view of the nature of man is dark, remember David's. 'I was shapen in iniquity and in sin did my mother conceive me.'" Augustine sat back. "Pelagius holds that we are born morally neutral, disposed neither to good nor to evil. The Bible tells us we inherit corruption."

"It seems a harsh teaching," Paulinus demurred.

"So it may be, but our Lord never was one to flinch in the face of a fact. Out of the hearts of men, he said, proceed evil thoughts, adulteries, fornication, murder, theft, blasphemy, pride and foolishness. All these come from within to defile us."

"If I am forced to agree," Paulinus murmured, "I must still contend that these evils start with the will."

Augustine smiled. "Paulinus, may I ask you a question?"

"Please."

"If, as Pelagius says, man is free to perfect his nature if he so chooses, how is it that no man has ever done so?"

Paulinus looked out of the window at a tree shaking in the storm. "We need time," he said. "The world is still young. Beyond every sea lie new horizons, perhaps even new lands. Like restless mariners we will push our frontiers farther and farther, and I doubt not that new discoveries will be made even at the edge of the world. So it may be with our moral development. We must give ourselves time to voyage in our spiritual bark. How do you and I know that the centuries to come will not produce a race of perfect men?"

At this point the servant appeared at the door. "Some person to see you, Your Reverence."

"Who is it?" Augustine inquired, a trace of impatience showing at the interruption.

"A widow, Your Reverence, one of your parishioners who says she needs help."

"Give her something to eat," said Augustine. "I will come to her presently."

Turning away from the door, he faced Paulinus again. "We are living in the present, dear friend," he said. "Every day of my life I have dealings with people afflicted with countless infirmities — people with broken hopes, empty lives, bruised spirits, dreams shattered like a vessel's shards. As with me in my youth, they are looking for pleasure. As with me in my youth, they have fallen headlong into the quicksand of sorrow and confusion and error. What do they need to rescue them from their sufferings? The prospect of a race of perfect men in some century they will not live to see? You know that it is not the answer. Their need for deliverance is now."

Paulinus acknowledged the argument with a nod of his head. "But in justice to Pelagius, Your Reverence will not deny that he believes in divine grace."

"Yes, he does believe in grace — in a way." Absent-mindedly Augustine picked up his reed pen and toyed with it. "He believes in grace the way a physician believes in the healing power of the herbs he prepares for people not feeling well. But that was surely not the grace spoken of by the great Doctor of the Gentile world. 'You he quickened who were dead in trespasses and sin.' *Dead,* mark you, not just ill." Augustine sat down again. "Your Pelagius speaks of grace as a mere *aid* to the improvement of our lot, but Paul says, 'By grace are ye saved through faith, and not of yourselves; it is the gift of God, not of works, lest any man should boast.'"

Paulinus was silent but again a shadow of skepticism crossed his face.

Perceiving it, Augustine leaned back in his chair and spoke softly. "My dear Paulinus, I too tried to find the answers to life's questions in the citadel of my own reason. I tried to quench my thirst at the springs of learning. No one ever burned more than I to be satiated with the shadowy loves of this earth. I think I know something of proud dejectedness and restless weariness and bitter, bitter vexations of spirit. I know what it means to turn away from God's unity and be torn piece-meal. You can imagine, then, with what bliss I learned of Him who is most merciful, yet most just; fairest, yet most strong; never new, never old; who changes not, yet changes all things — of Him who by one mighty, electing act of mercy reached down from Heaven and drew me out of many waters, snatched me from the depth of my death, and caught me sweetly to His breast. Tell me, dear Paulinus, was not this grace?"

When the spate of eloquence had spent itself, conflict showed painfully in Paulinus' face and there was yearning wishfulness in his voice when at last he spoke. "I wish I were capable of such faith as Your Reverence has."

Augustine sighed. "Do not forget that faith too is a gift. We can appropriate it only on the Giver's terms."

"And the terms are . . . ?"

"That in true agony of heart we break with sinfulness and rest on the mercy of God's one Mediator, Who was delivered over for our offenses and raised for our justification. You had that faith once, my friend. Pensioners of a false belief have been trying to rob you of it. Do not let them make you their victim."

Alypius got to his feet as the servant appeared to announce the noonday meal. Smiling, Augustine, too, stood up. "Alypius is the most well-balanced cleric I know. He takes due thought for the outer man, as for the dinner." He moved around the table and, as Paulinus rose to join them, threw his arms around the men's shoulders and drew them toward the door. "It is raining, my brethren, and rain always reminds me that we are like water spilled on the ground that cannot be gathered up. We have talked of sober things this morning. We shall continue to speak of them when we have eaten. Paulinus, if I seem overanxious for your spiritual welfare, know that it is because I seek to pass on to you the message of one dearer to my heart than life itself. One who said 'Oh, how I long that we shall meet above in the glory of my Father's house.' Now let us nourish our bodies so that our spirits do not altogether flag."

It was several months later that Alypius wrote again from Thagaste:

"You will rejoice to know, my own brother Augustine, that Paulinus has renounced the Pelagian error. Your conversations with him were the deciding factor. I have heard you say, 'When once you have fallen into the hands of a poor doctor, you are afraid to trust yourself to a good one.' My fear was that Paulinus, so deceived was he by the Pelagians, might never again heed the counsel of a dispenser of truth. I was wrong, thanks be to God. This excellent man and his wife, Theresia, have given themselves afresh to the service of Christ. I understand that in the Pelagian camp there is loud weeping and wailing and gnashing of teeth. It is said the devil shrieks while he watches his empire topple."

Chapter 41

*The eloquent are listened to with pleasure, but the
wise are heard with healthful results to the soul
(Teaching Christianity IV, 28, 61).*

The flight of the Roman patricians to North Africa
forced a pressing problem on the clergy there, for the
practice of looting had spread not only to the non-
Christian populace but to the pious as well. Men supposed to be free from the love of money targeted on
hapless refugees and stripped them of their worldly
goods. Hippo was not to escape its share in the
wretched business.

Augustine denounced the avaricious fiercely. "Ah,
you eagles soaring at dizzy heights!" he thundered
from above the altar. "You see schools of fish swimming
in the waters below. Alas, your eyes are not satisfied with
seeing. No! You must dive into those unsuspecting
schools and with gory beak and talon wrench the spoils
of the sea from their setting. You ransack! You rob! You
plunder! Then you present yourselves at the house of
God and pass through the motions of mourning!"

Through preaching and discipline, Augustine succeeded in checking the evil, but he was not able to
stamp it out completely. And it was one such victim of

Rome's debacle who was to confront him with a moral issue within his own congregation.

Among those who escaped Alaric was a branch of the family of the Anacii — Albina, her daughter, and her son-in-law, who settled in Thagaste. Genuinely devout, they united with the church, and profited greatly from the teaching of Alypius.

Soon after their arrival, Albina wrote to Augustine, of whom she had heard much, and invited him for a visit to their new home. And since Augustine could not go to them, they came to him, Alypius accompanying them.

It was a flattering gesture, and the church of Hippo swelled with pride. Albina's mother-in-law was the famous convert to Christianity, Melania. Upon her conversion Melania had renounced her social connections to become an ascetic. And Albina's daughter, often called Melania the Younger, at thirteen had married a man called Pinianus, himself wealthy and highborn. There were rumors that Pinianus' estate had been half dissipated in litigation when he had fled Rome, but that did not dim the luster of having the Bishop of Hippo entertain such aristocracy.

Augustine, who habitually condemned the sin of pride from the pulpit, looked on with displeasure as his people strutted before envious Donatists and Pelagians, boasting of the distinction that had come to their leader. Still, he welcomed the four guests at his episcopal residence with due courtesy.

"I regret that such terrible circumstances have forced you from your home," he said to the patricians. "But allow me to confess that, if misfortune had to separate you from Rome, the providence of God was kind to send you to Hippo ."

Albina, elaborately mantled in silk, acknowledged the compliment gracefully. "Our Heavenly Father has been good to us," she said. "Some of our relatives and friends were robbed of their last denarius."

"I fear our military governor is responsible," Alypius said. "I understand he has stationed soldiers at the docks to relieve refugees of their resources the moment they land."

"That is true." Pinianus spoke with a slight lisp, and Augustine thought his mannerisms a trifle effeminate. "We happened to have a friend in Carthage who paid the guards to let us come in unmolested. Otherwise we too would be without funds."

"There is something worse than theft and blackmail," said Augustine. "Many who cannot pay in gold are being sold into slavery." His face darkened. "These Greek slave traders are ulcers in the body of humanity."

In spite of himself, Alypius could not repress a smile. He has never overcome his prejudice against the Greeks, he reflected.

"Oh, it is all exceedingly distressing." Pinianus folded ringed fingers on his lap. "We thought to have left these dreadful villainies behind when we took our leave of Rome."

"I apologize for the conduct of my countrymen," Augustine said. "It is inexcusable — diabolical! It will inevitably call down divine wrath upon us."

"It is no fault of yours," Melania said timidly.

Augustine had been studying her covertly. She appealed to him much more than her husband did — perhaps because of the similarity of her name to Melanie's. And, he decided, even apart from that she possessed a quality strangely reminiscent of Melanie. Not physically: Pinianus' wife was fair, with high cheekbones, a diamond-shaped face, and a mouth wider than Melanie's. The resemblance lay in the cool shyness and wistful insecurity of the girl — an insecurity oddly out of place in one so rich and in need of nothing.

Her presence sent Augustine's mind back across the years. Back to that wonderful morning when, under the hibiscus bush in Malqua, Melanie had first melted before his brash overtures of love. How exquisitely, ravishingly sweet she had been, like the fragrant alyssum that bent its petals over the mountain streams at Thagaste. . . .

"I think it is nearly time for vespers," he heard Alypius saying.

Several evenings later, an unexpected event took place. A score of male worshipers intercepted Augustine in the atrium as he was about to leave the Chapel of the Martyrs.

"My lord Bishop, we are here to request you to ordain Pinianus to the priesthood," the spokesman said.

Augustine was aghast. "What prompted this?" he demanded.

"We are persuaded that he is a man of God and would be a worthy addition to our church —"

Augustine regarded them narrowly. "Are you sure it is not his money that interests you?"

"It is not, Your Reverence," the spokesman protested.

"But Pinianus does not even reside in Hippo. How could I contemplate ordaining him?"

"If he were ordained by you, surely he would take up his residence here."

Still convinced that material advantage lay behind the suggestion. Augustine asked, "How do you know Pinianus would be willing to receive ordination?"

"We have talked with him, Your Reverence," a second man answered. "We are a committee delegated by the church to proceed in this matter. Even now, one of our number is speaking with Pinianus to learn of his final decision."

"And what of Bishop Alypius? Have you taken it up with him? After all, Pinianus is in his diocese."

Somewhat to Augustine's surprise, the mention of Alypius' name had the effect of pouring oil on flame.

"Not Alypius!" a third man cried belligerently.

"*Bishop* Alypius," Augustine corrected him sternly.

The man colored. "It was Bishop Alypius who wooed Albina and her family to Thagaste. Perhaps had our leaders been more resourceful, we might have had them as permanent residents in Hippo from the beginning."

Augustine sighed, almost too discouraged to continue the discussion. The men were pressing in closer on him, and he was conscious of their hostility.

"See here, my friends," he said, "do you not realize that Pinianus is a married man?"

"Others have given up family life to serve as clergymen," the spokesman answered. "Why not Pinianus?"

"It is a high sacrifice," Augustine said. "Too high, unless one is called by God."

"How do we know Pinianus has not been called by God?"

"Brethren, let me tell you this." Augustine held out his left arm as he had when he lectured as a rhetorician. "I refuse to ordain the man against his will. I shall give up my diocese rather than ordain him merely because you wish me to."

"And yet Your Reverence himself was ordained against his will," put in a man who had not yet spoken.

"No. Bishop Valerius appealed to me to consent, and because I was able to reconcile it with my conscience, I did so."

He turned from them heavily, made his way down the aisle between the two naves, and up the steps leading to the apse, where he let himself down into the *cathedra velata*, the chair reserved for bishops. This pressure from the committee affected him more deeply than he would admit. He asked himself if his ministry in Hippo did not amount to a total failure, if in the pattern of his private life and his preaching he had labored in vain and spent his strength for so little spiritual influence.

Murmuring together, the delegates swarmed up to the recess before the apse. Then again the spokesman addressed the bishop. "Your Reverence, excuse me, but it has occurred to us that if you yourself cannot conscientiously ordain Pinianus, we can persuade another bishop to do so."

"That I would fight to the death." Augustine's mouth tightened. "I would resist it unto blood."

There was an angry buzz. "But, Your Reverence —"

At that moment the member of the committee appointed to consult Pinianus came back.

"What is his answer?" the spokesman demanded.

"Pinianus says he will not serve as a priest. He says that if we force ordination he will leave Africa."

Cries of disappointment greeted this announcement.

"He is a coward!"

"Let him go back to Rome!"

"Bishop Alypius has coerced him into refusing!"

Augustine sat back in the *cathedra velata*. More than one of the men eyed him resentfully, aware that their attempt to force the issue had failed.

The messenger signaled for silence. "Pinianus asks Your Reverence to go to him," he said to Augustine.

In silence the committee watched the Bishop of Hippo rise to his feet. He moved down the steps to the recess and up the aisle, leaving the church without a word or a backward glance.

An hour later he returned to the chapel, haggard with fatigue. He paused in the atrium and the committee surrounded him, clamoring to know what Pinianus wanted.

"He has made you a double promise," Augustine said. First, though he will not submit to ordination, he has agreed to take up his residence in Hippo. He will not go back to Thagaste. Tomorrow he will send for his personal effects and look for a house here — provided you will not compel him to be ordained to the priesthood."

The men looked at one another inquiringly, many of them nodding their agreement.

"Second," Augustine continued," he gives you his word that if he ever feels called to the priesthood he will receive ordination here in the Basilica of Peace."

"We thank you, Your Reverence," the spokesman said heartily. "We appreciate Your Reverence's cooperation ."

"And now, my brothers in the Lord, I pray you excuse me." Wearied by the strain of petty conflict, Augustine's voice was low. "I have writing to do on my book before I retire. God grant you all a restful sleep."

It was midnight when he entered his study to resume work on *The City of God,* almost three when he lay down to catch a few hours' slumber before the next day's demands.

The church was thrown into an uproar when, early the following afternoon, Melania quietly slipped out of Hippo and returned to Thagaste. Wrathfully, the committee stormed into Augustine's study.

"Your Reverence, we have been betrayed!" the spokesman cried. "Pinianus is a liar and a covenant breaker, and we demand that he be disciplined at once!"

"Excommunicate him!" another shouted.

Frankly puzzled at this development, Augustine parried for time. "Good people, calm yourselves. Let us not make the mistake of the physician who was in such a hurry to treat his patient that he spilled his medicine on the floor. I perceive that you feel there is need of haste. There is indeed, so we must move slowly." He enlivened the paradox with an indulgent smile that pacified his irate parishioners. "I gave you my word I will write to Bishop Alypius and to Pinianus; I myself do not understand what has happened any more than you do. But if the broken promise can be mended without coercion, I promise you that it shall be."

With this the committee had to be content. Augustine initiated a wearisome correspondence in which he maintained a delicate balance between the Scylla of his offended churchmen and the Charybdis of a patrician family accustomed to independent thought and action. Alypius threw his full support behind him.

The results of the correspondence were not altogether profitless. Pinianus wrote to the church at Hippo apologizing for his unceremonious departure from the port. He had decided to separate from Melania and enter a monastery, he announced. He had lost his wealth to corrupt Roman politicians; perhaps it was divine retribution for the sin of breaking his word. He reckoned himself unworthy of the priesthood, and begged the members of the church to pray for him.

Augustine's conscience was clear. He respected Pinianus and Melania personally; but far better, he told himself, that the incident came out as it had than for the church to acquire an aristocratic priest with means but no vocation.

Finally, through Augustine's diplomacy, a new link of affection was forged between him and his congregation. No one knew better than the Bishop of Hippo that the allegiance of men could be captured and held for his God by trivial means as by the most impassioned sermon one could deliver from the altar.

Chapter 42

*It is to their own sins that men ought to attribute
the fact that Africa is undergoing such calamities
(Letter 185 to Boniface).*

The tyranny of time caused Augustine to realize that
if he were ever to complete his writings he would have
to curtail certain of his duties. He had become a prodigious author, turning out hundreds of books, essays,
treatises and tracts on a wide variety of subjects. He
toiled sixteen years over one book alone: *On the Trinity.*
Still he longed to be able to concentrate on this field of
service, but could not because of countless interruptions.

With the encroachment of old age, he decided to
delegate to Heraclius the burden of his administrative
and judicial tasks. Serving as a deacon, Heraclius
quickly learned to assume many of the local responsibilities, thereby freeing his bishop for more important
labors in his study.

Now Augustine elaborated ideas he had long wanted
to work out. He wrote commentaries on the Bible. He
expounded Christian doctrine. He counterattacked
the Pelagian scholars, directing eight books against
Pelagius himself, and six against Julian. Then he con-

cluded *The City of God,* the most powerful assault on paganism ever enunciated. It was a massive work, in which the author forged a two-edged sword for Christian hands to wield offensively and defensively — a sword which flashed across the empire like that of David over Philistine heads, striking theological opponents to the ground. It was a wonder of the Roman world how one man could produce so mighty an instrument. It fired the imagination and drew the admiration of enemy as well as friend. Henceforth in the public mind Augustine ranked as the foremost ecclesiastical scholar of his day. He was seventy-two when the book was published.

In spite of interruptions Augustine went about his work serenely. He was called in on church councils, and involved in public disputations; he had to answer letters from all over the empire; he found time to preach, lecture and instruct his school of priests and monks. Often men forced their way into his study, insisting that he give them his counsel on personal problems. Yet there was a lightening of his routine, and he rejoiced in the change. In the meantime, war clouds were gathering over Africa. Alaric was dead. Hordes of Vandals under Genseric ranged over Europe, conquering city after city in Gaul and Spain. They came to the Mediterranean, and turned covetous eyes toward the immense supplies of grain stored in the granaries of Africa. Only a powerful army under Boniface, Count of Africa, kept them from launching an invasion. With others, Augustine entertained the uneasy dread that soon Genseric would grow reckless and gamble on a victory over Boniface.

It was one morning during this period of tension that the Bishop of Hippo received a caller. Augustine was coming out of the refectory, having just breakfasted, when he was approached by Faustus, a young soldier, a nephew of Alypius, and a faithful member of the congregation.

"I am on my way to Carthage to rejoin my legion," the young officer explained. "I wanted to stop and say goodbye to Your Reverence."

"So good of you." Augustine took his hand and led him to the terraced garden behind the refectory. "Let us have a few minutes together before you go."

Here and there stood stone benches, ringed by beds of cactus flowers, marigold, and convolvuli, and sheltered by orange and lime trees. Beyond the garden, one of the two rivers that watered Hippo meandered toward the sea.

"Shall we sit here?" Augustine chose one of the benches near a fountain and let himself down slowly. "Ah me, it seems that of late some of my vitality has drained away."

"Your Reverence has led an active life." In his gleaming bronze helmet, flexible breastplate, and red toga slung over his shoulders, Faustus was a colorful figure. "The people of Hippo marvel that Your Reverence is still able to drive himself as he does."

"A worn-out mule drives itself simply because it does not know enough to stop," Augustine said, his eyes twinkling. "Now, Faustus, I am glad you came this morning. I have written a letter to Boniface, and I shall be obliged if you will deliver it to him in Carthage."

Faustus' handsome face brightened. "The Christians in his army could wish that Your Reverence might influence the Count in the matter of conduct."

Augustine sighed. Some years before, Boniface had lost his wife, an earnest Christian, and had considered giving up his military career in favor of the monastic life. Augustine and Alypius had journeyed to Thubunae, in southern Numidia, in an effort to persuade him not to take the step. He could serve the cause of Christ better by protecting the churches against the onslaughts of the Donatists, they argued, than by retiring to a monastery.

Boniface yielded to their persuasion, retaining his post at the head of the army. Great was their disappointment, therefore, when they learned that shortly after their conference, he had begun to engage in extortion and plunder. Another sign of his moral defection was his marriage to a Spanish beauty of Arian convictions. More than that, it was public knowledge that he maintained a harem in Carthage, and that he was drinking heavily.

"Boniface is a good soldier and a shrewd general," Faustus went on, "but in private life he is a bad example to his men."

"Alas, I fear it is all too true. That is why I have written to him. Tell me, Faustus, what made you join the army?"

Faustus was pensive. "Well, a few years ago Your Reverence preached a sermon on warfare. You pointed out that the Lord was pleased to give David strong testimony as a warrior. There were other examples, like Cornelius and the Roman centurion, of men who could serve God without quitting the army, Your Reverence said."

"Yes, Faustus, this is one subject on which I changed my views — for I used to reason that one could not follow the Prince of Peace and take up arms. I even persuaded my friend Evodius, Bishop of Uzala, to leave the service. It was the fury of those roaring lions, the Donatists, that made me re-examine the position of Scripture on warfare, and brought about a shift in my convictions. And I must tell you that in the light of what appears to be a mighty struggle with the barbarians, I am grateful to God that we have soldiers like you fighting for the empire."

Faustus stood up. "Your Reverence is encouraging. With the blessing of the Church, we are able to throw ourselves into combat with our whole heart."

"The Lord be with you." Augustine also rose. "Endure hardness as a good soldier of Jesus Christ, my lad." He held out his hand in farewell.

The young soldier hesitated. "Your Reverence —"

"Yes, Faustus?"

"My dear wife —"

Augustine put his hand on the young man's shoulder. "I know what you are going to say. Claudia is afraid you may not come back."

Faustus nodded. "And if she is right —"

"If she is right and it pleases God to call you to everlasting glory, rest assured I shall comfort her with the comfort that abounds in Christ."

"I would be grateful."

"May it not come to that. And now let me seal my letter to Boniface and bring it to you. Be sure to remind him that my prayers are with him constantly."

Augustine was concerned for Boniface for reasons other than moral. He had reliable information that the African general was in disfavor with the Empress Placidia. A political rival had accused him of treason before the Court of Raven, and an open rupture with the government would inevitably result in consequences disastrous to the empire in Africa, as well as to the Church. It was with this in mind that Augustine had penned the letter to him, resting his appeal on a spiritual basis:

> Let your character be adorned by chastity in the marriage bond, adorned by sobriety and moderation, for it is a very disgraceful thing that lust should overcome one whom man finds unconquerable, and that wine should overwhelm one whom the sword assails in vain. If you lack earthly riches, let them not be sought in the world by evil works; but if you possess them, let them be laid up in heaven by good works. The

manly Christian spirit ought neither to be elated
by their accession nor depressed by their departure. Let us rather keep in mind what the Lord
says, "Where your treasure is, there will your
heart be also," and certainly when we hear the ex-
hortation to lift up our hearts, we ought un-
feignedly to make the response which you know
we do make.

But Augustine's admonition proved to be too late,
and now events moved swiftly. After publicly denouncing Boniface as a traitor, the Empress Placidia sent an
expeditionary force to Africa to arrest him, whereupon
the Count appealed to the Vandal Genseric for help.
But just as Augustine had given up all hope of a recon-
ciliation between the empress and her general, Placidia
changed her mind. She rescinded the denunciation,
recalled the expeditionary army, and begged Boniface
to resist the Vandal invasion. Augustine added his plea
to hers; Boniface reversed his stand, and sent his legions to check the barbarians, who had crossed the
Straits of Gibraltar and were landing on the African
beaches.

Ten days passed. The citizens of Hippo anxiously
waited to learn the outcome of the early engagements.
On the evening of the tenth day, the wife of Faustus
came to the bishop's study while he was at prayer. Her
face was ravaged by weeping, and Augustine had no
need to ask what had happened.

"Faustus has fallen in battle," he said.

"Why?" she cried, beating her breast. She was under
twenty, tiny of stature, and with child. "Why did it have
to be Faustus? Why Faustus?"

"Sit down, Claudia," he said gently.

She rocked herself to and fro. "Please, Your Reverence — no. Why, why, why? I want to know."

The aged bishop drew in a long breath. "That is what I asked when I lost my son." He stepped to the bookshelf and selected a scroll containing an Old Testament portion.

He unrolled it lovingly, and leaned over it, his short-cropped silver hair glistening in the light from the oil lamp. "Listen to this, my daughter. It is the story of another tragedy. David was called on to give up his son. Let me read:

> Therefore David said unto his servants, Is the child dead? And they said, He is dead. Then David arose from the earth, and washed, and anointed himself, and changed his apparel, and came into the house of the Lord, and worshiped: then he came to his own house: and when he requested, they set bread before him, and he did eat. Then said his servants unto him, What thing is this that you hast done? you didst fast and weep for the child, while it was alive; but when the child was dead, you didst rise and eat bread. And he said, While the child was yet alive, I fasted and wept, for I said, Who can tell whether God will be gracious to me, that the child may live? But now he is dead, wherefore should I fast? Can I bring him back again? I shall go to him, but he shall not return to me.

Augustine straightened and looked at the girl, his face luminous. "You do see it, do you not, Claudia? You *shall* go to *him*, go to him who has gone to be with Christ. You shall go to him, who, being absent from the body, is present with the Lord. You shall go to him, go to your beloved Faustus, who has fought a good fight, and finished his course, and kept the faith. You shall go to him, where there is naught but plenitude of joy and pleasures forever more, where together you will eat of the tree of life which is in the midst of the paradise of

God, where together you shall bask in the pure light that streams from the countenance of the Sun of Righteousness, and where together you will serve God day and night in His holy temple. This being so, tell me, dear Claudia, need you and I understand the *reason* for loss?"

Composed now, the bereaved young wife inclined her head ever so slowly.

"So now," Augustine said, "let us kneel and thank our merciful Father for the memories of those we have loved — and lost for a little season."

Chapter 43

From this earthly city came the enemies against whom the City of God must be defended (The City of God I, 1).

The legions of Boniface were powerless to stem the tide of invasion. The Vandals routed the African army, then swarmed over the inland provinces like a plague of locusts, spreading destruction and terror.

In the face of impending disaster, Augustine called a conference of Church leaders to deliberate on the course of action that should be followed. They met in the Chapel of the Martyrs in an atmosphere surcharged with tension. Many of them were old and infirm. Augustine himself was then seventy-five, and, suffering from a severe cold, spoke with difficulty. Alypius and Possidius were also present, together with about thirty other delegates.

"Brethren, I need not tell you that the days of tribulation are not over," Augustine said soberly. "Once more the Kingdom of God suffers violence, and evil men are seeking to take it by force."

"How do we know Boniface did not betray us?" one of the bishops asked. "How do we know he did not surrender to the Vandals?"

"I have reason to believe that Boniface threw everything he had into the battle," said Augustine. "No, brothers, let us face the truth. This is the day of divine retribution. God's words through his prophet are being fulfilled: 'My sword hath drunk its fill in heaven: behold, it shall come down upon the people of my curse, to judgment.'" He paused to cough. "But now the question we must decide is: what are we to do in the shadow of such affliction?"

"Affliction indeed," Possidius said bitterly. "In Guelma the barbarians have slaughtered men and women, mutilated little children, burned our houses, our barns, and our fields of grain, and wantonly cut down our orchards. It must surely be the most insensate pillaging heaven has ever witnessed."

"In my diocese," another churchman took up the plaint, "they seized our priests and dragged them at the end of ropes along the highway until they died."

"And as if murder and looting were not enough," Alypius put in, "these wretched Arians force their heresy on our prisoners."

Indeed, this was a crucial issue before the assembly. The Vandals had embraced Arianism, a rejection of the orthodox view of Christ's full deity as espoused by Athanasius at the Council of Nicea a century before. It was as if they carried their religion in their battle axes, bloodily imposing it on the communities they overran.

"Yes, it is our very faith that is in peril," Augustine said heavily. "And it is for that reason I have asked you here. If we are to stand together against the enemy, we must agree on a policy and abide by it in the face of all hardship and persecution."

The Carthaginian bishop rose to his feet. "It is my contention that we who are in high places in the church should withdraw to the desert and preserve our leadership for the time when it may once again do

God's work in peace. Did not our Lord say, 'When they persecute you in this city, flee ye into another'?"

"Not to the abandonment of His flock," Augustine countered sternly. "Only if we might shepherd them into greater safety would we be doing the will of the Lord. And since this cannot be, let us acquit ourselves like men as well as the ordained of God, and remain with our congregations to strengthen and comfort them in their distress, if need be to die."

"But what is to become of the Church of Christ if its leaders are slain?" protested the delegate from Carthage.

Augustine regarded the man fixedly. "Brother, remember the man named Uzzah who stretched forth his hand to steady the ark of the covenant when it was shaken. The Lord was greatly displeased and struck him down. The Church is the ark of the covenant, but it is a living covenant between the priest and his congregation. Shall now the priest abandon them and flee to safety in order to preserve merely the letter of God's law? We are not saints, my brethren, that we should withdraw into the wilderness to save our own souls. We are ordained to administer the business God has with humanity, to serve people in peace and in war alike, in times of terror or through intervals of security. And if it be God's will that some of us perish, Jesus has promised that Hell itself shall not prevail against His holy Church — He will raise up another generation of those to be ordained who will bear witness to His truth as long as the world shall endure."

There was a pause after Augustine's voice was stilled; then the debate continued. But the Bishop of Hippo's fiery conviction, his forbearance and eloquent persuasion, his burning zeal to do the right things, gradually overcame dissent, and by the end of the day the assembly of ecclesiastics had concurred that they should remain where it had pleased God to place them, and continue to minister to their communities.

The convention was about to break up when Augustine's personal servant, distraught, ran into the chapel with a message for his master. Augustine read it slowly, all eyes fixed upon him; then, lifting his head as if loath to share the news that it bore, he addressed the delegates gravely.

"Brethren in Christ, all of our cities have fallen but Carthage, Cirta, and Hippo. Boniface and the remnants of his army are now retreating to Hippo."

With a rustle of robes, the delegates rose to their feet.

"All is lost!" cried the Bishop of Tibilis. "It is all over!"

Augustine raised a trembling arm. "No, brother Bishop, all is not lost as long as the Lord is in the midst of His people. If we stand fast in our faith, now is the time to bear testimony to it. Let us go forth to our congregations and lighten their fear and despair — that is our task. Jesus has planted the seeds of his truth. It is we who must nurture them, that they may spring up unto everlasting life. Pray with me now that the Lord may deliver us from the hand of the barbarian — if that be His will. But if we may not be delivered, let us pray to endure whatever may be put upon us." The frail figure turned away to cough. "I am old, brothers in God, as are many of us who are here assembled. We have not long to tarry on earth. Let us, then, fear no evil. May we be faithful unto death, that the Redeemer may grant us the crown of life."

And as Augustine knelt, the bishops also fell to their knees.

Chapter 44

You, the supreme Good, need no other good and are eternally at rest, because you yourself are your rest (Confessions XIII, 38, 53).

Throughout the nightmare of the summer of 430, the Bishop of Hippo was heard by thousands, some days preaching morning, afternoon, and evening. The Basilica of Peace provided a bizarre setting. Stripped of its adornments and sacred vessels, the bleak temple, packed to overflowing with eager listeners, became to many the House of God and the Gate of Heaven. As the bishop sat behind the altar, arrayed in his black robe with its leather girdle, pouring out his heart of love to his flock, the only music often was the coarse songs of the soldiers surrounding the city walls.

"My suffering lambs, tell me, what difference does it make what kind of death puts an end to life, when the one from whom it is taken away is not obliged to die again? Since, with all the risks that daily threaten life, every mortal is, in a measure, exposed to every kind of death and is uncertain which of them he will meet, I ask which is preferable: to suffer one form of death once for all, or to keep on living in constant dread of all?

"Amid such a general massacre as that taking place all around us, it is not even possible to bury corpses. Genuine faith is not too horrified by this calamity, since it holds fast to the prophetic assurance that not even devouring wild beasts can harm the bodies of those who will rise again and from whose head not one hair shall perish. Truth Himself would never have said, 'Fear ye not them that kill the body and are not able to kill the soul,' if whatever the enemy might do to the bodies of the slain could in any way imperil the life to come. 'Precious in the sight of the Lord is the death of his saints.'"

Thus Augustine constantly admonished and encouraged the faithful.

By August, the army had to requisition the basilica and convert it into a hospital. But Augustine continued to expound the Bible to wounded soldiers inside and to civilians outside, preaching until he was exhausted, and then preaching again. He spoke until his voice was reduced to a whisper; then, after the last service at night, he would sip a bowl of broth, repair to his study and pray, write letters, or prepare more messages for the morrow.

In addition to the horrors of war, an epidemic struck the city, and within a few days the Bishop of Hippo was numbered among its victims. A burning fever interrupted his labors and sent him to his bed.

But even in his stricken condition he was not granted the comfort of privacy. Suffering men and women besieged his bedchamber, pleading for his blessing. Fever victims crawled into his presence, begging him to pray for them. The clergy came to entreat his advice.

When at last his physician put a stop to all intrusions, he sensed that his departure was near. He asked a servant to write out the penitential Psalms on parchment and pin them to the wall over his bed. So many times had he declared that no believer, clergyman or layman, ought to leave the world without engaging in a "general confession," he knew that he must now apply to himself what he had taught. For hours his eyes, undimmed by age, would be fastened on the parchments, his lips repeating the verses:

> Blessed is he whose transgression is forgiven, whose sin is covered. Blessed is the man unto whom the Lord imputeth not iniquity, and in whose spirit there is no guile. When I kept silence my bones waxed old through my roaring all the day long. For day and night your hand was heavy upon me; my moisture is turned into the drought of summer . . .

> Have mercy upon me, O God, according to your loving-kindness; according to the multitude of your tender mercies blot out my transgressions. Wash me thoroughly from my iniquity, and cleanse me from my sin. For I acknowledge my transgressions, and my sin is ever before me . . .

More than once a servant stepped into the room to find the cheeks of his master wet with tears.

The twenty-eighth day of August was clear and warm. The Vandals, angered that the defenders continued to hold out, began pelting the ramparts with huge rocks. Inside Hippo, gaunt-faced citizens told each other in frightened tones that resistance was almost at an end.

When Augustine's physician called on him at noon, the bishop was delirious. His eyes were glassy, and his pulse slow.

"Has he eaten or drunk anything today?" the physician asked the servant who hovered at the side of the bed.

"No, sir."

The low murmur of conversation seemed to draw the patient out of his oblivion. He gazed up at the physician and asked, "Have they sent for Alypius?"

"Bishop Possidius has sent for him, my lord Bishop."

"Good. May Possidius come in?"

"Yes, Your Reverence."

The physician nodded to the servant, and the man slipped away and presently returned with the Bishop of Guelma. The physician quietly withdrew.

"Possidius?" Augustine said.

"Yes, Augustine." He bent over the wasted body.

"My soul thirsts for the living God. When —?"

"In God's hour," Possidius said, placing a cool hand on the fevered brow. "Remember that our times are in His hands."

"Yes, yes." The glazed eyes were raised to the parchment overhead. "'Lord, all my desire is before you,'" Augustine read, "'and my groaning is not hid from you. My heart pants, my strength fails . . . fails. . . .'" His voice trailed off, and his breathing was labored. "What is to become of Hippo — and of my precious, priceless sheep? What, Possidius?"

"We must commit all to the Shepherd."

"To the Shepherd. Yes, to the Shepherd. Hippo will be laid waste — like Thagaste — Thagaste and Carthage. But the City of God, never. God is in the midst of her, and she shall not be moved."

He closed his eyes, and Possidius wondered if he had lapsed into a coma. "May I get you something, Your Grace? Can I do anything for you?"

Augustine appeared not to hear him. Then his lips moved and he was behind the altar once more, urging his hearers to make their calling and election sure. "He who is our life has come down to us. He has suffered our death — annulling it by the fullness of His life. Will you not ascend with him and live?"

Alypius opened the door and came in. He and Possidius exchanged murmured greetings.

"How is he?" he asked.

"Failing," Possidius whispered.

Alypius leaned over. "Augustine, I am here."

The sick man roused himself and looked up. His smile had a touch of the electric quality of his youth. "Alypius! I thank God you have come."

"How are you, beloved friend?"

"It is well with me. I shall soon cross the Jordan and enter the Land of Promise. How glad I am you are here!"

Augustine tried to raise a hand, and Alypius clasped it affectionately, restraining his tears. "You had better rest, dear fellow."

The sunken eyes closed once more. Augustine's breathing grew more labored. The two men heard him say, "How wonderful, how beautiful and lovely are the dwellings of your house, Almighty God! I burn with longing to behold your beauty in your bridal chamber Jerusalem, holy city of God, dear bride of Christ, my heart loves you, my soul has already long sighed for your beauty. The King of kings is in the midst of you, and his children are within your walls. His children . . ." The haggard countenance was luminous with a strange light. "Yes, little mother, and you are there, you whose heart I ruptured ten thousand times, you who watered your pallet with rivers of tears — and you, Adeodatus, gift of God, my own son, I see you too — and you, Nebridius, faithful friend, I see you in the royal courts —"

Alypius and Possidius stood close together, scarcely breathing as they heard the dying man's last enraptured words.

"And you, my sweet nightingale — for you too the winter is past and the rains are over and gone, the flowers appear on the earth, and the time of the singing of the birds has come. Alypius!"

The Bishop of Thagaste bent over the bed. "I am here, old friend."

"Tell me, Alypius, does not the nightingale modulate her voice delightfully? Is not her song the very voice of spring?"

"It is indeed, my dear fellow."

The Bishop of Hippo grew silent, and the two watchers thought he had slipped away. But a few minutes later he rallied and returned to his vision.

"There are the hymning choirs of angels, the fellowship of heavenly citizens. There is the wedding feast of all who from this sad earthly pilgrimage have reached your joys. There is the far-seeing choir of the prophets — there the number of the twelve apostles — there the triumphant army of innumerable martyrs and bold confessors. Full and perfect love reigns there, for God is all in all. They love and praise, they praise and love God forevermore. . . . Blessed perfectly and forever blessed shall I be too, if, when my poor body shall be dissolved, I may stand before my King and God, and see him in his glory — as he himself has deigned to promise, 'Father, I will that they also whom you have given me may be with me where I am; that they may behold my glory which I had with you before the world was.'"

He caught his breath and again the bishops were sure he had spoken for the last time. They were wrong.

He raised his head ever so slightly, opened his eyes and seemed to stare through the ceiling. Serenely, and in a perfectly normal voice, he said, ". . . *shall — meet — above — in — the — glory of our savior's — house.*" A laugh burbled in the throat that had been a source of affliction all his life, his head fell back against the pillow, and his breathing stopped.

Possidius turned away and tiptoed out of the room, leaving Alypius at the bedside with bowed head.

As the Bishop of Guelma closed the door, a servant was approaching the chamber with a cup of broth in his hand.

"I think I would not go in, were I you," Possidius said to him.

"Why, sir, is he asleep?"

Possidius drew a deep breath, and answered, "Yes, your master is sleeping in peace."